ORION'S BELT:
BAPTISM UNDER FIRE

BOOK TWO IN A SERIES

JOHN PETER FERRIS

ISBN: 0-9882991-5-1
ISBN-13: 978-0-9882991-5-3

DEDICATION

This second book in the Orion's Belt trilogy is dedicated to my wonderful readers who make the writing so gratifying.

Included is my devoted family who endured my incessant keyboarding as another Sci-Fi military thriller was born. As always, I herald our great American military while blending a theme of anti-terrorism with the genre of science fiction.

Note: Baptism Under Fire picks up right where Birth of the Hunter ends, and I suggest you read the first to fully understand the sequel.

This book is also dedicated to Lieutenant Michael Murphy and his fire team as well as the QRF team shot down in the Chinook helicopter as they were coming to the rescue.

There is more to do in defense of our great nation, and again I praise the fighting men and women who put their lives on the line. Perhaps we all can live vicariously through the bravery of the heroic characters within these pages.

Again, stay safe.

CONTENTS

ACKNOWLEDGMENTS

First of all in the inspiration of this book came about after my 34 years of construction work as a mason, carpenter, and other careers in the building industry. Because I became disabled by arthritis and an accidental injury, I decided it was time to try to accomplish my life's passion to write Science Fiction thrillers that are exciting enough for the Silver Screen. Helping me along with this project, I give a fond and great thank you to my formatter, book cover illustrator, and website designer Holly Chervnsik. Also to one very patient and fantastic editor and project consultant, Melanie Saxton. Also to my business manager and loving daughter, Melissa Padro. But the one who gave me the greatest inspiration of them all, my dear & sweet kind mother Ellen Ferris, who without her, my daughter, and my two new friends, this would have not been possible. Also to my sister Theresa who is very sick. I love you dearly & will always be by your side.

PREFACE: THE IDES OF MARCH

As Julius Caesar contemplates the unrest in the Roman Senate, he confides in Cicero, the adjutant senator of government affairs. Not knowing of the conspiracy to have him assassinated, Caesar decries to Cicero there can be no one but him to rule. The Republic must be disbanded and all power and loyalty should be admonished to him.

He tells Cicero before venturing forth on a military campaign in the East, "With you and my true friend Brutus, we shall compel the governing bodies of the Republic to bow to my manifest. My mandates and mine alone shall benefit a grateful Rome for time immemorial."

Cicero knowing the complacency of the rest of the Senate deceives his Emperor with the blatant lie: "Caesar, the Senate accepts your infinite wisdom without reservation. Let us go and meet with your loyal friends and ministers. They await your presence in the vestiges of the courtyard."

Cicero leads the First Citizen of Rome to the courtyard in the open solarium of the Senate building. A senator comes forward and begs clemency for a member of his family. As Julius Caesar refuses the request, conspirators begin stabbing his body in frenzy of bloodlust and maniacal hatred.

Brutus, the one soul whom Caesar believes is his only friend and confidant besides Mark Anthony, is the last one to drive his dagger home. Caesar's nephew Octavian waits in the wings, for Caesar has taken him as a son and prides him with imperial fortitude.

The conspirators believe the Roman people will welcome their treachery with open arms. But it is not to be. The assassination backfires as a call for their heads is heralded through the streets. Octavian, reeling from the murder of his uncle, calls for retribution and polishes the laurel crown of power.

The conspirators, who prayed to the gods for the opportunity to slay Caesar, are now punished as their wish is granted.

Hail Caesar!

INTRODUCTION

Their diabolical plans thwarted, the Al Qaeda terrorist network begins plotting their next move, regrouping in the capital city of Sanaa, Yemen.

The so-called cleric known as Abdullah Musheen relaxes in the ancient palace of the Khaleef of Islam. Here mineral baths are rumored to heal the afflicted, and some say the crystal waters from the nearby palace are holy.

Bearing stolen intelligence from the American Embassy in Oman is Musheen's number two man, Omar Khaldif. They look at photographs of the failed assault in Manhattan. Abdullah Musheen stares at the image of the man defying gravity and despised how easily he does away with Musheen's operatives!

"The West has finally manufactured a cyborg robot," observes Musheen.

"Yes, your Excellency, but the robot was destroyed along with Amal over New York Harbor," Omar quickly replies.

Musheen looks at Omar, concerned. "But how do we know they don't have others like this?"

Omar reassures him with an evil laugh. "Then we'll set a trap for them and capture one. From that, my brilliant brother Mustaffa will duplicate their robotics and then modify it to our bidding."

A sound coming from the garden instantly quiets both men. Her Royal Highness Shaleem Khodeef, the daughter of the Khaleef of Babylonia, approaches. The royal family has been a closely guarded secret from the times of Mohammed's ascension into heaven in 632 A.D., although most of the sultans and the maharajahs throughout the Middle and Far East know of its existence.

The talisman worn around the Princess' neck is known to all as the Star of Arabia, passed down from mother to daughter for centuries. It is rumored that the ruby faceted to the amulet was put there by King Solomon, himself.

Shaleem's face shows frustration and annoyance. While her many maidens fuss over her alluring silk gown she motions them to stop. They bow their heads.

"Abdullah, I thank you for your concern for my safety and well-being. But I will not be a prisoner wherever I go. You found the need to bring me to the nation of my father's murderers, but then you abruptly rushed me home on a flight only three days after we arrived," spoke the unhappy princess.

Musheen watches her closely as she continues.

"I am going to disguise myself by wearing my burqa and we will go to the bazaar. Is that clear, Abdullah?"

"Yes, your Highness." Musheen bows, then adds, "But we still must deploy the guards. The Western imperialists will do anything to capture and desecrate any one of the Royal daughters of the Khaleef."

The Princess becomes even more annoyed and tells Musheen, "I need to be amongst my people, Abdullah. My father did not bring me up to be a timid mouse hiding in a hole."

Musheen gives Omar a sly look and makes a hand signal. The evil cleric then tells the Princess, "Your Highness, I just sent Omar to ensure your guards are doubled for your trip to the markets so that you may enjoy your people."

Shaleem's face shows a bright, beautiful smile of jubilation. She grabs a burqa veil and silk Vella shawl, then summons her ever-present ladies-in-waiting.

Omar returns. "The limousine awaits," he informs Abdullah, then leads them to a secluded area of the palace. From a passageway accessing the street, a bodyguard opens the door to the limo and helps the princess as she is seated. The ladies-in-waiting enter with Musheen.

So glad are the women to be out of their captivity, they begin to laugh and joke with the entourage. But their enjoyable travels down the secluded desert road ten miles outside of Sanaa is short-lived.

All the sudden, men in American military uniforms appear from both sides. They wear scarfs to protect them from the swirling desert sand. One American soldier lifts a RPG7 to his shoulder and fires at the princess' armored limousine. The grenade just misses and lands about fifteen feet in front of the vehicle.

Musheen screams to the driver, "Ali, go back, go back! Turn us around. The car will not be able to make it through those American devils!"

Machine gun fire hits the fenders of the limousine as it speeds off and veers away from the vicious assault.

Musheen grabs the hand of the crying Princess and comforts her by saying, "Shaleem, I would give my life for you!"

"These infidels will pay for what they have done today," Shaleem cried. "I'll never, ever not listen to you again, Abdullah. I know now only to trust your judgment."

As the limo speeds back to the palace, the American soldier who shot the RPG-7 removed his scarf to reveal none other than Omar's brother Mustaffa.

CHAPTER ONE: TACTICAL TERRITORY

On a secret airfield in the outskirts of the city of Dusseldorf, a supersonic attack aircraft landed on a German airfield owned by Pearson Global Technologies. The Viking Avenger had just completed its maiden flight in three and a half hours.

The pilot, Lieutenant Commander Vanderkamp of the newly formed Global Garrison, was flight-weary but elated with the Avenger's smooth flight.

"Vanderkamp is one of the best pilots I've ever seen," observed Carl Bingham, an ex-colonel in the US Air Force.

"Duly noted," replied Commanding officer Captain James Malloy.

There meeting the team stood Hans "Hansy" von Dietrich and Klaus Steubern alongside two Mercedes limousines. The vehicles waited to transport them to the main headquarters on the other side of the secret compound.

The funeral for the fallen of the Global Garrison's team was scheduled for tomorrow at 10:00 hours Berlin time. Gunther Wilhelm Schroeder was killed when his Humvee took a hit from an RPG7 rocket propelled grenade. He was driving while Gunnar Mientz rode shotgun through the bush in Kenya.

The other ambushed teammate, Gerhardt Moeller, had been picked off by a sniper while carrying Gunnar to cover him from enemy fire. His funeral was scheduled for Saturday morning at 11:00 hours Berlin time.

The whole team greeted Hansy and Klaus with reverence for their fallen comrades. Gunnar, whose life was spared, awaited his friends back at the main building of the compound. Still recovering from his wounds he was temporarily and impatiently stuck in a wheelchair.

The limousines pulled away from the tarmac and headed for the compound. Valets and stewards converged at their arrival to help the

Garrison with luggage and bags. Once unloaded, the limos headed for the Corporation's main building.

As they pulled up in front Malloy noticed British SAS Special Forces Major Percival Nelson. Behind him stood Colour Sergeant Patrick Tinsdale and two Nepalese Gurkha guerrillas. The British Special Forces had used the guerrillas dating back to World War II. Their history was legendary. Troops would talk of their sneaky forays into highly fortified enemy Japanese camps, where the guerillas tied the shoe laces of the enemy just to let them know they were there.

Stealth was what these lethal and elite warriors were all about. Another distinction was their lethal Kukri knives, with a bend resembling a boomerang. These weapons could nonchalantly cut a man's head clean off.

Professor Pearson exited the limo and instructed the valet staff to have their luggage sent over to the Liberstraum Hotel in the heart of the city. Earlier he had set aside reservations for the entire Garrison before they left New York. He figured they all deserved the excursion, for they'd been through hell the last couple of days.

With the Christmas holidays only three weeks away, Pearson needed to talk with his top scientists stationed in Berlin. Professor Heinrich Kruger and his other top scientist Joseph Stellarnberg waited to meet with him at the Corporation's Ball in Berlin, to be held Saturday night. Stellarnberg was known for his work in propulsion and avionics. Werner von Braun and his protégé Goddard taught Stellarnberg the physics and mathematical equations in the dynamic field of rocket science. Now at the age of sixty-two, Joseph Stellarnberg was undeniably an academic force to be reckoned with.

Heinrich Kruger studied nanotechnology with Professor Pearson and Dr. Darfuir over eighteen years ago in Innsbruck, Austria. But Kruger went on to Vienna, Switzerland to study robotic engineering. Kruger had already been working for the Corporation for ten years when he heard about the terrible death of Pearson's wife Arlene, a victim of breast cancer. From that point on Pearson, Darfuir, Kruger, and Carl Livingston had been experimenting with every possible application of science to rid the planet of cancer.

Pearson knew that these two elite scientists would propel the Corporation into greatness. But feeling a little nervous, Pearson wondered how his two good friends would react to Project Icarus, initiated without consulting them.

But first things first. It was now time to pay respect and honor to the two brave German warriors who gave their lives for the safety of the world.

Malloy approached Major Nelson and his military attaché, handing his friend from the British SAS a manila envelope containing dossiers on the Al Qaeda operatives. These were the murdering terrorists the Team was trying so desperately to apprehend.

The major gave Malloy a courtesy salute and opened the envelope to get a quick look. The major then turned and signaled one of the Gurkhas to open the door. The Global Garrison entered the building one by one.

Claire stared at the Gurkha with a look of the bewilderment, seeing him hold the door with his left hand while his right hand saluted stiffly. His eyes were fixed in a trance, staring into nowhere. She walked up to Orion and asked, "Johnny, are those two strange men part of the Garrison? They give me the willies."

"They're known as the Gurkha guerrillas," he snickered, amused at her apprehension. "Their training is the most relentless and strenuous known to man, resembling the torture we go through in our B.U.D.s training. And if they are part of the Garrison, I'll sleep a little safer at night."

Claire looked back at the Gurkha as he let go of the door to follow the Garrison. "But they still give me the creeps."

Orion and Bobby began teasing her with ghoulish sounds until she ran to catch up with her older sister.

"Johnnie and Bobby are being assholes again, Lanny," complained Claire.

"Don't worry, sweetie. I'll get even with them for you later," comforted Lanny.

Claire smiled and quickly turned around to pose her middle finger towards them. Everybody laughed as they entered an area identical to the roundtable back in the Hamptons.

Sitting in a wheelchair towards the right side of the table was their wounded comrade Gunnar Mientz. The entourage surrounded Gunnar and joked around with their loyal friend. But when Orion approached him, Gunnar slowly and painfully stood to hug the hero who saved his life in Kenya.

"Johann, I do not understand how you were able to do these things I saw you do, but I don't care! You saved my life that day," stated Gunnar, his eyes welling with tears.

"Gunnar, you're my buddy and I know you would've done the same for me."

"I sure would have Johann, but I still owe you my life."

"No you don't! Good friends never do. Otherwise they were never really friends in the first place," replied Orion.

Gunnar hugged Orion tight and greeted his other buddies in the newly formed platoon.

Malloy introduced Lanny, Claire, and Valerie to him, plus Hansy and Klaus. Gunnar flashed a devilish smile when he saw how they looked in their battle dress uniforms, especially the females.

"Skipper, do you have any more like these gorgeous liebchens hanging around our organization?" Hansy laughingly asked Malloy. "Please tell me you do!"

"Not at the present time, Hansy. But I know how you three crazy Krauts are into the frauleins," replied Malloy. "Be careful all three of these ladies outrank you."

Gunnar momentarily frowned at that dilemma.

"But later as the unit grows, I'm sure all three of you hooligans will find something to keep your asses occupied, added Malloy." Hey, Ensign Valerie Queen has made a list of therapeutic exercises that will move your rehabilitation along."

Gunnar frowned again, shooting Hansy and Klaus a look of crumpled confidence. After all, Ensign Queen was beautiful . . . and a bit intimidating! But he knew he had to follow the orders of Malloy whether he liked it or not.

Malloy instructed the platoon to take their places just as they were assigned back in New York, then introduced them to Major Percival Nelson and to the platoon. Some already knew Major Nelson while others didn't, so Malloy made the introductions before he handed over the floor.

Bobby Palladin's good friend Colour Sergeant Patrick Tinsdale handed the major a compact disc filled with intelligence on the current activities of the Al Qaeda network. Nelson put the disc into a computer at the far end of the table as Malloy toned the lights.

Suddenly illuminated, a shootout with a small contingent of enemy insurgents filled the screen. Coalition forces appeared as the firefight was recorded by a combat reporter. The camera shook all over the place, then held still for the next couple of action shots. The sound of a RPK from one of the insurgents made everyone uneasy in the security room, for anyone who had been in combat in Iraq or Afghanistan knew that this was a formidable weapon, much larger and firing even more robust rounds than the 7.62 of the AK-47. When switched to automatic fire, the sound instinctively alerted everybody to hunker down fast.

Suddenly the camera fell to the ground and the recording angled with the action facing upward. Insurgents came into view leading three women to the safety of a small Fiat only thirty feet from the lens of the camera. One of the insurgents opened the back door, then turned so that his face was in complete view of the camera.

This was the first glimpse of Abdullah Musheen's face. Everyone took notice of the image as well as the voice that yelled to the driver to take off. Yes, the voice matched that of the same Al Qaeda terrorist whose image was picked up by the Rigel one satellite over New Jersey. Only at that time, Musheen was wearing a mask.

As the Fiat drove away, looking out the window was a horrified Princess Shaleem screaming and crying that her father had been gunned down. Then as the incursion ended, a distraught American soldier looked down at the now-dead combat reporter. His face registered disgust as he yelled to his unit, "God dammit, they got away and poor Daryl here took one in the head."

The soldier, seeing that the camera was still on, picked it up and began videoing the ghastly scene outside the palace in the street. Many of the team surrounded the fallen outline of a man dressed in royal clothing made of silk and cashmere. The team's leader, a staff sergeant Marine, spoke into the camera.

"This is what we are faced with. These evil bastards killed this poor man and they probably robbed him, too. Then they kidnapped the women that were with him, using them as human shields so we couldn't fire on them as they made their getaway."

The Marine screamed as he was hit by a projectile and the picture faded to black.

A somber Malloy turned on the lights as everybody felt anger and frustration.

"Well ladies and gentlemen, the good news is we have a face to match the voice," commented Major Percival Nelson. "This recording was turned over to the Provost Marshal's office in the Green zone in Baghdad two years ago. Seems this cheeky fellow is still on the loose and it looks like he means business."

A few from the table muttered under their breath, wanting to take out the terrorists who caused so much bloodshed.

"From our intelligence we also know he's of Yemeni descent. MI-6 has conferred to me that his name is Abdullah Musheen. His last transmission picked up by our Corporation's satellite allowed us to run his voice to our databanks. We have a 98.7 accuracy on the voiceprint."

Major Nelson continued, "Captain Malloy has given us pictures of the dead, compiled from the two assaults in New York City. These photos will be forwarded to British intelligence to try and determine what the Al Qaeda network might be up to next."

Then the major with a face much like a school principal catching students cutting class said, "Now ladies and gentlemen, I need all of you to turn your attention to the telly."

A Gurkha, Kada Bondi, turned on the TV set on the other side of the room. His comrade, Lunsi Paal, observed from the opposite corner. Both had left the British military after fifteen years of loyal service to her Majesty the Queen. Nelson recommended them highly to Malloy and Pearson for recruitment into the Global Garrison.

As Kada Bondi pushed the channel button on the remote, the image of Mark Blundenberg, the mayor of New York City, appeared.

"Turn up the sound," Major Nelson instructed Kada. Instantly the mayor's voice boomed, "We have no idea who the heroic commandos are who came to the rescue of our fellow New Yorkers. The White House has informed both me and our Commissioner of Police that they are a secret operations team."

A flurry of flashbulbs and microphones could be seen on the screen as the mayor continued. "Now as for the man... or robot ..." The mayor shook his head, ". . . flying above Time Square Plaza, we were told this is a top military secret. I'm in the dark just like the rest of the world."

The media protested, demanding more information.

"What I do know is our great city owes them our deepest gratitude for coming to our rescue as our people were under attack," continued the mayor. "So to those men and women I say, 'God bless you for your bravery in protecting us.'"

Pictures of the team firing on the terrorists appeared. The man or robot came out of a Black Hawk helicopter and swooped down to easily throw a car at the evil operatives. The news report told of eighteen civilians, including women and children, being killed in the vicious assault. Three police officers also gave their lives to protect the city they loved so dearly.

A New York reporter, Erica Tolletell, informed the viewers that the president would address the nation at eight o'clock EST.

Major Nelson signaled to Kada Bondi to turn off the television. With a big smile he commented to the room, "Pip, pip, well done. Check that. Good guys one, bad guys zero."

The audience gave a chuckle, proud of their part in saving New York City.

I've been in contact with your Admiral Fischer and he has told me everything in confidence. For all of you who don't know me, Captain Malloy will assure you of my complete cooperation regarding the clandestine nature of our newly founded militia."

Malloy nodded agreement from his seat.

"I retire at the end of this year," continued Major Nelson. "At that time I will climb on board with the rest of this very prestigious group of warriors to rid the world of the Al Qaeda network."

Light applause scattered from around the table.

"In the meantime, my Colour Sergeant and two of our finest warriors from Nepal will be joining the Global Garrison by next week," stated Nelson. "Many of Lieutenant Orion's men from the Afghanistan campaign already know Sergeant Tinsdale."

Palladin smiled at him and shook his fist in the air. "Hoo yah, Paddy!" he yelled enthusiastically.

Major Nelson's eyes gave Bobby that 'Who told you to speak?' stare, and Palladin immediately apologized. "I'm sorry, Sir. It's just that me and Paddy are old drinking buddies."

Nelson laughed. "Oh, don't worry. I'm sure both of you will reacquaint yourselves with that indulgence at the Grand Ball in Berlin on Saturday night. Now where was I before I was so rudely interrupted?" Major Nelson checked his notes. "Ah yes, now I would like introduce the members of the Global Garrison to the other two members of our cause."

All eyes were riveted on the new guys.

"The man to my left has been with me for the last nine years, Staff Sergeant Kada Bondi. And now to your right is Corporal Lunsi Paal, who was the top of his class at graduation, scoring above everybody to take the prize, a ceremonial Kukri, from Field Marshall Tunstall."

The group politely applauded.

"He's been under my command for the last five years and I assure you, ladies and gentlemen, he is more than qualified."

Claire whispered to Lanny, "I don't care what he says, they still give me the creeps."

Malloy gave her a strong stare to keep her quiet.

The major turned the floor back over to Captain Malloy, who welcomed the four men to the Garrison and went over the protocol he expected from everyone.

"I'm the commanding officer and if someone thinks they can't handle my rules and regulations, now is the time to speak."

He waited exactly five seconds, then headed over to the DVD player and inserted another compact disc. The screen lit, revealing a recording of the maiden flight of the Viking Avenger. The Bellatrix 1 satellite zoomed in on the entire flight from the Hamptons. After one and a half hours, the orbit passed out of the range of the camera. At that point, the Rigel 1 satellite was able to take over recordings for the rest of the flight.

At the beginning of the flight the Viking Avenger reached 25,000 feet as a plasma energy coil enveloped the aircraft. It glowed from the ionization of the hydrogen atoms being temperature controlled from an onboard satellite-directed supercomputer. Once the plasma kicked in, the molecular structure of the super jet's epidermis became invisible to all types of radar.

The plasma energy coil also dramatically reduced fuel consumption. Even the fuel itself put out a stronger boost through an infusion of nitrogen atoms with ionized plasma. Everybody in the room saw the aircraft handling smooth as satin, gliding 50,000 feet up. The onboard computer showed no real vortices trails from the wings, and this was at Mach seven.

Claire began to really appreciate her role as head pilot of this unbelievable aircraft, even more so when she witnessed the immense power of the energy coil. When activated, it became the same purple color as the powered-up body of Orion—John Orion, the "robot" heralded in the news story they had just watched.

Malloy went to the door and yelled down to the hall to Professor Pearson, "Yo Jeffrey, we're ready for you now."

Professor Jeffrey Pearson, who had been studying a portfolio of the data from the Icarus Project, put the paper back into a folder and stood up. He sped down the hall into the security room, and with a face of jubilation walked to the head of the conference table.

"Well ladies and gentlemen, it seems that all the data and equations for the plasma coil were perfectly dead on."

His happiness emanated the room. "Those eight hours times four endured by Lieutenant Orion have revealed information beyond our wildest dreams."

He looked directly at each of them and continued, "The super nano-probes of Orion's newly constructed body has revealed our mistakes and corrected them, as programmed. From there we were able to make modifications in the plasma energy coil, which performs ten times better than we ever thought it would be capable of."

Orion listened intently, knowing "he" was an experiment that could shape the fate of the world.

"From these modifications," continued the Professor, "We were able to conserve more ionized plasma energy than previously configured. John, when you were under the regeneration cycle, your neural-sympatic impulses captured all the data from the super nano-probes, right onto our encrypted compact discs."

"That's great news, Professor," quipped Orion. "I guess now everyone will want a piece of me."

Everyone smiled, with exception of the Professor.

"Johnny, when Dr. Darfuir and I decoded the data, one thing became crystal clear: This information must never fall into the hands of any evil entity."

"Clandestine," stated Orion.

"Completely clandestine," confirmed the Professor. "In fact, when we flew here today we didn't have a legitimate flight plan. No radar technology could ever be capable of picking up our resonance signature."

"Seriously?" asked Orion, surprised at the breach in normal aviation protocol.

"I'll have to make a real good bullshit story for the FAA when we get back," said the Professor, who finally cracked a smile. The crowd followed suit.

"But the good thing is, no one can actually say that we've violated anybody's airspace. How can we be prosecuted without any evidence?"

More laughter resounded in the room, and it felt good. The Team had been through so much and a little humor cut the tension.

"We have continued to perfect your battle dress suits, by the way," added the Professor, addressing the warriors. "Plasma energy can be introduced from the Viking Avenger right into the clothing through a special conduit. It transfers energy from the plasma energy coil to the suits."

"Yeah, and if anyone in a suit gets close enough they can hover alongside me," added Orion.

"True, but remember that transferring too much energy from the plasma coil could take away power from the force field that protects it," cautioned the Professor. "And another thing," he continued, "If Orion uses too much plasma energy protecting others, he'll have to be put on the electronic generator for at least two hours so the super nano-probes can revitalize his weakened body."

"That's no fun," observed Orion.

"No, that's no fun at all," agreed the Professor. "Ladies and gentleman, try not to rely on Orion's abilities. It could leave everyone vulnerable to attack."

CHAPTER TWO: PURSUANCE

The meeting broke with permission for the Team to get out of their battle dress suits. It was time to head for the Liberstraum Hotel in the heart of Dusseldorf.

"Oh Malloy, I'm taking Lanny, Claire and Valerie with me," said the Professor. "I'll go over medical and legal issues with them."

"Sure thing, Professor," said Malloy.

As everyone filed out of the security office, Malloy began making urgent phone calls. First he dialed Captain Joshua Golon of the Israeli Defense Force. "Golon, how are you?" greeted Malloy.

"Good to hear from you, Malloy," responded the Captain.

"We just arrived in Germany. I'm looking forward to our meeting in Berlin early Saturday afternoon."

"That works out perfectly. I'm bringing somebody I'd like you to meet."

"Looking forward to it. See you then," said Malloy, who was a bit skeptical. Yet he trusted his Israeli friend's judgment in matters of security. He immediately called Admiral Fischer in Norfolk.

After three rings the admiral picked up.

"Admiral Fischer? What's the news?" asked Malloy.

"Got some info stateside," answered Fischer. "Admiral Ford and Admiral Mancuso had a long debriefing on the two Al Qaeda attacks."

"Yes? And?" urged Malloy.

"Admiral Ford already knew that the convoy carrying uranium belonged to Pearson Global Technologies," said Fischer.

"And?" pressed Malloy, more than worried.

"Since the Corporation supplied United States with more than a sufficient amount of ore, they understand the reasoning for hiring mercenaries to protect it."

Malloy blinked, somewhat insulted. "Tom, my men are more than just

11

common merc's for hire. If they weren't, do you think all of them would travel to Germany to pay respects to the families of the fallen?"

"Jim, I'm not questioning you . . . "

Malloy heatedly interrupted, "I'm their boss, Tommy. But these men are also my friends. One of the survivors is being rehabilitated right here in our hospital compound. And one of his comrades gave his life carrying him to safety."

Admiral Fisher cut off Malloy right there. "I trained you, Malloy, remember? But Jim Ford is a friend of mine and I thought he was a good friend of yours, too. He's in a pickle and still has to explain it all to the Pentagon, or it's his ass, too."

"So it's delicate," reiterated Malloy.

"Damn straight, it's delicate. And it's complicated. Remember, we're dealing with a bureaucracy called the United States government. But I asked you to trust me . . . so trust me! And give us a break, will you?"

"I'm sorry, Sir. It's just this past week has been so exhausting for my mind and body," apologized Malloy, his voice hoarse from the effects of a very demanding tour of duty.

Admiral Fisher grunted. "So what? You're a goddamn Seal, one of the Best in the World. SO BUCK IT UP."

"Bucking up, Sir," said Malloy, duly embarrassed.

"Just another evolution," quipped Fischer, repeating the well-used phrase so familiar to those who worked special ops.

"Shit, you're beginning to sound just like me, and that is real scary, Sir," responded Malloy.

Both friends shared a laugh for a minute before tackling the business at hand.

"I explained to Admiral Ford that the attack in New York City was thwarted due to intelligence from the Corporation's satellites, plus working in conjunction with the Israeli Defense Force and Naval Intelligence," explained Fischer.

"Good. They need to know our intentions were to safeguard the country," agreed Malloy.

"As far as Orion is concerned, no questions are being asked for the sake of national security. This is now to be kept secret all the way to the joint chiefs and the president and his executive branch."

"Information blackout," agreed Malloy.

"Information blackout, exactly," confirmed Fischer. "From now on, any covert action you implement should first be passed along to me. From there I'll decide if it's in the best interest of Naval Intelligence to join in on the operation." Fischer was dead serious.

Malloy said, "You'll be given an encrypted satellite magna phone operable only by eyebrow and voiceprint recognition. I'll send it to your office in Norfolk by week's end."

"I'll be watching incoming packages," said Fischer.

"And I'll send all the intelligence I receive from Captain Golon as soon as I get it."

"I'll be looking for that too," said Fischer.

"And I want to be kept in the loop if any enemy chatter is heard from any of the military spy satellites," requested Malloy.

"Affirmative," Admiral Fischer confirmed. "We'll cooperate to systematically destroy those Al Qaeda bastards."

Malloy hung up and with a smile called Marilyn Carmichael back in New York. They talked for about twenty minutes before Malloy mentioned he had to get back to work. "I'll be taking you out for nice quiet dinner and a show when I get back to the Big Apple," he promised.

"You bet you will," cooed Marilyn, making Malloy hope the days passed quickly.

As he hung up, Malloy couldn't help think of his deceased wife Cynthia. She was the love of his life, killed when her flight from Des Moines, Iowa to New York City crashed shortly after takeoff in a cornfield twenty miles from the airport. It was utterly devastating, compounded by the fact that in the year 1992 Cynthia was six months pregnant with their baby boy.

After the accident Malloy walled himself up and used work to distance everyone from his personal life. The result: Malloy became one of the most formidable S.E.A.Ls that ever came out of Coronado, California.

By the next decade he stumbled upon Orion and Billy Stokes during their CRT B.U.D.s training. Malloy had just been given his first command at Little Creek, Virginia when he accidentally ran into both as they were caught stealing food from the mess hall. In both of these young men Malloy recognized a little bit of himself. From that point on, he rode both of them through all three phases of their training. After graduation, Malloy assigned Orion and Stokes to his new command in Umm Qasr, Iraq. But before they were dispatched, he sent them both to flight school for helicopter training. Orion became a fairly good pilot, but Billy Stokes was an unbelievably good pilot.

In fact, Billy was so good that the school kept him around for another three weeks for advanced training while Orion shipped out to Iraq. Malloy kept both of them under his wing and treated them like the son he would have had, if not for his wife's untimely death. The thought brought him back to Marilyn Carmichael, who reminded him so much Cynthia. Marilyn's devotion to her children, amazing good looks and gentle heart was the clincher.

Malloy remembered first meeting her and her husband Eugene at a community barbecue in their neighborhood. Cassie Carmichael was only six, and the Carmichael's other two children weren't even born. But Malloy remembered their devotion to their beautiful baby girl, so similar to the joy he and Cynthia anticipated while waiting for the birth of their own little boy.

Upon hearing the news he was leaving for Afghanistan in a few days, Marilyn had told him to take care of himself. But this was close to seven years ago, and almost three years later to the date his men were ambushed in a mountain twenty miles east of Kunday, Pakistan. That's when he was forced into retirement for the good of the Navy.

"Boy, it still feels a little uncomfortable going after Marilyn when her husband was just so recently murdered," muttered Malloy to himself. He planned on taking it very slow, because he knew how vulnerable the distraught woman was. He had lived through it, being widowed himself. But he could not deny the chemistry between them.

Jeffrey Pearson also noticed this at the hospital and triage unit on the compound back in East Hampton. That's why he gave Marilyn a secure phone to contact him or Malloy at any time. Marilyn loved staying at the Professor's lake house not too far away from the compound. But unknown to Malloy, she already had a lot of his things brought to the lake house, storing them in a separate bedroom for his return.

Now back in Dusseldorf, Malloy changed out of his battle dress uniform into some comfortable casual wear. He finished his shower in the private bathroom of the security office. Finally ready, he took the security elevator down to the main floor. As the door opened, he spotted Bobby Palladin and Trudy joking around with Gunnar in his wheelchair.

As soon as they saw Malloy, they stopped instantly.

"Hey, you're off duty. I don't give a shit what you do on your own time," he announced.

Professor Pearson rounded the corner and smiled at his friend, happy to see him relaxed for a change.

"So how's Marilyn doing?"

Malloy's face turned red. "How should I know? I don't keep ta... ta... tabs on her!"

Hearing the stammer made Professor Pearson smile even bigger.

"Right. Okay James. I thought maybe you had time to call her and cheer her up."

Malloy laughed and with his head hanging low replied, "She's fine, Jeff. We're going out for dinner when I get back." Then changing the subject he added, "Let's all get some R&R at the hotel."

Everybody cheered for the captain, for rest and relaxation was on the mind of every red-blooded warrior on the Team. Lanny, Claire, and Valerie all come over and put their hands on Malloy's shoulders, then planted big kisses on his cheek.

But Claire, not being able to help herself, whispered, "Yo Skipper, she's beautiful and perfect for you."

Malloy shot her a subtle 'mind your own business' look, and Claire hurried up to catch up with the girls. But she still couldn't resist turning around for a quick wink.

Malloy, who felt a paternal tug, smiled and waved.

Outside they all went, waiting on the three Mercedes-Benz limousines to take them to Hotel Liberstraum in the center of the one of the most beautiful cities on planet Earth. As Orion and Lanny were just about to step into the limo, a courier from inside the complex ran over to the Professor and handed him a fax from New York.

Pearson read it and began to laugh before getting into limousine.

"Professor, what's so funny this time?" asked Lanny, curious.

Pearson smiled and handed over the fax.

Lanny read it as the limo took off for the center of the city. Her eyes were worried as she handed the message to Orion.

"Oh shit! Walter should never have let them watch TV!"

Malloy, with a look of surprise, asked Orion, "Who's 'them,' and what the hell are you talking about?"

Orion handed him the fax. "Walter was watching my dogs just as Channel 4 news broadcasted my voice. The puppies went nuts! I haven't been around my little buddies much and, hell, I feel I've been neglecting them."

Malloy's bewildered face replied, "Puppies? Those fucking mongrels are goddamn wolves!"

"Hey, watch it!" warned Orion with a glint of humor. "They're like, well, my children!"

"Every time I'm around them, they look like they want to eat me!" replied Malloy.

Lanny instantly corrected Malloy. "Skipper, you're so wrong about Romulus and Remus. Me and Johnny never would let our babies hurt anybody! Isn't that right, Johnny?"

Orion turned his head to hide his expression from Lanny.

"Oh, I guess he forgot to tell you that he and Walter have been secretly training 'your puppies' in jungle warfare," quipped Malloy. "On top of that, he didn't tell you that Walter, who is Billy Stokes' uncle, trained German Shepherds and Doberman Pinschers for the Army."

"What?" cried Lanny, who whipped her head around to glare at Orion.

"I'd hate to see what would happen if those two got loose on the public," added Malloy.

Lanny punched her boyfriend in the shoulder. "What have you and Walter done to my babies?" She put a hand over her mouth to quiet an anxiety attack. "When we get back, I don't give a darn about moving back to East Meadow. Now I have to reverse the damage you two have done to my babies!"

Orion, who had slid down in the seat, tried to make himself as small as possible.

"They're like our children, Johnny. How could you do this to them? How could you do this to me? How could you do this to us?"

"Malloy's just exaggerating, sweetie," lied Orion to his one true love. "Walter and I are training them to protect the house. Jungle, schmungle just where do you get your crazy ideas, Malloy?"

Malloy just grinned, enjoying the hot water Orion had fallen in.

"You're sleeping on the darn couch tonight, John Patrick Orion!" Lanny was near hysteria.

The Professor, her surrogate father, jumped in. "Sweetheart, since you'll be living at the compound, we'll build an area for your dogs so they'll be able to roam around, free from their killer course work."

"Gee thanks, Professor," Orion groaned. "Just throw fuel on to the fire, why don't ya?"

"Now Lieutenant, are there anymore little secrets you would like to tell the woman you love?" asked the professor.

Orion stared at the Professor. "Hey doc, I was only doing it to keep Lanny safe when I wasn't around," he hedged. "Okay, maybe I went a little overboard by asking Walter to help me with their training."

"Humph! That's an understatement," sniffed Lanny.

"But I didn't want two pussy lapdogs!"

"Seriously? Johnny, it's not like I dress them up in matching outfits and bows!" protested Lanny.

"I'm sorry, baby. I'll make this up to you. Please forgive me for over-training your puppies."

Lanny wiped away her tears and looked at him lovingly. "I will this time, Johnny. But remember, I'm going to be your wife one day. So don't you dare ever do anything like this again!"

Orion pulled her closer to him and gave her a big kiss on the lips. "I promise, sweetheart. It will never happen again."

She cuddled up even closer, but said, "You're still sleeping on the couch tonight!"

Orion gave Malloy a dirty look and blurted out, "Oh, dammit."

Lanny immediately sat up straight and scolded Orion. "Did I just see you give your commanding officer a dirty look, Lieutenant? Are you pushing for the whole weekend on the couch, because that can be arranged! While you're doing PT, the rest of us are taking in the sites!"

Orion, startled, replied, "Noooo!"

Lanny snapped back, "No WHAT, Lieutenant?

"Er . . . I mean, no, Ma'am. Er . . . I mean, no, Sir. I mean . . . Oh dammit, Lanny, you know what I mean!"

Lanny grinned. "Just screwing with you, honey, for upsetting my little sister." She winked at Claire. "Now your buddy Bobby is next."

Everybody in the limo broke out in hysterical laughter. As the limo passed the statue of Hindenburg, Professor Pearson exclaimed, "Oh, I wouldn't want to be in Bobby's shoes. Seems we have our own little Kaiser in this automobile."

Meanwhile, Orion smiled at Lanny, admiring her kindness for all living things. It was a huge part of the reason he loved her so much.

The Professor piped up. "We'll introduce Romulus and Remus to their new home at the complex. In all seriousness, both wolves should be trained to guard the closed fenced-in areas of the residential homes of the complex."

"Lanny and Walter will be right on it," smiled Orion. "Emphasis on Lanny, so her babies won't morph into killers."

Lanny smiled up at him once again, adoration in her face. When all was said and done, she loved her wild man and his military ways.

As the limo traveled toward their destination, everyone soaked up all the beautiful Bavarian architecture.

"If we get a chance, I'll show you all the sights of the city," promised the Professor.

The entourage pulled up in front of the Liberstraum Hotel and the group entered the luxurious building. Valets and bellhops greeted everyone as they arrived in the lobby area.

Malloy looked at his watch and checked the clock on the wall. "Synchronize your watches to 21:10 hours Berlin time," he instructed the group. "The wake is tomorrow night at 19:00 hours, and everyone be ready in the lobby at precisely 18:15 hours."

"Yes, Sir," the Team responded.

"From the lobby, we'll be transported to the funeral home across town. Even though you're on your own time tomorrow, I want you in the dining area for breakfast," instructed Malloy. "And keep your identity a secret wherever you go."

Malloy asked the Professor for an itinerary of what and where their plans were for the day. "And don't get inebriated," he cautioned. "I need all of you sober when we meet Schroeder and Moeller's families. There will be hell to pay if you show up drunk." After these stern orders, Malloy added that he wanted them all to enjoy the sights and people of Dusseldorf. But he also knew too well what happened whenever Orion and Paladin hung out with Hansy and the rest of his German counterparts.

Von Dietrich assured Malloy, "I'll make sure to keep an eye on them as they tour Dusseldorf."

Malloy sarcastically told Hansy, "But who's going to keep an eye on you?"

All of the entourage held back the laughter until Malloy walked away. A few headed for the cocktail lounge for a quick night cap, but most of them took the elevator up to their suites on the fourth floor.

Time 01: 30 hours. Dusseldorf. December 2, 2010.

Time 06: 15 hours. Dusseldorf. December 3, 2010.

Just waking up from a refreshing night's sleep, Claire called Lanny whose room was down the hall. After about four rings Lanny picked up the phone which noisily resounded next to her bed.

"Hello Lan, it's me, your little sister Claire."

Lanny rubbed her eyes. "Hi Sweetie. What's up?"

"Bobby's in the shower and I'll be ready in about five minutes. I hear that all the men are taking off to the south side of the city."

"Oh really? Should we tag along?"

"I think me, you and Val should go shopping in the center of the city. Lanny, you won't believe the elegant clothes and jewelry in Dusseldorf!"

"I just looked at one of the hotel brochures and from what I see we've got a big day ahead of us," Lanny enthused, telling Claire to meet her at the hotel cafe in about fifteen minutes. Then she hopped in the shower while Orion began his daily workout regimen.

Four minutes later, she told her man about her shopping plans.

"I don't like the idea of you traveling around the city without a bodyguard," complained Orion.

Lanny hugged him. "I'm a big girl now and can take care of myself!"

Orion smiled, because when he first met her she had just knocked a 240 pound man to the ground a bigot who was pushing a helpless gay man at a motorcycle rally. But he also remembered 'taking care' of some of the bully's buddies when they tried to intervene.

"Hey, I'd still feel better if one of the guys in Garrison went along," said Orion.

"Malloy said it would be all right. And don't worry, Johnny. The Professor will be going along, and not only does he speak German, he knows every inch of Dusseldorf," replied Lanny.

"Oh, I feel SO much better now that you've got a trained Rottweiler with you," uttered Orion.

"Okay, maybe you can join me, Claire, and Val as we shop for dresses and shoes all day in the city. The boys don't need you around they'll just be blowing off steam and strutting around with their stupid testosterone, drinking, misbehaving . . . "

Orion thought for a second. "You know, I guess you'll be all right with the Doc riding shotgun. But make sure you call me if there's any trouble."

Holding back her laughter, Lanny kissed Orion, knowing she got one over on him.

"We'll meet up in a tavern called the Rats Keller about two miles from the hotel. Is 17:00 hours okay with you?"

Orion smiled, glad to see she was getting better at interpreting military time.

"Fine with me," he agreed.

He headed for the shower as Lanny finished putting on just a touch of makeup. She then hurriedly put on a Donna Karan dress and brushed her raven hair. After this quick touchup in the mirror she grabbed her purse and headed out the door.

Dusseldorf: Time: 06:45 hours.

Dusseldorf: Time: 16:15 hours.

After a day on the town with the male entourage of the Global Garrison, Orion looked at his watch. It was time to head for the center of the city.

"Hansy," informed Orion, "We're supposed to meet Lanny and the girls at some pub called the Rats Keller on Rieger Street. You know of this place?"

"Yeah Johann, it's a very nice place for food and drink. But every once in a while you'll get some unruly individuals . . . but you can say that about almost any place that serves alcohol."

Hansy noticed the look of concern in his buddy s face. "Don't worry," soothed Klaus. "Most of the people in this area of town are good-natured."

They loaded Gunnar's wheelchair in the trunk of the Mercedes SUV, then headed toward the tavern.

Meanwhile, the Professor and the girls were just pulling up in front of the pub in a limousine packed with the day's shopping fiasco. They noticed the outside had quaint little tables equipped with two sturdy wooden chairs placed across from one another, perfect for ambient dining and drinks.

"Take our packages to the Liberstraum Hotel, and then come back for us in about two hours, please," instructed the Professor to the driver. A casual gray tweed jacket perched upon the Professor's shoulders, one the girls had picked out for him.

Claire looked at her father and smiled. "You look so debonair, Poppa, in that nice jacket. The ladies won't be able to resist you now."

The Professor blushed. "Why would some attractive, sophisticated lady want with an old biddy like me?"

Lanny quickly kissed him on the cheek. "Poppa, you're a very handsome man inside and outside, and any decent woman with a brain can see that for herself. Anyone else doesn't deserve you, anyway."

Valerie with her English accent just a little more noticeable said, "That's right, Professor. They can bloody well stuff it in their bum for all I care."

They all laughed because Valerie had a double dry martini just before they arrived and she seemed to be letting down her hair. Valerie was still a mystery to Lanny and Claire—she just seemed to arise out of nowhere.

They decided to go inside since the temperature outside was a nippy 60 degrees. The Professor, even though he didn't drink, loved the smell of the tavern and the Bavarian cooking inside.

They were greeted at the door by a big, robust man named Bader who instructed a smiling girl named Holly to take them to a table reserved for twelve.

The Professor commented to Holly in German that she looked so quaint in her Bavarian dress and hat.

"Why thank you, Sir. You can speak to me in English, for I understand it very well. You see, I'm going to college in Oxford, England.

"Ah, your grasp of English is uncommonly good," noted the Professor.

"Yes, I'm on Christmas holiday for the next month and am helping out my uncle who owns the tavern."

"We must stick out like a sore thumb to everybody," commented Lanny.

"No, not at all! My aunt Ingrid over by the bar has known the Professor for years, for this is where he comes to eat."

Pearson looked over and spotted a blonde woman waving to him. He instantly smiled and waved back.

"Now I know where you got your good looks!" complimented the Professor.

Holly blushed as she handed them the menus.

"Professor, when you and the ladies are ready to order just let me know. In the meantime, would all of you care for something to drink?"

"We're waiting for our party to arrive. But in the meantime I'll have a lemonade," said the Professor.

Lanny ordered an iced tea, Claire ordered a Coca-Cola and Valerie just wanted water to shake off the Martini.

"And you'll want sauerbraten for your entree and our very special strudel from your friend, the cook, for dessert, correct?" added Holly, whose aunt had filled her in on his preferences.

"Tell Gerta to put strawberries on it," winked the Professor.

In the midst of this tranquil setting barged in a bunch of ominous-looking bikers. Amongst the five of them were two tall, husky men who seemed to stay just a little behind the other three.

Bader seemed nervous as he led the motley crew to a table far away from the Professor's entourage. But it didn't stop the shortest of the bunch from looking over to his right and spotting the table with the Professor and the girls. He whispered something to his comrade next to him in a derby hat. His comrade laughed and relayed some kind of message to the big men behind him. They all began to laugh as the man with the Derby tipped his hat and shot an evil grin towards the Professor's table.

Claire immediately gave all of them a look of disgust.

Just before sitting down, the short one grabbed his scrotum and wagged his tongue like a dog back at Claire. He and the rest of the men at the table began behaving like juveniles, making sexual innuendos and gestures amongst themselves.

Lanny kept her composure. "Just ignore them," she advised so that they could put their minds on something else.

But the Professor called over the Holly and asked if they could be seated at the back end of the tavern, further away from any chance of the girls being bothered.

Holly, completely understanding the situation, approached her Uncle Bader to accommodate them. Bader arrived with Holly and two busboys to escort the Professor and the girls away from the offending bikers.

The busboys moved two medium tables next to the large one already there. A giant red and white checkered tablecloth was thrown into place as another waitress and busboy arrived with glasses and dinnerware. A rolling cart topped with a beautiful flowered centerpiece arrived, compliments of Ingrid as an apology for their inconvenience.

Holly smiled and told the Professor that Gerta beamed when she heard how much he thought of her special strudel. But just as Holly walked back towards the kitchen, the troublemakers appeared and sat down adjacent to them.

"This part of the dining area is reserved," explained Holly politely. Bader, seeing the commotion was just about to unleash, made his way between his niece and the bikers. The largest one threw Bader into the booth behind them. The short one, Garth, smiled and said to Bader's assailant, "Kurt, please take it easy. I'm sure Chubby here didn't mean for us to leave."

Garth looked angrily at Bader. "So, you were mistaken, weren't you, Chubby?"

But before Bader could answer, Valerie stepped out of her high heels and shouted, "I want you all out of here, you little troublemaking runt."

Surprised, the bikers watched as a small, beautiful, strawberry blonde girl walked over to them.

Valerie grabbed a pepper shaker and catsup bottle on the way. Lanny pulled out her cell phone to call Orion while Claire yelled, "Val, get back here. What are you doing? Let's just leave!"

But Valerie, barefoot and brave, ignored Claire and unscrewed the top of both the catsup bottle and the pepper shaker.

Seeing this, Garth laughed to his buddies. "Get a load of this piece of ass. She wants to eat us!" They all start laughing hysterically.

Just as Valerie was only feet from the big one, Kurt reached out and tried to grab her by the arm. Ensign Queen immediately threw the pepper into his face. She then jumped in the air and front snap kicked him so hard in the jaw that he crushed the table behind them and fell unconscious.

In that instance, the other four surrounded her. Garth pulled a fixed blade from his coat pocket and waved it.

With a devilish laugh, Valerie squirted the catsup all over him. He charged her, trying to stab at her as he approached. At the last second she spun away and kicked him straight through the window. Glass flew everywhere as the other three charged her at the same time. As the first one was just about to grab her, she slithered to the floor and swept his legs right out from under him. His head slammed into the table right next to the girls, knocked out cold.

As Valerie sprung up, the other big guy lifted a chair over his head. But Ensign Queen, still holding the glass bottle of catsup, slammed the point of the bottle into his sternum. She then punched him with ferocity square in the groin, toppling him to the floor screaming in pain.

The last one standing decided to pull out a Glock 9 mm handgun. But soon as he cleared it from his jacket, Claire hit him as hard as she could with the catsup bottle, directly onto the crown of his woolly head. As he fell, Valerie grabbed his weapon and ejected the magazine and bullets in one smooth motion.

From behind she heard, "Oh wow, boy, do I really love you!" There stood Trudy with most of the men from the unit.

Valerie smiled and walked over, and just before kissing Trudeaux replied, "Of course you do, Mikey."

Trudeaux, in astonishment, replied, "Remind me never to get you mad at me."

Everyone in the tavern broke out into applause. Valerie headed over to Claire, who could not believe what she had just witnessed. She hugged the brave heroine. "Thanks, girlfriend, for watching out for us all."

"No big deal," smiled Val.

But Claire, still in amazement, replied, "I love you, Val. But let's not forget to thank the Heinz Catsup Company!"

Lanny piped up, "Where in the world did you learn to fight like that?"

As everyone laughed, Captain Malloy appeared from behind Trudy. "Everyone, this mystery lady is Valerie Queen, former British Secret Service with MI-6."

Everyone shot her a look of respect.

"Her uncle Fenly Tunstall sent her to me after she came back from a mission where two of her compatriots were set up and killed by the Al Qaeda network."

"More fallen, thanks to the terrorists," observed the Professor. "Thank God you were not harmed."

"It's all in the training," responded Val.

"If I were you, Gunnar, I'd do whatever physical therapy she tells you to do," observed Malloy.

"I'll be careful not to give her any guff," agreed Gunnar, wide-eyed at the warrior lady.

Malloy turned to Lanny and Claire. "And you two ladies, pay attention to her. She is now your hand-to-hand combat instructor."

"I could learn a few things, that's for sure," commented Lanny.

Bader Friedrich, the owner of the pub, called in the German police and led them to the moaning and busted-up bikers. The police handcuffed them while EMT workers loaded them on gurneys for their journey to the hospital.

After the police questioned Valerie and the girls, the Professor told his friend Bader, "Can we get our old seats back? And by the way, I'm going to pay for all the damage."

A grateful Bader led the group to their original seating.

"I'd like everyone in the tavern to join us. Meals this evening are compliments of our group," continued the Professor.

"That's not necessary! You don't need to pick up the tab for the entire restaurant!" exclaimed Bader. "For you have done us a service. These men have been bullying people all over town and a small attractive woman just beat the daylights out of them. We should be treating you to a meal!"

Lanny looked over to see Gunnar flirting with Holly Friedrich.

"Can Holly can join us, Bader? Is it possible to give her the rest of the night off?"

Bader saw how smitten Holly was with Gunnar. "Holly, my liebchen, why don't you take the rest of the night off and keep this nice German boy company."

Everyone noticed a twinkle of happiness as Holly kissed her uncle Bader on the cheek and untied her work apron.

The Professor approached Bader and Ingrid with a traveler's check. "Do not try and give this back to me, Mr. and Mrs. Friedrich. This is how friends take care of one another."

He then pointed to their niece Holly and Gunnar Mientz, commenting, "Besides, I have a strong feeling that one of my employees will be frequenting your establishment quite often."

Ingrid looked at the check and her eyes bulged out of her head.

Professor Pearson whispered, "Just remember what I said. We're friends!"

Ingrid hugged him. "We love you, Jeffrey." Then thinking for a minute she added, "Why don't you go in the back and surprise Gerta? She'll be delighted to see you!"

"You know Ingrid, with all the things happening in my life right now I think I will go back and say hello to that beautiful sister of yours."

As the Professor turned, he yelled out to the crowd, "Ladies and gentlemen, please enjoy yourselves tonight. Drinks are on me, and please take very good care of the people serving you . . . because your dinner and your desserts are on me, also!" He repeated himself in German and the entire tavern screamed with applause as the Professor made his way towards the kitchen.

A tear formed in Valerie s eye, and Lanny and Claire immediately asked her what was wrong.

"With all the evil in the world and all the suffering I've seen, I wonder why God has placed me in an organization where the boss is the most kind and loving man I could ever know."

"Welcome to the family, Valerie, and you're stuck with us," assured Claire.

"Orion stood up and tapped his Pilsner glass with his spoon. "Everyone, can I please have your attention. I would like to make a toast to the newest member of our family. Let's all give our warmest welcome for a very extraordinary woman, Ensign Valerie Queen."

Everybody stood as Trudy came over and kissed her with passion while tears ran down her eyes.

Coming out of the back, the Professor held Gerta Schmidt's hand. They too began clapping.

"Jeffrey, who is she to you?" asked Gerta, nodding to the heroine, Valerie.

He smiled and said, "Oh, just another one of my daughters."

Gerta with a puzzled look and asked, "What?"

"I'll explain everything to you later." He then yelled across the pub, "Welcome, sweetheart. I'm so glad to have another one of my daughters on board with us. Now girls, keep the men in line."

Valerie, with more tears, looked over and waved to the Professor. Wiping her eyes, she and Trudy sat down with everybody else.

Captain Malloy reminded the unit that the wake was at 19:00 hours, and it was now 15:30 hours. "So be ready at 17:15 hours to go back to the hotel and change to proper attire for the rest of the evening," reminded Malloy. "And Orion, make sure nobody disgraces the unit by showing up drunk."

"Skipper, alcohol has no effect on my brain anymore. Just makes me piss a lot."

Aggravated, Malloy shot back, "Listen, Lieutenant. You're supposed to be leading by example. So at least do your job as my lead combat officer. Is that clear, Lieutenant?"

"Crystal, Captain.

Malloy headed for a private area where he could call Marilyn out of earshot of the group. But just before leaving, he told Orion, "I hope you piss your fucking brains out tonight!"

Both of them broke out laughing. Then the Team began to enjoy their meals along with the people in the pub, for the people of Dusseldorf really knew how to have a good time. The spectacular food and hospitality was unbelievable.

Lanny looked over and caught a glimpse of Gunnar sneaking a kiss with Holly. She nudged Orion and he looked over as well.

"Way to go, Gunnar," he said quietly as he and Lanny beamed at each other with contentment. Their lives had been so blessed with the people they loved.

After a wild and exhausting week, Malloy was glad to see the Global Garrison Team of elite men and women enjoying themselves. People who previously didn't know each other were now family, and this family was dedicated to bringing prosperity and peace throughout the world.

Malloy and his two counterparts of peace and stability would use force as a last resort, as was stated in their adopted charter for all who wished to be part of the Global Garrison effort. Membership required an oath to the preservation of peace throughout the entire world. Hatred and bigotry would not be tolerated at any price.

For the rest of the night they would pay homage to their fallen comrades who died in the line duty. It was time to show love for the family and friends left behind.

Time: 18:00 hours. December 3, 2010.

JOHN PETER FERRIS

CHAPTER THREE: A GRIM GOODBYE

Time: 06:15 hours. December 4, 2010.

A light suddenly emanated from the fourth floor of Hotel Liberstraum. In room 425 Lieutenant John Orion began his daily regime of exercises. His girlfriend Lieutenant Commander Lanny Cromwell patted him on his butt twice as she headed for the shower.

"I've always loved that firm ass of yours, Johnny."

Orion smiled and stretched as she passed him. "You got a lot more than just a nice ass, baby," he resounded, training his eyes on her well-endowed breasts.

Lanny, just before she walked into the bathroom, dropped her see-through sheer black negligee. Orion sweated like a sauna room as she closed the door only slightly. As a shower turned on, Orion strolled into the bathroom and shut the door.

From the inside came the wail, "NOT NOW, JOHNNY . . . We've got things to do . . . Ohhh . . . "

The door opened slightly and a pair of blue boxer shorts flew out.

Meanwhile in the room next door, Claire and Bobby finished making love in the shower and felt a thump on the shower wall. Faintly, they overheard Lanny moaning in ecstasy as Orion made love to her.

"Doesn't my sister have any scruples?" asked Claire. "There are other people in this hotel!" She turned back to Bobby and added, "She's screaming like a tiger in heat!"

Bobby couldn't help himself and busted out laughing. "What are you talking about? You were just screaming like a pack of hyenas!"

Claire's eyes opened wide. "OH SHIT! My sister's going to think I'm a real whore." She fidgeted nervously. "Come on Bobby, let's get dressed real quick so they think we were having a pillow fight, instead."

Bobby Palladin's face showed disbelief. "Yeah, sure. PILLOW FIGHT,

YOU SAY?" He couldn't believe his beautiful, seemingly dim-witted girlfriend was the captain of the Viking Avenger AND a practicing lawyer!

But that's what Bobby loved about her. Not only was she one of the hottest-looking blondes he'd ever seen, but she also made him laugh with her cute little quirks.

As they entered the bedroom, Bobby spun her around as one towel wrapped around her body and another turbaned her head.

"I love Claire Vanderkamp. I really do," professed Bobby, looking deeply in to her soft eyes.

"And I love Bobby," she replied.

They kissed like nothing existed but them in the universe. As they finished, Bobby pulled on his boxer shorts and saluted.

"Master Chief Palladin requests permission to get dressed, Ma'am."

Claire laughed and walked right up to his face, then slid her right hand down the front of his boxers. "Seems when you salute, you really know the meaning of it, Master Chief Palladin."

Bobby tried to grab her, but Claire stopped him dead in his tracks and pushed him away.

With a look of frustration he complained, "Claire, WHAT THE HELL WAS THAT? You grab me there and then expect me to control myself?"

Claire turned around as she finished adjusting her black bra. "I'm your superior officer, Master Chief Palladin. You will comply, and when I ask for your opinion, I'll give it to you."

Bobby yelled, "AWW, SHIT," and barged into the bathroom, slamming the door.

Claire sat down at her dressing table and looked into the mirror with the giddy smile and whispered to herself, "Thanks big sister that worked. PAYBACKS ARE A BITCH, aren't they!"

She then put on her mascara and eyeliner, hearing Bobby bellow with frustration in the background. The biggest shit-eating grin of a lifetime appeared on her face.

Meanwhile, Lars Olsen and Benny Kramer arrived back at the hotel, having just been relieved of guard duty on the Viking Avenger across town. After they left, Malloy put a lockdown on the base and airfield so the entire unit would be able to attend the burial services of their fallen comrades.

They met Captain Malloy in the lobby. He asked if they rotated watches with each other in order to get some sleep.

"We did it by the book," confirmed Lars.

Malloy gave them the key to their suite on the fourth floor. As they exited, Malloy saw Gunnar being pushed towards the elevator by Holly Friedrich.

A chewing out was in order. "What the hell do you think you're doing, Gunnar? Don't you know that she's the niece of your boss' friends?"

The couple jumped, startled.

"And you, young lady," continued Malloy, "Does your aunt and uncle have any idea where you spent the night?"

Holly with a look of astonishment replied, "Mr. Malloy, I meant to tell them. But I had a little too much to drink. Besides that, I'm twenty-one and I am a big enough girl to take care of myself!"

Benny and Lars laughed like crazy hearing Holly tell off the Skipper. Malloy's face turned red and he yelled to both of them, "Oh, you find this funny, do ya?"

Both hurried to their room and shut the door fast.

The captain was just about to talk again when he heard moaning out of Trudeaux's room.

"Just what the fuck is going on here? This is a first-class hotel, not a brothel."

Gunnar and Holly couldn't help themselves and busted out hysterically.

At that moment Orion and Lanny opened the door and walked out into the hall to hear the Skipper ranting and raving. Then out popped Bobby and Claire.

With frustration still written all over his face, Malloy face-palmed and exclaimed, "I thought I had made provisions for the girls to be in one room and the men to be paired off in separate rooms." He stared at the guilty culprits and added, "What do you think our boss is going to think when he finds out we've turned the Liberstraum into a fucking cathouse?"

Malloy then pounded on Trudy's door and yelled, "Ensign Trudeaux and Ensign Queen, get dressed and get your asses down to the dining area. Now."

But right at that moment, the Professor opened his door and peered into the hall, swathed in bath towel. "Jim, what seems to be the problem?"

Before Malloy could speak, Gerta Schmidt came up from behind the Professor. "Is everything all right, Jeffrey?" Gerta was wearing only a towel and her hair was all mussed up.

Holly Friedrich's face showed shock. "Aunt Gerta, OH MY GOD! What you doing here?"

Gerta blushed. "What am I doing here? What are YOU doing here?"

Malloy dropped his head in disbelief. "OH GOD, WHY ME?"

Everybody laughed hysterically at the Captain's expense.

Malloy hit the stairs. "I GIVE UP, I GIVE UP."

The Professor pushed Gerta back into the room before she commenced with more scolding. He smiled at Holly. "Come on you two, get out of here while I calm her down."

Holly pushed the wheelchair as Gunnar told the Professor, "Thank you!"

"JUST GO GUNNAR, NOW." The Professor closed his door as Holly pushed the down button to summon the elevator.

The door to Michael Trudeaux's room opened and, still putting on their shoes, the couple looked around to see Gunnar and Holly waiting for the elevator.

"What's going on with the Skipper, Gunnar?" Bobby asked. "Sounds like another one of his tirades. What did we do wrong now?"

Gunnar explained the situation as the four got into the elevator. As they reached the ground floor, the door opened slowly to reveal all of them boisterously laughing.

But as they got off, Malloy was standing there with his hands on his hips, staring at them with contempt. "Is something funny there, boys and girls? Do tell, because I think I could use a good laugh right about now."

Trudy wiped the smile off his face immediately. "It's not that, Skipper. I'm just telling Gunnar, here, a funny story that happened to me back in New Orleans."

Malloy, knowing all of them were full of crap, put on a face of disbelief. "SURE, ENSIGN. Now get into the dining area and fill that lying mouth full of food."

All four of them passed the captain biting their lips to control the laughter that threatened to erupt again.

Malloy began to calm down just as the Professor and Gerta got off the elevator to the lobby. Pearson put his right hand on Malloy's left shoulder. "Jim, lighten up a little on them. These kids are in love. Besides, they're grown adults and they're on their own time."

Malloy agreed as they headed into a beautiful dining area facing east. It was glorious to behold the sun coming up in the distance. The picture windows to the north of the room were a sight to see.

The Skipper sat down with the Professor and Gerta, who had already seated themselves next to Gunnar and Holly. The hotel waitresses all bustled around to take everybody's order.

Suddenly Malloy's cell phone rang. It was Marilyn Carmichael! Immediately Malloy turned his chair away and whispered, "Hi, honey . . . What? You got the dress that the girls helped me pick out for our date? Oh yeah, honey, they're the greatest . . . Yep, well, I figured you'd like something like that . . . Oh yes, the girls have great taste in clothes . . . Okay, baby, I'm kind of busy right now . . . Yes, I miss you very much, too . . . Okay sweetheart, I'll call you later . . . Bye-bye."

Malloy turned back around to see Lanny, Claire, and Valerie with their arms crossed over their chests looking slightly resentful. He immediately collapsed. "Thank you, girls. I don't know what I'd do without any of you."

The girls got out of their chairs and surrounded Malloy. "We love you, Uncle Jimmy," said Claire. "But sometimes you're a real grouch."

As they returned to their seats Claire said a little too loudly, "She better put out when he gets back or all of us are in trouble."

The men cracked up and Malloy yelled, "Oh yeah, you think it's funny. Ha, you guys didn't buy me a dress." Then he thought for a second. "Wait just a minute . . . that didn't come out right. I meant, buy Marilyn a dress."

Still laughing hard, Lars continued, "Don't worry, Skipper. We'll pick you out a real pretty pink one next time."

Captain Malloy couldn't stop himself and busted out laughing. At that time Benny Kramer came into the dining hall and walked right over to the Skipper, then handed him a folder with four large photos inside.

"Kyle was able to make duplicates of the satellite photos and sent them to you and Vice Admiral Fisher at the same time," said Benny.

Malloy opened the folder and a look of concern flitted over his face.

Orion noticed and asked, "Skipper, every time I see you put on that face it worries me. Everything okay?"

Malloy looked at his lieutenant. "I'll fill the Garrison in on this after the services. It might be something, and then again, it may be nothing at all." He grew quiet, thinking intently before adding, "I'm going to call Tommy Fisher when our burial duty is over. Come on gang, let's eat. I have a feeling that today is going to be draining on us, anyway."

Malloy and the Professor quietly conversed about the photos, and the group noticed the wheels in Malloy's head spinning. Orion, having been personally trained by the Skipper, knew the units were going to be on alert even if it was nothing. But looking around the room and seeing everyone dressed in black brought back horrible memories of Billy Stokes' burial.

Orion stared into a void in space.

Lanny snapped him out. "Johnny, are you all right, baby?"

Orion shook his head. "Oh, I'm fine, Lanny. As long as I have you, I'll always be fine."

Lanny knew when her man was telling a white lie, but she really understood this one.

Benny, too, noticed the look on his buddy's face—the same face Orion had after Billy was killed in Afghanistan. But Benny also remembered how Orion froze, unable to take his eyes off his dying best friend. Benny and Malloy had snapped him out of it back then, and Orion regained his composure. He was able to take off and fly the unit to safety.

Benny came over to Orion and sat across from him. "Jonathan, you going to be all right today?"

Orion smiled. "How can I not be, Benny? You are here with us again, and you've always been my right-hand man. If it wasn't for you and Kyle creating a diversion that day, none of us would be here right now."

Benny patted Orion's shoulder in sympathy.

"It seemed lonely trapped in a corner and everything seemed bleak, but the WIZARD appeared with his magic and showed us how amazing he really is," declared Orion.

Benny interrupted him. "It's just redirecting the human mind to see what it thinks when it wants to see something different, and nothing more." Benny paused thoughtfully, then continued. "Remember, you're the only one who could fly the chopper that day. If it wasn't for you, none of US would be here, either, John, believe you me. It feels good to be back with you and our old unit once again."

Orion looked at him and let out a whoop. "Hoo Yah!"

Benny assured Orion that since he was his right-hand man, he'd be standing next to him at graveside. Then he sat back down with Lars, Hansy, and Klaus.

Orion glanced over and spotted Lars, who looked concerned as he spoke with Benny. Orion figured Lars also vividly remembered that day, for Lars was yelling at Orion to lift off just as he just spotted three enemy Taliban insurgents setting up an 80 mm mortar to fire at their chopper.

It was bad enough that a RPG-7 grenade exploded only 30 feet from them. But somehow, Benny and Malloy got Orion to snap out of it and they all got the hell out of there.

Lars looked across the room at his buddy, and thumped his chest twice to ask if Orion was okay. Orion slapped his right hand over his heart to convey he was all right. Lars lip-synched, "Hoo Yah," and Orion did the same with a smile of pride.

Entering the dining hall came Mike Maguiness, Carlos Alvarez, and Calvin Thomas. They sat adjacent to Orion and Palladin's table.

Bobby yelled over, "Maguiness, you are a full-fledged Ranger and not just Airborne. Maybe someone should have told you not to wear a Nasty Nick and Sapper patches on your rucksack. I wasn't born yesterday, Mike."

Maguiness looking like the cat that just swallowed the canary, replied, "Ask Malloy. He's the one who told us to appear as rookies."

Bobby replied sarcastically, "There were no rookies that day in the jungle of Kenya. All of you set up perfectly as a fire team unit and laid down a suppressed amount of fire, almost similar to how we trained."

Malloy interrupted by yelling, "Well somebody is observing and keeping on their toes. All of you except Kyle have grown soft these last few years. I've got to see how much you lazy schmucks have forgotten what is essential and not essential since you left the Navy."

Bobby looked annoyed. "What about you, Skipper? You've been out a while."

Malloy, with a devilish grin, replied, "I'll remember you said that, Master Chief Palladin."

Bobby said under his breath, "Me and my big mouth. I've got to learn to keep it shut around him."

Malloy shouted, "Maguiness, take those damn patches off that ruck of yours. No more advertising. We cannot compromise anything about us ever again. Is that clear, Chief Warrant Officer Maguiness?"

"That's a Roger, Sir," said Mike.

Orion put his hand over his mouth and leaned towards Bobby. "Him and his fucking games. Well, here we go, ROUND TWO."

Palladin, putting his hand over his mouth, said, "Tell me about it."

They all went on to enjoy their meals as the clock on the wall read 08:00 hours Dusseldorf.

Time: 09:10 hours. Dusseldorf.

Three Mercedes limousines pulled up in front of the luxurious Liberstraum Hotel. A doorman pushed Gunnar Mientz as Holly Friedrich opened the car door at the rear. Trudy poised himself next to Holly to help them in.

From the limo behind, Calvin Thomas and Lars Olsen were the first to enter. But from the third limo, the front passenger door opened and out stepped Lunsi Paal. He opened the rear door and out stepped Major Percival Nelson.

The major walked up the stairs of the hotel as Kada Bondi stood sentry at the rear of the limo. Both of the Nepalese men were dressed in black Dolce and Gabbana suits and exhibited a style of prestige and elegance as they awaited for the rest of the entourage to get into the limos.

But inconspicuously the Ghurkas were equipped with Uzi Mach 11 submachine guns well hidden inside their suit jackets. This was because immediately following the burial ceremony the entire entourage would be converging back to the base. From there they planned to board one of the Corporation's Gulfstream Lear Jets. Then they would fly east to Berlin for the Corporation's vital meeting with other members of the company.

Later that evening, a Grand Ball would be held in one of the capital's most beautiful hotels.

Kada and Lunsi were simply a precautionary guard, as the entourage had to be prepared for the unexpected. Once in the air the Ghurkas would be able to enjoy the fun with the rest of their comrades.

Finally, Captain Malloy was the last to be seated in the second limo. The Professor came down the stairs with Major Nelson and both climbed into the last car as Kada came from behind. Lunsi shut their door and scurried up to the passenger side of the limo to climb in with the rest.

The three limos departed for the church located close to the western part of the city. The burial site was not far from the church and was right next to the Rhine River along its banks. Gunnar was there to ensure his comrades would be buried facing the east side of the Rhine River. Gerhardt was the one who carried him to safety after Gunnar was thrown from his GMV armored Humvee. Doing so cost Gerhardt his life at the hands of an Al Qaeda sniper.

The night before the rest of the unit met with the families and loved ones of the fallen heroes. The wake really hit home, especially to the Professor. After all, those who died were in his employ when the convoy was savagely attacked.

But the families of Moeller and Schroder were proud of their men, especially when they learned the enemy terrorists were defeated. They were also glad knowing war criminals were captured and sent to The Hague to stand trial for their atrocities.

The fourth day of December was a calm and beautiful sunny day. But it would also be a day etched on all of the Garrison's minds. From this day forward Professor Pearson and James Malloy were going to do everything in their power to make sure all of the men and women in the Garrison would be protected with the best state-of-the-art weapons and body armor.

Pearson was still a little queasy about the reaction of two Corporation scientists after he shared the secret information with them in Berlin. Professor Heinrich Kruger and Professor Joseph Stellarnberg were at the top in their fields and might feel insulted that they weren't first asked their input on Pearson and Darfuir's decision.

But Pearson felt a little bit better that Professor Darfuir would be there to help him explain the dire circumstances. Darfuir was arriving in Berlin with Carl Livingston to coincide with the burial in Dusseldorf.

The three limousines turned down a busy street and heard the clang of a ship's bell somewhere in the distance. The church of St. Boniface was at the end of the hill, winding up around a botanical garden adjacent to it. People exited their cars wearing traditional black garb to memorialize the somber occasion. A priest greeted the weary mourners as they entered his cathedral for the funeral mass.

Two funeral coaches pulled up with two black Mercedes limos thirty feet behind. The Schroeder and Moeller families got out and some of the men from each family stood behind hearses for pall bearing duty.

Hansy led Trudy, Calvin, Benny, Carlos and Wilhelm Kruger's younger brother to the casket. Klaus lead Orion, Bobby, Lars, Malloy and Mike Maguiness to Gerhardt Moeller's casket. The entire funeral procession consisted of men all wearing black armbands with the new insignia logo of the newly formed Global Garrison.

Both caskets rolled out of the hearses and loaded onto the walking gurneys. Approaching them was General Dieter Ansbach, Colonel Franz Schubert and seven German soldiers and sailors for burial detail. General Ansbach handed a folded German flag to one of the seven and he and the others draped it across the casket as the women in the crowd began to cry.

Then Colonel Schubert handed another German flag to another one of the weeping women and repeated the same with the other casket. The burial detail stood at attention with three facing the other three, and the highest-ranking member standing between them, two feet in front of them. They stood six feet apart, perfectly parallel. They rolled the caskets on the gurneys to the first landing of the entrance of the cathedral.

The priest came down to join the altar boys, one on each side of him. He prayed in German as the procession bowed their heads. Then he waved the funeral incense over both flag-draped coffins.

The pallbearers grabbed the handles of the caskets as the seven color guards snapped to a salute, then followed the priest into the church. Family members wept as the caskets were brought in front of the altar.

The mass lasted forty-five minutes and the faces amongst the pallbearers were desolate. Orion grimaced as he saw the priest once more wave the smoky incense over the caskets. It reminded him of the cordite smoke around the chopper that day he and his team were ambushed in Afghanistan.

Lanny grabbed him by his chin and made him look straight into her eyes. "Johnny, you going to be all right, baby?"

Orion shook his head to bring himself back around. "Yeah honey, it's just starting to bring back painful memories."

Lanny hugged him as tight as she could, then snuggled even closer to him.

The priest motioned for the pallbearers to surround the coffins and be at the ready to exit the church. He invoked the final blessing and waved holy water over the caskets. Some of it hit Orion by accident, spooking him.

Standing at the middle of Gerhardt's coffin, Orion accidentally lifted the coffin in the air. Everyone in the church was completely stunned by the incredible feat.

Malloy gave Orion a look of concern as he tried to calm his friend down. "John, are you okay? Maybe you should sit this one out."

Orion regained his composure. "I'll be all right, Skipper. I'm not sitting this one out. Gerry wouldn't sit it out if our roles were reversed, either."

"All right Lieutenant, but stay alert. No more powerlifting, if you know what I mean," warned Malloy.

Orion complied with, "Aye aye, Sir."

Malloy looked at the priest and explained, "He has a robotic prosthetic." Then looking at the rest of the team he conveyed, "We've got to get it fixed. Sometimes it's got a mind of its own."

Palladin added, "Yeah, we'll have Carl and Dr. Darfuir look at it when we get back to Berlin."

But the eyes of the General and his men were still popping out of their heads.

The priest continued to lead the procession out of the cathedral as the organ music resumed. The color guard again paralleled themselves, then presented arms and saluted as the coffins passed through. The pallbearers loaded their fallen comrades into the hearses and boarded the waiting limousines for the final trip to graveside.

Lanny ran over to the Professor's limo and stuck her head inside. "He'll be all right, Poppa. I'll keep my eyes on him. This is just bringing back memories of his best friend Billy's death."

Pearson looked back at his daughter. "All right, sweetheart. But please relay to him this is very dangerous for us all. We can't arouse suspicions."

Lanny nodded. "I understand, Poppa. I'll make sure." She went back to rejoin her man in a limousine behind the Professor's.

The procession proceeded towards the Rhine River only five minutes away. Inside Lanny's limo she conveyed to Orion the importance of him being discreet. She comforted her man by telling him to glance her if he felt something going wrong. Lanny then reached into the breast pocket of his suit jacket and pulled out his sunglasses.

Putting them on him she said, "Wear these to be on the safe side. We can't have those beautiful baby blues turning purple, now can we, honey?"

Orion chuckled. "I don't know what I'd do without you, baby."

Bobby added, "Yeah purple boy, ix-nay on the purple-nay!"

Everybody in the limo gave a composed laugh of relief. The funeral procession turned onto the river road as the occupants got a glimpse of the mighty Rhine River. They began to see cemetery monuments as they headed north towards the entrance. The first hearse turned right as the rest of the funeral procession followed. Two giant steel gates opened wide and above them was written Sturbourg Cemetery.

As the first hearse entered, it turned left and then proceeded down an embankment towards the burial site. As the first hearse carried Wilhelm Schroeder along the narrow road, the gravediggers stood by a three foot high mound of dirt with a backhoe awaiting thirty feet back. Two mounds of dirt and two six-foot holes were visible right next to each other.

Another mound of dirt could be seen behind the second grave, only fifteen feet from a large and distinctive oak tree with an attached sign that read Gustav Hill. Overlooking the left was a full view of the Rhine River.

The procession slowly and somberly followed the priest and pallbearers to the gravesite. Gunnar was wheeled across the grass by Hans von Dietrich. Both of them asked the gravediggers to bury the coffins so they would be facing the Rhine.

The one in charge told them it would be their honor. The entire funeral procession surrounded both graves as the priest again consecrated the caskets with holy water. Father Peter Steiner first prayed in Latin and then continued in German.

A cool wind suddenly arrived at everyone's backs as cumulus clouds opened to let the full rays of the sun beam down. To everyone, it felt like a sign from God, as if he (or she) was welcoming the two heroes to heaven.

As Father Steiner continued, more tears appeared on everyone's faces. Orion, with his head bowed in reverence, slowly tried to compose himself, but instead went into a trance-like state, drifting back in time to the start of that awful day the terrible death of his best friend.

CHAPTER FOUR: DAY ON THE MOUNTAIN

DATE: September 14, 2006. PLACE: Kandahar, Afghanistan (Helmand Province), Mongoose SOCOM Headquarters.

Flashback: Inside of bivouac tent on the office side of the Compound a Navy Lieutenant JG shook his buddy to wake up for their morning run. Time: 05:15 hours.

"Come on, you lazy shit. Do I have to change your diaper, too?"

John Orion slowly opened his eyes. "First let me put another load in there for you, Billy. We would want to gyp you at a latrine duty, would we?"

Billy laughed. "Come on pal, we got to set an example for the enlisted men. Oh by the way, the towel-heads shot more rockets into the air base last night. After you and Lars muster the men, the Skipper needs us in the operations tent."

Orion ignored him, but Billy persisted. "Yo brother, come on! I still want to eat sometime in this century."

Orion yawned and stood up, then pulled on his Navy gray sweat suit and Nike sneakers. He turned the Silver point on his watch to coincide with the minute hand and left his bivouac to meet Billy outside as they began to run.

"You know, you're really supposed to set your watch when you're actually running, bro."

Orion shrugged. "What are you, my mother now?"

"Hell no," replied Billy as he ran alongside. "She used to spank us when we cheated. And your ass used to hurt a lot more than mine."

"Okay, Billy, I'll take five seconds off at the end of the run."

"Try ten. Remember, my mother used to wash our mouths out with soap for lying."

Orion, remembering, put his hand up to his mouth. "Ten it is."

Laughing, they controlled the cadence of the same run they took every day. It was configured by Benny and lasted approximately four miles.

Benny used to hold the record until he trained the kid, Kyle, who was only twenty-two-years-old. Chief Kramer took him under his wing to make sure he'd make it home to his loved ones. After amazing Kyle with his sorcery and magic, the kid loved him like a father . . . except this father was one of the most expert commandos on the face of the Earth. He was a little unorthodox, but that's what made Benny arise above the rest. No one could predict what he would do next.

Kyle was a speedster and took his training very seriously with the Chief. Benny instilled in Kyle the necessity to be aware of his surroundings at all times, and Kyle was an excellent student.

Coming to the end of their run, Orion asked Billy if he wanted to eat before they headed for the showers.

Billy, always hungry, told them, "What you think? That's a stupid question."

The smell of bacon and hot cakes filled the air as they entered the giant chow hall tent. Billy had the mess workers start piling up his plate with food. Orion grabbed his tray and loaded his plate with a lot of bacon and eggs. His sixteen ounce glass of milk was filled to the brim.

As they took their seats, they saw the rest of the unit plus a few Green Berets enter the chow tent. One of them, a Staff Sergeant named Frankie Collins, jokingly said to Billy and Orion, "You fuckin' SQUIDS keep eating like that, you're going to stink up the choppers."

"How else are we going to let you grunts know we're there?" laughed Billy.

"Better not do that on the water," commented Frankie. "Your ass bubbles are going to give you away."

Orion shouted over to Frankie, "You're a fucking pissa Frankie," as he dropped his fork in laughter.

The comradery amongst the warriors continued as the chow tent filled up. Frankie sat down with Orion, and Billy and began conversing.

"You guys hear about the raid we pulled off yesterday in boogie land? That guy Baraash's Intel was right on. That's the second time we've taken out a major Taliban stronghold."

Orion cut it off immediately. "Frankie, I still don't trust that guy. All of a sudden this shit is dumped on us like a birthday present. I think it's too convenient. Besides Frankie, they only found two bodies in a compound. How do we know those bodies weren't already dead when you called in the airstrike?"

Frankie, annoyed, replied, "C'mon Lieutenant. You know fucking well it was a good kill!"

Being great friends with Frankie, Orion retorted, "I'm sorry, buddy. You're right, it was a good kill. Congratulations, brother."

"I know, Johnny. It's been frustrating getting permission just to cross into Pakistan. But I think this guy's legit, answered Frankie, who thought for a second. "What's his name . . . Caresano. You know, that guy in the CIA. He said he had them checked out. Come on Lieutenant, go with the flow, and we might soon be out of this godforsaken hellhole."

Billy looked up at Frankie. "God, I hope so. I really do, brother."

The three of them joked as other members of the fire team sat down and joined them. They finished and looked at the clock on the wall. Orion told Billy that they could still meet up with them after their debriefing with the Brass.

The two best friends headed for the showers and got ready for the meeting with Malloy and the other Top Brass. After they got into their BDUs (battle dress uniforms) they headed for the Command Operations Center in the middle of the compound. As they walked into the tent they saw Captain Malloy standing next to CIA operator, Emanuel Caresano.

Pointing to a map on a topographical terrain of Pakistan was Colonel David Caldwell. Also standing around the table was Lieutenant General Andrew Spanks (logistics officer), Lieutenant Colonel Marvin Pollock, and next to him the so-called Taliban double agent Amal Baraash.

Malloy looked up and spotted his two finest officers enter the tent. "Come in, Lieutenants Orion and Stokes."

Orion gave Baraash a look of distrust as he and Billy approached the map.

Malloy explained that last night, a cell of Al Qaeda operators launched the rocket attack at the southern tip of the airbase. They were able to destroy a Kiowa Scout helicopter and badly damaged a Cayuse Loach. Dressed in Afghan Army fatigues, they kept the sentries busy while the others fired on the choppers. Baraash was able to retrieve Intel from the same enemy operators. He also conveyed they were regrouping with a large contingent of heavily armed insurgents in a hidden compound in Chaman, Pakistan.

Billy asked Malloy if the area had been reconned from the air. Lieutenant Colonel Pollack answered that a UAV predator drone had confirmed a large presence of Taliban insurgents not far from that exact location.

Billy looked at Orion. "You see brother, the picture tells the story."

Orion shook his head. "How goddamn convenient can you get? Everything right on a silver fucking platter."

CIA operative Manny Caresano barked at Orion, "What is your major malfunction, Lieutenant?

Orion looked back at both him and Baraash. "I've got a team of men who trust my diligence. They know I'm doing everything in my power to make sure they make it back alive. By the way, I don't trust your trained monkey over there."

Baraash with eyes popping out of his head said, "This is the thanks I get for showing my loyalty. I'm doing everything possible and putting myself and my family in danger. If Mullah Omar found out what I was doing, he would have all of my family killed and tortured. Now I feel I'm being slapped in my face and mistreated because I am Muslim."

Orion, disgusted, said, "You want me to stop playing the violin?"

Caresano slammed his fist down onto the map and said to Malloy, "Captain, this is your finest operator? I don't think we can use him on this mission. It doesn't seem he'll be able to execute our plan according to our details."

Captain Malloy then shot at Orion with a look of "What are you doing?" He asked Orion, "Lieutenant, do you have a problem executing my orders to the T?"

Orion stood at a stiff attention. "No Sir. I will follow your orders just the way you give them to me."

Malloy then looked at Caresano. "Is that good enough for you, agent Caresano?"

Caresano, annoyed, replied, "Fine with me. Just keep your tiger on a leash until it's time to deploy."

Billy, not liking the tone used against his best friend, glared at Caresano.

Malloy with the general and his team went over the mission to ensure the times and logistics would be carried out precisely. All the while, Orion snuck quick glances at Baraash to see how he reacted during the briefing. Every time Orion peered at him, Baraash defiantly stared back.

Colonel Caldwell told them their LZ would be two miles west of the compound in Chaman and that the time of the infiltration would be approximately 16:25 hours just as the sun was going down.

Two COBRA helicopters would accompany the SEAL team and break off as soon as they knew boots were on the ground. From there, Orion and his fire team would travel East about two clicks and make sure the recon from the Predator drone was copacetic with the intel Baraash had given them. Then Orion and his team would observe enemy strength and positioning. From there, Orion would have to determine what kind of airstrike would be necessary to take out the compound.

The team would be equipped with three SOFLAM special opposition forward laser acquisition markers. They would paint the lasers on strategic areas so as not to leave any trace of the enemy for retaliation. Orion was to first take reconnaissance photos because Baraash said Mullah Omar would be in charge of the planned Taliban assault. A UAV Global Hawk would be carrying laser guided cellulose acquisition bombs. But Command specifically wanted proximity devices on them so they would explode seconds before hitting the target. This was to make sure that the human equation was taken out. This also made it easier to identify the remains, if possible.

From there the team would go through the encampment and gather up any intelligence they could. But little did they know this was all a ploy by Baraash to get the $80 million Global Hawk into enemy airspace. They had two Stinger shoulder fired missiles with them so they would be able to take it out. The Predators and the Global Hawks were the biggest deterrent on Al Qaeda to wage war.

Orion's call sign would be TALON. Command's call sign would be Taj Mahal. The back-up QRF (quick reactionary force) sign was Firebird. The two Super Cobras from the Red Dog 773 unit were Pterodactyl.

Orion asked if there was a backup contingency plan and immediately Caresano shot that scenario down even before it could be addressed.

As the debriefing ended Orion went over to Captain Malloy and Colonel Caldwell. "I'm carrying out the mission, but under protest."

The colonel in charge of operations conveyed to Orion that his protest was duly noted.

Orion and Billy left the Command tent and headed back towards their team's berthing area. Billy started laughing, and hysterically said to Orion, "Trained fucking monkey, hah. You really don't like those Virginia farm boys, do ya?"

Orion smiled and replied, "I thought you'd like that one, pal. I still don't understand why Malloy won't let you tag along on this one, Billy. You think just like I do."

Billy wrapped his arm around Orion's shoulders as they headed for their hooches. "The Skipper told me I'd be flying surveillance immediately after your return. Besides, I think you've finally learned how to wipe your own ass by now."

Orion pulled away from his pal and punched him in the shoulder. "Fuck you, I can fly a helicopter almost as good as you."

Billy with a shit-eating grin wrapped his arm around Orion's shoulder. "That's the key word—ALMOST."

"C'mon bro, I got to give the heads up to our guys, and you know they're not going to be happy about this one, either."

Orion and Billy entered the Rec tent to find Trudy and Lars playing pool against Kyle and Benny. Bobby Palladin was in the corner lifting free weights. Orion told all of them to gather around the pool table. He then instructed the other soldiers and sailors to leave the tent.

Orion gave a quick go-over of the situation to his compatriots, and immediately Benny completely disapproved.

"As soon as the Brass is done in the Operation's tent, the Skipper will call for us and go over the plan in exact detail," explained Orion. "Carry on with what you're doing."

He then pulled Benny to the side. "Let's take a walk around the compound." The two left the Rec tent and began walking slowly around the base.

"I've been in too many operations that are totally based on what a so-called turncoat has to offer," Orion commented. "Just in case we're set up, will you be able to come up with a secret contingency plan? Can you reach down into your magic bag of tricks just to be on the safe side?"

Of course, this conversation was between him and Benny alone.

"I'll have something devised in time to carry out the mission," assured Benny.

Orion knew Chief Kramer wouldn't let him down due to of the prowess and integrity of the man.

Orion and the Chief headed back to the Rec tent to get some R&R.

Soon the captain called the team up for their debriefing. When they got back, Benny asked Kyle to follow him to their hooches. He figured there would be no better time to get the kid a little firing practice on the range west of the base, and took a Comm Unit with him just in case they were called on for an emergency.

Time: 10:40 hours. September 14, 2006.

Time: 16:04 hours.

Having just loaded a specially modified Seahawk helicopter, an elite group of Navy Seals hunkered down as they followed two Super Cobra helicopters into what they called "the valley of death." Lieutenant John Orion was last to board. He looked at his best friend Lieutenant JG William Stokes as the chopper lifted-off.

Billy, concerned, pumped his fist in the air at Orion and then saluted. Orion just barely saw him through the clouds of dust as they lifted off, and returned the salute back to his childhood friend. Looking east across the terrain, Orion noticed the sun was slowly fading at their backs.

Just forty minutes before, he had created a diversion to pull away the two guards on the tarmac by showing them hot naked pictures of gorgeous porn star Tela Patrick. As he lured them slightly away from the choppers, Chief Benjamin Kramer and his protégé second-class petty officer Kyle Duffy secretly loaded a duffel bag into the chopper.

The Seahawk was specially modified to fly in silence by improvising the fuselage which stealth technology. The Super Cobras were to follow them and until they were twenty clicks out from their landing zone. There they would hover until receiving a transmission from Orion informing them they were safely inserted.

Inside the chopper everyone double-checked their gear and firearms. Soon they were twenty miles into Pakistani airspace. That's when Orion filled in the rest of the team about Chief Kramer's precautionary plan, just in case of a double cross. Once they proceeded past the Cobras, they awaited confirmation of insertion. Orion would order the chopper pilot to veer north until they were two clicks in from the specified LZ.

There Benny and Kyle would fast rope down with their gear and bring what they snuck onto the chopper ahead of the mission. The chopper would then turn back southwest toward the original point of insertion. Since they were flying below the radar, Command would never be able to pick up the deviation in their flight path. This would also give Benny and Kyle ample time to get into position to recon.

As the Seahawk flew towards their objective Orion filled the pilot in on the small change of plans. The pilot seemed worried, but Orion assured him that he'd tell Command he forced it upon him in the event something went wrong. After all, once they were dropped off, the pilot's orders were to immediately return to base.

A blue light emitted, cueing them that it was ten minutes to insertion. The pilot looked at Orion and got a nod. The pilot radioed the Cobras to break off and hover. Then the Seahawk moved east in a straight line.

The pilot waited about three minutes before deviating his course northeast to insert Benny and Kyle into their newly designated position. The pilot, knowing the terrain, came upon the position Orion had specified. He then hovered as Benny and Kyle sent their gear and themselves into the valley of death.

Once they were on the ground, Orion gave Benny the 'proceed as planned' sign. Both of them were equipped with more than a normal man could carry and began to travel southeast towards the undetermined enemy encampment.

The Seahawk began its return to the original drop off point. Three more minutes elapsed before the pilot relayed to Orion that they were coming up on the insertion zone. Orion transmitted to Benny that they were now at the specified LZ, and Benny told Orion he should be in position about five minutes. Orion copied him and the rest of the fire team fast roped with their gear and firearms to the terrain below.

Immediately they grabbed the gear for an accelerated run to make up the time wasted on the contingency plan. While Orion and the rest of the team head for their positions, Benny and Kyle arrived just below a small hill that lead into the valley. Benny reached into his tactical vest for his Starlight Five night vision scope. Then silently and slowly he made his way to the top of the hill.

Benny trained the scope around an encircled area of the enemy compound. He carefully checked to see if Baraash's Intel panned out. Mostly he was hoping to have proof positive that Mullah Omar could be identified as being there.

Normally there would be about ten roving sentries moving about the compound, and the chief found it odd that no sentries were posted at all.

He decided to belly crawl backwards and contact Orion just as he heard in the distance two men speaking in Arabic.

Belly crawling back up the hill to recon the situation, Benny heard one of the men ask the other if everybody was in place.

The other man replied, "Just waiting for our company to arrive." He laughed in an evil way.

Benny motioned down the hill for Kyle to come up and join them. Orion and his whole team were dressed as enemy insurgents, and Benny made him and Kyle look even more raggedy in their dress than the rest of the fire team.

Then Benny gave a hand signal to Kyle that he was going to sneak up on the two insurgents and silently take them out.

Kyle nodded as Benny took his Knights M-110 with him and belly crawled silently towards the two Taliban insurgents. Circling around their backs, he slowly pulled out his combat knife and waited until both of them took their eyes off each other.

Then he struck, coming up behind the one closest to him. In one single motion, Benny put his hand over the insurgent's mouth and drove his blade into the base of the back of his neck. The insurgent made a grunting sound before he dropped to the ground, dead.

The other insurgent whipped around instantly and raised his weapon. A tiny "pop" sounded and the insurgent's head exploded from a deadly projectile. It was Kyle's silencer on his SABR rifle with 338 Lupua rounds that killed the bastard. The LWRL International weapons company makes an astounding rifle and second class Petty Officer Duffy loved it.

Benny smiled and motioned for him to come over immediately. As Kyle grabbed the gear, Benny hand signaled him to leave it. Kyle descended empty-handed down the hill with incredible speed.

Benny took off the hat of insurgent he just killed and put it on Kyle as he arrived. He then motioned for both Kyle and him to put on their cloaks, then grabbed the insurgent's AK-47s. They drug the bodies to the gear.

Benny hurriedly rifled through the secret duffel bag that had been snuck onboard the chopper. He put all sorts of items in his bloody cloak. This time he and Kyle drug the heavy bag back up the hill and left it just out of sight close to the top.

Benny pushed the Comm button by his neck and transmitted to Orion, "Talon, this is Wizard. You hear me?"

A squelching came back in his earpiece, and Orion replied, "I'm here, Wizard. What's going on in the Emerald City?"

"I see two wooden shacks with three canvas trucks parked about forty feet apart," informed Benny. "I've infiltrated the compound in the Northeast corner."

"Is there is any proof of the Taliban chief in the area?" asked Orion.

"Not so far, but there is another enemy activity that could warrant it," replied Benny. "Funny, there are three spools of concertina wire on the compound. Two are almost empty, and the other is half empty."

Orion wondered what the enemy was doing with American-made razor wire and checked his watch. He decided to start moving in on the Taliban encampment and transmitted back to Taj Mahal Command Base that they were proceeding as planned.

Back at the command base Malloy and the Top Brass, with Caresano and Amal Baraash, were looking at the map on the table. They received Orion's transmission from a loudspeaker above:

"Taj Mahal, this is Talon. Beginning operation Houdini. Enemy encampment verified, over."

Malloy replied, "We hear you, Talon. Execute with extreme caution, over."

"That's a copy, Taj Mahal. Over and out."

Orion signaled for the team to move into the bushy area fifty feet from the entrance of the compound.

Back at the base, Amal Baraash told Caresano he needed to use the bathroom due to a queasy stomach from the thought of people being killed. Baraash covered his mouth like he was about to throw up. Everyone in the room looked disgusted. Caresano told Baraash to leave the room and get sick outside.

As Baraash left in a hurry Caresano laughed. "I guess these Towel Heads really don't have the stomach for this after all."

Immediately Malloy and Billy Stokes gave each other a look: IS THIS GUY REALLY THAT NAIVE?

Back around the enemy encampment Orion's team spread out and reached into their MOLLE packs, then removed their SOFLAMs for target acquisition. Once in position Orion conveyed to Command to send in the Global Hawk.

Command contacted Bagram Airbase to begin the operation. Master Sergeant Kim Parks confirmed and began to remote the joystick that controlled the unmanned aircraft. With radar control, she maneuvered the Global Hawk now flying over Marut, Afghanistan. Marut was fifty miles Northeast of Chaman, Pakistan, and within ten minutes the aircraft should arrive, just about in line to fire with lasers painted on their designated targets.

Back in the Northeast corridor at the edge of the compound Chief Kramer looked for anything out of the ordinary with his night vision scope.

At Command headquarters the intensity of the operation's room was at a level of anxiety. All the sudden, an explosion to the east of the base came roaring at a high decibel level. Automatic weapons sounded off in the distance.

Malloy told Billy to check what was going on while the rest stayed put to await Orion's call for extraction. Billy exited the tent to spot GMVs and other vehicles by a giant hole in the fence firing at a vehicle escaping in the distance.

"What happened?" Lieutenant JG Stokes asked the guards, who pointed over to a dead Army Corporal. "We saw that guy Baraash kill him as he set explosives to breach the outer gate. When he approached the scene, they opened up on him with AK-47s and had him pinned down."

Billy told them not to follow because this could be a set up for an ambush. He high-tailed it back to the Command tent to let the Skipper know what was going on. Out of breath, he reached the tent just as Chief Kramer noticed men climbing out of holes camouflaged with plywood and burlap canvases. The canvases were slightly covered with dirt to give the impression of solid ground.

Benny couldn't believe how many men came out of the holes. Many emerged from the hilly area just out of their fire team's position. They had their eyes trained on them for some time, and Benny was thankful that Orion went with his instincts and asked for a backup plan.

With the insurgents unaware of Benny and Kyle s presence, Benny told Orion over his Comm, "Fall back! It's a trap!"

Orion immediately gave the sign to break off and fall back. They ran about a hundred yards from that position to a fence when concertina wire came springing up in front of them. Orion seeing that they were now trapped radioed ahead to Command and let them know they were in trouble. As he did, the bullets flew all around, forcing them to take cover.

"TAJ MAHAL, THIS IS TALON. WE VE BEEN SET UP. Send Pterodactyl and Firebird, OVER."

Back at Command, Billy had just entered the tent and heard his best friend's desperate cry for help. His eyes and mouth showed his rage at the CIA operator Emmanuel Caresano. "YOU MOTHER FUCKER, I'm going to kill you when this is over. Captain, we got to send them in NOW!"

Colonel Caldwell looked over at Malloy. "Send the Pterodactyls with the Firebird(QRF) team."

But as this was going on, the Global Hawk had just entered enemy airspace. Over the next hill, Benny saw an insurgent lift a shoulder-fired Stinger weapon and aim it into the sky. Next to him was a man in chieftain s garb and headgear holding a laptop and using a Global positioning device to pick up the Global Hawk.

Benny immediately signaled Kyle to grab the M-32 grenade launcher out of the duffel bag. Kyle came running up as the Taliban chief noticed what was going on and began to run. But before he left, Benny heard him tell the other insurgent that the missile was locked onto the Global Hawk, and to fire immediately.

Benny grabbed the grenade launcher from Kyle and fired it before the insurgent could lift it to his shoulder. A gigantic explosion rocked the hill nearby as the Taliban chief got away in the distance. Benny looked around, but Kyle was nowhere to be seen. At that moment, Benny conveyed to Orion that the enemy had Stinger missiles.

Back at Command headquarters, everyone in the Operations room heard the same thing. Immediately, Caresano told Colonel Caldwell to delay that order. "We can't risk our aircraft being shot down from Stinger missiles, especially the $80 million Global Hawk."

Billy started to charge Caresano, but General Andrew Spanks shouted out, "STAND DOWN, LIEUTENANT STOKES. I'm sorry to say, this asshole is right. And I'm sorry son, I can't risk the lives of 34 men."

Then he looked angrily at Caresano. "And you are relieved of any command, and you are under arrest following a board of inquiry. He then looked at Lieutenant Colonel Pollack and told him to place Caresano under arrest.

Billy still complained and threw a glass, smashing it across the map in front of them. He ran out of the Command tent and Colonel Caldwell ordered him to return, which Billy ignored.

Caldwell looked at Malloy. "If Stokes does anything foolish I'll have him locked up, too."

Captain Malloy reassured them and tried to calm Billy down, exiting the Command tent. Outside he saw Billy running towards a Seahawk helicopter at the ready to extract the team. Malloy caught up as the chopper's Flight Officer held a 92-F Beretta pistol at Billy. The Flight Officer asked the pilot to come over as Malloy arrived.

Malloy held up his hand to the Flight Officer. "Don't worry, Mike. I've got this covered."

The Flight Officer, Michael Turner, relaxed his grip for a second and took his eyes off Malloy. Malloy quickly put him in a sleeper hold while Billy knocked out the pilot. They both jumped in and Billy piloted the Seahawk chopper east. Throttling at full speed, he said to Malloy, "Thanks, Skipper. You know both of us are going to Leavenworth for this one."

Malloy laughed. "Well, if we make it back alive, at least we'll be able to keep each other company."

Back in the Northeast corner of the hill, Benny launched six tear gas grenades into the enemy's firing positions. He then reached into his bloody cloak and pulled out three red and three green smoke grenades, loading them into the M-32. Then he headed toward the position just outside of his team's position.

All the sudden, Kyle appeared with the unconscious Taliban Chief draped over his left shoulder. He could hear the Seahawk chopper coming in from the west.

Aboard the chopper, Billy and Malloy kept hearing General Spanks scream over the radio, "RTB, RTB, RTB. If you don't, I'll have you both court-martialed."

RTB meant return to base and by the General's tone, he meant it. Immediately.

Below on the ground Benny told Orion, "Get ready. They're getting us out." He pressed his Comm button. "Kyle, are you ready, my apprentice?"

From Benny's ear piece came, "That I am, Mr. Wizard."

Benny fired the first three smoke grenades fifty feet east of the position of the fire team. Red smoke instantly engulfed the entire compound. An explosion directly behind went off, exactly where Kyle was hunkered down with the unconscious Taliban chief.

Orion and the team saw an opening in the concertina wire and escaped through it. Benny came running up as the Seahawk was coming into sight and fired the three green smoke grenades just a little west of there.

Billy's voice reached Orion's earpiece. "Talon, there's no Firebird. But I guess this will do."

Orion with a big smile on his face said, "I love you, brother. First ten beers are on me." The smile on the entire team was insurmountable.

The chopper sat down and Malloy helped bring the prisoner on board. Kyle then took the duffel bag that seemed only half full and centered it in the blasted opening of the razor wire. But just then, more bullets were shot by the desperate enemy. They got close to the chopper.

Benny yelled to Kyle, "Leave it! Let's get out of here!"

Kyle pushed a Claymore mine next to the bag and ran. Benny reached into his bloody cloak, but this time pulled out fragmentation grenades and loaded six of them into the revolving cylinder. He immediately fired two just a beyond the dissipating green smoke.

Malloy yelled to Billy, "Okay Billy Boy, take us home."

Billy smiled at Orion and at that exact moment a stray bullet pierced Billy's neck.

In a state of horror and shock, Orion and the rest of the fire team watched as Billy slumped over.

Orion screamed in agony, "OH GOD, NO. PLEASE, OH GOD NO! BILLY! BILLY! NOOOOOO!"

Then more bullets came at a faster clip. Lars Olsen pulled Billy out of the pilot seat and checked to see if anything could be done. But everyone knew he was dead, instantly.

Malloy screamed at Orion, "Johnny, you're the only one who can fly this thing. Come on, they're almost on us."

Orion shook like a leaf and stumbled into the pilot seat crying hysterically. "I don't know if I can do this. Oooh . . . BILLY!"

Benny looked outside the chopper and faintly saw the insurgents appear. Coming over to Orion he calmly said, "Jonathan, take a deep, deep breath. That's it, now overcome your hurt and concentrate. You'll be able to save all of us."

Orion took his advice and the Seahawk climbed into the sky. About fifty feet off Kyle noticed an insurgent aiming an RPG-7 at them. He yelled to Bobby Palladin to aim at the Claymore hidden at the opening in the razor wire. Palladin with his Barrett M-107 fired, and an unbelievable explosion killed every one of them.

Orion headed west towards the base, but looked back to see if some kind of miracle occurred to bring Billy back from the dead. Benny blocked his view and reminded him that the safety of his other five brothers-in-arms was still in his hands.

Orion closed his eyes to regain composure, gripping the controls tightly in both of hands. He finally screamed out in despair, "BILLY!"
***

When Orion opened his eyes, he was standing at the funerals of Wilhelm and Gerhardt. Everyone around him seemed to be in a state of suspended animation. He felt a slight tap on the shoulder and swiftly turned, not quite believing what he saw. His childhood friend stood there smiling with his hands and palms folded across his chest. A purple glow surrounded him the same way it did when Orion defied gravity.

"Johnny Boy, this shit has got to stop. Too many people are counting on you now," spoke his friend.

Orion looked around and still everybody was frozen. Lanny looked at him with dire concern.

Orion then said to Billy, "Am I fucking dead, too?"

Billy looked up at the sky, shaking his head in disbelief. Still gazing upward, he talked as if someone was there. "So why was he chosen to save the Earth and everyone in the galaxy? What about this ability to figure things out in an instant?"

Orion asked Billy, bewildered, "Billy, who the hell are you talking to? And what the fuck is going on?"

He then looked over and saw Wilhelm and Gerhardt with their arms similarly folded across their chests. Orion waved to them and they smiled and waved back. Orion tried to walk towards Billy and noticed he couldn't move his legs.

Then Billy put his left arm around Orion's back and said, "You keep calling my name, brother, and I love you so much. I had to come and set you straight." He then pointed to Professor Pearson and said, "That man right there is probably one of the smartest to ever live. On top of that, Johnny, he's one of the most loving souls to ever live. Your destiny and his were determined a long time ago. His love for others is what gave you another chance at life. I just thank God that you met this unbelievably gorgeous woman to crack you out of your shell. She's also the reason you got another chance in the ring. John, you don't seem to understand that the man over there created a technology to save the world from deadly diseases, then created another man to help rid the galaxy of evil."

Orion asked with hesitation, "You're talking about me?"

Billy once again looked at his friend in disbelief. "Noooh, fucking Lucille Ball. Of course I'm talking about you! Johnny, I'm okay. What happened that day on the mountain was horrible, but I chose the right way to live. God has taken good care of me and then some. Oh, and if you tell anybody you've seen me, then Lanny's heart will really be broken. That's because she'll think she's losing you . . . because you'd be losing your mind. CAPISH?"

Billy hugged him and said that during the next year Orion would be blessed with the best news he'd ever had. "You could probably consider yourself a Guardian Angel, but remember Lanny is still in control. This is God's plan."

Orion asked, "Why did he pick me?"

Billy instantly answered, "What makes you think God is a he? That, Johnny boy, you will find out another time." He began fading away and the two warriors Gerhardt and Wilhelm began to do the same. "We're counting on you, brother. God's counting on you, and she told me herself."

Billy then disappeared as Orion's jaw dropped. "GOD'S A SHE?"

Billy appeared again laughing. "Just fucking with you, brother. One day you'll know."

Then he was gone.

Orion laughed to the air, "I won't let you down." As he looked straight ahead, everybody began moving once again and Lanny asked, "Who aren't you going to let down, baby?"

"You of course, Lanny. I love you so much." He put his arm around her and squeezed her tight.

Lanny was glad to see him in a good mood, but reminded him that they were at a funeral. Just as Orion slapped her on the ass the seven men in the burial ceremony fired off three shots for their twenty-one gun salute. It amazed her that the shots didn't faze Orion one bit.

With a hearty smile she asked, "Have you had some kind of epiphany or something? Are you sure everything is alright, Johnny?"

Orion looked deeply into her loving eyes. "Awww Lanny, everything is just great."

They heard, "PRESENT ARMS." Then everyone made their final salute to their fallen comrades.

Time: 12:16 hours. December 4, 2010. Dusseldorf.

The funeral procession broke up and the Global Garrison headed for the Corporation's second of its six headquarters established around the planet. Each one was equipped with hospitals to help those who could not help themselves. All of them had private airports with runways long enough to accept any type of aircraft. Professor Pearson and the team headed for Germany's capital, BERLIN.

Time: 14:00 hours. On to Berlin.

JOHN PETER FERRIS

CHAPTER FIVE: BRIEFED IN BERLIN

A Gulfstream Learjet belonging to Pearson Global Technologies landed at the international airport in Berlin, Germany. Dressed in elegant evening wear, the women of the Global Garrison walked down the ramp to three waiting limousines. Standing next to the last limo was Dr. Kamal Darfuir, the assistant executive officer of Pearson Global Technologies. Immediately the girls start waving and walked towards him. The men exited with Orion and Hansy shoulder holding Gunnar Mientz as he carefully deplaned down the ramp.

Pearson and Malloy were the last to depart, while the pilot Carl Bingham waited to taxi the jet for storage until the next day when they'd head back to Dusseldorf. Pearson and Malloy approached the last limo, then piled in and informed the entourage that they'd meet them at the hotel. Malloy told Orion and Lanny that he'd need them at the Berlin office to debrief the two Corporation scientists on the prior six day's events.

The chauffeur opened the right rear door. As they entered their attention was drawn to two elderly men in tailor-made suits sitting across from them. The Professor got in last and introduced Orion and Lanny to Professors Heinrich Kruger and Joseph Stellarnberg. The limousine headed downtown towards the more secluded eastern end of the city for the secret and confidential meeting of the minds.

Kruger told Captain Malloy that an Israeli Army Captain awaited him in the building and instructed him to contact Admiral Fischer before they attended the Ball that evening.

The limo traveled a good ten minutes, then made a right turn into an underground garage. As they pulled up a giant steel door slowly opened. The limousine entered as lights begin turning on to reveal an intricate laboratory with state-of-the-art scientific machinery and laboratory equipment.

The limo came to a stop and the chauffeur opened the door. Lanny looked around and saw medical and surgical equipment she didn't recognize. Some of the machines were high-tech top secret lasers known only to a privileged few. Even Orion was in awe of the laboratory and thought the gadgets looked like something from a Star Trek movie.

It turned out that Professor Heinrich Kruger was not annoyed at all when Pearson brought them all up to date, although Professor Stellarnberg was a little on edge. After all, his life's work was rocket science and the effort to propel the world back into the space race. But after meeting John Orion and Lanny Cromwell, he didn't blame them for saving Orion's life, especially Lanny with all her charm and knowledge of human anatomy. He was quite impressed that she knew so much about the impact of trauma on the body and how tremendous G-forces affected the brain.

Dr. Darfuir reiterated all the stages of the ICARUS PROJECT with Professor Krueger, including the topic of Orion's body and the super nano-microbes. Looking at the computer screen, Professor Stellarnberg and Professor Pearson witnessed the amazing transformation, seeing for themselves how Orion's face morphed into a transcendental state. On the screen his body glowed that eerie purple color of course, and all eyes turned to peek at Orion in the flesh.

Soon the computer revealed how the electro-magnetic accelerator was accidentally left on ten minutes past proper duration more than any human body could withstand.

Kruger asked Orion, "John, did you not feel the toll taken on your insides as you passed out?"

Orion thought for a moment. "Yeah, I do remember feeling like I was going to explode. But I utilized Malloy's SEAL training. In underwater surf, our bodies are slammed and we become disoriented. We are taught not to panic, but rather to concentrate and keep our composure. That's how I survived. I concentrated and overcame all the pain and discomfort in my body."

At that moment, the elevator bell rang and the door opened. Out stepped Captain Malloy and Captain Joshua Golon, looking concerned as they approached the others.

"Good to see you, Jim," said Kruger. "I was just asking our most amazing young man how he coped with the extreme pressure his body endured during the ICARUS PROJECT. He tells me it had a lot to do with the intense training he was put through."

Orion told the Skipper that he had shared with Kruger details of the Blackened-out Ditch and Don training that helped them all overcome the tremendous bombardment of pressure. Malloy further explained to Professor Kruger that this conditioned the individual not to panic, which prevented drowning.

Kruger let everyone know that if Orion hadn't concentrated and overcome the pressure, he would not have survived his ordeal. He asked Orion to join him at a complex-looking machine which would monitor his vital body organs none other than the nano-particle omitter and detector created by Professors Darfuir and Kruger about ten months ago. On the exam table connected to the machine was a cradle cap to explore the neurons in the brain. An EKG had been set up to monitor the heart, while an unusually thick cord with a probe would check all vital organs.

As Orion neared the table, Malloy told him the probe was a colonoscopy device that would enter through his anus.

Orion immediately zoomed to the other side of the laboratory, screaming, "NOBODY IS PUTTING THAT THING IN MY ASS!"

As Malloy exploded in hysterics, everybody else was shocked at Orion's powers. Kruger calmed Orion, assuring him that the probe would be inserted in another Icarus Device at the bottom of the table. Orion sighed with relief, then noticed Lanny and the others laughing uncontrollably. Realizing he made himself look ridiculous, he finally accepted his fate with a smile.

Professor Kruger placed the cradle cap on Orion's head. Lanny assisted by hooking up the five probes to the EKG. Then Professor Kruger lifted the Icarus Device laying on the shelf at the bottom of the table.

Orion asked why he didn't have to wear his special suit, and Professor Kruger explained the machine would only probe the super nano-microbes in the body. But it could also stimulate the nano-microbes to see how they reacted.

Professor Pearson helped Orion into the modified Icarus Device. Once he was totally secured, Professor Kruger attached the probe to the machine and turned on the power. Eerie purple lights immediately surrounded Orion's entire body with the familiar illuminating aura.

Kruger and Stellarnberg were immediately mystified.

"Jeffrey, this is way beyond our wildest dreams," exclaimed Kruger. "This young man's entire body has reoriented itself into an entity all its own."

As they looked at the screen, everyone witnessed Orion's atoms and molecular structure arranging in a manner no ordinary human would be able to withstand. The super nano-microbes by themselves managed to manufacture hundreds of unknown super nano-microbes.

"Jeffrey, you told me his body creates a force field that is impenetrable when it senses a threat," Kruger again commented. He then whispered something to Pearson, who whispered it to Malloy.

Orion with his back turned away from Malloy didn't see him pick up a wooden chair. Professor Pearson nodded to Malloy, and with look of regret Malloy hurled the chair at Orion.

Immediately, the force field protected both him and Lanny, who stood next to him. In fact, the chair broke into pieces.

"OH MY GOD!" shouted Kruger. "Jeffrey, look on the screen. I'll play it back for you. This is incredible!"

Everyone stared at the computer. Super nano-microbes reacted at an incredible speed to form a barrier, all the while supercharging around Orion and Lanny.

Lanny asked Professor Pearson and Kruger, "But why do they also protect me?"

The professors could only speculate that it was her DNA earlier introduced into Orion's body from one of the tears that had fallen onto Orion from Lanny's eye. The questioned loomed: Had the super nano-microbes chosen to combine with Orion because of Lanny's gentle nature?

Orion, pissed, exclaimed, "WHATEVER! Don't be throwing any damn chairs at me. You know, me, THE GUINEA PIG!"

Professor Kruger looked apologetic. I'm sorry about that, John. But if you knew it was coming, we would not have been able to track how your body's metabolism would react.

Orion shot Kruger a look of approval, but still reiterated, "Okay this time, Doc. But please, no more surprises."

Professors Kruger and Pearson smiled to reassure him. "You got it. No more surprises." They kept him on the particle machine and recorded stimulation factors and capabilities data. The computer's mainframe captured it all.

Finally after thirty minutes they removed the cradle cap and Icarus Device. Lanny unhooked the EKG lines from the pads sticking to Orion's body. Professor Kruger informed Orion that they would resume more tests once they were back in New York on Monday.

Professor Pearson instructed everyone to grab their things, because they were now heading to the Maderdoff Hotel to attend a gala extravaganza at the Johan Strauss Grand Ballroom in the heart of beautiful Berlin.

Lanny's face lit up with joy, having heard from Claire of the extravagance of the ballroom. Professor Pearson shared that at some of these functions, royal couples had been known from time to time to be present. Orion's heart melted as he observed how happy his girl was.

As they prepared leave, Kruger pulled the compact disc from the computer and put it in a case, which he handed to Professor Pearson. It was promptly tucked inside his suit jacket.

The group climbed into the limousine and headed west toward the center of Berlin.

Time: 18:35 hours.

Time: 19:50 hours. Maderhoff Hotel, Berlin.

They entered the main lobby of the Maderhoff Hotel and the entire entourage prepared to enter the Grand Ballroom in the west wing. Two giant doors similar to those back at the Citadel in East Hampton were made of red Oak with walnut outer lacing, scrolled around the edges and center. The left door had "Johann" embroidered into the lacing, while the right door was embroidered with "Strauss." Dignitaries and people of importance from around the world filed in as doormen from inside the Grand Ballroom opened the doors slowly to receive their distinguished guests.

As they entered the giant room the orchestra played Bolero by Ravel. Lanny Cromwell felt chills running down her back as she and Orion walked arm-in-arm. The waiters were dressed in formal uniforms and wore white gloves.

Claire noticed Kada Bondi wearing a very elegant Armani suit looking not at all frightening. Nor did he give her the creeps as he had the first time she saw him. Major Percival Nelson had Lunsi Paal with him to greet the Global Garrison in an area specified for them.

The giant ballroom could easily fit more than a thousand people comfortably. Twenty-four chandeliers hung from a forty-foot ceiling, positioned perfectly. Everything from the top to bottom was shining and the Global Garrison could practically see their reflections.

Orion and Lanny mingled with the other guests as Professor Pearson introduced his group to renowned people from all over the world. Gossip permeated the air, for the dramatic rescue in New York City had occurred just a couple of days before. Orion put on a nonchalant act and appeared disinterested at the whole melee. As he drank a bottle of Becks beer Lanny noticed a look of disgust on his face.

"Johnny, is all the talk getting you down?"

Orion shook his head. "HELL NO, BABY. It's just I can't get a buzz on from beer anymore. I can drink all I want, and nothing happens."

"Then why the hell are you drinking again?" Lanny asked.

Orion took a quick swig. "Because I love the taste of it."

"Well, okay, that's good. Maybe you'll behave yourself tonight, Johnny."

Orion took another swig. "I doubt that."

Lanny raised a finger to his face and scolded, "I swear to God, John Patrick Orion. You do anything to upset me tonight and I'll cut you off from you know what."

Orion looked seriously concerned. "Okay honey, I promise to be good."

More guests poured into the humongous room as the thirty-piece orchestra played Scheherazade. A small commotion revealed that someone very important had arrived. Lanny and Valerie walked over and spotted men in black suits looking around very cautiously. Four of them surveilled, then hand signaled two others standing by the doors.

Lanny spilled her glass of phony non-alcoholic champagne as Prince William of Great Britain strolled in with his future bride, Kate Middleton.

Walking next to Kate was her sister Pippa.

Valerie, being from England, was completely star struck as she helped Lanny clean the spot on her new Valentino evening dress.

"Oh my God, Val. The future king and queen of Great Britain are here in the same room with us tonight!"

To their amazement, the royals walked right up to Professor Pearson and Dr. Darfuir. Instantly Lanny, Valerie and Claire shot across the room to get in on the action.

Claire arrived just ahead of the other two. "Hi Poppa." Then trying to be non-invasive, she continued, "Your Majesty, what a delight to make your acquaintance." But before she finished, Lanny and Valerie moved in next to her. The royal guards advanced nervously, but Prince William waved them off with a smile.

Professor Pearson raised his eyes brows. "Your Majesty, I'd like you to meet my three inquisitive and nosy daughters. The little blonde who has almost introduced herself is Claire. Next to her is our raven-haired Lanny. Next up is my recently adopted daughter from England, Valerie."

The Prince and Kate looked confused but seemed to shrug it off.

"Where is Kendra?" the Prince quietly asked Professor Pearson. "I remember meeting her when you and my father were at this very same gala some time ago."

The Professor explained that Kendra was back in the states studying hard for exams.

By this time the girls had already aligned themselves in Kate and Pippa's circle. The ballroom slowly but surely became packed as the orchestra took a half an hour intermission. A disc-jockey took over, enticing the girls to place requests. All five girls headed out to the middle of the floor as music from Joss Stone began to play. They shook up the crowd as they moved in sync to the beat.

Lanny pointed to the table where the boys sat and gestured for them to join in. Kate even summoned Prince William to the floor and he complied immediately, telling his guards to relax and not to worry. They danced for about another three songs before some of the men asked to be excused.

Orion and Bobby both joined the Prince for a beer while Benny and Trudy walked towards the hors d'oeuvres tray. Lars and Kyle stuck it out on the floor, flirting with a plentiful array of girls.

More commotion came from just outside the giant doors as Oprah Winfrey and her entourage entered the Ballroom. Just as the Prince and Kate had done, Oprah walked right up to the Professor and greeted him.

Lanny, standing next to Kate, exclaimed, "Poppa seems to know almost everybody who is somebody."

Kate smiled. "Come on, girl would you like to meet her? I just happen to know her."

Claire, standing next to Valerie, set puppy dog eyes on the future princess. "Katie, can we come too?"

The future Duchess of Cambridge smiled and beckoned the girls to join her. As they approached the Professor, he raised his eyebrows again and happily introduced his girls to the queen of daytime television.

Captain Malloy in a secluded corner discussed business with Captain Golon and some other military-looking individuals. Malloy noticed Benny returning from the restroom and waved him over to join them. Orion and Lars talked with the Prince about flying since the Prince was an accomplished pilot.

All the sudden, the prince was tapped on the shoulder from behind. Now they all got a good look at the notorious brother of William, Prince Harry. All joked around as more dignitaries arrived throughout the evening.

Orion's neck felt a chill that raised his neck hair a bit. Looking over to the ballroom doors he noticed that diplomats from Liberia and Guinea had entered. Both were dressed in polished military uniforms of their own nationalities and immediately became chummy with the delegation of diplomats from Libya. Orion, always on alert, excused himself and moved within twenty-five feet of them. Concentrating and adjusting his hearing, he zoomed in on their conversation.

Speaking in Arabic, the Libyan diplomat chattered as Orion recorded every word. After about five minutes a Liberian bodyguard caught a glimpse of Orion and wondered why he was slipping glances toward their delegation. The guard tipped off the diplomats and pointed to Orion, who acted as inconspicuously as he could.

Orion rejoined Lars who was still joking with the two royal brothers. Lars noticed the look of concern on his buddy's face and asked if everything was all right.

"I don't know, I'm going to see what Benny makes of it. But that'll be later on," said Orion. "For now gentlemen, let us rejoin the party."

Prince William wondered what to make of his new friends, all employees of his father's friend Jeffrey Pearson. The delegation from Saudi Arabia arrived with three of the country's Royal Crown Princes leading the way. He excused himself to greet them as a matter of royal etiquette.

Behind the Saudi delegation came the Oman delegation, followed by Qatar. Finally the delegation that sponsored the gala arrived from Jordan.

Beautiful Queen Noor of Jordan and the Consulate of Germany led by President Merkel made a proposal: a world cruise for children of dignitaries. The idea was for children of each national delegation to invite an impoverished child from the same country to be guests on a luxury liner. The children would visit countries throughout the Mediterranean and the Gulf of Aden.

Professor Pearson represented the United States. The cruise was to take place on June 2nd to commemorate the birthday of the Prophet Mohammed. The children would learn of the different cultures of all the countries participating in the event. They would also be chaperoned by adults (preferably women) throughout the voyage. The journey would begin in Monaco and end in Qatar six days later.

The Professor had already chosen Claire and Kendra to chaperone the children of the United States. Professor Pearson and Kruger also used this event to push funding for the increased use of nanotechnology in the fight against cancer. The two Professors were determined to do whatever was necessary to bring whoever they could on board. Eighty percent of the delegations at the event usually invested fully in Pearson Global Technologies experiments. The other twenty percent were generally undecided, because secret terrorist organizations needed them to fund the supply of armaments and bombs. But in recent years they had difficulties collecting donations, since most people recognized the selfishness of their motives. The terrorist organizations coveted ultimate power for themselves instead of their people.

In the ballroom Captain Malloy and Golon checked out the undesirables. No one had seen hide nor hair of Benny for the last twenty minutes. Another half an hour elapsed before he emerged from the smoking lounge area. Orion found that strange, since Benny had never smoked in his life.

Orion grabbed Lanny away from the other girls and pulled her onto the floor for a slow dance. Smiling, he asked her something that had her shaking her head no. Finally Orion took her hand and led her to the orchestra, then requested something of the conductor who nodded and smiled. Orion walked away while Lanny nervously stayed behind. Orion approached their entourage and asked them to head towards Lanny, who was about to sing.

Klaus and Trudy looked at each other in bewilderment and followed Orion towards the orchestra pit. The lights dimmed and a blue spotlight highlighted Lanny as the violins started to play. Everyone recognized her song as You're Still the One by Shania Twain. The crowd was completely mesmerized by the beautiful voice and Lanny looked straight at Orion as she sang with emotion. John Orion's heart melted all over again as he gazed into her gorgeous eyes. Even the orchestra peered at one another, noticing that she sounded better and better as the song progressed.

As Lanny finished, the lights dimmed and the violins stopped. The applause from the crowd was almost deafening. Then the lights went back on and the crowd applauded even more loudly as the raven-haired beauty appeared again.

Orion walked up to the conductor, whose face was astonished, and told him Lanny's name. Maestro Fritz Hammerson instantly grabbed the microphone saying, "Ladies and gentlemen, I give you Ms. Lanny Cromwell." He threw her a kiss as Orion lead her back into the crowd. Tears showed as the couple neared Professor Pearson. Lanny hugged her father as he smiled down at her.

"Why the tears, my dear? You sing like a Nightingale."

Orion cut in. "Doc, when she was a little girl her father had her sing with him to help her overcome her shyness. He coached her because she never thought she was any good. But as the years went on she broke the grip of shyness, singing and playing piano with her father. But tragically he was killed when she was only fourteen. From then on she's been silent, until I overheard her a one day in the shower. I've been encouraging her to sing, but until this evening she would only sing to me."

The Professor took his right index finger and lifted her chin. "Lanny sweetheart, you know I consider you my daughter. If I asked you to sing for me, would you?"

Lanny hugged him and looked into his eyes. "But Poppa, that's why I'm able to sing. I will only sing for the three men in my life: my daddy who is with God, my boyfriend who is taking too long to propose to me, and this charming gentleman who has made me his daughter."

As they hugged even harder Orion's face turned red. He had caught Lanny's remark loud and clear.

The Professor grabbed her hand and put it into Orion's. "Lieutenant, I think you should take my daughter out on the dance floor and begin discussing your future with our family."

Orion smiled and led his girl as the rest of the ballroom followed suit.

The Professor looked at the door and noticed Gerta Schmidt entering with her niece Holly Friedrich. He immediately excused himself and walked up to both of them. Malloy appeared, pushing Gunnar and his wheelchair to meet them also. The Professor kissed Gerta's hand and offered up his arm. Holly leaned down and gave Gunnar a quick kiss on the cheek as her aunt looked on.

Valerie s eyes squinted as she told Holly, "That's not the way to kiss your boyfriend! Hello!"

Gerta turned her head pretending to see something interesting and pulled Professor Pearson away for a walk. As they left Valerie said to Gunnar, "Okay Corporal Mientz, I expect you to show this fine young lady a good time tonight."

Gunnar quickly replied, "That I will, Sir. I mean, Ma'am."

Valerie giggled. "Oh shit, Gunnar! Both of you have a good time tonight."

All three of them laughed as Valerie left to rejoin Trudy.

Gunnar asked Holly about the flight from Dusseldorf and she explained they were delayed about an hour. They were also in a hurry because the replacements at the restaurant were late showing up.

A waiter with a tray of champagne came by and Holly grabbed two glasses. Both of the lovebirds toasted their relationship by taking a sip of Moet Chandon and then sealing it with a kiss. After that the night went on and the Global Garrison had the time of their lives.

Orion, when he got a chance, pulled the Skipper alongside Benny. "We have a lot to discuss later," he informed.

This grandiose gathering happened only once every four years and would bring almost every nation of the world together. The major philanthropists contributed generously to causes that benefited mankind. It seemed this year's charity event had significantly helped Pearson Global Technologies. Many of the same people at the event were at Professor Pearson's demonstration the week before. Pearson had also told the same people that the Corporation was about to test their new innovation in plasma energy and space vehicle propulsion.

The stockholders knew of his integrity and honor and usually plowed money into the stock, for it had always made a quite considerable profit. Now with the Christmas and Hanukkah season only weeks away everyone prepared to spend time with their family and friends.

New buildings in the five compounds around the globe would begin to break ground in March. This would facilitate the new accommodations for the expansion of the Global Garrison and would build the top secret laboratories needed to advance their knowledge, some made purely by accident.

The party continued until 01:00 hours at which time everyone filed out, anticipating their flight back to Dusseldorf that would leave at 10:00 hours later that morning. But this time, Gerta and Holly would accompany them on the Learjet.

The Professor handed affidavits to Claire so she could scan and file them in the supercomputer back in Dusseldorf. Being the Corporation's head secretary, she was only one of three people who had the access code. He also gave her the data disc from the laboratory in Berlin.

Malloy ordered everybody to their rooms and instructed them to have a good time. It appeared that he had calmed down quite a bit since he phoned Marilyn earlier that evening. All the rooms were on the fifth floor and the hallway echoed the consistent sound of closing doors. The hotel lights then turned off one by one.

Time: 01:25 hours. December 5, 2010.

Time: 0515 hours. December 5, 2010. Berlin.

Lieutenant John Orion awoke and began his morning regimen of exercises which he always tackled before his daily run. He didn't want to bother Lanny since he and the rest of the platoon were running together on the streets of downtown Berlin.

Once done with his usual routine of stretches and calisthenics he quietly left the room to go downstairs and meet his comrades in the lobby. He and Bobby were the first to arrive. Little by little the rest of his platoon trickled in. Trudy showed up with Valerie, both in gray sweats like the rest of them. Valerie let Orion know that as soon as they got back to the states, Lanny and Claire would be doing the same regimen under her guidance. Malloy told her that everyone must comply with the daily physical training, no exceptions.

Benny lead them all out into the street and they began their fifteen minute run. Orion turned the bezel on his diver's watch counterclockwise to position it with the minute hand. Benny ran alongside him and jokingly asked if Orion still cheated by five seconds. Orion laughed and replied that Billy stopped him from that ploy. Benny patted him on the back as the platoon cadenced their run. Everyone was impressed that Valerie kept right up front with Orion. After the fifteen minutes elapsed they arrived back at the Maderhoff. All of them headed for the hotel dining area.

Time: 06:10 hours. December 5, 2010.

Time: 09:15 hours. Berlin.

Heading for the airport in Berlin, Professor Pearson and the entire Global Garrison entourage said goodbye to one of the most beautiful times of their lives. It was time to journey to the base in Dusseldorf and the awaiting Viking Avenger, gassed up and ready to fly back home to East Hampton. Gunnar and Holly would be separated for the next five months because she had to go back to college in England and he was facing a hard and stressful rehabilitation stint. Gerta Schmidt, who was now romantically involved with the Professor, made plans to see him in the spring. For the time being, she'd train a replacement cook at her sister's restaurant .

Professor Pearson made plans for extra security to be posted around the giant complex of the Citadel and the airports. Higher fencing would safeguard them from the prying eyes of the public. More guards would be stationed around the entire perimeter. Additional housing units and facilities for the Garrison and scientific staff would break ground in the middle of March, 2011.

Beginning in January, Lanny Cromwell and Valerie Queen would tackle their piloting licenses. Valerie would also be training Lanny and Claire in extensive hand-to-hand combat training. They would be well-versed in weapons and explosives training.

The men would practice everything from CQB close quarter battle to combat diving, just to name a few. Claire would continue practicing with Carl Bingham in the flight simulator for the Viking Avenger. The scientists Pearson, Darfuir, Stellarnberg and Kruger would be completely enveloped in their top secret work.

For the next five months the entire complex in East Hampton would be the busiest on the whole planet. Medical and pharmaceutical departments as well as construction and protocol would commence at a non-stop pace. The scientists would further develop the Icarus Device to rid the human body of all known diseases and experiment with high intensity magnetism and rocket propulsion. From the data recorded in the Corporation's super computer they would make full use the technology given to them. Hopefully in the next five months they'd make breakthroughs to benefit all of mankind.

Captain Malloy was intent on keeping everything well-guarded and was vigilant against those who used their evil ways to create chaos for all of mankind. He told the members of the Global Garrison not to call each other by their real names when in battle dress uniform. Alternate protocol names were designated for each team member. Even when out of uniform and incognito they could never use their combat names.

Special use of battle dress masking around their eyes and nose areas would conceal their identities from others. Only the scientists and Malloy alone would actually know their true identities. Malloy put considerable thought into perfecting suitable pseudonyms for each of them.

From the secret base and airfield in Dusseldorf, Germany the battle jet Viking Avenger lifted-off at lightning speed to disappear in the sky, heading for East Hampton, New York.

CHAPTER SIX: SPRING AHEAD

April 30, 2011. East Hampton, New York.

Almost five months had gone by since the Global Garrison returned from Germany. Construction began five weeks prior on the entire compound of the Pearson Global Technologies jus complex. New housing and scientific laboratories seemed to be sprouting out of the ground as the warm spring weather invigorated the soul. Malloy had an Olympic-sized swimming pool installed in the area about a mile behind the secret airfield. Next door a specialized group of construction workers built a Dive Tower to accommodate the combat divers in their extensive training.

Eighteen new housing units were almost completed to house the new members of the elite fighting teams. Closer to the Citadel complex were secretly modified laboratories being constructed under heavy guard.

Orion's mother along with her lifelong friend Millicent Stokes had been relocated to a quiet secluded area of the compound. Adjoining their house was a smaller abode used as living quarters by Walter and the two wolves. A special fenced-in kennel prevented prying eyes from looking in. When Romulus and Remus howled at the moon at night, the noise scared the residents for miles around the complex. Orion and Walter knew on what nights to kennel them and suppress the sound of their howls. On those nights the full moon appeared in the sky, but see-through bubble wrap surrounded the kennel enclosure and quelled the cacophony of noise.

Orion introduced his dogs to each individual member of the Garrison, slowly fostering trust. Only Malloy was still on edge with the canines due to a harrowing event in Vietnam.

Lanny and Claire moved along exceptionally well with their hand-to-hand combat training, courtesy of Valerie Queen. Valerie had also made sure they were well-equipped and familiar with the M4 assault rifle as well as the MP 5, 9 mm submachine gun. But Valerie and Claire were also brought up-to-date by Lanny in the art of field triage, learning to treat wounds and administer first aid.

Lanny and Valerie were now single-engine plane pilots and busily training for jet aircraft. Claire was still the only one besides Carl Bingham who was able to handle the elaborate controls of the Viking Avenger. Lars had been training in a special simulator as a backup in case of emergency. Fourteen new members had been inducted into the Garrison including Major Percival Nelson, the two Gurkha guerrillas Kada Bondi and Lunsi Paal, plus New York City Police Lieutenant Jim Ferris and two ten-year veterans of the Navy SEALs.

Admiral Thomas Fischer informed Malloy of their prowess in operating the new technical weapons now being used in Special Ops. The other eight members were slowly being brought up the speed in their new jobs. But until they were completely evaluated by Malloy, they were not privy to anything top secret.

Next to runway one a gigantic magnetic rail was being constructed. This was to facilitate a Top-Secret experiment that would launch the Scram-Jet parked behind the Viking Avenger. In the last five months, Professor Joseph Stellarnberg had modified it based on research from the Corporation's supercomputer. A group of many scientists were brought into the experiment and hoped to have a first test flight at the middle-to-end of summer. Because this experiment required escaping the intense gravity of Earth's pull every precaution was being made to ensure safety.

Time: 10:45 hours. April 30, 2011. East Hampton, New York.

Waking up just hours before, the entire Global Garrison units took in some weekend R&R at the pool. Their training wouldn't resume until Monday.

Gunnar was especially excited, since Holly had a week's break from the college in England. She was expected to arrive in a private Corporation jet in about an hour. Since the airfield was only a mile from the pool, Gunner planned to meet her when she landed. He was now good as new. With determination and drive, his rehabilitation had made him a new man.

Valerie Queen had never let up and brought him back to the condition of excellence. She had more than proven herself as a vital member of the Global Garrison. No one would ever know how badly Gunnar's body was incapacitated from the vicious assault in the jungles of Kenya, Africa. The pool was especially helpful as he recuperated. The constant swimming made him more limber than he was before the attack.

Valerie kept constant vigil on his workouts and diet regimens and even called him a pussy from time to time to motivate his inner drive. She was just as vigilant at instructing Lanny and Claire in Tae Kwon Do, Tang Soo Doo and the use of a rattan in the art of Escrima. This was the way she was taught, so she implemented it and pushed harder than anyone to prove that she was one of the boys.

The pool phone rang in manager Peter Kobb's office, who yelled over to Gunnar, "That was the Control Tower. Aircraft approaching from the east. Arriving forty minutes ahead of schedule. It's her."

Like a happy little boy, Gunnar became nervous and paced erratically. Valerie and Lanny grabbed his arms and led him to the awaiting Cadillac SUV, then drove him straight out to the tarmac. They saw a lone Learjet coming in from the east. Lanny pulled out a wheelchair that Gunnar was recently confined to and opened it. Gunnar sat down like he had done so many times before.

The Learjet came in on runway four and landed as smoothly as silk. The jet taxied to the edge of the tarmac where the three comrades waited in suspense. The cabin door opened and out walked Bader Friedrich and his wife Ingrid. The flight crew deplaned as Bader and Ingrid met them at the bottom of the ramp. Ingrid told Gunnar jokingly that Holly was nervous and dolling herself up before she exited the plane.

Finally appearing at the cabin door, Holly gradually made her way down the ramp towards Gunnar in the wheelchair. She smiled with glee as she approached him at the bottom. But just as she got there, Gunnar stood up and ran to her. She was so startled she practically fell over before he reached her, but Gunnar was too fast and caught her.

"Oh my God, Gunnar! You can walk!" Holly clamped her lips around his and passionately kissed off the lipstick so painstakingly applied just minutes before.

Gunnar whispered to her in German, "Wait until you see what I can do later." With his arm around her, he led her to the Cadillac SUV. As he entered he noticed her Aunt Ingrid's face, which reflected that she heard exactly what he whispered. Uh oh.

Gunnar grimaced and bowed his head as he entered the car. Ingrid laughed and smiled as she followed. Gunnar, being a gentleman, invited them to accompany him and Holly into town later to see the Hamptons at its best.

Ingrid instantly replied, "I'm pretty sure neither of you wants us around for what you have planned later. We'll be fine. Jeffrey and Gerta are taking us into New York City for the day."

Gunnar replied in German, "Are you sure, Mrs. Friedrich? We could postpone our plans for the day."

Bader leaned over to Gunnar and hissed in German, "Shut up, STUPID, while you're ahead of the game."

Valerie spoke German fluently and from the front laughingly said, "Yes, shut up, STUPID, while you're ahead!"

Everyone broke out in laughter, causing Gunnar to blush. Lanny and Valerie drove to the main house to make arrangements for their living quarters. After that, Lanny called Orion at the pool and told him the Professor had given permission to use the cabin cruiser for a fishing expedition that day. She also let him know the Captain was taking Marilyn and the kids to the aquarium for the day and would not be aboard.

Bobby and Claire were loading the boat as they spoke. Hansy and Klaus were bringing their dates as well. Lanny informed Orion that she and Valerie would swing by the pool to pick up him and Trudy. Klaus left to pick up his date and would then to swing by and get Hansy and his girl.

Glancing at her watch Lanny told her boyfriend that they should be ready to leave the dock in just about an hour. Gunnar was not coming for reasons well known to everyone. Claire had already packed food and drink for the day. After they returned later that night, they'd reunite with Gunnar and Holly in Southampton.

Time: 11:15 hours. April 30, 2011.

Time: 20:30 hours.

It was a great day of fishing and fun. Orion and the rest of the crew now got ready for a night on the town with the rest of the entourage. Mike Maguiness and his fiancée Colleen planned to meet them in Southampton. Calvin Thomas and Carlos Alvarez had flown to Texas the night before to meet up with their girls. Being from Texas and Arizona, they were not yet comfortable with the New York lifestyle.

Mike Maguiness and his girl were from Boston, Massachusetts. Being just five hours away from the Hamptons they were more at ease with the Northeastern way of life. He and Colleen were already departing the city for the Long Island Expressway. Gunnar and Holly were eating at a seafood restaurant when Maguiness called and asked directions to the nightclub.

"You're only an hour away," informed Gunnar. "We'll meet you and Colleen at the Bijou Club in the northern part of the town." Gunnar provided good directions and hung up his cell phone. He and Holly stayed about another forty minutes then paid their bill and headed out to the Bijou, which was always packed on a Saturday night with people from all over the East End. Gunnar and Holly arrived at about 10 o'clock and asked for a table to accommodate fourteen people. The maître d' told Gunnar that a Captain James Malloy had already made reservations.

Gunnar smiled. "We'll finally be able to meet the Skipper's love interest," he told Holly.

Ten minutes went by before Mike and his girlfriend Colleen poked their heads into the club. Gunnar stood and waved Mike over. Then everybody from the Garrison clambered in. It was now 22:20 hours 10:20 p.m. and everybody was just getting settled when Orion's cell phone started to play Popeye the Sailor Man. On the other end was Billy Stokes' Uncle Walter. "Out of nowhere your dogs began to howl like there was no tomorrow," informed Walter.

"Let them prowl the grounds, and just as a precaution notify security." Orion hung up and let Lanny know the dogs were acting up.

Malloy overheard. "You're nuts for keeping two big Alaskan wolves for pets in the first place!"

Lanny sneered at the Skipper. "They just need time to get used to their new home."

Malloy flashed back to his unfortunate "dog" experience in Vietnam and shook his head, then threw his left hand up to shrug off a full explanation.

All of the entourage entered the dance floor and to the surprise of everyone, so did the Skipper with Marilyn. Suddenly a commotion at the bar interrupted them as people began to cheer like crazy. A crowd assembled around the flat screen TV by the bar. Popping out of the crowd came Bobby Palladin, tearful with joy.

"Skipper, Johnny, Mikey and everyone, check out the television!" he yelled across the dance floor.

An announcement flashed on the teleprompter: OSAMA BIN LADEN BELIEVED TO BE KILLED BY U.S. MILITARY FORCES. THE PRESIDENT WILL SOON ADDRESS THE NATION.

People screamed at the news that the evil bastard was finally dead. The bartender turned up the sound as the place grew quiet. Wolf Blitzer reported that an assault by Navy SEALs had killed the head of the Al Qaeda network.

Trudy in jubilation yelled to Malloy, "Skipper, it was our guys who got him. Yo, Orion, what a payback."

Malloy immediately ran over to Trudeaux and stared at him angrily. "Are you out of your fucking mind? Don't mention any of our names. Get everybody together at the table. NOW, ENSIGN."

Trudy, realizing his mistake, grabbed Orion by the arm and put his head down. "I'm sorry, brother. I guess I lost my head in the spur of the moment."

Orion hugged him. "Fuck that, Mikey. I'm glad the mother fucker is dead. If the Captain doesn't like it, too fucking bad. Tell him to explain it to Murphy's parents. And what about the QRF team that was also killed? I'm going to say something to him right now."

Trudy grabbed Orion. "Thanks brother, but the Skipper is right. My fuck up could result in a grave situation. We all know to follow protocol."

Orion thought for a second. "Hoo Yah."

Orion was the last to sit at the table. Malloy shrugged his shoulders and began to speak.

"Trudy, I'm sorry about getting in your face, but you guys have to understand. God knows I'm glad that piece of shit is finally dead. But gentleman and ladies, let's not forget what we're trying to do. How can we protect the good and innocent people of this world when we accidentally drop our guard and give away our identities. For the rest of the night, people, we are going to celebrate like there's no tomorrow. But come Monday, I will put in Fail Safe to protect us all. So come on guys and girls, back on the dance floor, and that's an order."

Everybody instantly raised their glasses. "HOO YAH."

The night went on with the president confirming the death of the man who brought so much hurt and misery not only to the United States, but to almost every other part of the planet. Jubilation ignited the world, but the Global Garrison knew the mission was by no means completed. Still, the faces of the platoon showed tears of joy and solace.

Time: 23:50 hours. New York. April 30, 2011.

Time: 05:30 hours. May 2, 2011. East Hampton, New York.

After a great weekend of mingling with their significant others it was time for members of the Global Garrison to get back to training. Captain Malloy called for everyone to be present at a briefing in the hangar of the Viking Avenger. As Orion and Lanny shut off the TV, they noticed the news still reported the well-carried-out assault on Osama bin Laden's compound.

Orion said to Lanny, "I hope this country doesn't think everything is going to be peaches and cream from now on."

As they began their run around the newly devised track just finished the week prior, Lanny replied, "I don't think so, Johnny. But that evil man had been able to avoid capture for years and his network was still able to kill innocent people at their leisure. Let the people of our country revel a little longer. They certainly deserve it."

Unexpectedly running up from behind came Carlos Alvarez with Kyle Duffy and Lars Olsen.

"Kyle, what the hell you doing here?" asked Orion.

Kyle running in perfect cadence replied, "I was just granted leave on Friday and planned to head home to San Diego when the Skipper asked me to join everybody here, instead. I guess something is very important. Besides, what's the big deal? I hear the girls in New York are just as pretty as the ones in California. I'm from Stanford anyway, so I'll see how the Hamptons add up."

Lanny laughed. "Kyle, Claire and I are both from Long Island. I don't think we turned out that bad, do you?"

Kyle blushed a little. "Are you kidding? If I could find somebody as pretty as you and Miss Vanderkamp I'd be the luckiest guy on Earth."

"Awww, Kyle. Thank you, sweetie! With your qualities I'm sure you'll have no problem in New York."

They came to the end of their first lap and saw Claire and Valerie enter the track. Bobby, Maguiness, Trudy, Calvin, Kada, Lunsi and two of the new guys, Darnell Crawford and Jimmy Wong, had finished their run twenty minutes ago. The rest of the teams led by Senior Chief Kramer left an hour earlier to do CRRC (Combat Rubber Raiding Craft) training out in the ocean. They brought two Zodiac 470 Kevlar wrapped rubber boats and left early on two Mach-five attack boats so they would be back in time for Malloy's briefing set to begin in hangar four at 10:00 hours. Everyone in the Garrison had to attend.

Benny had Hansy, Klaus and Gunnar. Staff Sergeant Calvin Thomas instructed the other eight members of the Garrison to load the two Zodiacs onboard the C-130 Spooky. Once they got to the drop area they would deploy out the back of the Spooky. Then in the water they would commence with training as the C-130 flew back to base. The two Mach 5 assault boats were already out there and would pick them up at the end of the maneuvers. From there, they would head back to the canal adjacent to the complex.

Pearson and Malloy were able to buy the Mach 5 assault boats with some wrangling from Vice Admiral Thomas Fischer. But they were still having some trouble with the Navy Department on the purchase of a SSGN modified class submarine. The Navy was a bit contentious with Professor Pearson, wanting him to give up some of his top secret findings. That would never happen, but Pearson promised he would help out with their new technology to combat global terrorism at any cost. Pearson also assured them that his Corporation secrets were no way harmful to the security of United States. The Navy's Appropriations Committee would take another six months to vote on the purchase of the submarine. In the meantime, they said they would evaluate the decision based on the cooperation of Pearson Global Technologies cooperation.

The rocket propulsion department of Pearson Global Technologies was now working with NASA on a launch system that would not expend an excessive amount of fuel when escaping Earth's gravity. The railing system next to runway one (currently being constructed) would be a super powered electromagnet combined with plasma technology.

Professor Pearson was waiting on Professor Stellarnberg to finish three optical mirrors to be launched in separate Titan rockets. Two of the mirrors would travel to Venus, then use their gravitational force to increase their speed as they traveled to Mars. Once the optical mirrors were close enough to Mars' orbit they would jettison their booster rockets and establish themselves as satellites around Mars itself. The third optical mirror would be launched to establish its own satellite orbit around Venus. Once all the mirrors were in perfect position, Pearson's team would launch the Scramjet Perseus to see if the stand-alone use of super plasma electromagnetic energy could be applied without expending the precious rocket fuel needed in space.

Currently eighty-five percent of the vital fuel was burned up in Earth's atmosphere at escape velocity propulsion. Stellarnberg and Pearson's system could be the answer to that problem. If Perseus worked they would construct other numerous cargo launch vehicles to carry payloads of different components. This would enable them to build a space vehicle for a manned mission to the red planet. The optical mirrors would be used to amplify the power of the Sun and convert it into super plasma energy. Perseus would have at its back a reflected buffered mirror to catch the plasma rays, which in turn would propel it five times as fast as could expanded fossil fuels. But because it would be traveling so fast, they would then use the mirror around Mars to slow it down with the optical mirror deployed in front of Perseus.

If this worked, the time frame of six to eight months it took to reach Mars would be drastically reduced to just three weeks. Professor Pearson was guaranteed by the United States government that with his Corporation's cooperation with NASA, they would not pry into his other top secret and confidential matters. This was guaranteed by the executive branch of the presidency.

Jeffrey Pearson proposed this compromise when they began asking too many questions about what happened the day of the attack on New York City. Admiral Fischer helped in making the deal go down, saying he would be the liaison for the military to ensure safety protocol.

Meanwhile, the three platoons of the Global Garrison had finished their daily run and were piling into the cafeteria for a well-deserved breakfast. Captain Malloy had prepared briefing notes and new rules that would be put in place later that morning directly after 10:00 hours. Kendra, who was now working with her sister Claire in the legal office, was the only one who knew what was written on them. This was because the Skipper dictated it to her and she typed it out.

Marilyn Carmichael, who had a doctorate degree in psychology, was now working for the entire Corporation. Having witnessed so much pain in her own life, she and Jim Malloy were settling in as a fine couple. Both were each other's rock, proving that opposites attract. The members of the Garrison loved it when she was around because Malloy was not as pushy in her presence. But the Captain still ran a disciplined ship and Marilyn didn't interfere unless his actions were detrimental to someone's psyche.

Having just sent her kids off to school, she arrived to join everyone in the dining room. Marilyn and the girls were always doing things together and when she entered the room they immediately called her over. Claire, being the most inquisitive, asked if anyone had a clue about this morning s briefing. Marilyn laughed but told her even if she did, she would not be able to reveal its content.

Orion reminded Claire that if that Skipper knew that she was even asking, she'd be in big trouble. Claire's face became worried, but Marilyn smiled and assured her the Skipper wouldn't hear anything from her.

Everybody finished their meals and headed out to their jobs for the day. Most went to the gym to work out until it was time to head to the briefing. Valerie grabbed Lanny, Claire and Kendra for more training in the martial arts. Kyle went upstairs to the Skipper's office to fill him in on Intelligence that had been recently acquired from Admiral Fischer.

Time: 07:55 hours. May 2, 2011. East Hampton.

CHAPTER SEVEN: PROTOCOL

Time: 10:00 hours.

Inside the auditorium of the Citadel the members of the Global Garrison patiently awaited their Commanding Officer, Captain James Malloy. He finally arrived and with him was Kendra holding everyone's dossiers. Coming in from behind them were the scientists Kruger, Darfuir, Livingston, Stellarnberg and, of course, the boss Professor Pearson.

Captain Malloy began by stating how annoyed he was with the entourage on Saturday, especially the breach in security as the real names of individuals were shouted out in a public place. He let them know in no uncertain terms that henceforth they would refrain from this breach at all times. The idea of being clandestine meant exhibiting restraint in everything they did.

He had picked a call sign name for them all and explained that they would be given a piece of paper with everyone's new names. Their task was to memorize, and then destroy, the papers immediately. Anyone guilty of an infraction of this protocol would be relieved of duty.

Malloy asked Orion to come to the front of the room. He then explained that five months ago back in Germany Orion had picked up a conversation with the Libyan, Guyanese, and Liberian delegations without them knowing it. Malloy asked Orion to demonstrate.

Orion closed his eyes and concentrated, then opened them in a trance of glowing eerie purple. From out of his mouth came the exact voice of the enemy delegates in perfect replication in Arabic and some Farsi.

Professor Darfuir and Benny, who spoke both languages fluently, begin to translate the conversation. After Orion finished everyone looked as though they had heard a ghost come into the room. No one knew of this particular power exhibited by Orion except Benny, Malloy and the

Professors. Lanny's mouth dropped open in awe, for not even she knew of it.

The conversation was hard to interpret but had something do with kidnapping someone or something of importance. One thing bothered them the most, and that was the mention of Abdullah Musheen's name in the talk. Professor Darfuir knew this man tried to kill his sister and told him all to be very vigilant. If they heard anything through their resources they were to bring it to the attention of the Skipper immediately.

Malloy and Professor Pearson handed out many different assignments to each individual to carry out specifically. They then passed out the sheets of paper with the new names of the Global Garrison's protocol. It read:

GLOBAL GARRISON
Commanding Officer James Malloy: SKIPPER
Orion: TALON
Lanny Cromwell: LADY BEE
Lars Olsen: TANK
Bobby Palladin: GALAHAD
Michael Trudeaux: DUKE
Valerie Queen: DUCHESS
Benjamin Kramer: MERLIN
Kyle Duffy: PUMA
Kendra Pearson: BARONESS
Marilyn Carmichael: ISIS
Cleopatra Stokes: CHERRY
Kada Bondi: CUDA
Lunsi Paal: LUNA
Klaus Steubern: CLAWS
Hans von Dietrich: MUSTANG
Gunnar Mientz: GUNNER
Holly Friedrich: GOLDIE
Perceval Nelson: FALCON
Jim Ferris: WOLFMAN
Joshua Golon: DANTE
Mike Maguiness: MAVERICK
Dave Caldwell: JUPITER
Carl Bingham: CONDOR
David Banks: ALBATROSS
Liam Faraday: RAVEN
Donald Tremaine: FIREBIRD
Walter Cosgrove: LUPO
Calvin Thomas: RHINO
Carlos Alvarez: ZORRO
Vice Admiral Thomas Fischer: EAGLE ONE

Vice Admiral James Maguire: EAGLE TWO
Vice Admiral James Ford: EAGLE THREE
Fleet Admiral Mark Mancuso: EAGLE FOUR
Flight Engineer Joseph Coffey: COCHISE
Former SAS Colour Sergeant Patrick Tinsdale: GRIFFIN
First Class Petty Officer Darnell Crawford: BOOMER
First Class Petty Officer Michael Wong: MANTIS
Lieutenant Seka Sharon: NIGHTINGALE
I. D. F. Staff Sergeant Guri Hertzig: SHOFAR:
I. D. F. Chief Science Officer Carl Livingston: POINDEXTER
Rocket Propulsion Physicist Joseph Stellarnberg: TITAN
Micro-Nano-Technician and Biologist Heinrich Kruger: SATURN
Chief Executive Officer and Scientist Jeffrey Pearson: NEPTUNE

Captain Malloy reiterated that they had day to learn everyone's new name. After that they were to burn the paper and use only the designated names. The Professor or Malloy would let them know when to use their real names, especially the girls at business meetings and charity events.

Malloy conveyed that his was the easiest—SKIPPER—and that their code names were to be used when they were in their secret BDUs (battle dress uniforms). Only two people besides Kyle Duffy knew who they really were, and that was Vice Admiral Thomas Fischer and his executive officer, Donald Tremaine.

Malloy explained, "Fischer told US Naval Command that he didn't know our identities, but let them know we would cooperate with them only through him. Otherwise we'd stay underground, which would be detrimental to them. By using Fischer as a conduit, they could reach out to us for help and vice versa. Then he added, "Fischer trained me to be this way, so now you know why I can be such a prick."

Palladin then accidentally murmured, "TELL ME ABOUT IT!"

Everybody in the room cracked up and Malloy instantly walked over the Palladin. "Well for one thing, Galahad, if you paid more attention to protocol I wouldn't have to be such a prick."

Bobby, bewildered, looked up at the Skipper. "Who the hell is this Galahad?"

Malloy quickly faced everybody. "Need I say more, ladies and gentlemen?"

The Skipper, with a smile, relayed to Palladin, "Bobby, look at the paper Kendra just handed out."

Bobby looked down and a second later blurted out, "Ahh, this isn't fair. I didn't even have a chance to look at it."

The laughter got even louder than before. But the Skipper put on his infamously serious face. "People, I never want to hear that kind of fucking excuse again. I'm training all of you to be the most skilled operators on the entire planet. You look at everything and become acquainted with it immediately. When it comes to the business of the day, children, I better never hear that excuse again. AM I MY CLEAR ON THIS?"

All, including the Professors, screamed out, "Hoo Ya, Skipper."

Malloy looked at Kendra. "Are we ready, Baroness?"

She smiled back at her uncle. "Yes we are, Skipper. I prepared the dossiers as you instructed."

Malloy looked at Captain Golon. "Dante, the floor is yours."

Kendra passed out the folders and Dr. Darfuir turned on the flat screen in front of the room. On the screen was a photograph of Mustaffa Khaldif.

Captain Golon read from the dossier, "People, this individual is a Yemenis Al Qaeda operative known as Mustaffa Khaldif. He used to go to school right here in the good old USA and studied robotic engineering at Texas Tech. After five straight years he became the best scientist in his field and went to France to study at the University of Versailles, this time in the field of micro and nano-computer technology."

Golon moved his hand in front of the screen just as an image of Omar Khaldif, Mustaffa's brother, appeared. "This right here, ladies and gentlemen, is his older brother, Omar Khaldif. This guy is very dangerous. He once was a bodyguard for Zawhari, the number one man right under the recently deceased bin Laden. This man is an explosives expert. He dabbles in everything from semtex to RDX and HMX. For years he taught the Al Qaeda network how to make shaped-charge IEDs out of artillery shells. He's an expert at booby-traps and wouldn't think twice of killing innocent women and children to gain power. But most of all, he's the number two man behind the most evil man on Earth itself."

The captain waved his hand across the screen again. "ABDULLAH MUSHEEN," he announced as a new image appeared. He looked at Benjamin Kramer and said, "Merlin, can you take it from here?"

Merlin explained how he was able to infiltrate into their network by gaining the confidence of Amal Baraash and Rajhid Hussein. He told them the whole ordeal leading up to the attack on New York City. Benny had them look real hard at the picture of Abdullah Musheen. "Remember, this man didn't mind using women and children as a diversion for his evil plan. If I didn't get to Professor Darfuir's sister in time, the innocent would have died and they would've won."

He exhaled and took another deep breath. " We must find this piece of shit and rid the Earth of him forever. If we don't, many more innocent people will die due to our failure to act. We have their voices on data recording computers. Whoever from now on is on satellite watch, you must listen and watch for voice recognition chatter. If any of these three assholes are picked up by satellite transmission, a purple warning light will immediately activate. You then must record any conversation being broadcasted over the airwaves."

Benny looked hard at his audience. " Now remember, ladies and gentlemen, we just liquidated their boss. So don't be naive and think they're not going to retaliate. Watches will be assigned to everyone. You will all alternate 24/7. I'm now going to give you back to the Skipper. Captain, they're all yours."

Malloy got them all up to speed on the ongoing intelligence he received from Kyle and the Vice Admiral. The military's secret spy satellite had picked up photographs of an attack on a limousine and its entourage. The units watch as men dressed in American army uniforms parallel-ambushed the convoy. They watched a lone soldier with a red polka dotted scarf wrapped around his face raise a RPG 7 at the lead of the limo. They also watched as what appeared to be a dead shot at the limo strike far away from its intended target. The limousine and its entourage quickly turned around and headed back west.

The Pegasus satellite zoomed in on a man who shot the RPG 7 and they all saw it was none other than Mustaffa Khaldif. The satellite locked onto the fleeing limo until it came to a stop. As the rear door was open by the chauffeur, out stepped the devil himself, Abdullah Musheen. Behind him were beautiful silken-draped women leaving the limousine in a hurry.

But then out stepped a gorgeous raven-haired woman who seemed to be shaken up and crying. They headed into a passageway as the picture faded to black.

Malloy and Golon told everyone to get some intelligence on the women who was escorted by Musheen into the passageway. Malloy told them to check with INTERPOL, and even Al Jazeera s foreign press secretary to see if they could come up with something.

Golon told them that even the Mossad and the IDF drew blanks when it came to this woman.

Golon and Malloy concurred that if they could just figure out her identity things might just begin to fall into place. Twice they'd seen this woman's face, first two and a half years ago when her frightened face was recorded as Abdullah Musheen made his getaway in a Fiat. Now they saw her with Musheen, but this time it is in a staged phony firefight to make it look like Americans were involved.

When Malloy finally dismissed the units Benny noticed Lars was fixated on the photograph of Shaleem Kholdeef. He walked over to Lars, " What's wrong, Tank? Looks as if you've seen a ghost."

I think I have, Merlin. " She's been constantly visiting me in my dreams."

Benny gave his friend a confused look. " What is she doing in the dream? She tried to kill you?"

Tank shook his head. No, not at all Merlin. We're both always making hot sensual love with each other.

Merlin picked up her photo. " Well, be glad it's only just a dream. This black-haired beauty comes from well refined Arabian stock. The clothes she's wearing are only worn by royalty. Now look at you, a six-foot-five blonde Scandinavian Viking. Oh, I'm sure her parents would approve."

"Maybe so, but I swear to God she's the exact girl in my dreams," said Lars.

Benny seemed concerned. " Maybe you should talk about these dreams with Isis."

Lars fired back, "Come on Wizard, I told you this in confidence. The team will ride me to no end."

Benny smiled. " Your secret is safe with me." He looked back at the picture. " Well, I must admit you have impeccable taste in women."

Lars put the photo back into the portfolio and headed with Benny to get some coffee at the cafeteria. They arrived to see everybody surrounding an astoundingly beautiful African-American female. Orion hugged her as they both smile at each other.

" People listen up! I'd like all of you to meet Cleopatra Stokes. This is Billy's baby sister."

Cleo immediately interrupted. " Baby sister? I'm only one year younger than he was."

A silence then surrounded the cafeteria. But instantly Orion changed the subject to ease Cleo's remembrance of her brother.

" So little sister, what brings you out to East Hampton?"

With her right arm wrapped around Orion's waist she said, "First of all, you've kidnapped both of our mothers and now I have a two-hour drive here from Astoria. Plus I quit my job at the CDC in Atlanta at the request of one Captain James Malloy. So big brother, you're stuck with me. I now work here in the laboratory below the Citadel."

Lanny's face lit up with joy. She came over to hug her once more and introduced Cleo to the other girls.

"Mama Rosa and my mother want you and Johnny to adopt a grandchild for them," Cleo told Lanny, who couldn't have children.

"First of all, he still hasn't proposed to me. Secondly, right now we are definitely too busy to even think about it!"

Cleo then decreed to her, " When you're about to approach forty and haven't experienced the joy of motherhood, I'll think back to this day and say I TOLD YOU SO."

Lanny kissed Cleo on the cheek. " You're right sis, but can we change the subject in the meantime?"

Cleo nodded. "Okay, what else can we talk about? What's up with my brother Johnny? Sometimes he's so dull and dreary, it makes me wonder if anything exciting ever happens in his life. Am I right, Lan?"

Lanny bit her lip. "Oh, you have no idea, Ms. Stokes."

Everyone snuck glances at one another and laughed silently amongst themselves.

The Skipper appeared in the cafeteria, spotted Cleo and kissed her on the cheek.

"Get her acquainted with everyone," he ordered Orion. "She is now a member of the Global Garrison."

Orion grabbed her and began introducing her around a little at a time.

While this was going on Dr. Darfuir entered the cafeteria with his girlfriend Tiri and his sister Lamarra. Both women ran the Corporation's day care center on the complex.

Kyle Duffy couldn't keep his eyes off Cleo and she definitely noticed him. He got nervous as they approached the table he shared with Lars, Benny, Dr. Darfuir, Lamarra and Tiri Palaat. Lars was seated right across from Lamarra. When Cleo arrived, Lars noticed Kyle giving her goo goo eyes grabbed him by his shoulder to introduce him.

Lars said to Cleo as his portfolio hit the floor, "I think my little buddy here has the HOTZ for you."

Cleo smiled as Kyle turned red in embarrassment. "Don't worry about it, Puma. This here lioness has got the HOTZ for him too."

"How do you know my call sign? I was just told it an hour ago," asked Kyle.

"The Skipper brought me up to par on all your names," Cleo explained.

Suddenly Lamarra screamed out, "BY ALLAH, where did you get a photograph of the Princess Shaleem?" She stared down on the floor at a large photo that had spilled out of Lars portfolio. Shaleem's face stared right up in her.

Everybody gathered around her and the picture. Dr. Darfuir asked his sister how she knew the woman.

"I was her teacher and Nana until she was killed three years ago, and practically raised her by myself since she was a little girl. The Khaleef only trusted his precious daughter with me. After I was widowed in the Iraq-Iranian war, the Khaleef, who knew my husband Kusa and loved him like a brother, asked me to come and stay with them and help raise Shaleem, a gentle soul like her mother."

Orion instantly pulled out his cell phone and called the Skipper. As Malloy picked up Orion said, "Skipper, get down here right now. We've identified the woman in the photograph. Grab Dante and the Professor, too. You're not going to believe this one."

Time: 13:04 hours. May 2, 2011.

On the other side of the planet a Russian-made submarine loaded supplies brought to it from Dow boats forty-five miles out of Yemen and the Gulf of Aden. The captain of the sub was none other than the

Chechnyan war criminal Vladimir Kozlovski. Talking with them on the bridge of the conning tower was Mustaffa Khaldif. The submarine had just been recently fitted with underwater stealth technology to prevent being discovered by NATO forces.

Mustaffa created an enclosure around the screws (propellers) which made it almost impossible to pick up its hidden signature. Kozlovski s crew raced to get the cargo on board, before any satellites could pick them up.

CHAPTER EIGHT: THE DEVIL'S MIND

May 2, 2011. Time: 22:10. Sanaa, Yemen.

Just outside the coast of Yemen, a refurbished Russian-made submarine had just loaded its cargo just forty miles north of the Gulf of Aden. Dow boats from Somalia earlier converged on this area to meet up with it.

Captain Vladimir Kozlovski, the commander of the boat, was also wanted by the Soviet government for stealing it. Kozlovski was born in Chechnya and only two years into the rebellion had double-crossed the Russian Navy. With the help of another Chechnyan-born Soviet naval officer he was able to sneak the sub away right under their noses. The other naval officer was captured by Orion and his men and was presently being held in prison at The Hague. His name was Meadiav Bosloff and the Soviet government wanted to get their hands on him badly. But they would have to wait until he was tried for crimes against humanity. After his capture the Al Qaeda network made sure that Kozlovski would not be next. He had been kept in a small town only five miles from the port city of Mocha, Yemen.

The submarine, while being modified, was well camouflaged from any satellite detection. Musheen had talked Princess Shaleem into requisitioning the funds for it and got more money than he bargained for. Since the so-called attack by the American military on her limousine, she had been handing money over to Musheen like it was candy. She even set up a trust fund for him under another one of his aliases, Narum Burunah. The fund was in Euro and American currency, supposedly made up of over $100 million dollars.

After paying for the renovations on the sub and giving him the trust fund, Princess Shaleem told Abdullah not to ask for any more funding unless it was a matter of life and death.

On board the submarine Damocles Kozlovski and Mustaffa Khaldif were going over Musheen's plan to create chaos in the Mediterranean and the South China Sea, all at the same time. On June 4th around 10:00 hours in the morning, twenty-four canisters laden with sarin gas would be released on the population of Ragusa on the island of Sicily. Thirty minutes later inside the country of Malaya, thirty-two canisters would be released on the population of Pekan, Indonesia. Twenty-four of them would be laced with the deadly sarin gas. But the other eight would contain the deadly yellow strain of mustard gas.

The canisters would come in the form of 80 cube diving tanks. So as not to cause suspicion, diaphragms and regulators for scuba gear would be attached. When the time came, the Al Qaeda operatives would wear protective chemical warfare suits. They would wrap rubber bands around the mouthpieces of the regulators to let the deadly gas into the atmosphere. From there they would drive to the coastal areas of the country and make their escape by boat. This would be the diversion they needed to commandeer the luxury cruise liner Queen Beatrice.

From there they would kidnap and transfer the children and chaperones to the awaiting submarine Damocles. By adding the mustard gas to the equation with Malaya, Musheen knew this place would be a number one priority. The deaths would become more frequent than in Sicily. This would keep NATO forces busy while they make their getaway from the Queen Beatrice.

They would travel to the Gulf of Sidra and unload the children in Tajura, Libya and conceal them in the El Hamra mountain hideout they completed back in April. The hideout was equipped with high-tech surveillance and detection equipment. From this strategic vantage they could pick up anyone coming and going in that area. After this was done Abdullah Musheen would contact Zawhari so they could make their demands on the countries of the world.

When Zawhari made his broadcast, Musheen would then execute the second part of the operation. They would blow up two major hotels with high profile tourists in the capital city of Doha, Qatar. This would be the sign to the rest of the world that they meant business. If the demands were not met to Al Qaeda's exact specifications, they would execute one child at a time each hour, on the hour.

The kidnappings would take place on June 4th, three hours after they left port in Cyprus. The Queen Beatrice would be only two hours from the Suez Canal before they would take over the ship. Only a devil's mind would conjure up something so heinous and evil. At the time of the hijacking the terrorist would set the autopilot inside the bridge of the Queen Beatrice. This would cause a crash only two hours away. But in this case, once the kidnapping was complete they would increase the ship's speed from twelve knots to twenty-five knots. The terrorists then would chain the door to the bridge closed and lower themselves with ropes to an awaiting Donzi speedboat to make their escape.

The luxury liner would be poised to make the canal in one hour instead of two. Leaving the ship with no steering or communication also put the entrance to the Suez Canal in dire straits. A ship moving at that speed without detection would be impossible to slow down, unless they got to it within ten minutes of the canal itself. This time, the devil created chaos and mayhem at three areas instead of two.

Musheen coordinated the attacks strategically knowing nobody on the face of the Earth could stop his evil plan in time. The Damocles just received weapons and high explosives to be taken to the mountain hideout in Libya. The submarine could not travel to the Suez Canal and would take a southerly route around the Cape of Good Hope. It then would stop and refuel in Benguela, Angola on the West Coast of Africa. From there Kozlovski would travel north to Buchanan, a port city of Liberia. They would refuel for the final destination to Tajura, Libya.

Kozlovski and Omar Khaldif estimated the voyage would take twenty-six days. They didn't want to rush the trip because anything faster than cruising speed on the Damocles might be picked up by NATO Naval forces. The Damocles proposed time of arrival in Tajura would be on May 28th, given a day or two. This would give them four or five more days of preparation. As long as Kozlovski stayed at cruising speed, the modifications by Mustaffa Khaldif around the screws would make them undetectable by sonar.

Some of the deadly sarin gas had been stored in two places since April of 2011. Twenty-four canisters were on Tioman island which was one hundred and fifty miles north of Singapore, Malaysia. Stored with them were canisters of mustard gas. The other canisters of sarin gas were in the El Hamra mountain hideout.

The gas was to be moved north to the island of Sicily on the American Memorial weekend. The Damocles would move north out of the Gulf of Sidra to a designated spot eighty miles south of the island of Malta. The canisters would be jettisoned from the torpedo tubes on the Damocles. A diving excursion boat would be topside when the canisters were deployed. They would be wrapped in shrink-wrap and a flotation airbag would inflate and carry the deadly cargo to the surface.

From the diving boat they would travel north to Pozzallo, Sicily where the boat was registered. The sarin gas would be hidden in the forecastle until it was time to release the gas. Everything hinged on the Damocles remaining undetected.

A recent uprising in Cairo, Egypt had centered attention on that region of the world. But from that uprising a rebel contingent of insurgents decided they had had enough of Qaddafi in Libya. Even in Yemen, an Al

Qaeda stronghold, people wanted to overthrow the government. Tunisia was the first to get rid of their dictator. Everybody in that region of the world was finally fed up with absolute tyrannical rule.

Tajura was just a little east of the capital city of Tripoli, Libya. But the mountain hideout was still thirty-five kilometers southeast from there. Musheen was given full cooperation from Qaddafi to the mountain area. Cut off, he really didn't care because the place was so desolate and had no strategic value, anyway. Not even nomadic tribesmen cared to travel there.

But to Abdullah Musheen it was the perfect place to carry out his diabolical plan. The mountain hideout was at least forty miles from the Gulf of Sidra and could pick up anyone approaching from the coast. Eighty feet up from the bottom of the hideout was an opening in the mountain wall, twelve feet from top to bottom and almost thirty-five feet across. But the opening consisted of a five-and-a-half-foot wall across the thirty-five foot stretch. On top of this wall was a steel door that opened to reveal a six-and-a-half-foot opening, which would enable them to fire on any approaching aircraft or terrain vehicles.

The outside was made to look as if it were part of the mountain. The opening had two SAM surface-to-air missiles batteries. It was also equipped with heavy fifty-caliber machine guns with seated mounts, able to move left and right and up and down. But as usual, the Al Qaeda devil would escape back to Yemen as soon as the captives were all secure. The monster, himself, would not compromise being caught at any cost.

But the Global Garrison knew he'd never quit his domain of terror unless captured or killed. But for now, they'd just wait for the Al Qaeda network to slip up and give away their whereabouts. On May 7th Pearson Global Technologies was sending Titan rockets carrying a new and more sophisticated satellite into orbit. The satellite would be called Saiph 1 and would be used in top-secret missions for the Global Garrison. Disguised as a weather satellite it would send data back to Earth about climate and temperature changes. But it would send on another relay an encrypted amount of messages from listening devices secretly planted around the Earth.

Pearson got the approval from NASA for their use in calculating dangerous weather around the entire planet. By letting NASA use entry into the Saiph 1 satellite, they then gave approval for the launch of the buffered optical mirrors on two different Titan rockets in August. This would clear the way for the launch of the top secret Scramjet, with the cooperation of NASA. That in turn would clear the way for the plasma propulsion tests for the journey to Mars.

Pearson and Malloy agreed on this satellite because of its multitasking capabilities. Malloy needed it for the surveillance of Al Qaeda, while the Professor needed it for the use of atmospheric detection of the Earth's climate change. But as good and evil began to prepare for the future, an observatory in the Hawaiian Islands picked up strange and unusual violet lights omitting time signatures in sequence from space.

Time: 02:17. Pearl Harbor. May 3, 2011. Mokalahia observatory, Hawaii, USA.

Time: 02:25 hours. Pearl Harbor.

Dr. Dave Hewitt and his colleague Professor Ron Yamans had just picked up sightings of strange celestial behavior and began to converse about the strange phenomenon.

"Are you sure, Ronnie, on your findings?" asked Professor Hewitt.

"Without any reservation, Dave. The strobe sequences are exactly fifty-four seconds apart, and from what I see it's still omitting the same behavioral patterns we noticed eight minutes ago."

Professor Hewitt turned on a recording video camera built into the 2 x 2 telescope. Dr. Yamans followed up by positioning another smaller telescope with the video capability. With the help of a computer he positioned this smaller one towards the Oort celestial cloud. This cloud helped scientists measure distance in miles of any celestial object from the sun s position in the solar system. But the main telescope was positioned towards the reference point of the Kuiper Belt.

Both scientists would compare readings of both to get the closest possible configuration. After about fifteen minutes the computer signaled a reading that concurred with both of the telescopes. It seemed they picked up signs of a new star forming in the exact vicinity of the strange glow of purple. In this area of deep space it had always been difficult to establish readings because of the mixture of the Oort cloud and the Kuiper Belt transcending trajectory findings. The belt was, most of the time, in front of the Oort cloud viewing sequences.

But because of this new phenomena, Hewitt and Yaman could see new planets that had formed in orbit around this new star. What puzzled them was movement in that part of the galaxy that was distorted. The movement of objects in no way had a pattern that could be established as regular and fixed projections. In fact, it was possible to conceive that they were UFOs.

Now that Professor Hewitt and Yaman reviewed their findings they called the Hakeliah Observatory on the island of Maui. From there they told two colleagues of what they were witnessing. After hearing of the strange phenomenon, the colleagues positioned their high-powered telescopes in an attempt to conclude the same findings.

Time: 03:40 hours. Honolulu Time. Hakeliah Observatory. May 3, 2011.

Time: 05:15 hours. New York Time. East Hampton. May 3, 2011.

Almost six hours earlier Talon (Lieutenant John Orion) and Lady Bee (Lieutenant Commander Lanny Cromwell) had just arose fifteen minutes earlier. They did so in order to run together with their beloved pet wolves

Romulus and Remus. Talon brought the dogs to the brand-new track the Corporation built for the firm and security units.

Lanny yelled to the dogs soon as they were released from their enclosure, "Romy, Remy, come boys. Come to mama."

The two very large Alaskan wolves bounded up to her with their tails wagging and tongues protruding with happiness.

"Good babies, good boys," she giggled with delight.

Orion mixed in with them, hugging and playing. All the sudden the dogs began to growl and showed their frightening fangs. Orion looked towards the fence opening of the track and saw his unit starting to arrive. Duke and Duchess (Trudy and Valerie) stopped in their tracks when they saw the wolves were not in their pen.

Lanny looked at her dogs. "Easy, boys, they're our friends."

The wolves stopped baring their teeth.

"Now just come over nice and easy," Orion instructed Trudy and Valerie. Once they get to know you and see you mean no harm, they'll take to both of you like one of the family."

Valerie came first and knelt down next to Lanny. She began petting both of the animals and they took to her right away. Then Trudy came over, but he showed signs of apprehension. The wolves picked it up right away.

Orion held up his hand, warning for Trudy to stop. "These dogs are very intelligent, Duke. Relax as I call them to us."

He whistled and the dogs rushed over to them. After about three minutes the dogs adapted to Trudy and wagged their tails and licked him, too.

At the opening in the fence the rest of their comrades had frozen in fear. Orion and Lanny initiated them one by one so the dogs could get used to everyone before their workout. The dogs seemed to take to the women more than the men, especially when the girls talked softly to them.

After their first lap around the track the animals ran and played with the entire unit. As they made their way around the track for the first lap, Walter appeared behind the fence, smiling towards Orion and Lanny. He gave them a thumbs-up and Orion, still running, returned him a salute.

Orion thought the world of Walter, especially because he was Billy and Cleo's uncle. But he also showed Orion how to train these remarkable animals. Walter Cosgrove joined the Navy in 1980 and in 1981 became a gunner s mate in the Riverine Navy. Three years later he would be indoctrinated into the Military K-9 Corps. Walter became highly trained in hand-to-hand combat, explosives and weapons training. But his main love was being around the remarkable animals that he had trained.

Walter met Captain Malloy while bringing over some attack dogs for his SEALS to train with. When Orion and his nephew Billy were about eight-years-old he would tell them stories of the magnificent Navy SEALs. From that day on all the boys wanted to do was become Navy SEALs. Walter weaned them into preparing for the most treacherous training in any military organization on the planet. He even got them into the ROTC program to make way for them to become officers. After high school and two years of college, both of them enlisted right away.

Walter was able to pull some strings and have them sent off to CRT, commonly known as B.U.D.s training, in Coronado, California. That was ten years ago, right before the attacks on the World Trade Center and the Pentagon. The boys were then transferred to the amphibious base in Little Creek, Virginia and finally met Captain James Malloy. Malloy knew Walter thought the world of the boys, so he took them under his wing. He drove them into the fearless and unstoppable forces they had become.

It just so happened that Orion, since childhood, always had in his heart a love for wolves. When he left the Navy after Billy died, Walter helped him obtain Romulus and Remus. Walter not only taught the wolves, but he also taught Orion how to be their handler. Orion and Lanny brought them up as their pups and Lanny always called them her babies, since she knew she couldn't have children of her own.

Now Walter, peering through the fence with pride, knew that Orion and Lanny would bring the dogs to love the Garrison, also. Mama Rosa and Millie were also acquainted with the wolves because Orion always took them over for visits with his two moms. Anyone not acquainted with these fierce animals would pay the price for trying for hurting the ones they loved. The dogs were good-natured and also strictly obedient, but fiercely protective.

Kendra was playing with them as they finally came to the end of their run. The wolves really took a liking to her.

"Hey little sister, since my two boys here seem to be crazy about you why don't you come with me and help me put them in their enclosure," suggested Lanny.

Kendra replied, "That would be my pleasure, sis."

The rest of the unit headed for the mess hall as Lanny and Kendra brought Romulus and Remus to their protective pens. Before they left the dogs they fed and give them refrigerated water containing phyto-nutrients and vitamins. The water was flavored and the dogs loved it. Plus, the entire Global Garrison drank the same water for revitalization. Since the entire complex started drinking it everyone had been motivationally better in their daily lives. Even the scientific and medical staff were participating and drank the concoction at least twice a day. Any sign of being sluggish or tired had completely vanished. Now the entire Global Garrison swore by it.

That was a good thing, because the agenda for the Garrison today was a seminar in the field of health and nutrition. Lanny and Dr. Darfuir were training the Garrison for emergency treatment triage in the battlefield, showing them everything from tourniquets to applying sulfur dressings, then injecting the drug morphine.

Everybody thought it was funny when Lanny used Orion as a guinea pig. She pretended like she was giving him an injection, and Orion used his power to make the syringe stab the ceiling tiles, instead. It even got funnier when she punched him in the shoulder and he used his force field to block it. Then he snuck in a quick kiss and immediately reactivate his force field.

"If you keep this up, wise ass, wait till you see how my force field activates in our bed tonight," whispered Lanny devilishly.

Orion immediately complied and Lanny finished her demonstration. After that, the unit went to hanger four to be fitted for the new headgear for their battle dress uniforms. There was a new adaption made solely for their own safety. Even though they wore masks over their eyes and noses (velcroed into their high collar clips), that was not good enough to deter chemical or biological warfare attack. At the back of their heads was a flap rising up just two inches shy of the top of their heads. It was put there to fasten the mask that hid their identities.

Captain Malloy had Carl Livingston show them how the new battle helmet, equipped with computer imaging and gas mask, was applied to the bottom of the protruding flap at the back of their uniforms. Malloy explained that this piece of equipment was vital, especially since intelligence had been picking up lots of chatter from the satellites. Apparently al Qaeda was preparing to dispense chemical weapons on the populace. Carl let the unit know that once the helmet was completely on, they were to punch in a code on their forearm band, right below their tactical watches on their left wrist. This then would activate all countermeasures for the suits to react.

A buffered lining at the bottom rim of the battle helmet would become snug and the collar of the battle suit would be cohesive with it. Any kind of pathogen would gather in the ports on top of the helmet. Immediately this data, gathered for spectrum analysis, would be forwarded to the main computer. This would be vital in discovering how to combat whatever deadly toxin was determined.

Malloy discussed in code the pickup of this Al Qaeda intelligence with the Professor, who immediately began devising a state-of-the-art battle helmet. Pearson promised them he would make sure they were protected with the very best implements he and his scientific staff could devise.

Time: 07:55 hours. EST New York. May 3, 2011.

Time: 15:57 hours. Mocha, Yemen. May 3, 2011.

Inside a well hidden laboratory in Yemen, Mustaffa Khaldif went over his plans with his brother Omar. Their new attack robot had been designed to fight any android or cyborg the West had conceived. Mustaffa spoke into the microphone on his wristband and from the other side of the room a giant door raised into the ceiling. This revealed an enormous ten-foot robot made of titanium and tungsten.

Mustaffa summoned the robot by speaking into his wristband. Once the robot reached him, he ordered it to destroy a fork lift in front of them. To their amazement, it decimated it into tiny pieces. Now Mustaffa and Omar believed they had what would destroy the American's latest weapon.

CHAPTER NINE: SWEET CHILD OF INNOCENCE

Time: 07:10 hours. June 2, 2011. Monaco, southern port of France.

The luxury liner Queen Beatrice was preparing to leave port in about an hour. The docks were filled with reporters from all over the world to witness a party of dignitaries partake in a peace initiative. Queen Noor of Jordan, Chancellor Merkel of Germany, Princess Amira of Saudi Arabia and, of course, Oprah Winfrey of the United States all began to commemorate this historical voyage. It seemed the world was starting to change for the better. Oppressed countries in Africa and the Middle East were crying out for democracy. The people of these regions were sick of living in poverty and squalor. Even Slobidan Milosevic had been captured and was being held in The Hague for war crimes.

The global economy had a recent shakeup and scare, but the people of the world were now reaching out to each other to peacefully coexist. Even though they weren't there yet, at least decent and compassionate people were doing their best to see this vision succeed. Today they hoped this gesture of philanthropy and willingness to share in the common good would lead by example.

This would be the real first effort to blend Middle Eastern and Western values in a way that brought their cultures together respectfully. Many of the kids were not familiar with each other's ways and this was a chance for them to see how each other really were. Most of the chaperones were on board as the delegation from the United States arrived on the pier.

The chauffeur stopped the limousine and opened the rear passenger door. Out stepped Kendra Pearson who was followed by two small children representing the United States. Behind them came Professor Jeffrey Pearson, and then his adopted daughter Claire Vanderkamp. The little girls and the Professor's daughters were all dressed in beautiful cotton lace dresses, as though they were going to church.

One of the little girls was an honor student from Parsons, West Virginia. Her father entered her in the contest for gifted children whose parents had recently lost their jobs due to the recession. Her name was Carly Sinclair and her father had been in a coal mining accident about two years ago. After going through six strenuous months of rehabilitation he found out his job at the mine was no longer being held for him.

Carson Sinclair was also father to three other beautiful little girls. His wife Lucy was a stay at home mom who sold garments inside their small home to make ends barely meet. Carson in his 92 Chevy C-20 pickup truck searched from dusk to dawn for scrap metal to cash in at a town called Elkins, about forty miles south of their home. Carson rarely got to see his family during the week, but made sure he was home every Sunday to bring his wife and daughters to church no matter what.

As Professor Pearson and his four daughters went over the entries they noticed immediately how hard Carly studied and applied herself to any challenge that came her way. All four of Pearson's daughters convinced him they had found their candidate. With that done, Lanny called the Sinclair household and gave them the good news. Not only did Carly get to go on this historic voyage, but she also got a $50,000 scholarship to a college of her choosing after graduating from high school.

But Pearson being the man he was also told Carson that Pearson Global Technologies would hire him for an environmental position within his billion-dollar Corporation. Jokingly, he also had Lanny inform Carson that the Corporation wanted to keep Carly in their sights. This was to ensure that the talented little genius would work in their science division.

The Associated Press and media from all around the world were there to take pictures of the event from start to finish. The Professor brought over another little girl to Claire and Kendra. Her name was Nancy Cullen and she belonged to a wealthy shipping magnate family whose name was influential around the world. Garrett Cullen was probably one of the most generous philanthropists, next to Jeffrey Pearson. Garrett and Pearson had been friends and business associates for the last eight years.

But little to Claire and Kendra's awareness, their father had secretly put Kada Bondi and Lunsi Paal aboard as stewards for their protection. Malloy told Kada and Lunsi to be inconspicuous because Kada made Claire feel uneasy.

The time was slowly nearing the cast-off ceremonies and Claire and Kendra began walking Carly and Nancy up the gangway of the Queen Beatrice. People cheered as Carla Bruni led Queen Noor of Jordan to the speaker s podium twenty-five feet from the entrance to the ship. Chancellor Merkel, Princess Amira, and Oprah Winfrey stood around the Queen as she began commencement ceremonies, smiling and tapping on the microphone. Unfortunately, it squelched and assaulted everyone's ears. The ship's

Captain Edvard Milson waved to the crew member operating the sound system so the volume would be lowered.

The Queen smiled. "Ladies, gentlemen, the good people of Monaco and the good people of the world, we are here today to witness and participate in a global effort to share our different cultures and ways of life with the children of the Earth. Too many times we hear that we are not doing enough to reach out and understand one another. Now our concerns for peace around the globe may protect innocent children from paying the price of disgraceful warfare and bloodshed that shamefully discredits us all. We, as women and mothers, have come here to make you hear our voice. We, as a global existence, are sick and tired of the relentless bickering amongst our countries. When things are not what you like or your religion doesn't meet another's way of thinking, you simply disregard our children's safety and aim rockets and bombs to quell your stupidity without thinking of the consequences. Today, right here and now whether you damn well like it or not, children from around the world and through all walks of life are participating in a lesson about respect and decency. These children will learn the value of respecting one's fellow man."

Oprah whispered to Queen Noor. The Queen quickly laughed and continued, "One's fellow man AND WOMAN."

Everyone broke into laughter.

"With this, we challenge all of us to do what these amazing young little boys and girls are about to endeavor. So good people of the Earth, let us join in cheering for the commencement of the Voyage of Tranquility."

Aboard the Queen Beatrice and all around the pier people were throwing confetti and cheering the great Queen's speech. The ship's air horn blew the signal, ALL ASHORE THAT'S GOING ASHORE. The Queen was led down the gangway to the pier by dozens of bodyguards as the rest of the dignitaries from around the world followed suit.

When they get to the bottom, Professor Pearson looked up at his daughters and smiled with pride. The riggers prepared to signal-up and have the tugboats tow them into the Mediterranean. As the Queen Beatrice left slowly, Kendra and Claire blew kisses to their father. He did the same.

The Professor got into the limo and instructed the driver to head for the airport. He had to get to the base in Dusseldorf to meet Joseph Stellarnberg and test fire the jet engines of the new battle aircraft, Blazing Trident. The Blazing Trident was sister to the Viking Avenger and had an extra special ability. This aircraft worked like the E2-C Hawkeye with radar jamming capabilities. Its maiden flight was supposed to be this Friday, the 4th of June.

Lars Olsen had been training to pilot it for the past six months and he knew he was ready. The entire Global Garrison was in Dusseldorf for this momentous occasion. Malloy and the scientists were hoping to do joint flight operations with the Viking Avenger by the end of the following week. But for now, the main implement was to have Lars as the pilot and Liam Faraday as the copilot to test fly the Blazing Trident at 06:00 hours that morning. Since Claire was chaperoning the Voyage of Tranquility, Carl Bingham would pilot the Viking Avenger in her place.

Meanwhile at the base in Dusseldorf John Orion was showing members of the Garrison the engagement ring he bought for Lanny in town the night before. Valerie stared at the beautiful three carat Marquis diamond.

Orion asked, "Do you think I picked the right shape?"

Valerie replied instantly, "Oh, did you ever, Talon. Lady Bee is going to be floating on air."

All the sudden Lanny entered the hangar and caught only what Valerie had to say. "I'm going to be floating on air, Duchess? Why is that?"

The rest of the Garrison blocked Orion from Lanny's view as he quickly tucked the bright bobble back in his pocket.

Valerie cleared her throat. "That's because Talon has picked the best restaurant in all of Dusseldorf to have your graduation dinner. You two are going to celebrate your graduation. Congratulations on being able to pilot the Avenger, Lady Bee."

As Lanny adjusted her mask to the flap on the back of her uniform she said to Orion, "Talon, what the freak are you doing? You know we can't afford the Ballantine. I love you, baby, but your e still not careful with the money."

Orion looked down and growled silently, then lifted his head to reply. But before he could utter a word Captain Malloy came in and said, "Commander, don't worry about it. The Corporation's footing the bill. Your father's really proud of you, as all the rest of us are."

Lanny responded, "I don't know what the big deal is, Skipper. We all know that Lady Hawke is the only captain of the Viking Avenger. Plus, I think she should be here for that since she was the one who taught me."

Orion shook his head and face-palmed. "See what I got to go through?"

Lanny gritted her teeth. "What you got to go through? WHY YOU!"

But right then and there Malloy screamed out, "ENOUGH, ALREADY! This is not up for discussion. Do you hear me? OH GOD, can we please have one fucking peaceful day. If you two keep this up I'll have Isis counseling you for hours at a time. Do you hear me?"

Both Orion and Lanny looked at each other and smiled, then faced the captain. AYE AYE, SKIPPER!

Malloy looked around at the rest of the Garrison only to see them laughing hysterically. He showed a tiny glimmer of laughter himself, but instantly reverted to the business at hand. "Okay knuckleheads, our first order of business. Everyone is to participate in ocean drop today. You're going out in the Spooky. You're doing sonar buoy recovery. We'll have two separate boat units. You will be dropped forty miles out of the Med. From there you will deploy your CRRCs and use your ULTs (underwater listening transponders) to locate and recover the buoys. You will be graded by Lieutenant Commander Lady Bee in one boat crew and in the other boat crew you will be evaluated by the new promoted Commander Talon."

Lanny's mouth opened wide as she looked towards the Skipper. Malloy said in a soothing voice, "Come on, girl, you know this was coming. We all did."

Orion was smiling and grinning like he had been handed the keys to a SLS-AMG Mercedes-Benz. Malloy told him, "Okay Talon, get them geared up and on the tarmac in fifteen mikes."

Orion yelled out, "All right, you heard the Skipper. Fifteen mikes and wheels up."

The Garrison headed to their gear lockers in the barracks adjoining the hangar. Orion approached Lanny with a grin a mile wide. She smiled and put her arm around his waist as they walked towards the C-130 Spooky.

"Congratulations are in order there, Commander."

Orion's smile grew even wider. "Why thank you, Lieutenant Commander Lady Bee."

She stopped and looked up at him. "Do you think this means you can boss me around?" Her face turned to a serious gnarl as she awaited his answer.

Orion became flustered. "Well of course not, baby."

She reached up and kissed him. "Then wipe that ridiculous freaking smile off your face."

Orion complied instantly as they continued their walk. But sneaking a look towards the sky he whispered, "Why me, why me?"

Even though she was looking the other way, Lanny surprised him with, "You're just lucky, I guess."

Orion knew he didn't say it out loud and was startled.

Malloy's phone sounded off a text notification from Eagle One, Vice Admiral Thomas Fischer.

Time: 09:45 hours. Dusseldorf.

Time: 08:45 hours. Tajura, Libya.

After having just met with Moammar Qaddafi, Abdullah Musheen left in a Jeep heading west to Gabes, Tunisia. From there he would fly back to Sanaa, Yemen as his henchmen prepared their diabolical assault on the world. Qaddafi just told Musheen he could not guarantee his men safety in the mountains because the capital city of Tripoli was under constant attack from NATO forces.

Musheen then told him that the area of his operation was so desolate and so far away from the bombing he didn't need protection. He also told Qaddafi that if all went well, the attack on his cities would instantly cease.

He assured him the West would be eating out of his hand, but would not divulge his sinister plan to him. However, he reassured Qaddafi it was the checkmate in bringing the West to their knees.

Leading the assault this time was an up and coming operative called Faraz Saphan. Saphan was exiled from his Pashtan tribe in Afghanistan for testing the opium products he smuggled on little children. After six months of finding children dead in abandoned poppy fields, the Afghan cops pursued him to the southeastern corridor of Juwain, Afghanistan. But this was to no avail. He was able to sneak across the border into Iran. From there, with help from fanatical Jihadists, he made his way to Mocha, Yemen.

Since then Abdullah Musheen had preened and prepped him in his diabolical scheme. Now with only a forty-four hour wait, the evil henchmen boarded a private jet for Tunis, Tunisia. From there Faraz Saphan and a group of his terrorists would board a fishing vessel to take them out to sea. Once out in the Mediterranean, they would meet up with the submarine Damocles. From there it was only an eighteen-hour waiting game until they resurfaced to commandeer the Queen Beatrice.

On board the Queen Beatrice were fourteen more of his Al Qaeda operatives, many of them working in the galley as scullery helpers and service technicians. But three of them were women who registered on board as cruise directors and bartenders.

Musheen went to great lengths to forge their passports and job descriptions. One of the women known as Saberah Shazad was a cruise maître d and had immediate access to Captain Edvard Milson's quarters on the bridge. She was the one to initiate the attack on the ship and had a package containing a remote-controlled bomb consisting of two pounds of semtex. When the time came on Friday morning, she was to use it to blow up all radio communications with the outside world.

Time: 19:30 hours. Dusseldorf. June 2, 2011.

Landing an hour before, the Global Garrison got out of their battle dress uniforms to board a shuttle bus to the center of town, then went on to the Liberstraum Hotel. Lanny still seemed annoyed that her boyfriend was now promoted to her superior. But she handed Orion the test scores for the operation in the Med that day.

Orion looked them over and said to Valerie, "Well Duchess, seems you've outdone some of the men. Most women, I presume, wouldn't be able to pull themselves back up onto the zodiac. It seems you've exemplified yourself in our UDT maneuvers."

Valerie, sitting with Trudy and looking exhausted, replied, "Thank you, Sir. Can't let you men have all the glory."

Lanny interrupted. "Yes Talon, seems we are not just for male sexual desire."

Orion immediately pulled Lanny next to him. "Baby, you know me better than that. I treat every man or woman as an equal. Honey, what's the matter with you today?"

Lanny snuggled up to him. "Everything is happening so fast. I guess I'm a little frustrated. God, I miss Claire and Kendra already."

Orion pulled her a little closer. "Baby, they're only gone for ten days. Before you know it you girls will be shopping and gallivanting at Lord and Taylor and Saks Fifth Avenue."

"Honey, you always know what to say to cheer me up. Oh, I have to get out of my uniform. The salt water smell is all over me."

As they left the hangar the new guys to the Garrison were washing seawater off the two zodiac 470s.

Time: 19:55 hours. Dusseldorf. June 2, 2011.

Time: 20:40 hours. Liberstraum Hotel, Dusseldorf.

Valerie Queen led Lanny down the stairs in front of the Liberstraum Hotel.

"Val, what did Johnny tell you before he left me here all alone?"

Valerie, keeping a straight face, told her, "The Skipper called him to an emergency meeting. Now come on, sis, relax and have a good time tonight."

Lanny was dressed in a knockout lavender Oscar de Laurenta evening dress and looked stunning. Valerie was also decked out in a Versace lace and ruffles evening wear. Her dress matched her gorgeous strawberry blonde hair.

Little did Lanny know that Orion was dressed as a waiter at the Ballantyne where he would surprise her and then propose in front of all of their friends and relatives.

The limousine pulled out and Lanny wondered why the Skipper picked this night to pull her man away. They drove on for about eight minutes before the limo pulled up in front of the five-star restaurant. A valet immediately opened the door and Lanny and Valerie stepped onto the red carpet leading up the stairs into the Ballantyne.

"Val, I still think this place is too expensive. Just because I can now fly the Viking Avenger doesn't mean I deserve this."

"Lanny, you know how Poppa is. Nothing is too good for his daughters."

Lanny and Valerie made their way up the stairs as the doorman opened the door to let them in. Eric, the maître d', and an assembly of waiters were there to greet them as they entered.

"Good evening, Ms. Cromwell and Ms. Queen. You're seated right next to your father near the gold curtains by the picture window. Can I get you ladies something to drink?" asked Eric.

Lanny replied, "Thank you, I'll have a tall glass of lemonade and my sister will have double martini with two olives."

Valerie smiled but quickly said, "Yeah, but make sure it's Patron vodka!"

As they were led to the table everyone kept congratulating Lanny, who wondered why everybody was making such a big deal out of this. The waiters had them seated and another put their drinks in front of them.

Valerie quickly took a sip. "Lan, I'll be right back. I told these people Patron and now I'm going to complain to the management. Lanny tried to stop her, but Valerie quickly ran away."

From behind the curtains Orion came out holding a metal tray. Lanny, still looking down at her drink, heard, "Madame, would you care for something more sparkly?"

Lanny was annoyed and started to say, "I don't drink alcohol. SO PLEASE, NO... " But at that moment she looked up to see her man dressed in a waiter s uniform.

Orion instantly dropped to one knee and spun the tray on his index finger, then waved his other hand so that it instantly stopped. There in front of Lanny was a purple velvet ring box and inside it was the beautiful marquee diamond ring. Orion looked into her eyes and saw she was sobbing.

Lanny, with tears pouring down her cheeks, put her hand over her mouth, trembling.

Orion, now in tears himself, began with, "MS. LANNY BEATRICE CROMWELL, I can't go on another day without you being my wife. Lanny, will you marry me? I love you, and will love you for all eternity."

"Of course, I'll be your wife! I will love you for all eternity also."

Both of them immediately kissed with a feverish passion. The entire place erupted in applause and cheers.

Lanny's face became aggravated.

Orion asked, "What's wrong, baby, something bothering you?"

Wiping her eyes she replied, "Claire and Kendra should be here. It just doesn't feel the same without them."

Right then and there people who were blocking a big flat screen television moved aside to reveal Claire and Kendra looking straight at them.

Claire with tears in her eyes said, "I'm right, here big sister, with your other sister."

Kendra, smiling and crying at the same time said, "Do you actually think we'd miss our big sister's engagement party?"

Then Kendra turned her head to face everyone on the ship's dance floor. "Everyone, let's hear it for the future Mr. and Mrs. John Orion!"

Thunderous applause and cheers come from the screen. Then from the side door Walter came in pushing Mama Rosa s wheelchair with Millie Stokes right next to her.

Mama Rosa and Millie were both in tears and Mama Rosa said, "Lanny, you get over here right now, my daughter, and give your mother a big hug."

Millie yelled to Orion, "Don't you keep that poor girl waiting, ever again. Do you hear that, young man?"

Orion hung his head down and replied, "I won't ever do that again, Mama Millie, I promise."

Professor Pearson came over with Professor Darfuir and both began hugging the couple.

Claire yelled from the screen, "Johnny, Lanny, I'd like to introduce you to these two bright and beautiful little ladies."

She put Carly and Nancy in front of the screen and the two girls started congratulating them.

"You know what? I'm going to be needing two flower girls for my wedding. Do you think you young ladies would be interested?" asked Lanny with a twinkle in her eye.

Carly and Nancy jumped up and down clapping.

Lanny and Orion smiled as Lanny said to them, "I guess I can take that for yes."

They both started yelling, "YES, YES, YES, YES!"

"Nancy and Carly, how is the trip and so far?" Lanny wanted to know.

"Oh, Ms. Cromwell," responded Carly. "This is the best time of our lives. The other children from around the world are really so great. We are all becoming best of friends. All the bad things that other people say about some of them are a bunch of hurtful lies. The boys and girls from the Middle East are the same as us and they want the same things as us."

"Now I know I've picked the right girls for my wedding," answered Lanny. "That's the problem, girls. People don't reach out enough to realize this. But as long as you remember to treat others as you would want to be treated, the Earth would be the greatest place in the universe next to heaven."

Claire cut in, "Lanny and Johnny, the children have to be in bed in another hour. So we're going to leave you to your most magical night. Love you, sis."

Kendra reiterated the same. "Love you, Lan."

Lanny, with more tears, blew them a kiss. "I love both of you too."

Professor Pearson ordered everyone out on the dance floor and said to enjoy the evening. He couldn't help but flash back to how it all began. A skeptical man had been hired by his best friend James in a desperate maneuver. The mission was to bring Kendra Pearson home safely, for Professor Pearson feared his only child would be lost on the streets, a victim of heroin. Then a registered nurse, Lanny Cromwell was hired by the Corporation to help rid the planet of cancer and disease. How serendipitous that both Kendra and Lanny met under these circumstances and forged an instant bond. Both of them had suffered just as he had in anguish and tribulations. Now, whatever the future might bring he would be there as the father who loved them both unconditionally.

Pearson further contemplated what God had in store for all his family and friends. As he daydreamed, he felt a tap on his shoulder from behind. Turning, he saw Lanny smiling up at him.

"Well, Poppa, are you going to leave your oldest daughter hanging on for a dance?"

Jeffrey Pearson, with tears in his eyes, replied, "This old man will never, ever leave you hanging, my sweet Lanny."

She just smiled and buried her head into his chest.

Time: 21:45 hours. Dusseldorf, Germany. June 2, 2011.

Time: 09:15 hours. Tioman Island, 150 miles north of Singapore. June 3, 2011.

Al Qaeda operatives had just killed the captain and his crew of the commercial fishing boat Shangri-La. They were taking the bodies out into the South China Sea to feed them to the sharks. Pora Saleesa was Al Qaeda's number one man, who Musheen had picked to carry out this part of the plan. Saleesa was a monster and didn't hesitate to maim and murder. His absence of conscience made him the perfect candidate for the mission. The time to carry out this most despicable act suddenly drew near.

CHAPTER TEN: ASSAULT ON A QUEEN

Time: 10:00 hours. Dusseldorf, Germany. June 3, 2011.

Captain Malloy just got off the phone with Vice Admiral Fischer who was calling from Norfolk. Back in the states Fischer, known to the Garrison as Eagle One, had filled in the Skipper on radio and computer chatter picked up by the military's top secret satellite, PEGASUS. Malloy decided to let his men and women enjoy a big breakfast before summoning them for an emergency briefing.

Commander Talon and the rest of the elite Global Garrison began pouring into Malloy's office and conference room. Across the room was the big screen that only the three Pearson Global Technologies satellites could communicate with. From the screen they saw Fischer looking back at everyone in their new battle dress uniforms. As soon as they were all seated Eagle One started to talk.

"Good morning, Global Garrison."

"Good morning, Sir," the group replied.

Fischer continued, "Very impressive uniforms there, captain. I like the way the masks are attached in the back and cover the eyes and noses in the front. Thank God someone had the brains to included nostril holes."

Everybody gave a quick laugh.

"Okay, ladies and gentlemen. Let's get to the business at hand. From the chatter we've picked up over the airwaves and Internet, I'm really glad that all of you are in Europe. Al Qaeda operatives are increasingly talking in code, and we've been able to decipher a lot of it. But only bits and pieces in the messages speak of the chemical warfare attack. The problem is that our satellite is picking up what seems to be multiple attacks. We've had one transmission in the Med, and from there they sent voicemail to someone in Singapore with the very same and frightful message."

Merlin then asked Eagle One, "So does your intelligence crew think the message is a diversion to throw us off? Or do you think it's viable enough to put the entire sixth, fifth, and seventh fleet on full alert?"

The admiral, recognizing Benny's voice, replied, "No doubt about it, Merlin. This is the real thing. Some of the radio chatter claims that failure will not be tolerated at any cost. The sources from our agents say it comes from Al-Zawhari, and what do you know, our boy Abdullah Musheen himself. Your Skipper and I had devised a plan we hope your big boss will agree to. After what almost happened in New York City last November we don't want to be caught with pants down again."

Orion stood and said to Eagle One, "Sir, we are going to do everything in our power not to let you down."

Admiral Fischer replied, "I know you won't, Talon, and congratulations on your promotion, Commander."

Orion smiled. "Thank you, Admiral."

Lanny stared at the ceiling, frowning. The Admiral noticed and exclaimed, "Lady Bee, congratulations to you and Talon. Oh, by the way, if your dad and his colleagues are on board, I think you may be flying something very special today."

Lanny's mouth opened in astonishment. A big shit-eating grin tugged at her pretty lips. At that moment, Professor Pearson, with Dr. Darfuir, Professor Stellarnberg and Professor Kruger entered the room.

Captain Malloy told the Garrison to wait in the hangar and that he'd be there soon once the meeting with Eagle One and the scientists concluded.

Lanny grew weary knowing her father assigned Lars to be the captain of the Blazing Trident. As they piled into the elevators, Orion put his arm around his fiancée and said, "Cheer up baby, and always think positive." He kissed her to boost her spirits. Lars tried to look her way but caught her frowning from time to time.

A good forty-five minutes elapsed before the Skipper, followed by Professor Pearson and the scientists, walked into the hangar. He held something behind his back and the suspense was killing Lanny.

Malloy called her and Lars over and they moved to the front.

Professor Pearson spoke to Lanny. "I'm sorry, sweetheart, I know how bad you wanted to be on the fire teams." He hesitated before continuing. "All of that is impossible now."

Lanny's head bent in disappointment as her father said, "That's because you're the new pilot and Captain of the Blazing Trident."

Lanny couldn't control herself and rushed into the arms of her father. But then she stopped and in bewilderment asked, "What about Tank? He's more qualified than me."

Lars laughed and replied, "I'm a Seal. I don't want to be flying. I want to be in the thick of it with my team. Otherwise I would've joined the Air Force."

Lanny walked up to Lars. "I know you're just doing it for me, Tank. Come here, you big lug." Lanny hugged him, making a comical sight since his head was a good twenty-four inches above hers.

Orion laughed and joked with Lars, "Yeah, where s my hug, you big lug, how about some loving here?"

Lars frowned. "Fuck you, Talon. Sometimes you can be a real asshole."

Malloy cut in and said with a twinkle in his eye, "Enough, already. Lady Bee, get into the cockpit. Duchess, you're on Rio radio intercept officer and navigation. Tank, get in the copilot's chair. Wheels up in 15. Everybody else gear up, shit heads. Let's move. NOW!"

From behind Professor Pearson's back Malloy pulled out the pilot s special head bonnet and handed it to Lanny. "Make me proud, Lady Bee."

She kissed him on the cheek. "Will do, Sir." She saluted the Skipper and he returned it. She then headed to the ladies locker room to don her G-suit.

Pearson never conceived of Lanny flying one of the super jets. He really wanted her in the lab, but noticed her mind was always on what the units were doing. So by having her learn to fly in the simulator he got the best of both worlds. She excelled in both the scientific field as well in the air as an amazing combat pilot.

The Garrison was now on the tarmac and Malloy gave Lady Bee her flight plan. She was to take off first and fly to the Mediterranean, then keep a steady course until Condor (Carl Bingham) linked up with them. From there they would practice invasive and radar-jamming maneuvers while Viking Avenger let the Garrison do an ocean drop.

But on this particular flight Orion wanted to test one more of his incredible powers. Being able to change his molecular structure, atomic weight and temperature, he was going to add an invisibility cloaking along with the force field. He would first attempt this feat from the Blazing Trident since it had the E-2C Hawkeye capabilities. Once the two jets had rendezvoused in the Med, they were to fly close winged support until it was time to deploy the insertion teams. Orion chose this crucial time to try his experiment.

As soon as he boarded the Blazing Trident he put on the Guardian component the ICARUS DEVICE. He laid down on the small regeneration bed which had been engineered to enhance the power traveling throughout his entire body. A smaller version of the electron generator at the laboratory in the Citadel was implemented in both battle aircraft. This way, it didn't matter what super jet Orion was in. With dual access he would always be able to regenerate himself at any time thanks to Malloy, who always thought of every little detail.

Inside the cockpit of the Blazing Trident the airfield tower communicated with Lanny. "Blazing Trident, this is tower. You're all clear for takeoff. Winds are coming in from the Southeast at eight knots.

Visibility ceiling is at 12,000 feet, OVER."

Lanny signaled to Lars to program this data into the onboard computer. "That's a copy, Tower. Now taxiing to runway two and ready to commence maiden flight of SST battle aircraft Blazing Trident, OVER."

Lanny told the strike team in the back to prepare for takeoff. The air-traffic controller in the tower then gave the same instructions to Condor piloting the Viking Avenger. Carl taxied out to runway four and awaited Lanny's takeoff.

Lanny pushed forward on the throttle and the super jet sped down runway two.

Lars pitched the rocket boosters and the blazing Trident was airborne. As soon as Lanny climbed to about 30,000 feet she glanced over at Valerie, her navigator, who smiled and gave her a thumbs up. Lady Bee returned the thumbs up and set a course for the middle of the Mediterranean.

Five minutes elapsed when over the headsets they heard, "Blazing Trident, this is Viking Avenger coming along your Portside. Do you copy?"

Lanny hit the transmission button. "Read you loud and clear, Viking Avenger. Keeping steady the course until you're ready to commence flight operations, OVER."

Carl asked, "Is Talon ready for peekaboo insertion? OVER."

Lanny smiled. "That's affirmative, Condor. Ready when you are, OVER."

Both jets flew side-by-side as they headed for the deck. At only fifty feet above the water Lanny radioed to Talon in the back. "Talon, we are now in position for Peekaboo."

Over the intercom on the Blazing Trident came, "I read you, baby, now initiating cloaking sequence."

Orion concentrated for a second on the sea below where a luxury liner was poised as the two battle aircraft came zooming into clear sight. Aboard the Queen Beatrice sightseers were in awe as they watched the super jets approach. Claire and Kendra were with the children and saw both aircraft pass the cruise liner, then disappear into thin air.

Kendra immediately ran to her sister and asked what had just happened, but Claire put her finger to her mouth. "Shhh, it's probably one of Poppa and Johnny's experiments. It might even be a hologram to make us believe we saw them."

Everybody aboard was buzzing about it and the cruise director Saberah Shazad replayed it on her video camera. Instantly she ran to a man in a waiter s uniform and with a face full of concern began whispering. People all over the promenade deck speculated that it was probably a new NATO weapon.

Claire noticed the reaction of the cruise director, who was without a doubt of Middle Eastern descent, and became concerned. As soon as the woman finished talking with her waiter friend on the deck she slowly made her way past Claire, Kendra, and the children. But as she did Claire eyed her up and down. The cruise director quickly looked away.

But also watching from an open hatch was Cuda and Luna (Kada and Lunsi) and they didn't like what they saw. They silently disappeared into the ship's corridors without detection.

Claire used her cell phone to secretly take a picture of the so-called cruise director. She then went back to the business of keeping the children happy and entertained.

The crowd on the promenade deck slowly returned to fun and relaxation. Claire decided to leave the kids with Kendra so that she could slip away to her cabin. But she spotted the same waiter again, the one with whom the cruise director seemed to be in cahoots. Claire snuck up on him then aimed her cell phone his way to get a clear picture of him, crossing her fingers that the waiter was unaware of her moves.

"I'll be right back," she told Kendra and rushed off to her cabin down below.

Back at the base in Dusseldorf, Professor Pearson, Malloy and their two scientists from Germany were monitoring the two super jets. All of them were elated with the results of the stealth operation. Suddenly a beeping sounded on Captain Malloy's laptop. Malloy opened it to see encrypted numbers. He hit the access button and Claire appeared on screen.

"What's so important, Lady Hawke, that you needed to encrypt your transmission?"

"Skipper, I was just out on the deck of the ship when I saw our two super jets fly by, then suddenly disappear. But that's not what concerns me, Sir. What I want to report is the reaction of two ship employees."

Malloy, startled, said, "Did everybody on the ship witness this?"

Claire, frustrated, replied, "Yes, Skipper, but people assume it's a NATO experiment. Some of them even think they witnessed a hologram." Claire got even more flustered. "I want to report a woman who is definitely of Middle Eastern descent and who also is the assistant cruise director. She immediately ran to another one of the crew, also of Middle Eastern descent, and they both began acting strangely. I picked up on it right away."

Claire paused for a second, then continued, "Sir, I'm sending you pictures I took of both of them just to be on the safe side. I think we should look into it."

Malloy nodded. "Good girl. It might be nothing, Commander, but you're my operator and I'm going to send these photos out over the wire. By the way, what did you think of the flight ops?"

Claire gave him a giant smile. "It was fantastic, Skipper. I've never seen anything like it."

Malloy laughed. "That's the idea, Commander. All right sweetheart, go back with your sister and if anything comes up I'll get back to you right away."

Professor Pearson walked to the front of the screen. "Yeah honey, just watch your back and at any sign of trouble get back to us immediately."

Claire threw him a kiss. "Okay, Poppa. Love you."

Pearson smiled. "Love you too."

The screen faded to black. Claire Vanderkamp headed back to her sister on full alert.

In the galley the cruise director arrived to talk to some of the scullery and kitchen staff. One of the bartenders also arrived just as she was about to speak. She threw him a dirty look.

"If I tell you to report to me right away, Bareen, I mean RIGHT AWAY. Do you understand me?" she demanded.

The bartender, Bareen Farkur, shrugged his shoulders. "Saberah, are you on some kind of power trip? You know I can't just leave without having someone cover my station. I know Faraz put you in charge, but you're way out of line now."

Saberah Shazad regained her composure. "I'm sorry, Bareen, but you weren't topside when those two giant attack aircraft came in at incredible speed. I've never seen anything like that before."

"I used to be in the Egyptian Air Force," he commented. "NATO is constantly using the Mediterranean to show off their new weapons. This is nothing to be concerned with."

Saberah's eyes almost popped out of her head. "Both of them just disappeared before my very eyes."

Bareen walked over and put his arm around her shoulder. "Saberah, I've seen this done before with a convoy of ships. They set up mirrors and then use refracted images to make the mind believe this."

With a frown she answered, "But Bareen, why all of a sudden do they choose to demonstrate this only eighteen hours before our operation?"

Bareen smiled again. "Like I told you, beautiful, they are constantly operating over the Med all the time. Now calm down and we'll discuss the operation tonight in your state room." Bareen grabbed her ass and gave it a pat.

Saberah smiled. "Okay Bareen, but I think we should still be on guard."

Bareen reassured her as she walked away, "That we will, Saberah. See you later."

As she disappeared up the stairs one of the scullery work said to Bareen, "Why the fuck did Faraz put a woman in charge in the first place?"

Bareen answered, "Assad, he had no choice. There was only one opening for cruise director and it had to be a woman, and Saberah was hired instantly. Do not worry, Assad. I'll fuck her tonight as usual and the little slut will stay in line. In the meantime, make sure all preparations are ready for tomorrow."

Assad replied, "You can count on me, Bareen. ALLAH AKBAR."

"ALLAH AKBAR, Assad," responded Bareen.

Time: 15:30 hours. June 3, 2011. Dusseldorf, Germany.

Time: 14:45 hours. June 4, 2011. Pekan, Malaya.

Time: 09:45 hours. June 4, 2011. Ragusa, Sicily.

Time: 11:45 hours. June 4, 2011. Doha, Qatar.

An hour earlier a fishing vessel left Tioman Island and was now docked in the port city of Pekan, Malaya. Unloading 80 cubic inch scuba tanks were a group of men wearing what looked to be yellow raincoats with closed-in headgear. Other people on the dock wondered why they were dressed like that in scalding hot weather.

At the same time in Ragusa, Sicily a commercial diving boat was doing the exact same thing. Two men on the boat were on watch just in case the harbor police showed up unexpectedly. Both were armed with AK-47s and had dozens of grenades as backup. Three men were dressed in yellow chemical suits and were stacking tanks that other crewmen were transporting off the boat.

Inside the Shah Jahan Hotel and three miles away at the Caprice hotel in the city of Doha, Qatar, men dressed as auto mechanics pushed their large red Snap On tool chests next to the center columns of the buildings. Inside the tool chests were wired RDX explosives set to go off by remote control. Each chest had 200 pounds of the deadly composite material.

Time: 09:52 hours. June 4, 2011.

On board the bridge of the Norwegian luxury liner Queen Beatrice, the assistant cruise director came through the door carrying a strapped cargo bag over her shoulder. Saberah Shazad s arms were free to carry a tray of styrofoam coffee cups.

She smiled at Captain Milson. "I got you coffee, just the way you like it, Sir. Cream with no sugar. Everybody else, the galley told me to put two sugars in each."

The helmsman, Ensign Garr Lundgren, told her, "God Saberah, you know just what to do for us all the time. Will you marry me?"

As the crew on the bridge started randomly grabbing the coffee a submarine surfaced on the starboard side. A minute went by then a horn from the ship's wheelhouse blew twice. All the sudden, inside the bridge the crew begin convulsing and foaming at the mouth. Saberah had laced the coffee with sodium cyanide.

As they began to fall to the floor she pulled an Uzi submachine gun from her cargo bag. Captain Edvard Milson's face reflected horror as he watched his crew die right in front of him. He looked towards the emergency alarm button, but Saberah screamed out, "Just try and go for it, and you'll join the rest of the crew."

The door flew open and Bareen Farkur entered with four of his henchmen. "Saberah," he screamed. "What are you waiting for? Blow the communications console."

Saberah fumbled through the cargo bag and finally pulled out a taped bomb with a pound and a half of C-four. She set the timer and Bareen, with a Beretta to Captain Milson's head, led everybody out of the wheelhouse.

Looking up from lounge chairs on the promenade deck, Claire Vanderkamp and Kendra Pearson saw the armed terrorists leading the captain outside. Ten seconds later the small bomb ripped a hole in the top of the bridge. Screaming and panic erupted all about the forward deck.

The terrorists began shooting their submachine guns in the air. The Damocles submarine was now visible to everyone on deck. The terrorists ordered everyone to put their hands on top of their heads. One of the chaperones that had befriended Claire and Kendra yelled back at the one called Assad. "I will not! How can you people do this in front of innocent children?"

Claire with her hands on top of her head pled to her friend, "Lena, just do what they say. Come on, I beg you. It's not worth your life."

Assad looked back at Claire then glared into Lena s face. "Listen to your friend, you stupid cunt."

Lena shot him the middle finger. "You don't scare me, you coward."

Assad instantly put the gun to her head and killed her on the spot.

Kendra screamed out in horror and began shaking. "Oh my God Claire, they're going to kill us all. They're going to kill us all."

But climbing onto the ship from a makeshift gangway came Faraz Saphan. He yelled out to everybody, "Do not worry, we don't want to kill anyone. Just cooperate and we will be gone before you know it." Faraz then yelled to Bareen, "Hurry brother Bareen, time is of the essence. Get the ship's manifest and separate the rich brats from the useless ones. We have fifteen minutes before they send a reconnaissance aircraft. Have a Pallazzi put the rich cargo on the submarine. Then lower the launch and disable the motor."

Climbing on board was the Princess Shaleem. She overheard the conversation and immediately said, "Faraz, do not even think I'll let you leave helpless children to their own fate out at sea."

From behind her came Omar Khaldif, Musheen's right-hand man. He said, "That is right, Faraz. You will put their chaperones aboard with them. Plus our dear Captain will accompany them so they don't become marooned out at sea. Now Shaleem, do your thing so no transmission can reach the ship."

Shaleem grabbed her amulet and concentrated with closed eyes. Two of the terrorists then began lowering the captain's launch to the water below. One of them smashed the prop with the fire extinguisher just as it began its descent. Faraz stopped them from lowering the launch once more, saying he needed to inspect it to make sure no one was hiding in it. He disappeared into the cabin, when all the sudden a loud gunshot was heard. Faraz appeared again a minute later.

Omar Khaldif asked him about the shot. Faraz laughed and explained that he killed a large rat hiding in the forward hold.

Saberah said to Faraz, "We're wasting time. We need to get all the children off the boat."

Two of Bareen's henchmen appeared on deck with Carly Sinclair and Nancy Cullen. He yelled at Claire, because he found them inside her stateroom. But Carly told him they stayed behind to play each other in a chess match. The henchmen let them go and they immediately ran to Claire and Kendra.

Faraz studied the ship's manifest and saw that one of the girls from the American delegation was none other than Nancy Cullen, daughter of one of the richest men in the world. He told Kendra to get on board the captain's launch and start helping the children into the boat.

Claire knew she had to get to her laptop and pleaded with Saberah to allow her to go back to her stateroom and get her life-saving insulin. She also told Saberah that she really needed to use the restroom. Saberah told her to use the restroom on the launch, but that she understood about the insulin. She instructed Assad to take Claire to retrieve the insulin. But Bareen overheard, and seeing how hot-looking Claire was offered to accompany them to make sure she hurried.

With a smile he waved his submachine gun, indicating she should lead them to her quarters. But he already knew he was going to rape and kill her as fast as he could. As they reached her stateroom Bareen, with a smile, opened her cabin door and motioned for her to go in. As she did, Bareen yelled for his man to grab her. The terrorist wrapped his arms around her from behind and Claire immediately slammed her right heel into the toes of her assailant. She then smashed her elbow across his jaw, sending him to the floor. Bareen tried to shoot her but she was on him already with a jumping front snap kick.

As Bareen went sailing into the clothes dresser his henchman slammed a porcelain lamp across the side of her head. Claire went down unconscious and the two Al Qaeda terrorists held her tightly across the study desk. Bareen reached under her dress and ripped off her panties, throwing them across the floor.

Claire started to revive, only to find her hands duct taped behind her. One henchman laughed with glee as Bareen dropped his trousers and underwear, then came up from behind her.

Bareen teased, "Ohhh Blondie, I'm going to love sticking it to you and you're going to love it."

Claire screamed at top of her lungs as she felt his body begin to mount her. Suddenly, he fell on top of her back and rolled to the floor, dead. Claire arched up and heard two quick shots. The man holding her fell to the floor. There with his FMG machine gun was Kada Bondi, his gun barrel smoking. She looked down at Bareen to see Kada's Kukri knife in his back.

Kada grabbed its handle, put his left boot on Bareen's corpse, and pulled it loose. Claire was out of breath and gave Kada a giant smile of relief. "Oh Cuda, have I ever been wrong about you. Thank God you were here to save me."

A fleeting glance of happiness appeared on Kada's face before he announced they needed to move quickly. Luna had positioned himself in a place where he couldn't be detected and that the emergency beacon on his watch had been activated. But something was interfering with it.

They made their way to the stern of the ship and there in a nondescript corridor was Lunsi Paal, laden with ropes and a packed-up inflatable raft. Claire told Kada they have to go back because Kendra was in trouble.

"Your sister is okay for now because she was put into the captain's launch along with half of the children and Captain Milson. But Faraz shot and killed Sharisse Khamin, the chaperone from the delegation of Saudi Arabia.

Claire began to cry because Sharisse had become very close friends with her, Kendra, and Lena Franks from Austria. This day had been a nightmare for her. Not since the day her mother Margaret died six years ago had she felt so much hurt and bitterness.

"You're an elite warrior from the Global Garrison," Kada reminded her. "We need to get off the ship right now."

Claire agreed, thinking that terrorists must be jamming all communications from the ship. That meant if they got away from the ship, they stood a good chance in contacting the Garrison.

Kada pulled the raft out of the five foot cargo bag and tied one of the ropes to its rungs. He leaned it over the side and pulled the inflation tab. The raft immediately inflated and Lunsi secured two oars inside it.

The ship was now only moving at two knots, so when they lowered the raft it laid down smoothly in the water. Lunsi with a small ALICE pack shimmied down the rope and got in. Kada had Claire follow him, and she surprised everyone because she moved better than most men.

Kada hoisted his rucksack over his shoulder and made his way to the raft. He then pulled his Kukri knife and cut the line.

On the starboard side of the ship, Faraz asked Carly and Nancy, "Who is the daughter of Garrett Cullen?"

Nancy started to answer, but brave little Carly said proudly, "I am, and once my father finds out who you are, you're going to wish you were never born."

Faraz slapped her hard enough to cause blood to gush out of her nose. The poor little girl started to wet her pants, when Princess Shaleem came over and punched Faraz in the face. His nose began to bleed as she screamed, "NOW I've HAD IT, OMAR! How can you say this is for the greater good of all the people when you're cowards inflict pain a little babies? THIS STOPS NOW. I'm ORDERING YOU. DO YOU HEAR ME?"

Omar screamed at the top of his lungs. "You heard the Princess, release them right now. He bowed to Shaleem and took her hand to kiss it. But he crushed her fingers with a ring that held a knockout compound."

Shaleem's eyes bugged out of her head and she grew faint, then fell to the deck. Omar Khaldif reached into his robe and pulled out a bottle of chloroform. He poured it on her head scarf and wrapped it around her unconscious face. One of the terrorists duct taped it in place. Then they grabbed her limp body and threw her into the captain's launch.

Scurrying down to amidships they made their way to the makeshift platform at the base of the submarine. The last two terrorists lowered the launch to the water and set it adrift. Then Assad ran into the wheelhouse and pushed forward the throttle unit to full speed at 25 knots. He wrapped a thick chain and a giant padlock around the bridge doors so no one could get in again. They had killed every member of the crew and knew the autopilot course was set for the Suez Canal.

As the propellers began to pick up full speed Assad ran down to amidships to the makeshift gangway leading onto the Damocles. Once he made it to the sub s platform he cut the ropes. The gangway slammed into the starboard hull of the Queen Beatrice as the Damocles dove below the waves.

Time: 10:37 hours. June 4, 2011.

CHAPTER ELEVEN: AFTERMATH

Time: 10:08 hours. June 4, 2011.

A half hour earlier Eagle One had contacted the commander of the Global Garrison, Captain James Malloy. The units went to the General's Quarters on full alert after they were told of a deadly chemical attack on the people of Pekan, Malaya. As they boarded the Viking Avenger, Eagle One made contact again to inform them of the same kind of attack taking place in Ragusa, Sicily.

Immediately Malloy had the Blazing Trident deployed with half of the units separated to each super jet. Malloy and Pearson went to his security office to monitor the situation as it unfolded.

Within fourteen minutes the Viking Avenger was airborne and heading for the South China Sea. Malloy conveyed to Carl Bingham reports of twenty-three people dead already. The Skipper related to him that his aircraft unit must don chemical warfare suits with forty minute OBA tanks (oxygen breathing apparatus). He also instructed them to have Galahad and Merlin deploy one of their Zodiac 470s before their arrival. They were to parachute down with four other members of the unit, then sneak in as the Viking Avenger arrived.

Malloy wanted direct communication with the Avenger so he could keep Eagle One informed. Malloy was concerned that Al Qaeda had backup terrorists, and for this reason wanted a hidden insertion team.

"Based on the team s evaluation of the scenario, do we need to use an incendiary bomb to neutralize the gas?" he asked Carl.

Carl chewed on that one.

Meanwhile Lanny had launched the Blazing Trident four minutes following the Avenger. Malloy gave the same order to Orion's team. The Blazing Trident would arrive at Ragusa in twenty minutes. Eagle One had contacted the authorities in Pekan and Ragusa to notify them of the arrival of the elite secret forces.

Reports came that a shrimp boat in Ragusa, Sicily had quickly succumbed to the deadly gases as they returned from a night of fishing. The shrimp boat crashed into a harbor police boat, setting both vessels on fire. An enormous fire engulfed the pier and spread to adjoining boats.

Aboard the Captain's launch from the Queen Beatrice, Captain Milson noticed the boat was taking on water. Now he understood why Faraz Saphan had shot into the boat twenty minutes earlier. Laying on the deck were the lifeless bodies of Lena Frank and Sharisse Khaman. Marla Evans, one of the chaperones on the voyage, placed blankets over them to at least try and calm the children.

Captain Milson turned on the bilge pump to the boat, but without the battery recharging from a working motor it wouldn't last much longer. Soon everyone aboard the doomed boat used anything they could to help bail water.

Marla and Kendra saw the face of the princess turn blue. Kendra grabbed a fishing knife and cut the duct tape from her mouth. She and Marla propped her up so she could revive with some fresh air. Kendra then got a good look at her face and her memory instantly tied it to the face of the woman back at the debriefing and security office.

Captain Milson came over. "Why are you wasting your time with her? She came on board my ship with those other killers. As far as I'm concerned we should throw her over the side and let the sharks get her."

Kendra angrily screamed back, "OH YEAH, we'll just do that. We'll become just like those murderers who killed your whole crew. You're supposed to lead by example, Captain Milson. If you try and throw her overboard you'll be joining her too."

Police in Ragusa, Sicily were evacuating the nearby residents so close to the pier. People screamed and ran to their cars. The gas slowly made its way towards them. Police helicopters flew high so as not to succumb to the deadly gas. But all the sudden a magnificent jet came in flying out of the north and hovered only thirty feet above the water. The back vertical door opened and out hovered what seemed to be a man in a black type of suit. He swooped down on the containers of deadly gas with an eerie purple glow which surrounded his entire body. Then the glow surrounded the containers of deadly gas.

The man turned off the valves to stop the leak of deadly toxin on the town. He flew ten feet above them and hovered again, then pushed his open palms forward causing a pulsating electrical charge to burn the deadly gas into black smoke. His belt harness affixed to the suit strobed in a funny sequence.

Suddenly a Zodiac carrying eight men in chemical warfare suits arrived at the pier. The flying man landed on the deck of the pier and began talking to them. The men removed their protective gear only to reveal to the people of Ragusa black suits similar to those of the flying man. They also were in awe because their masks completely covered their eyes and nose areas. One of them had strawberry blonde hair behind her mask.

The crew of eight grabbed the Zodiac by its rungs and walked it onto the pier. They threw their chemical suits in, then reached down to pick up the Zodiac once again. The man with the harness belt ascended into the air. The back of the incredible jet opened once more and as the flying man stretched forth his palms. The eight men below him were now surrounded with the same eerie purple glow. The entire crowd couldn't believe what they saw next. All of the airborne figures hovered up in the air and receded into the back of the super jet.

Television reporters momentarily dropped their cameras in shock, but then picked them up to photograph something out of this world. As the door shut the voice of a woman came over the jet's loudspeaker.

"People of Ragusa, we are the Global Garrison. We have eradicated the deadly gas. But please wait until your police and emergency officials give you the all clear."

People rubbed their heads as Valerie rushed to the microphone. She repeated in Italian everything Lanny had just said. When she finished, Lanny, with her hand over her mouth, murmured, "Oh shucks, I forgot to translate."

Orion said, "All right, baby, now get us out of here."

Just as fast as the Blazing Trident had arrived, it zoomed off into the clouds leaving behind an awe-struck populace. People cheered, but still a lot of them were on their knees crying in anguish over the murder of their family members.

"Do you need to replenish your Guardian component (ICARUS DEVICE)?" asked Lanny.

"No need," answered Orion. "It really didn't put any stress on my body at all."

Just then, an encrypted message came over the console of the Trident. Orion grabbed the headset from Valerie and conversed with Malloy. "Captain, what's up? Galahad's unit needs us right away."

Malloy answered in disgust and worry, "Talon, Galahad and Merlin were too late to contain the area. Seventy-eight innocent people are dead. I had to pull them out and alert Eagle One. From there, Eagle Four ordered an incendiary strike on the pier and contaminated surroundings. NATO authorized us to use napalm first. Then we used a Daisy Cutter with explosives and phosphorus ordinance."

Malloy grew silent for a second then said, "I've got more bad news, Talon. We just got an emergency distress beacon from Cuda. Once that came in we immediately tried to raise the Queen Beatrice. Supposedly no

119

one can get through to her. Talon, I'm sending you the ship's last coordinates. The Professor's a nervous zombie right now. If we've ever needed the Garrison, now is the time."

Orion face grew angry and he clenched his teeth. "Skipper, I'm going to find our people. Tell the Professor I swear on my life I'll bring them home."

Malloy's voice grew hoarse. "Just watch your six, Commander. This was definitely a well-coordinated attack. It looks like we got caught with our pants down again."

Lanny spoke into her headset. "Skipper, we can't be in four places at the same time."

Malloy responded reassuringly, "I know, Lady Bee, but we're working on that. Now fly that bird and bring our people home."

"Aye, aye Sir."

Valerie showed her the Queen Beatrice s last coordinates and she immediately unlocked the autopilot and put a sequence of numbers to the console. Lanny tipped her right wing up and the Blazing Trident went left and headed towards the deck. She leveled off, as the super jet was only a hundred feet above the water.

Orion told her to reduce speed or otherwise they wouldn't spot anything from the air.

Meanwhile on the surface of the water, Kendra noticed three people in a raft slowly coming up on the port side of their sinking launch. The boat was also beginning to list to its starboard side. Claire spotted the two lifeless bodies of her dear friends Lena and Sharisse and began to cry, but then stopped so the children wouldn't panic.

Kada told Claire, "Missy Claire, there's only room in the raft for twelve people."

Claire kept her wits about her and replied, "Okay, Kada, let's just get the children in first, then my sister. Then we will have to coordinate people in the water at different intervals."

Captain Milson and Marla Evans began to help Kendra load the children onto the raft. The Princess looked almost dead as they brought her to the edge of the boat.

"There is hardly enough room in there for us," said Captain Milson angrily. "This evil bitch was with them when they boarded my ship. I say she's no goddamn good, and look at her, she hasn't got long to live anyway. Throw this piece of shit overboard and let someone who deserves to live take her place."

Claire asked Kada for his FMG submachine gun. Kada handed it to her and she unfolded and pointed it at Milson. "I don't care what you think she's done. First person that does to harm anybody here, I will shoot you where you stand."

The captain looked at her face and saw she wasn't bullshitting. They very carefully loaded the dying princess aboard the raft. Claire got a real good look at her and immediately knew who she was. She instantly looked at Kendra, who had her fingertip on her lips. Claire nodded to let Kendra know she understood.

The children began shouting, "LOOK OVER THERE! DOLPHINS!"

Marla Evans realized they were not dolphins, but rather SHARKS. The launch was now almost on its side and it seemed only minutes until it headed to the bottom. The weakened Princess slowly grabbed the talisman around her neck and began chanting in a strange foreign tongue. The metal around the large Ruby glowed just like Orion as she recited an ancient prayer.

Above the Mediterranean Sea a super jet prowled the ocean surface for any sign of castaways. Orion lowered the back vertical door and then told everyone to keep their eyes peeled for something out of the ordinary. Back in the cockpit, a radio transmission came to Lanny and Valerie that their comrades on the Viking Avenger were twelve minutes away from joining the search. Calvin Thomas came running into the cockpit and told Lanny that Orion needed her to reduce speed.

"The Commander is glowing purple. It's almost blinding everyone in the back," he added excitedly.

Orion transfixed his hearing to the surface below and heard screams of horror coming from the sea. His sensitive hearing registered, "OH, PLEASE MAKE THEM GO AWAY. WHY DO THEY KEEP CIRCLING OUR BOAT?"

Orion pressed the button on his headset. "Lanny, we're here, baby. They are right below us and in trouble."

Lanny instantly slowed and headed closer to the surface.

Inside the raft Kendra looked up and saw a purple glowing figure heading right at them. She yelled, "CLAIRE, LOOK!"

The silhouette of a glowing purple man slammed into the sea. The sharks were instantly scared off. Everyone on the raft sat spellbound as the battle jet Blazing Trident appeared and hovered twenty feet above them.

Marla Evans was about to faint. "God, is everybody seeing what I'm seeing?"

The children cheered as a man came hurtling up from below dressed in a black suit with long gauntlet gloves and shin high boots. His mask hid his face, but they saw his smile.

"Is everybody okay? Is anybody injured?"

Claire responded, "Ah, yes, Sir. Whoever you are, this poor girl is very close to death. Can you please help her?"

Orion loved the way Claire hid his identify. "Everybody hold tight to the raft. You're going for a little ride."

He raised his arms and opened his palms, then began to glow an even more of an eerie hue of purple right before their eyes. The raft began lifting towards the vertical door of the Blazing Trident. This time Captain Milson fainted while the kids cheered in delight.

They had almost reached the door when another similar super jet appeared next to them. In a state of shock they got off the raft and went inside the Blazing Trident. Aboard were men and women dressed just like the flying man and wearing the same type of mask.

Marla saw weapons of all sorts placed strategically about the plane. Orion went to the cockpit and told Lanny they had with them along with Lamarra's friend who was close to death.

Lanny told Lars to fly the jet while she tried to save the woman's life, then ran to the rear of the jet and asked some of the crew to put the dangerously ill woman on Orion's regeneration table. Lanny took a small flashlight and pulled the woman's eyelids open. Then she ordered Mustang (Hans) to get the oxygen bottle and breather mask. Lanny pulled a medical valise from under the table and withdrew an injection syringe which she loaded with 20 ccs of adrenaline. But as she tried to inject it, a bit of a force field tried to stop her. Lanny was still able to administer the injection but her stomach became nauseous as she threw the syringe in the waste container.

Orion, concerned, saw his fiancée grab her belly for a second time. "Baby, everything all right?"

Lanny finished putting the mask over the woman's face and replied to her man, "Yeah honey, I'm okay. I'm just hoping we were in time. This poor girl was exposed to chloroform perhaps too long. Everything is in God's hands now."

Captain Milson awoke and put in his two cents. "This girl is a terrorist. Who gives a damn if she dies."

Claire said, "Oh, you again." She turned to Lanny. "I don't know who you are, Ma'am, but this man suggested we throw your patient overboard so there would be more room in the boat."

Lanny looked at Captain Milson. "Is this true, Captain?"

Captain Milson shrugged his shoulders. "You bet I did, and I'd do it again."

Lanny instructed Hansy, "Sergeant Mustang, put this man in handcuffs. He's under arrest for violating the law of the sea. The charge is attempted murder. Now get him out of my sight."

Hansy grabbed Captain Milson. "Come with me, and if you give me any trouble you'll be swimming back to shore."

Milson, frustrated as he was being cuffed, asked, "How can this be? I was only looking at the interests of my passengers and crew."

Hansy replied sarcastically, "Oh if you're wondering, we're sailors, too. Under your command manual it clearly states you are to protect the lives of all who berth and work on your vessel. You made yourself judge, jury, and then executioner under your own rule of law. That makes you just as bad as those al Qaeda fucks. At least you'll get a fair trial."

Up in the cockpit Valerie Queen relayed an important message back to Dusseldorf. "Blazing Trident calling Global Command. Come in please, OVER."

Malloy's voice came over the console. "Blazing Trident, this is Global Command. We read you loud and clear, OVER."

"Global Command, this is Blazing Trident. Tell our boss that Lady Hawke and the Baroness are safe. We have ten of the precious cargo in tow. Ten more are still unaccounted for, OVER."

Back in Dusseldorf Jeffrey Pearson's eyes filled with tears of joy.

Malloy replied, "Okay Blazing Trident, you and Viking Avenger are ordered to return to base, OVER."

"Global Command, that's a copy, OVER AND OUT," responded Valerie.

In the back of the super jet Lanny held her patient's hand and prayed to God, hoping the princess knew someone was there for her. Orion looked over and smiled, confident in the beautiful human being he was going to marry.

Time: 13:13 hours. Dusseldorf. June 4, 2011.

The submarine Damocles had just arrived ten miles out from the shore of the city of Tajura. There to meet them in a dow boat was Mustaffa Khaldif and a group of Al Qaeda terrorists. They transferred the kidnapped children from the submarine.

Mustaffa embraced his brother. "We have done it, my brother. We will now bring the United States and the West to their knees. Allah be praised. We have done it."

Carly Sinclair with dried blood running from her lip looked over and tried to memorize every face she saw. The beautiful little girl tried to be strong and brave as she prayed to God for a miracle. She then pictured Claire and Kendra and her heart took on even more bravery.

Time: 14:15 hours. Tajura, Libya. June 4, 2011. Gulf of Sidra Time: 14:00 hours.

Thirty miles from the entrance to the Suez Canal, and having just been alerted twenty minutes prior by Eagle One, Orion switched over to the Viking Avenger to intercept the runaway ship Queen Beatrice. Orion arrived just in time and was able to freeze the mighty ship from moving while his right hand man, Merlin, boarded the ship with his unit to shut down the engines of the luxury liner.

The people aboard were mesmerized by the flying man who was able to stop a cruise liner in full speed propulsion.

As quickly as they arrived, the elite Global Garrison unit disappeared.

The Egyptian navy arrived to see the jet fly off into the distance. They were also impressed at the super jet moving away at such an incredible speed.

Time: 14:26 hours. June 4, 2011. Somewhere out in the Mediterranean.

CHAPTER TWELVE: THE DEVIL'S DEMANDS

After landing on the secret Command Base in Dusseldorf, Germany, the Viking Avenger and the Blazing Trident began taxiing towards the giant hangar made just for them. There waiting with a gurney was the medical and science teams of the Corporation. Professor Pearson was present and dressed in surgical scrubs along with Dr. Darfuir and Carl Livingston. They were going to open up Shaleem's chest and try and clean the poison from her lungs.

There was no time to transport her to the surgical hospital on the other side of the base. Lanny had notified her father that Shaleem's pulse was getting weaker at forty beats per minute and dropping fast. As they rushed her from the rear of the Blazing Trident, Lars Olsen picked her up and ran to the awaiting makeshift operating table in the hangar.

He laid her on the table and the princess' amulet glowed. Her eyes opened briefly to see Lars face over hers. She fell into unconsciousness but her face lit up with a smile. Lars, with a tear forming in his right eye, said to the Professor, "Doc, please do everything you can to save her."

Pearson seemed bewildered because he knew Lars had never before met this woman. But with a reassuring voice, he replied, "I'll do everything in my power, Lieutenant, but it's also up to her and the man or woman upstairs. I can only do so much. Now Tank, I need for you to get on the other side of the curtains so we can proceed."

Lanny had just changed out of her BDU and appeared in surgical scrubs to assist the team in the operation. She grabbed Lars by his arm. "Hey big guy, we're going to save her. Just hang in there, Tank." She led him to a chair on the other side of the curtains and sat him down. She couldn't believe how much the big guy was shaking and kissed his forehead. "Think positive, big guy."

Lanny then rushed to assist her father and probably the best surgical team from around the globe.

On the other side Dr. Darfuir made the first incision and a force field grew around Shaleem just as it did around Orion. Lanny's stomach began to ache a little as she reached out her hand to penetrate the barrier of the field. Her stomach stopped aching immediately as she touched the princess' hand.

Dr. Darfuir called to Orion, "Talon, get in here quickly. We need you."

Orion entered like a lightning bolt only to see the strange purple glow formed over the Princess and his fiancée.

"Talon, see if you can control the force field around Shaleem. Lady Bee has been allowed to penetrate it. I don't know why, but I need her to help me operate. So try and defeat the barrier if you can," said Darfuir.

Lanny watched her man as he concentrated, and the eerie color of purple began to envelop the entire surgical team. One of the staff put on a surgical mask, but the doctor told her it was not needed. Orion's amazing body was able to completely reject and destroy any kind of bacteria or deadly agent immediately.

The operation lasted two and a half hours. Finally, the princess' vital signs came back to a weak, but normal, reading.

Time: 16:20 hours. June 4, 2011. Germany.

In the city of Doha, Qatar were two groups of terrorists dressed as valets and auto mechanics. The hurried out of the parking garage of the Hotel Shah Jahan where they just set the bomb that Omar Khaldif would detonate by remote control.

Two miles down the road was the Caprice Hotel where a similar explosive device had also been set. Omar Khaldif showed his henchmen how to place the four shaped charges at the center columns of the hotels. Each hotel was to have two bombs fastened to the main structure beam. One explosive device was to be planted to the main column and the other would be fastened to the facade column at the edge of the hotel s parking garage. This was to create the domino effect and cause the other columns to pancake on one another.

But unknown to Omar Khaldif, his main man in charge decided it would be better if they just put all the shaped charges in the center column. Molaan Shavaaz, being Khaldif's most trusted right-hand, made this decision after they began to arouse suspicion from the other mechanics in the service area of the garage itself.

As the terrorists drove off in their Jeep Wrangler, Molaan opened his cell phone and called Abdullah Musheen, informing him that they were ready for his order to detonate the shaped charges.

Musheen told them to get into position and await his command. They parked only a mile and a half from the hotels and awaited the Evil One's instruction.

Time: 18:30 hours. June 4, 2011. Doha, Qatar.

Time: 16:45 hours. June 4, 2011. Dusseldorf, Germany.

The lungs of the Princess Shaleem had been detoxified and Professor Pearson and his surgical staff relaxed on the couches in the hangar that were used to sleep some of the weary pilots.

All the sudden, Zorro (Carlos Alvarez) dashed in with a determined face. "TURN ON THE TV SET! Look what's going on."

Gunnar grabbed the remote to the Sony flat screen and turned it on. A terrorist with a red polka dotted scarf covering his face appeared on the screen as Gunnar turned up the volume. They missed the first thirty seconds of the broadcast but heard him say, "PEOPLE OF THE WEST, and mainly your government officials and bureaucrats, today we have successfully taken your next-generation of pimps and whores you infidels procreated for your dominance. I am here now to make my demands on you if you ever want to see your precious little monkeys again."

The man on the screen turned his head and pointed, indicating to the camera man that he should fix his lens on the kidnapped children who were tied up and crying on the floor.

"As you see, we have their best interest at heart. Just to show you I mean business I now draw your attention to the monitor right behind me." The man whispered something into his cell phone and a resounding rumble from under the foundation of the two buildings could be heard. Smoke billowed out of the bottom as the structures trembled and shook. But after the smoke cleared it was apparent both buildings were still standing.

The man on the screen said in a choked up voice, "As you see, we have detonated explosives under two of your favorite playgrounds in our part of the world. This is just to show you all that I am capable of doing what I want. Next time, you will not be so lucky." The man became annoyed as he rattled on. "My first and main demand is that you bring to a specified meeting place $400 million in gold bullion. I will reveal to you the meeting place in five days. Along with that you will bring $100 million in precious diamonds and gems. Please don't try anything funny. If you do I will begin executing your children one by one for the world to see. If you try sending in your commandos we will cut off their lily-livered heads."

Then he gestured for the cameraman to come closer and focus in. "Now this is for that team of mercenaries who call themselves the Global Garrison. If you're thinking that you can out-think or fool me, you're terribly mistaken."

Just at that moment Claire entered from the back with Valerie and Kendra. They looked up and listened very attentively.

"I will kill every one of these fucking brats if I even pick up the smell of you. Also I see you've created another one of your cyborg robots. If you try using that thing against us... wait one second... " Musheen moved to the

127

children lying on the ground and picked up a little girl who was blindfolded and gagged. He drug her in front of the camera and continued. "Like I said, if you even think of using that thing against us I will personally cut the head off of... " He pulled off the child's blindfold. "Of little Nancy Cullen."

There on the screen was Carly Sinclair with one of her eyes turning black and blue. They didn't even clean the dried blood across her nose and lips.

The horror showed all over Claire's face as screamed out in agony, "OH GOD, how could I have left you behind? I should be there."

Bobby ran over as she lowered herself to the floor, crying uncontrollably.

Musheen continued, "Now Mr. Garrett Cullen, it seems you have been making quite a tidy sum of money from the oil that belongs to the people of Islam. Well, we want it back. So start conferring with your rich and powerful pals. Because if you do not meet my demands, by Allah, I will kill them all. In five days from now at exactly 6 o'clock on the morning of June 9th I will contact you with further instructions. Failure to comply or stall means immediate execution."

He then screamed, "Insha Allah" (God willing in Arabic).

The screen faded to black and Kendra said, "Oh my God, what happens if they find out that Nancy is really Carly?"

Professor Pearson replied with zeal, "I'll call Wolfman (Jim Ferris) back in the states and have him bring Carly's parents up to speed. Believe you me, he's ex-police and Lieutenant Major Ferris will know exactly how to prepare them."

Pearson then looked at Malloy. "Skipper, contact Garrett and tell him not to talk to the press. That little girl s life is hanging in the balance. Tell him I'll explain further in a little while."

Malloy replied, "Will do, Jeffrey."

Pearson started to walk away but stopped and asked Malloy, "What are you going to do now, James? It seems as if that evil bastard has tied all of our hands."

Malloy smiled and pointed to Orion and the units. "That asshole doesn't know we've got the best escape artists in the world. If you look closely, they're already devising a foolproof plan."

The Professor left and Malloy headed for the security office, but stopped by Lady Hawke. "Lady Hawke, take some time with Galahad and try and regain your composure. Take a walk on the beach or something. Then in two hours I want to see both of you in my office."

Claire, surprised, said to her uncle, "But Skipper, I belong here with the rest of the unit to help come up with a plan."

Malloy replied, "You do what I tell you to do. Galahad knows what I'm talking about. He'll fill you in on what your choices will be with this organization. You better think very carefully about your amount of resolve. Your boyfriend will explain."

Malloy headed for his Land Rover and drove to the other side of the base.

Claire and Bobby went to the locker rooms and changed into shorts and T-shirts. Claire was really nervous and worried she was being pulled out of the Garrison. After they changed Bobby met her as she exited from the women's side of the locker room. He saw small tears on the face of the woman he loved.

"Come on, baby, let's go down to the Rhine. I hear the sunsets there are some of the most beautiful in the world."

Claire was annoyed. "Tell me right now, Bobby. Is my uncle throwing me out of the Garrison?"

Palladin answered honestly, "I really don't know, Claire. The captain only does what he sees fit. But for now baby, I need my time with you. You have witnessed a vicious and incomprehensible attack. Just for now sweetheart, we're going on a walk along the shore. Let's just hold one another."

They drove on for another ten minutes before arriving at a beautiful crystal cove along the Rhine River. Bobby grabbed his iPod and exited the Cadillac SUV. Wrapping his right arm around Claire's waist he pulled her close. They walked silently for about five minutes before Claire tried to speak.

But Bobby put the tip of his index finger gently to her mouth. "Shhh… " He then laid a giant beach towel onto the sand and pushed the play button to start the music. He lowered her so softly to the towel as the Mazzy Star song Fade into You began to play. They passionately made love as their bodies became as one. Ten minutes elapsed before they rolled over, exhausted.

Claire whispered to Galahad, "I love you, Bobby. Please don't let the Skipper throw me out of the unit."

Bobby leaned over her naked body. "Claire, you were traumatized. The Skipper's worried, and so am I, that your emotions are leaving you vulnerable to attack. Baby, if your mind is not on the mission and you can't control your feelings, you're compromising everybody's life in the units. Can you realize that, Claire?"

Claire pleaded, "But Bobby, I was with those children and I feel somewhat responsible for this situation. Is it wrong to be human?"

Bobby reached in and kissed her. "No, of course not Lady Hawke. But what about your thoughts of losing me? Remember those strong emotions?"

Claire's eyes lit up like fire. "This ain't about me or you. This is about ridding our planet of scum who would kill innocent children for their own power and greed."

Bobby was transfixed at his girlfriend's face. She passed Malloy's test. Palladin reached into his shorts by the side of the beach towel and pulled out his cell phone. He pushed a speed dial number and he began to converse.

"No, you were wrong, Skipper. She's definitely been baptized. Yes Sir, that I will. See you in an hour."

Claire was bewildered. "What do you mean, she's been baptized?"

"The Skipper and Talon will fill you in when we're back in uniform on the base," replied Bobby.

Claire's eyes bulged. "Oh, this was some test that you and my uncle put me through, huh? Oh, and I guess you figured you would fuck me first before the test was utilized."

Paladin s face turned sour, but before he could say anything Claire finished with, "GOOD IDEA! That really was the best sex we've had in a long time."

Both of them laughed as they get dressed to return to the base. The Cadillac SUV headed east to the clandestine base as Claire snuggled up to Bobby. The thought flitted across Claire's mind that another good thing about the base was that it provided employment to most of the townspeople in the area.

Joseph Stellarnberg and his wife Francine lived two blocks from the outer edge of the base. Their two boys were attending college in Brandenburg. But now that it was summer, they were at home planning a visit to the United States.

The Stellarnberg family finished dinner and left the dining room for the comfort of the living room. Franz Stellarnberg asked his father a question as his brother Burt turned on the television. "Papa, do you think all this kidnapping and terrorism comes into play because of the presence of the Global Garrison? Really, who do these mercenaries think they are? We don't need a global police force. If it wasn't for them, the terrorists probably would've picked another place to do whatever is that they do."

His brother Burt answered sarcastically, "Franz, you can't be serious. Al Qaeda is only self-servient to their own agenda." Then he pointed to the television as Al Jazeera played a tape from the Egyptian navy.

The screen showed the super jet Viking Avenger lowering its vertical back door. Orion came out and flew towards the runaway luxury liner.

Burt snidely remarked, "Now, what would've happened if they didn't show up with whoever, or whatever, that is flying above the water?"

On the television screen Orion thrust his arms forward and it was obvious that he was concentrating. The colossal ship made a crunching sound as it slowed to a stop only thirty feet from where Orion hovered above the sea. The super jet moved in as one of his arms levitated Merlin,

Rhino, Gunnar, Zorro and Maverick to the deck of the periled ship. They cut the thick chain with a laser weapon and entered the bridge. Whatever they did, they did expediently. Within three minutes they were being levitated back to the jet by the flying man.

As the amazing jet flew away at incredible speed Burt reiterated to his brother Franz, "If the ship wasn't stopped it would've slammed into the entrance of the Suez Canal. Think of what the world markets would've went through after its main shipping arteries were disabled for weeks, or maybe months."

Franz responded, "Like always, my dear brother, those courses in economics have compelled your brain to think in a clearer picture. Maybe you are right. But still, do you think these bands of mercenaries can make a difference? This has all been tried in the past, and it didn't work."

Professor Stellarnberg cut in. "Well my boy, what are you, the glass half-empty or the glass half-full?"

Burt laughed with his father and brother. "We already know he's full of it."

Franz responded, "You are right as usual, my brother, and I should be very careful of what I say about them. I know I've caught glimpses of those aircraft flying over Dusseldorf."

Franz and Burt both stared at their rocket science father with a look of curiosity. Joseph Stellarnberg cleared his throat. "Let's watch something more relaxing. I think Europe's Got Talent is on now." He spotted his two boys smiling at him and buried his head into his daily newspaper.

Time: 20:35 hours. June 4, 2011. Dusseldorf.

Time: 19:00 hours. June 4, 2011. Dusseldorf.

Bobby and Claire arrived back at the base and immediately donned their battle dress uniforms, then headed to Captain Malloy's security office on the eastern side of the base.

As Claire got off the elevator with Bobby she felt a little nervous, but put on a face of determination before entering her uncle s office. She knocked on his door with anxiety threatening to take over.

From the other side of the door came, "You may enter, Lady Hawke and Galahad."

They stepped through to see the rest of the units waiting for them. Claire saw her empty chair next to Lanny's at the officer's side of the table.

Malloy said to her, "Come in, Master Chief, and you too Commander. You know your places. NOW SIT!"

Claire sat next to her sisters and saw them smile reassuringly.

Malloy immediately got to the point and asked Kada Bondi, "Sergeant Cuda, how would you surmise the performance of Lady Hawke against the Al Qaeda terrorists?"

Kada stood up and with a funny British salute said, "Even when caught off guard Ms. Lady Hawke still kicked their evil asses all over the room. She is a credit to our elite team and I would go to war with her in a heartbeat."

Claire smiled with contentment to hear him speak highly of her. She tried to respond, but Malloy held up his hand and silenced her.

He pointed to Orion. "Lieutenant Commander, Lady Hawke has been exemplary at her duties under stressful situations. Under the recommendations of our Master Chief Galahad, she is indoctrinated into our COMBAT READINESS UNIT. In other words little sister, you've passed. Will you please elaborate for her, Skipper?"

Malloy replied, "Commander Lady Hawke, all of us who have been in combat many times over know how to face a dangerous dilemma. Only those of us who have experienced it know the look of giving up versus the look of resolve. It is apparent you will do whatever it takes to be part of the unit. Lieutenant Commander Lady Hawke, you've entered the realm of no return. You have been BAPTIZED UNDER FIRE. Like the rest of us, you have demonstrated your commitment to our cause. I was really worried, though. I love you more than anything, Commander. But when you became hysterical and blamed yourself for the predicament of those innocent children I had no choice but to test your resolve. Lady Hawke, the way we win wars is to keep a clear head. Combat under pressure is resolved with a steady hand at the helm. Do I make myself clear, Commander?"

Claire gave a serious reply. "That you do, Sir."

Malloy continued, "My dear girl, you are the Captain and pilot of the most expensive and combat ready aircraft in the world. Nobody can fly her like you. Am I right, Colonel Condor?"

Carl Bingham spoke. "No question about it. I can't fly her as good as the Lieutenant Commander."

Lanny voiced, "Oh, believe you me, I know I can't."

"No my dear, but you sure are getting there," encouraged Bingham.

Malloy cut in. "Enough chit chat, boys and girls. To the business at hand. I need a plan and a backup plan on my desk by 13:00 hours tomorrow. Do I make myself clear, ladies and gentlemen?"

The whole room answered, "Hoo Yah."

Malloy then said, "Good. Now what the fuck are all of you sitting here for? Get out of my office."

Everyone ran for the door like there was no tomorrow. But Claire stayed behind and whispered to the Skipper, "Thank you, Uncle Jimmy." She kissed him on the cheek.

He smiled for a second but then responded, "You're still here? MOVE! Now get me some solutions, Commander."

She smiled and ran to the door yelling, "Aye Aye, Sir."

Time: 19:45 hours. June 4, 2011. Dusseldorf, Germany.
Time: 21:45 hours. June 4, 2011. Mocha, Yemen.

In the port city of Mocha, Yemen the al Qaeda terrorist Abdullah Musheen was in a tirade over the failed toppling of the two luxury hotels in Doha, Qatar. Musheen conversed with his second in command, Mustaffa Khaldif.

"How did your brother Omar pick such an incompetent idiot as Molaan Shavaaz to carry out the demolition? I can already hear Zawhari speaking to the Council about having me removed for incompetence."

Mustaffa replied to his leader, "My brother brought him in on the recommendation of his lieutenant, Faraz Saphan. Saphan assured him that Molaan and his cousin Saberah went through our training camps with flying colors. Something must have gone wrong."

Musheen slammed his fist down on the table inside the fish market building that he used to disguise his operations. "Of course something went wrong and I'm the laughingstock because of it. If your brother were here right now, I would personally execute him with my bare hands. As soon as Faraz contacts you, let him know the operation still goes on as scheduled."

Mustaffa replied, "Yes, your Excellency, but what of this Molaan Shavaaz? He's on his way here with three other operators as we speak."

Musheen, with an evil look said, "KILL HIM! And then his band of fools." Then he paused for a second. "No, wait. They're perfect for one of our diversion operations. Mustaffa, I need to know more about this so-called Global Garrison as well as the powers of that android and what its capabilities are. I've just thought of something. If we have these fools make an assault on another priority target we can set up hidden cameras at the target to observe and learn of this super weapon they've constructed. Once we know what we are dealing with, we will then know it's weaknesses and be able to destroy it."

Musheen studied the huge map of the Middle East and Europe strewn across the table in front of them. First he looked at the top of the map, but immediately became disinterested. Then he pointed to the picture of an oil tanker in an area just north of Tunisia.

He waved to Mustaffa. "Come here, my loyal friend. This is what I am proposing for that bumbling idiot and his men. The ship right here called the Syrene Majestic leaves the port of Bizerte, Tunisia on the seventh of June. Its main cargo of 80,000,000 gallons of number two crude is set for a voyage through the Straits of Gibraltar. The ship is supposed to go to Port Monmouth, New Jersey. Now I propose we bring the Global Garrison and that android out of hiding."

Musheen became enthused. "You see Mustaffa, from our own operator in Algeria we found out that they are also shipping magnesium and cobalt along the aft decks of the ship. If we can get an operator on board it before it leaves Bizerte we could then sneak onboard to plant hidden cameras. It is scheduled to reach the Straits fourteen hours after it leaves port, at six o'clock on the morning of the seventh. So that will be eight o'clock in the evening, but one hour before our man with his heavily armed trio of fools will set fire to the magnesium containers at the stern of the ship. They will open dozens of the containers and put sacks of powdered phosphorus in them and set it ablaze. We will tell these idiots that they will have plenty of time to make their escape. But ten minutes prior we will tip off INTERPOL and I'll bet my soul that this Global Garrison will arrive before anyone else, especially since the Syrene Majestic is about to cause havoc in the main shipping lane. We then will have a front row seat to observe the android and his operators as they come to save the day."

Mustaffa then asked Musheen, "Excellency, aren't you worried about them getting caught and giving up our location here in Mocha?"

Musheen laughed wickedly. "Oh my dear brother in arms. I'm counting on it."

Time: 22:10 hours. June 4, 2011. Mocha, Yemen.

Time: 20:10 hours. June 4 , 2011. Dusseldorf, Germany.

Professor Jeffrey Pearson had just called for Orion, Lanny, Bobby and Claire to meet him in his office on the eastern side of the base. As they entered Captain Malloy was leaving and said to them, "Enjoy your flight. I'll see you all back here on the sixth."

Orion, confused tried to speak, but the Skipper cut him off. "The boss will fill you in."

They walked in and saw the Professor on the phone. As he talked he motioned for all of them to take a seat.

"I understand perfectly, Professor Hewitt. Tell your colleague Dr. Yamans to call us if it shows the same spike in behavior. Lift-off is at 15:00 hours tomorrow. Yes, we are going to fly out of here in an hour. What's that? No, Dave, it's not impossible for us to rest and be ready for the launch. Let me get going, Professor Hewitt. I need to get ready for my flight. Yes, I'll soon be in touch. Okay, goodbye."

As he hung up, Lanny asked, "What was that all about, Poppa?"

"Well my dear family, it seems we leave within the hour for our home base. NASA will not approve the necessary appropriation funds for the scramjet launch unless they can observe our electromagnetic generated railing system in action for themselves. They say we've used too much of their precious time and they want to see the prototype handle the escape velocity of the Earth's gravitational pull. They also conveyed to me that if they can't see it by tomorrow they will go elsewhere. I also need you there, Commander. As we launch the scramjet you will be in a simulator that will record all G forces and body functional progress as the vehicle escapes the Earth's gravitational pull. Only we will know that we are recording your vital signs as it orbits the Earth one time. Inside the scramjet will be a dummy made of cellulose and gelatin mold. We will attach electronic indicators to the dummy to evaluate the stress of escape velocity and then reentry. But secretly we will have the supercomputer monitor your functions in virtual reality synthesis."

Orion asked, "Doc, what about Al Qaeda? What happens if they do something while we are in the states? There's no way we could cross the Atlantic in time."

The Professor replied, "I said the same thing to the captain. He told me not to worry and get back as fast as we can."

Bobby nodded his head and said to Orion, "The Skipper's right, Talon. There's enough talent in the Garrison to hold those bastards off. I know, brother, none of us have the amazing powers you possess. But we both know we have the best fighting team in the world."

"You're right, as usual," said Orion. "And besides, I want to see this spaceship launch, anyway."

Claire and Lanny said at the same time, "ME TOO!"

Pearson laughed. "That settles it, boys and girls. Get ready. Wheels up in forty-five."

As they left, the Professor called Stellarnberg and Kruger and instructed them to also get ready to leave, especially since they were the ones who built the propulsion system on the spacecraft. Plus Pearson knew they wanted to ride in the Viking Avenger themselves. Forty minutes later in their battle dress uniforms Orion, Lanny, Bobby and Claire greeted the Professors at hanger four on the west side of the base.

Claire finished putting on her mask and told everyone aboard to strap in. She and Lanny entered the cockpit to greet Lars, who this time was navigator. "Okay Tank, how's the air traffic out there right now?"

Lars replied, "The tower says we have a ten minute window for takeoff, Lady Hawke. Whenever you're ready."

Lady Hawke replied, "I'm ready right now, Tank. How's our special passenger doing?"

Lars looked worried. "She's in good hands with Dr. Darfuir. He still doesn't want to take her out of her induced coma until we are back at the Citadel."

Lanny put her hand on his shoulder. "Once we've leveled off you can go back and sit with her, big guy."

Lars said in a hoarse voice, "Thanks, Lady Bee."

Claire then asked Joe Coffey in the back, "Cochise, is everybody tucked in?"

Coffey answered, "Ready whenever you are, Captain."

Claire pulled to runway one and got clearance from the tower. She pushed the throttle forward as the jet hurtled down the runway. The Viking Avenger lifted-off at amazing speed and headed into the heavens.

Time: 21:15 hours. June 4, 2011. Dusseldorf, Germany.

CHAPTER THIRTEEN: LAMINATION OF LOVE

Time: 08:30 hours. June 5, 2011. East Hampton, New York.

Just getting into the United States at 01:10 hours, the crew and the passengers of the Viking Avenger enjoyed much needed time for some shut eye. Finally getting to sleep at 01:40 hours gave the crew and scientists almost six hours of rest. Even though the initial flight was just over three hours long, everyone still had a little jet lag.

Dr. Darfuir approached the Citadel's cafeteria escorting his sister Lamarra Balaash. He introduced her to the German Professors, then ordered breakfast for him and his sister.

Lars Olsen noticed something familiar about Lamarra but couldn't put his finger on it. The good doctor noticed Lars staring with curiosity at his sister, then whispered to her. They came over and sat down with the six-foot-five commando.

Lamarra looked at Lars and thought there was something familiar about him. She seemed puzzled and spoke to the blonde-haired warrior. "Mr. Tank, my name is Lamarra Balaash. I am the sister of your good friend here, Kamal."

Lars reached out to shake her tiny hand and a certain chill touched the back of his neck.

"My brother here tells me you're more than just infatuated with my sweet Shaleem."

Lars, being a gentleman, asked her, "Is she your daughter, Mrs. Balaash?"

Lamarra replied, "Oh I wish she was, and you may call me Ms. Balaash. My husband was killed in the Iraqi-Iranian war."

Lars immediately replied, "I'm sorry, Ms. Balaash. Sorry about your loss."

With a kind smile she responded, "No need to be sorry, Lieutenant. I lost him twenty-two years ago. Oh, that stupid war. Just a bunch of fanatical power-hungry leaders falsely claiming they do it in Allah s name. I don't know of any God who would condone killing, and if I were this God I would punish them for their insolence."

Lars smiled and said to Professor Darfuir, "Hey Doc, I like this lady. No wonder she's your sister. But Ms. Balaash, how did you come to know the Princess Shaleem?"

Lamarra sipped her coffee. "My husband was killed along with three members of the Kholdeef Royal family. Even though the Kholdeef's were only observers of that tragic war, the Iranian regime still wanted to wipe out the whole family. My husband Armanash killed three of the assassins, only to be picked off by a sniper as he hid the Khaleef from certain death. His Lordship Omal Hussein Kholdeef made me a member of his inner circle and trusted me as the caretaker of his most precious Shaleem. The Sultan blessed me with this and I am forever grateful. I love her as if she were my own."

Lars asked in bewilderment, "But Ms. Balaash, why was she helping the Al Qaeda network? it's hard to believe such a gorgeous and noble woman like her would have anything to do with those evil bastards."

Lamarra responded in a raw tone, "Lieutenant, I was told she was killed along with her father over six years ago. That evil shit Musheen made even me believe this. He mislead my entire mosque into believing he was for American way of life. I can just imagine what he made her believe."

Lars stood up as Lamarra began to cry. He put his massive hands on her shoulders. "Ms. Balaash, I am sorry if I made you cry. But I also want to let you know that I can't place it, but I've seen her in my dreams and my soul can't let go of her."

Lamarra put her small hand over Lars. "You know, I have this strange feeling that we've met somewhere before also."

Dr. Darfuir looked puzzled and decided to change the subject. "Okay both of you, before we have a reality show of the paranormal brought here, I figured I'd let you know we're waking Shaleem out of her induced coma this morning around 10 o'clock. So if both of you want to be there, I warn you not let our patient become too excited. If both of you promise that you're welcome to be there."

Both agreed to the doctor's demands and finished their breakfast. Lanny and Claire, who went to the room only five minutes prior, came over to join them.

Lars asked both, "Where are your other halves? What, they got punished and are not allowed out?"

Everybody at the table chuckled. Claire said, "No, you big galoot. Galahad is helping Talon with his special G-suit for today s launch. Tank, I know you've got a lot on your mind but would you like to go running with me, Lanny and the dogs? Maybe it would relieve a little of your stress."

Lars explained that the Professor was taking Shaleem out of her coma this morning. Lanny and Claire immediately asked the Professor if they could be there also. But the scientist said it wouldn't be prudent and might be harmful when she first comes to. Once his diagnosis of her condition was confirmed, he would then consider it.

Just then an orderly from the hospital approached Lanny. "Ms. Cromwell, you have a call from overseas, a Ms. Valerie Queen. You can take it in Dr. Livingston's office."

Lanny thanked the orderly and told Claire she'd be right back. Lanny entered Carl Livingston's office and pushed the lighted button on the big screen console. Valerie instantly appeared.

"Hey sis, have a good flight?"

Lanny smiled back. "Sure did, sweetie. I'm getting used to it. What's up girl?"

"Carson and Lucy Sinclair are arriving today at the East Hampton base. They've been filled in on Carly's condition. The Skipper has made arrangements for Marilyn to take care of their other three daughters while they fly aboard one of the Corporation jets to Dusseldorf. Okay sis, now listen very carefully. Merlin has come up with a beautiful plan to rescue the children when the time is right. Make the Sinclairs think that you're in the dark as much as they are. Reassure them that everything will be okay. The Captain knows how good you are at comforting people, especially when you were an emergency room nurse. So try and keep them at ease before they fly out later tonight."

"I'll do my best, Duchess," assured Lanny. "Believe you me sis, were going to bring those babies home to their parents."

A knock came from the door and Lanny asked, "Who is it?"

Claire walked in to see Valerie on the screen smiling at her. "Hey girl, what's up? Is everything okay?" asked Claire.

Valerie replied, "Just giving big sister here orders from the Skipper. She'll fill you in after. I gotta go now. Baby sister has a Kendo lesson from me in a little while. So I'll see both of you when you get back tomorrow. Love yahs."

Lanny and Claire repeated the same as the screen faded to black. Lanny then shared with Claire all that Valerie had told her. They both decided to be present when the Sinclair parents arrived.

On the airfield side of the complex the team of scientists watched as the technicians began securing the scramjet to the railing system. It was composed of chorominium, titanium, composite nickel and a synthetic form of tungsten and aluminum. The scientists prayed for a launch with no problems whatsoever. It was now 09:55 hours and the Tower had picked up a jet flying in from Houston, Texas filled with some of NASA s leading rocket engineers and scientists.

Also with them was General Arlen Douglas, the U.S. Army department chief of medical science and research development. He knew Professor Pearson very well and had tremendous confidence in the Professor's ability to astound the scientific field. Along with him was his liaison officer Lieutenant Colonel Marcus Henderson. Henderson was the coordinator of military funds, if approved by General Douglas.

A large steel cable had secured the scramjet to the tarmac just in case the winds began to increase. A Gulfstream Learjet appeared from the west as ground crews awaited their arrival. As the jet appeared, Lanny and Claire slowed their pace on their run in order to see the visitors coming in for a landing.

Claire stopped immediately as Romulus came over to lick her face. "Easy boy, come on, we got to head back home." She patted Romulus and said to Lanny, "The government boys are here, big sister. Let's get the puppies out of sight, at least until we know who we're dealing with."

Lanny looked to her left as the jet was about to pass overhead. "I see what you're talking about, Claire. Let's get invisible for a little while. Come on Romy and Remy, we go home now."

The wolves ran with both of them back to the caged kennel. Lanny and Claire hugged them and let them know they loved them. Lanny then punched in the alarm code to activate the lock-in. But it still had an automatic release if the emergency panels were pushed on from the main house.

Lanny then turned to Claire. "Come on sis, let's help out Poppa and the Corporation."

Claire, with a puzzled look, responded, "And what do we do to accomplish that?"

Lanny smiling devilishly replied, "We dress business-like, but we dress to kill. Do you catch my DRIFT?"

Claire's mouth opened wide, then a slight wink came from her eye. "You mean slutty-but-business-like."

Lanny's high-pitched giggle was contagious. "Yes my dear, but not too much cleavage."

Claire laughingly replied, "Lan, you're going to have more of a problem with that then me."

They ran towards their housing units to change out of their running sweats.

Back at the hospital complex Lamarra and Lars followed Professor Darfuir and his medical team to the princess' room. As they entered Lars saw how peaceful she looked and then grabbed her little hand in his. Dr. Darfuir stopped him and instructed him to sit in one of the chairs on the side. Lamarra waited by Lars.

The Professor had one of his staff inject the Princess with a syringe. They kept the oxygen going and within three minutes Shaleem began blinking her eyes. Lars jumped up as she opened her eyes completely.

The Princess, looking surprised, asked, "AM I IN HEAVEN? Your face seems to be always in my dreams."

Lars replied, "No sweetheart, but now that I know you're going to be all right, that's heaven enough for me."

Shaleem asked, "How is it that all I see in my dreams is your face, yet we have never met?"

Lars replied instantly, "Your Highness, I have been having the same kind of dreams and I can't explain them, either."

Just then Lamarra walked over and perched her face for Shaleem to see.

Shaleem screamed out in joy, "LAMMY! Oh Lammy, you're still alive. How can this be? Abdullah swore to me that you were murdered with my father."

Lamarra, with tears pouring from her eyes, responded, "SHASHA, my beautiful Shasha. That demon has lied to us all. His henchman Omar also tried to murder you."

Lars began shaking and then asked, "SHASHA? You're called Shasha?" Then he looked over at Lamarra and continued. "And she's always called you Lammy?"

Lamarra, puzzled, replied "Yeah, she's called me Lammy and I've always called her my Shasha."

Tears of joy rolled down Lars face as he said, simply, "Shasha, I am Cubby. Do you remember me? That was my nickname when I was little."

Shaleem's face filled with joy as she held his hand tight and began to cry.

Dr. Darfuir stepped in. "Everyone, this can't go on. You must leave. This is too much for Shaleem. I can't have my patient overexerted."

Shaleem grabbed Dr. Darfuir's lab coat sleeve. "Please doctor, I'm okay. This has just become one of the happiest days of my life."

The doctor was completely bewildered but said, "I'll let everyone stay as long as you don't try and get up or do something to injure yourself."

She smiled. "I promise, doctor."

Lamarra told her, "Well you better, because my brother Kamal is used to having his patients follow his orders."

Shaleem was even more surprised and told him, "I have never met you, but Lammy has bragged about you most of my life."

Dr. Darfuir looked over at his sister. "Oh she has, has she?"

Lamarra replied, "Don't let it go to your head, Kamal."

Shaleem then looked warmly into Lars eyes. "Well handsome, if Cubby was your nickname, what is your real name?"

Lars looks very deeply into her eyes. "It's Lars, your Highness."

She immediately said, "Lars, enough with the Your Highness shit. Just please call me Shasha like you always have."

Lars smiled. "Yes, your, I mean, Shasha."

Lamarra spoke to Lars. "I remember you now. The Sultan's family was on safari in Tanzania on one of the biggest game preserves there. Your family was not far from our camp that day when little Shasha wandered off."

Shaleem interrupted, "Lammy, I didn't mean to wander off. I saw a baby baboon just inside where the trees met the savannah. It was screaming for its mother, or so I thought. I was so concerned for the baby's safety that I followed it into the jungle."

Lars interrupted, "Yes, that's when I saw this beautiful but foolhardy girl enter the jungle. My father who was there sleeping at the time didn't notice me take his pump shotgun from the tripod. When I finally caught up with her, we began to talk. She told me she was a princess, but back when I was eleven all girls considered themselves princesses, especially girls as beautiful as her."

Shaleem smiled and interrupted, "No Cubby, it's now my turn to finish the story." She looked at him as a woman who deeply loves a man. "We were going into the jungle and I began to get scared. But Cubby, I mean Lars, made me feel so secure that day. I watched him as he took his knife and marked the back of trees every fifteen to twenty feet. We were only gone for ten minutes, but I guess it felt like hours. All the sudden we came upon the baby baboon and it was screaming for its mother. That's when we heard the leopard. We couldn't see it at first. That's because instead of stalking the baby baboon, he was stalking us!"

The princess drew a deep breath before continuing. "Cubby, I mean Lars, made me stay close to him. He raised the shotgun and poised himself to shoot. We knew the leopard was close but we didn't know how close. I began to cry hysterically, but my hero, still just a little boy himself, had the bravest face I've ever seen. The leopard leaped at me from the bushes as Lars blocked the scary animal. The cat was too close for him to get a shot off. But he smashed the barrel against the leopard's skull, which only made the big cat more angry. Lars took a quick shot and this time blew off its tail. The leopard then poised and went to pounce on me. But Lars fired and killed him as he was in midair. I ran to him crying and remember him saying, 'No one is ever going to hurt my Princess.' Even though we were so damn young, we kissed for what seemed to be an eternity."

Lars interrupted, "Yeah, that's when we heard men and dogs coming our way, screaming both our names."

Shaleem continued her story, "My father appeared with his rifle from the bushes only to see the dead cat next to us. Lammy was right behind him with my father's caravan. My father and my mother surrogate were so happy to see me alive that I didn't get scolded for disobeying them."

Lars interrupted once more, "Yeah, but I know if your father caught us kissing I would have been safer with the leopard. I remember when he looked at me and asked me if I killed the cat. I told him yes and he nodded in approval. He then took a medal he was wearing and gave it to me. My mother and father showed up right then and Shasha's dad told my father what I had done. I'll never forget as they carried Shasha off that day. I yelled to her that we would be together again one day. I remember that her father took the big cat's tail with him. Then and there I knew you weren't lying about being a princess."

He laughed, then started laughing harder. "Plus this beautiful girl who I've always loved got away with no scolding at all. Well, my father commended me on my courage. But I couldn't sit down for a week when he was finished with me."

Shaleem pulled him close. "Oh honey, I'm so sorry. But I was a foolish child then and I wanted to help the baby monkey. I'm still in love with you and I can't believe how large and handsome you've become."

"I love you too princess, and I'd take a hundred beatings for you anytime." He leaned over the side of the bed and kissed her for about twenty seconds.

Dr. Darfuir shouted, "No, no, no, no! She's in no condition for this. This is not a hotel room. She's too weak for sex, anyway."

Lars reassured him, "Doc, it was just a kiss for Christ s sake. I'm on duty in an hour, anyway. Calm down."

Lamarra interjected, "She is of royal blood. You cannot just have your way with her."

Shaleem yelled, "ROYAL, SCHMOYEL! This is the man of my dreams, so you get used to him being around." She looked warmly at Lamarra and asked, "Please Lammy, for me? You know I love you, too. I want him to have his way with me."

Lamarra kissed her on the forehead. "For you Sasha, I give you my blessing."

Shaleem thought for a second then asked Lars, "By the way my sweet, whatever happened to that medallion my father gave you?"

Lars put his fingers down his shirt and pulled out a large round gold medallion. On it were two sabers crossed against a crescent moon.

Lamarra and Shaleem recognized the sign of the Royal guard. Only the greatest of warriors ever received this from the Khaleef. Shaleem pulled Lars down for one more kiss, but said to him, "See? My father has already chosen you for me."

Lars smiled and whispered, "Okay, Shasha, now get some rest. My buddy and Commander need to go over something with you, if you're up to it, baby."

Shaleem responded with determination, "If it means to find and get rid of that lying piece of garbage Musheen, I'll do anything."

Lars hugged her one final time as Dr. Darfuir emptied the room. Darfuir and his medical team gave the princess a real going-over, then administered a light sedative to help her sleep.

At the other end of the housing complex Lanny and Claire peered out the window, waiting for their father's car to pull up. Soon a very big super-stretch limousine arrived and the girls ran out giggling towards the car. Claire carried a briefcase with her father's itinerary and agenda portfolios. Lanny carried a secured encrypted laptop computer with her. They scampered across the lawn in their expensive high heels.

The Professor walked out of the main house with Kruger and Stellarnberg, only to see two of his nosy daughters running up to him. "What are you two up too? Why are you dressed for an office meeting, and Ms. Cromwell, button up that blouse a little."

Lanny and Claire were all decked out, but Lanny was revealing a little too much of her ample cleavage. She buttoned one more loop and said to the Professor, "Sorry Sir, we were in a hurry getting dressed. I have your encrypted laptop and your satellite matrix phone with us."

Professor Pearson crossed his arms as Claire said, "And yes Professor, I made sure your agenda notes are all in order before you greet your colleagues."

Pearson replied, "Okay you two, how do I know that you're up to no good?"

Professor Kruger interrupted. "Oh, put a cork in it, Jeffrey. Can't you see they're trying to help us out? Your two gorgeous daughters are trying to make our clients feel at ease. A little shot of their legs and beautiful faces will keep them in check. Am I right girls?"

Lanny and Claire took out their glasses and put them on. "We are strictly professional, Dr. Kruger."

Pearson looked concerned and Lanny said, "Oh come on Poppa, please? We want to watch the launch. PLEASE? Besides, we're very interested in the success of the mission."

All the sudden Gerta came to the door and spoke one word. "GIRLS!"

The Professor turned to her and said, "It's okay Gerta, they can come with me."

Gerta shrugged and replied, "Okay, both of you better be on your best behavior."

Both girls yelled to her at the same time, "We promise, Gerta." They loaded themselves into the limousine and headed to the airfield where the jet from Houston had already landed.

NASA engineers were already examining the long giant ramp running two miles along side runway one. At the very end of the ramp the direction went two hundred feet straight up. For about a mile and a half the beginning of the ramp stayed off the ground about a good twenty feet in the air. Then it gradually raised eight inches every twenty feet for another thousand yards. The last five hundred feet shot up dramatically until it was almost at a perfect right angle.

At the very end of the ramp sticking up in the air was a buffered plasma mirror with both sides of the ends two feet in. They were both tilted at fifteen degree angle towards the center at the end of the ramp. On the back and front of the scramjet were the same buffered mirrors, installed to catch the immense plasma energy that would hurtle it into space.

This scramjet was much smaller, since it was the prototype. The other was three times larger so it could bring astronauts to the new spacecraft that would be going to Mars. Most of the NASA scientists didn't believe it would work in an oxygen gravitational atmosphere. But unbeknownst to them, much of the scramjet and buffered mirrors were enhanced with the element from another galaxy, chorominium. If Professor Pearson could just get the government contract for the delivery system, there was no telling what contracts his Corporation would be given after.

The Professor looked out the rear window of the limousine to see General Arlen Douglas chatting with Bobby and Orion. Over by the scramjet Lieutenant Colonel Marcus Henderson was up with Carl Livingston and some of the other rocket scientists on a motorized platform. This was so they could have a closer look at the spacecraft.

When the limousine stopped Orion saw Lanny and Claire get out first. Lanny held the rear door open as Professor Pearson and his fellow scientists disembarked. They walked towards the prototype of the Perseus spacecraft. As they got within ten feet of the vaulted platform Lieutenant Colonel Marcus Henderson shouted down to the Professor. "Jeffrey, what's the skin of this so-called space vehicle made of?"

Pearson with a grin replied, "Oh, that's top secret. All you can know is that the wings, fuselage, mirrors and engine components are all made of different elements of the Mendeleyev periodic chart. In fact, they've all been rolled into one to form one composite element."

Henderson said in a sarcastic tone, "Well, you could have just told us it was none of our damn business."

Professor Stellarnberg relayed to him, "That's exactly what he just did, but in a more appropriate manner."

Then the Lieutenant Colonel had the platform driver lower them to the tarmac. Once on the ground Henderson approached Pearson and his colleagues. He walked right up to Stellarnberg and in a challenging tone asked, "And with whom do I have the privilege of speaking?"

Pearson interrupted. "This is the scientist who built the Perseus spacecraft."

Henderson retorted, "He built this bucket of bolts?"

145

General Douglas overheard and yelled at the Colonel, "Know your goddamn place, Colonel! If you treat everybody like you're a top shit know-it-all, then you'll sit in a corner for the duration of the flight test. Do I make myself perfectly clear?"

Henderson lowered his head in embarrassment. "That's a Roger, Sir!"

The General stared him down for a second, but then said to Pearson, "How have you been, Jeffrey? You look more vigorous and alive since I saw you in November."

The Professor replied, "I've been fine, Arlen. The exercise regimens from one of my daughters have helped, and I've been taking an adaptogen compound with my meals every morning. Believe it or not, it's made to be a coffee."

Douglas asked, "Can you give me the name of it? I could use a little something to get me going in the morning, too."

Claire reached into the Professor's briefcase and retrieved a copy of the address in Utah.

The general smiled at the beautiful blonde. "If I remember well, you're Ms. Claire Vanderkamp."

Claire answered with a smile, "Very good, General Douglas. I'm flattered you remembered me."

The general replied, "Who could not remember the charming and beautiful daughters of my good friend. Am I right, Ms. Cromwell?"

Lanny's face showed surprise as she blushingly replied, "Thank you General, Sir."

He walked over to her. "Oh by the way Lanny, congratulations on your engagement."

In a soft and sweet voice she responded, "Thank you very much, Sir. It would be an honor if you could attend my wedding."

General Douglas grinned. "No, young lady, the honor would be mine."

He pulled the Professor to the side and asked, "Jeffrey, the last time I was here you we're working on a project to rid the world of cancer and disease. Have you had any breakthroughs?"

The Professor put on his poker face. "Well Arlen, I could show you what I have done up to date. But if you must know, the pressure on me with the Perseus Project has taken me away from the Icarus Project."

The general nodded. "Let's see what you've done so far, and Jeffrey, if the test flight today is a complete success you'll most likely have more time to spend on something more important, like the Icarus Project."

Pearson shrugged. "I really do hope so, Arlen. Okay, let's get everybody together and we'll all go to my laboratory. The launch is set in three and a half hours. I'll let security know we're coming."

Everybody boarded the large stretch limo and headed for the laboratory. Orion looked at Bobby with concern before they both got in. But Bobby gave him the hand signal to stay calm, then he got in himself. The entourage journeyed along the narrow road through a mile of woodlands which separated the complex from the airfield and hanger. They entered into the Main building of the Citadel and headed for the large elevator door. Instantly they descended to the well-guarded subterranean complex below.

There to greet them at the door was Cleopatra Stokes. She led them to the main laboratory and as they entered they noticed two tables made from centrifuge aluminum. The electron generator looked different than it did back in November. It now seemed to be more sophisticated. From the data recorded during Orion's regeneration periods, the generator worked at a phenomenal rate of power. On each table, though, was a Guardian component made for a large animal testing instead of human testing.

General Douglas said in earnest, "Well Jeffrey, seems you graduated from little rabbits. What are you using now for test subjects?"

Professor Pearson replied, "Like I told you General, the Perseus Project has the Icarus Project on hold somewhat. The harnesses have been configured this time for a Golden Retriever with leukemia and bone deterioration. The other one is for an English mastiff with parvo and signs of distemper. Dr. Stokes, here, has been keeping them alive until we get a chance to move forward. This is what we were in the process of doing when we received the call from Dr. Von Kleist."

Professor Otto von Kleist looked concerned. "I had no idea of your work here, Professor. Please accept my apology. It's just that my boss at NASA has had me under the gun."

Pearson smiled. "Apology accepted, Professor. Allow me to tell you what we are trying to achieve with this delicate project." Professor Pearson explained the genetics and nano-robotics involved in the project that would restore damaged and diseased cells long before they could multiply, and subject the host subject to an agonizing death. He then shared that in his past experiments the diseased and damaged cells were eradicated. But the nervous system of the host subject would then contract Parkinson's or a blinding twitch, which would develop in a short period of time. He explained that this time they had been able to use a pressurized headgear to relieve the stress from the great power of the electron generator.

Professor told Von Kleist and General Douglas that they were still months away before they could initiate the experiment again. The General cracked a joke about experimenting with the device on his wife and the entourage laughed in unison.

All the sudden Professor Pearson's cell phone rang. Claire answered and listened for a second. "Yes Gerta, he's right here."

Pearson took the phone. "Yes honey, we'll be there shortly. See you then, hon." He handed the phone back to Claire and said, "Seems my girlfriend Gerta has prepared some of the best Bavarian food you'll ever taste. Am I correct when I say that girls?"

Lanny, Claire, and Cleo replied at the same time, "That's for sure, Professor."

He pointed the way towards the elevator. "Shall we, my esteemed ladies and gentlemen?" They walked to the elevator door and ascended to the main floor. Before they left Orion picked up the strange harnesses that the Professor had spoken about. He then put them down and hurried to catch up with the group before the door closed.

They went back to the main house for a Bavarian treat prepared by Gerta with the help of Millie Stokes. Mama Rosa and Millie traded stories during the afternoon lunch of what it was like raising Orion and Billy. Cleo added how both of them played dirty tricks on her when she was real little.

The general and the staff from NASA got a kick out of Orion's embarrassment over his young antics. But Cleo professed her love for him as another one of her brothers.

After dinner, the Professor called Dr. Darfuir to join him so they could show their guests most of the vast building complexes that made up the compound.

Time: 13:40 hours. June 5, 2011. East Hampton, New York.

Time: 14:45 hours. June 5, 2011. East Hampton, New York.

It was only fifteen minutes to launch time and the entire complex had been put on lockdown. Security was on high alert. Bobby helped Orion attach the different wired probes on his body before he got into his G-suit. The prototype was a UAV unmanned aerial vehicle but the probes on the cellulose gelatin dummy were coinciding with the ones attached to Orion. While Orion was in the simulator, the probes from the dummy transmitted to his body the same pressurized reaction that the dummy was taking in.

The scientists from NASA had a plasma laser and a satellite waiting in orbit to fire at the front buffered mirror of the Perseus space vehicle. This was to slow down the spacecraft from hurtling out of control from the unbelievable speed expected from the configurations of Stellarnberg and Kruger. Once the Perseus spacecraft had cleared the vaulting ramp the two mirrors fixed to the end of the ramp would aid and guide the plasma laser beam to the back mirror of the Perseus spacecraft.

Professor Pearson told Orion that a Portison helmet was affixed to the dummy. Once the tremendous pressure built up in the dummy s body the inside of the helmet would inflate a liquid carbon fluoride compound to protect the brain of the astronauts as they were delivered into space. Pearson conveyed to Orion that he might feel pressure, but doubted it because of the force field would instantly react to anything that conflicted with the safety of Orion's body.

The Professor also told him a refrigerated compound was now being introduced into the Perseus spacecraft. This was because, just like in the

Viking Avenger and the Blazing Trident, the outer skin and protected windows of the vehicles would become superheated. They needed to be cooled so that no one would be burned by touching any of the windows.

It was now five minutes and counting as scientists and technicians awaited the spectacular show. A buzzing sound of tremendous proportion began to reverb throughout the gigantic ramp as the electromagnetic generator was turned on.

Pearson asked Orion if he was ready in the simulator. Orion gave him the go sign and the final countdown began. People from all over the entire compound were outside waiting to see the spectacular launch they had worked so hard to bring to life. As the last twenty seconds showed on the digital clock by the launch ramp, a purple glow surrounded all of the ramp and the Perseus prototype. Then the clock reached zero, and the spacecraft hurtled down the ramp at lightning speed. It shot up at such an accelerated speed it blurred as it left the top of the ramp. Within ten seconds a three-inch round purple beam shot out of the end of the launch ramp and hit the mirror of the spacecraft, propelling it at speed faster than light.

Pearson and the other scientists studied the computer readings as the craft escaped Earth's compelling gravity. The Portison helmet deployed the liquid compound and the readings instantly stabilized. The scientists hollered with joy, for the launch was now nothing short of a complete success. Even Larry at the front gate was jumping with exuberance.

Lieutenant Colonel Marcus Henderson walked up to Professor Stellarnberg. "Looks as if I really did put my foot in my mouth."

Stellarnberg responded as the prototype spacecraft did one orbit around the globe. "Soon as we get this baby back here you can buy me a drink."

Henderson giggled. "It would be an honor, Herr Professor!"

From out of the sky fifteen minutes later, the spacecraft came in for a smooth landing on runway three. Orion, now out of the simulator, came over to congratulate the man of genius that had saved his life. Lanny and Claire hugged him so tightly he looked like he was about to fall over.

The Professor and Orion secretly conferred with one another and Orion told him that as far as he could tell, the spacecraft was safe for human travel. He told him the Portison helmet worked better than first expected. Orion showed Professor Pearson the data from the simulator that had come back and forth from the spacecraft.

General Douglas congratulated the three Professors and said he was recommending the Perseus Project immediately to the Mars program. Professor Otto von Kleist concurred and told them he was looking forward to working with them from now on.

Pearson had the technicians uncouple the equipment and put it under lock and key in hanger four. The Perseus prototype was already on its way there.

In the background could be heard the sound of wolves howling as the electromagnetic generator was shut off. Lanny laughed and hugged her father, then yelled in the direction of the howling. "That's it Romy and Remy, Grandpa has done it again."

Employees of Corporation started laughing as the scientists from NASA looked puzzled, as did General Douglas and Lieutenant Colonel Henderson. General Douglas asked Lanny, "What was that?"

Lanny grabbed Orion and answered, "That's our babies, Sir."

Pearson tried to explain further but the general laughed and told him there was no need. The General told the scientists from NASA that they had to get back to Texas as soon as possible to give the Appropriations Committee the good news. Their jet was already pulling out of hangar two and started heading for runway three as the group of scientists and military men got into the limousine.

The Professor waved them a quick goodbye as he surveyed everyone around him. The incredible achievement had finally come to pass. He laughed as Romulus and Remus began howling once again.

Time: 17:05 hours. June 5, 2011. East Hampton, New York.

CHAPTER FOURTEEN: CANIS MAJOR & CANIS MINOR

Time: 21:20. June 5, 2011. East Hampton, New York.

The work around the launch ramp still had about an hour to go when one of the rods from the electromagnetic generator refused to budge. Anthony Bustamante, lead foreman in the construction and disassembly of the Perseus Project, was not at the site. Professor Pearson had him at the lab to go over the film part of the experiment that took place earlier that day.

Trevor Rollins called to Bustamante to get permission to recharge the stabilizer rod that had locked itself in place. Bustamante felt a vibration from his cell phone and looked at the screen: ROLLINS, URGENT. He asked the Professor to excuse him for a second and then answered.

"Trevor, what's so urgent that you need to bother me during a meeting with the boss?"

The Professor overheard his foreman and began to eavesdrop.

"What do you mean, the stabilizer rod has locked itself in? Did you try the manual release on the loading mount? You did? And nothing still happened? Yes, that is odd. Yes, Trevor, I know starting up the generator is the only other way to move it. How much of the undercarriage have you moved?"

Bustamante listened for a minute then said, "Yeah, you did the right thing by calling. Hold on, I'll talk to the Professor himself."

As Anthony explained the dilemma the Professor became concerned and called over to the recreation hall. He asked the hall manager to page Professors Stellarnberg and Kruger. The line was silent for about thirty seconds before Stellarnberg answered.

"What's up, Jeffrey?"

The Professor filled in the man who had built the main sections of the ramp.

Stellarnberg responded, "Well from what I can evaluate, the stabilizer rod must've picked up some sort of magnetic field and then it locked itself. I put this mechanism in place as a precautionary safety measure. We need to head back out to the launch site and see if we can reverse the containment field. Okay, we'll be out front."

Bustamante hung up and went with Pearson to the Rec hall. The crew out at the ramp had to stop work immediately. Ten minutes went by before a black Land Rover appeared from the other side of the woods. The vehicle pulled up to the locked stabilizer rod. Stellarnberg spotted Trevor Rollins pointing to the undercarriage of the ramp.

"You can try the manual override one more time if you like, Professor. But that baby is locked in there tight."

Stellarnberg yelled back to him, "Trevor, I'm going to depolarize the containment field to release the safety lock. The lock is made of centrifuge aluminum, but the bushing clamp that holds it in place is made up of cobalt and steel. We're going to take two negative charge lines from two different batteries, then apply them straight to the clamp and bushing. For safety reasons, I need everybody back behind the acrylic composite shield once we have turned the electron generator back on. When the generator reaches 4000 on the containment diaphragm it should automatically expel itself of the coupling."

"I guess that's why you get the big bucks, Doc. That's genius. I would have never thought of that in a million years," commented Rollins.

Pearson spoke. "Joseph, the power plant only has one battery. I think you're going to need one of those fourteen foot forklifts over here. Their batteries are definitely big enough for the unlocking process."

Stellarnberg agreed and told Bustamante to bring it alongside the power plant. He took out booster cables and hooked one of the negative ends to the bushing clamp under the ramp. Then separating the booster cables from the other set to the power plant, he hooked that negative cable directly to the bushing. They then set up the two-inch thick acrylic composite shield around them and the power plant.

Pearson relayed a message to the hangar crew by two-way radio. Inside the hangar they turned on the enormous electron generator. It began to drive up power to the four-inch lines leading from the hangar out of the launching ramp. The lights around the ramp turned on instantly and the containment diaphragm needle began to rise slowly.

Stellarnberg told the crew to keep behind the Shield. "Trevor, be ready to hit the switch to the induction coil once it reaches 4000," he further instructed.

It now read 2000 and those strange eerie purple lights began to glow.

High buzzing sounds started to omit from the ramp as the diaphragm indicated 3000. The stabilizer rod began to vibrate as the diaphragm meter neared 3700. It finally reached 4000 and Trevor Rollins flipped a switch to the induction coil. But instead of releasing the stabilizer rod, the buzzing sound became deafening. The four-inch electrical lines going into the undercarriage of the ramp were now jumping up and down six feet in the air. The huge forklift rose eight feet in the air as everyone covered their ears. Professor Pearson tried to call the hangar to cut the power, but the pain in his ears was too unbearable.

The two wolves in the background began howling, seeming to know something had definitely gone wrong. As some of crew passed out a streak of purple light came into view. But before anyone could figure out what it was, the giant forklift hurtled like a scramjet across the compound.

Orion arrived and with his incredible strength yanked the stabilizer rod from the coupling like it was a yo-yo string. He pulled a high-voltage line from the undercarriage as easily as a child opens a wrapped present. A sound of an explosion ricocheted over the other side of the woods and everybody whipped their heads around to see a plume of smoke rising from around the kennel area.

Orion's eyes narrowed dangerously. He ran towards the woods, then leapt into the air and glided to the other side with ease. Pearson and the other scientists jumped into the black Land Rover and sped to the other side of the woods. They pulled up to see Orion yanking cinderblocks, two by fours and fencing from the area where he just flipped over the forklift. Security guards showed up as Lanny and Claire raced barefoot across the lawn.

When Lanny was halfway there she heard Orion scream, "OH GOD, PLEASE, NOoooh!" From out of the rubble he pulled what looked to be a lifeless wolf. Tears spilled from his eyes as he laid Remus on the ground.

Lanny reached the devastation. "OH MY BABIES, OH MY GOD, MY BABIES!"

Orion reached the other wolf who was in extreme critical condition.

Lanny, hysterical, held Remus body close to hers. Orion carried his beloved Romulus over to Remus and laid him nearby just as Cleopatra Stokes arrived from the main house. She was still in her lab coat and wearing a stethoscope. Orion, grief stricken and in shock, fell to his knees.

Cleo dropped down to examine the wolves and listened for any signs of life. After she checked them both she informed Lanny that both were alive, but just barely.

Professor Pearson urgently ordered, "Bring our four-legged family members to the operations center, stat. Call Dr. Darfuir and Livingston and have them to meet us there immediately."

Lanny, trying to keep her composure, said to Orion, "Oh my God, it feels just like that awful day in November."

Orion looked at Cleo, who had overheard and seemed puzzled. He clarified, "Cleo, there is something you should know..."

Cleo, seeing the dogs were fading fast, told him, "Later big brother, our boss might have something up his sleeve. Come on, let's get your two boys over to the lab."

As they loaded the wolves into the Land Rover, Cleo glanced at the forklift on its side and the vast amount of cinderblocks and lumber piled onto it.

"Boy, all of you worked so quickly getting that weight off of them. It may have saved their lives."

Lanny whispered to her fiancé, "You haven't tried to explain things to her yet?"

Orion, surprised, responded, "I thought maybe you were going to do that for me."

Lanny broke down and started to cry because Romulus opened his eyes for a second and whimpered to her in pain. "Mommy is right here, babies. Hang in there, boys. Daddy is here too. We love you and help is coming." Lanny closed her eyes and prayed, just as she did the night Orion was about to die.

The Land Rover raced to the main complex as a medical team assembled. Two separate gurneys awaited the animals. The medical team raced through the open doors to the private elevator, then descended to the secret laboratory below. The medical team along with Orion took Remus first because there was no room for both gurneys. Orion followed the medical team into the same room where they saved his life seven months before.

The team immediately went to work removing the impaled foreign matter. In rushed the other gurney and they began to work fast on Romulus, as well. Professor Pearson wouldn't allow Lanny in because she was too emotionally involved. Five minutes flew by.

Remus' team grabbed and opened a large steamer trunk, pulling out one of the Guardian components that were initially made for the first two dogs. As they hooked the first one onto Remus, the other team prepared the second one for Romulus. But this time Dr. Darfuir pulled out two Portison helmets similar to the one used on the Perseus spacecraft.

"John, they can't know when it's time to react to the enormous magnetic field. You're going to have to be hooked up with them. It's the only way we can stop their brains from becoming vegetables," Professor Pearson informed.

Cleo automatically yelled, "WAIT, WAIT, WAIT! Are all of you out of your minds?"

Bobby and Lanny grabbed her as a medical team hooked lines from

Orion's Icarus harness. They put Orion in a Portison helmet so he could communicate with both dogs.

Cleo was now trying to break loose as Lanny reassured her, "Cleo, he's going to be fine. Do you think I'd let him do it if I didn't know he'd be all right? I guess you're going to find out now, anyhow."

Cleo calmed. "Find out what Lanny?"

Lanny lowered her head for a second and replied seriously, "Remember when those terrorists tried to attack New York City?"

Cleo, even more bewildered, said, "Yeah. SO?"

Lanny continued, "Do you remember seeing on the news the robot who came to the rescue and threw a car like it was papier-mâché?"

Cleo once again said, "Yeah. And?"

Lanny pointed into the room. "THAT WAS NO ROBOT! It was my Johnny!"

Cleo looked like she saw a ghost. "HUH? You're kidding, right?"

Lanny just shook her head. "Come on sweetie, I'll try and fill you in on the way up to the observation gallery."

They took the spiral stairs up to the top of the gallery. Cleopatra Stokes felt like she was stuck in some zany dream as Lanny and Bobby shared a quick synopsis of that fateful day. She had a hard time believing anything like that could be true.

Then from the floor below the technicians turned on the electron generator. The eerie purple glow filled the room and only the staff in purple scrubs stayed behind. Orion's harness glowed in tandem with the wolves harnesses. Carl Livingston made sure to set the timer for exactly five minutes. The remaining staff left.

Two minutes elapsed as everyone filled the observation gallery. They watched Orion and the two dogs start to levitate two feet into the air.

Cleo's mouth opened wide at the spectacle below her. "Oh my God, I can't believe what I'm seeing," she exclaimed.

The two wolves simultaneously grimaced, just as Orion did seven months ago. They were definitely reacting to the operation as the five minutes ticked down. With about fifteen seconds to go all three test subjects rose another foot. But to the right side near the timer, Romulus' tail hits the dial and sent the generation cycle into another eight minutes.

Everyone saw it and the medical staff rushed back down to the operations and tried to get the door open, but to no avail. The energy being given off stopped them from entering. From inside they finally heard the electron generator power down.

Lanny quickly opened the door to see her man taking off his helmet. "ARE YOU OKAY, BABY?"

"Never felt better, and don't worry, our two boys here are going to be just fine."

Over the loudspeaker could be heard the sounds of both dogs whimpering, although still in an unconscious state.

"Go ahead, talk to them, Mommy. They hear you just like I did seven months ago," encouraged Orion.

"Romy, Remy, it's Mommy. Can you hear me?"

Instantly both wolves whimpered.

Lanny flew into the arms of her father. "Thank you Poppa, I'll never forget this. She hugged him with all her might."

"If there is one thing I won't put up with, it's having to see my little girls cry. They're not out of the woods yet and I think they'll have to endure the same regeneration cycles just as your future husband did."

He noticed Orion petting the two beloved animals. "John, will they have to regenerate just like you did?"

"Well somewhat, Doc. The supercomputer has relayed to me that their cycles will be five hours instead of eight. And the rest periods in between will be two hours instead of one. I think it's because of their small anatomies. The computer also told me they need a solution of glycol and glucose fed to them during the two hour recuperation cycle. You better let me do it because I'm probably the only one who can get an intravenous catheter in them. I've already detected their force fields booting up."

As Orion and the Professor prepared the solution for the intravenous bag, Cleo tapped on Orion's shoulder. "When you have the time, you have a little explaining to do. Oh let me take that back. YOU HAVE A LOT OF EXPLAINING TO DO."

Orion, remorseful, replied, "Yeah Cleo, I know. But that is exactly what I was trying to do before."

With a tear forming around her eye she said, "Are you sure everything's okay? I lost one brother and I'll be damned if I lose you."

Orion handed the Professor one of the finished bags, then hugged Cleo. "Baby sister, you're not going to lose me. As a matter of fact I'm having a hard time making sense of all this. I no longer feel pain. My body is increasingly stronger and healthier day by day. For heaven's sake, I was able to stop a 100,000 ton ship in its full speed capability. I threw that twelve ton forklift you saw outside like it was paper. I'm scared, Cleo. This is still frightening to me. I feel like a freak. I'm a good man and I'm so afraid that somebody innocent will get hurt because of my new abilities. I must've seen Marilyn and her office over twenty times this year alone."

"I see Marilyn every day at work. Why hasn't she consulted me?"

"She's a doctor of psychology. You know she can't release anything about my therapy."

Suddenly Cleo's uncle Walter Cosgrove entered the room and said to both of them, "My sister Millie just told me what happened. How are our boys?"

From the loudspeaker came the sound of whimpering. Walter s face was flabbergasted. "Johnny, is that them?"

"Yep, that's them. They know you're here and it's a long story, Walter. But I'm pretty sure they're going to be fine."

Claire entered. "I just got off the phone with the Skipper. He knows about Romy and Remy and he's glad they pulled through. But were all flying out of here at 07:30 hours in the morning. It seems Al Qaeda is about to strike again soon and he wants all of us back as of yesterday."

The Professor told Carl to make arrangements for the wolves to be hooked up to the electron generator inside the Viking Avenger. He informed Cleo that she was accompanying them on the flight. He needed her there when they removed the Icarus Devices from both dogs, especially since they had done something different in the operation: They modified the harnesses to extract the proteins that cause the genetic imperfections from their bodies. Anything that could cause any type of disease such as distemper, parvo, leukemia or a mutant growth had been extracted. Pearson wanted Cleo and other biological scientists from his team to be present. They would be in charge of isolating the harnesses soon as the regeneration cycles were over. He wanted the harnesses stored and put away until they were able to study the contagions in an isolated, germ-free chamber.

"I'll help babysit," offered Walter, who had helped train the wolves alongside Orion.

"Fine, and you can sleep on the Avenger on the way to Germany," agreed Pearson.

With a face loaded with excitement Walter asked, "You want me to go too?"

Pearson smiled and pointed to Romulus and Remus. "Not just me. They want you there."

Over the loudspeaker both dogs whimpered again and the Professor said, "SEE?"

Time: 23:40 hours. June 5, 2011. East Hampton, New York.

JOHN PETER FERRIS

CHAPTER FIFTEEN: ON THE HUNT

Time: 11:06 hours. June 6, 2011. Dusseldorf, Germany.

The Viking Avenger arrived at the base in Germany only a half hour ago. Rain wasn't in the forecast but it seemed to be coming down anyway. The Princess needed to have blood drawn to see if her white blood cell count was back to normal. Lars accompanied her to the hospital facility on the eastern side of the complex. But he needed to return as quickly as he could for the briefing that he, Percival Nelson and Joshua Golon planned to submit to Captain Malloy.

Lars kissed her on the cheek and told her he'd probably be back after six o'clock tonight. Then he bolted out the door of the hospital and headed for the Jeep that Trudy and Mike Maguiness were waiting in. He hopped in the front and the trio traveled across the base to the conference hanger.

Trudy asked Lars, "How's she doing, Tank? I heard it was touch and go there for a little while."

Lars replied, "I know she's going to be fine, buddy. She's still a little weak but knows now that a lot of people love her. Shasha has always been a trooper in the face of danger."

Maguiness interjected snidely, "Just like you, ha, Cubby?"

Lars instantly turned and gave him a dirty look, then growled.

Trudy conveyed to Maguiness, "You should be very careful, Maverick. Tank has been fighting alongside me for years. You'll learn that little cubby bears grow up to be ferocious grizzly bears. This grizzly is more dangerous than any you've heard of. You got that, Sergeant Major?"

Maguiness replied in a hoarse voice, "Sorry about that, big guy."

Lars replied instinctively, "It's okay, Maverick. I just have a picture of Omar Khaldif in my head. Now all I want to do is kill the man that tried to kill my woman."

Mike put his left hand on Tank's shoulder. "I'll be emptying my rounds into him right alongside you."

Lars placed his right hand on the one over his shoulder. "Hoo Yah."

They drove into the hangar to find everybody assembling for the briefing. Tables and chairs were set up alongside the computer flat screen for the presentation. From his back-office came Captain Malloy, followed by Nelson, Ferris and the unit's new addition, Patrick Tinsdale. Bobby Palladin was ecstatic because he trained at sniper school with him.

Tinsdale was one of the best paratroopers anyone had ever seen. In England they call him the Flying Griffin. Once in a nighttime HALO jump he didn't deploy his parachute until he was 900 feet above the ground. He then silently drifted in behind the sentry on duty and released the pins holding the canopy just as he was within ten feet of him. Tinsdale tackled the guard to the ground. It was only war games, but no one had done anything like it.

Tinsdale spotted his old buddy from the past and waved to him. Paddy smiled and gave Galahad the thumbs-up.

Malloy then said, "Okay, ladies and gentlemen, park your asses down as I give the floor to Falcon (Percival Nelson)."

Everybody sat as the major pulled out a download key from his pocket and inserted it into the computer on the table in front of them. On the screen appeared the stolen Soviet submarine sailing on the surface just outside what Qaddafi called the Line of Death. The Damocles was headed north only sixteen hours after the kidnapping aboard the luxury liner Queen Beatrice. Major Nelson told the units that passengers aboard the liner talked of a submarine taking the children as hostages and then disappearing beneath the waves. Then they found the entire crew murdered.

"We definitely have a problem if the children are being held hostage in Libya," commented Nelson. "Right now the good people of that country are trying to overthrow Qaddafi's regime. Our NATO forces have been helping the rebels by bombing strategic positions of the Libyan Army s artillery. They've already destroyed their airfields and harbors. So we're thinking they must have snuck the children into Tunisia under the cover of darkness. From there it's anybody's guess where they were transported. Wolfman will take it from here."

Wolfman (Major Jim Ferris) waved his hand in front of the screen. "The Damocles is now sailing the surface just outside the Gulf of Aden. My friend at the FBI forwarded this satellite image taken back on the 2nd of May. If you look real close, guess who's on the conning tower with Kozlovski? Here, let me enlarge the photo."

In front of them was none other than Mustaffa Khaldif laughing with the Chechnyan war criminal.

Ferris continued, "Since May, this submarine has born the name Damocles on its hull. It was last seen heading south past the Horn of

Africa. For almost a month we've been trying to lock on to its location. We're not sure how, but they were able to elude NATO's naval forces. Since we know it didn't go through the Suez Canal, it's evident the sub took the long way around the African continent. We then put two and two together. Since a submarine was reported leaving the scene of the kidnapping, we can interpret that Kozlovski is still working for Musheen. We are now on constant watch for any sign of the Damocles. Along with the military's Pegasus spy satellite, all three of PGT's satellites are taking more photographs from space."

Both men looked at Dante (Joshua Golon) and gestured for him to take over.

"The Israeli Secret Service, also known to you as the Mossad, has agents in Algeria and Tunisia," began Golon. "As of the night of June fifth, an operative we call Nightingale noticed the Damocles while she was aboard a yacht anchored outside Bizerte, Tunisia. I am told from there she had other operatives follow a bus south. But once it crossed over into Libya they had to back off. So we know they're being held in Libya. But our problem is precisely, where? Now through our spy satellite SHOAH we captured this photograph just south of Tajura, Libya."

Golon pointed to the image of a battered-looking bus. "Nightingale and her team say this is undeniably the same bus. To the south is nothing but vast desert mountain area. To the north and east the country is at war. Musheen is no idiot. Those kids are his only bargaining chip. They have to be tucked away somewhere safe from the chaos. But in the meantime, boys and girls, the Global Garrison will fly stealth and camouflaged Sordis coming in from the south of the country. They might hear us, but we are completely oblivious to their radar and tracking systems. Simultaneously in the Mediterranean, NATO will be using a naval task force led by the USS ANTIETAM as its command ship. They will be trying to locate the rogue submarine Damocles. Now listen up, people. June 9th is almost upon us. Let's bring our kids home safe."

Dante waved for Lars to come up and speak.

"I know what some of you are thinking. What's going on with the Iraqi princess? Is she friend or foe? The Skipper and I are getting her full cooperation. She's divulging what she knows about the Al Qaeda network. Don't judge her too harshly, guys. We are going to get to the bottom of this, hopefully with her help. I'll be with the first Sordi when the Viking Avenger leaves. When I return later this evening the Skipper, Talon and I will try and get Intel on these evil bastards. I got a feeling she's going to be the nail in their coffin."

Lanny spoke out. "We're with you on that, Tank. She is one of the gentlest souls I've ever come across. We're with you all the way, big guy."

Lars blew a kiss towards Lanny. "Thanks, Lady Bee. She'll be glad to hear that you said that."

Orion yelled, "Okay, everybody, enough. Let's get to work. Duty roster is posted in the lockers. Let's show the world we're a force to be reckoned with."

Everybody stood. "Hoo Yah! GLOBAL GARRISON!"

The units split into their assignments as the Viking Avenger's engines began to fire up. Wolfman boarded the Viking Avenger with Claire as pilot and Tank as copilot.

Time: 13:20 hours. June 6, 2011. Dusseldorf, Germany.

Time: 19:30 hours. June 6, 2011. Dusseldorf, Germany.

Just getting back from six hours of reconnaissance flyovers, Lars got out of his battle dress uniform to meet up with Orion and the Skipper. Claire told him she'd join them shortly after she gave their Intel to Wolfman.

At the eastern side of the base Lamarra arrived at Shaleem's hospital room with flowers. Dr. Darfuir came in about five minutes later with a laptop and an access encrypted key. Captain Malloy and Orion both also arrived with flowers and Shaleem gave them a beautiful smile. They told her that Lars was on his way. Shaleem told the Skipper that they could start without Lars there.

"NO WAY!" exclaimed Orion. "We don't want to piss off that monster of a boyfriend of yours." Orion handed her carnations and kissed her cheek.

For about five minutes the group chit-chatted and got a little more acquainted. Then Lars entered the room carrying one wrapped red rose with baby s breath complementing it. He walked up and pulled a box of Godiva chocolates from behind his back. Kissing Shaleem hello, he handed her the rose then looked up at Malloy. "I guess whenever you're ready, Skipper."

Malloy asked if Shaleem was up to the task. Shaleem, with a face of the determination, gave an affirmative. The Princess directed him six years back to the Iraqi war in full swing. She told him that most of the time the royal family was in hiding because Saddam wanted to share his power with no one. Musheen was then a trusted advisor for her father. Lamarra was the caretaker and knew sooner or later the Republican Guard would catch up with them.

Even though the people knew the Khaleef could not venture into the politics of the country, Saddam still wanted all royal and ancient bloodlines to be eradicated. Her father, a multibillionaire, realized his wealth would not protect him for long. She told of the time Musheen came in one morning, informing her father that the Americans were hired by the newly elected government of the people. The mission? To have them arrested for sedition with the enemy.

Shaleem shared that her father felt betrayed, having done so much for the Americans in the past. She explained that Musheen and Baraash had made plans to get her family out of the country and that Mujhadeen warriors would sneak them into the palaces of Yemen. Ultimately, she and her two servants were taken to an awaiting car that would transport her and the royal entourage safely out of the country. She remembered that Amal Baraash took her from their compound when they were under attack from the Americans. Baraash had placed her and her two servants in the car and went back to get her father and Lamarra.

Lamarra was told by Musheen that Shaleem had been sent to America the day before. She was told the Khaleef was given sanctuary by the Americans and that she was to prepare the mosque in Hoboken for his stay.

Tears poured from the eyes of the Princess. She stuttered and trembled. Shaleem remembered the loud gunfire as Baraash and Musheen came running to the car. She was told that the Americans had just murdered her father and Lamarra.

Now breaking down and unable to stop weeping Shaleem slumped down, but Lars grabbed her and pulled her tight to his body. There was not a dry eye in the room. Even the hard-nosed Captain Malloy had a hard time keeping his composure. But he turned on the laptop by putting in the encrypted key. On the screen was the attack she just spoke of. Gunfire was heard and in the background Baraash and Musheen were shooting down an alleyway. Both of the men jumped into a Fiat and sped off with the Princess in the back of the car.

Shaleem cried out, "That's IT! That's exactly where it happened."

Orion looked carefully into the mirrors of the Fiat and asked Dr. Darfuir to play the scene back in slow motion. Once again they heard a lot of gunfire. Then Baraash put the women into the back of the car. More gunfire.

Orion yelled, "STOP! Back it up just a little."

Dr. Darfuir rewound to just before the gunfire blasted. The first shot rang out and Orion yelled, "STOP right there."

Malloy, puzzled, said, "Right where? What the hell are you talking about?"

Orion told Dr. Darfuir to zoom in on the broken side view mirror on the driver side. He then told him to back it up a few more frames. On the screen, as clear as day, were Musheen and Baraash pointing their AK-47s at Shaleem's father. Then with regret Orion told the good doctor to play it out.

Instantly the screen showed the murder of Shaleem's father by the two evil al Qaeda operatives. Shaleem screamed in horror and buried her head in Lars chest. Lamarra had to be helped to a chair because the same bastard told her that the Al Qaeda network had murdered Shaleem the day after she left for America.

Lars stood up and looked into the face of the two terrorists on the screen. "I'm going to make sure all of them pay for this." He reached down and kissed his crying girlfriend. "THIS I SWEAR BY ALLAH." He looked at Malloy and Orion and they promised, "SO DO WE."

Time: 20:15 hours. June 6, 2011. Dusseldorf, Germany.

CHAPTER SIXTEEN: HERE COMES THE SUN

Time: 07:05 hours. June 7, 2011. Dusseldorf, Germany.

Members of the elite units of the Global Garrison sat down for a hearty breakfast. Having just said goodbye to his wife for the day, the renowned Aero-dynamic physicist Joseph Stellarnberg arrived at the front gate of the highly secured base. As he pulled up one of the guards waved for him to come in and pull his car off to the side. Staff Sergeant Carl Moedel walked over and handed Stellarnberg a slip of paper.

"Must be really important, Carl, for it to arrive this early in the morning."

Carl replied, "That's why I pulled you over, Professor. I thought if were that important you'd probably want to read it right away."

Stellarnberg thanked Carl then pulled up the tab on the message. As he opened it the large letters URGENT hit him full force. He read quickly as a cloud of concern hovered on his face. He folded the message and tucked it in his suit pocket. He drove to the main building for breakfast and was greeted by Lanny and Kendra as he entered the building.

"Good morning, Professor Stellarnberg," said Kendra.

"Good morning to you too, Baroness." He turned his attention towards Lanny. "How are your two boys coming around, Lady Bee?"

Lanny's face lit up. "They're doing great, Professor. They have only one more day on the electron generator."

Stellarnberg smiled. "Are you and Talon available this morning at any time? I would like to talk with both of you when your father comes in."

"Sure, Professor. We're not going on patrol with the Trident until 13:00 today. Is something wrong?" asked Lanny.

Stellarnberg shrugged. "No, not at all. But Professor Kruger and I would like to go over some things with you both."

Lanny responded, "I'll tell him soon as he comes in from his run."

Stellarnberg with a puzzled look asked, "Why are they running late this morning? I thought they started at five."

Kendra answered, "This morning they all got together to plan a surprise party for Carl Livingston. My dad was with them this morning to help them plan."

Stellarnberg responded, "Thanks for letting me know, girls. I had no idea it was his birthday. I'll let Heinrich know and will keep it under wraps. He really is a brilliant man."

Lanny agreed, "He sure is. He was instrumental in saving Johnny's life."

Kendra opened the door. "Come on, sis and Professor, I'm famished."

The trio headed into the lobby then made a beeline for the cafeteria.

On the other side of the world two astrophysicists were pouring over four different diagrams that came out of their computer. The observatory was on the island of Maui in the Hawaiian Islands. The two scientists compared diagrams rendered on November 27, 2010 against a diagram that came in just two days ago at about 22:00 hours, New York time.

Dr. Theodore Bertram nodded and said to his colleague Dr. Sato Yamaguchi, "I concur with you on these statistics. The fractal geometry is the exact thing we witnessed last year. This indicates the Earth is about to receive another jolt of cosmic energy in two to three days. Sato, we have to warn our colleagues Dr. Hewitt and Dr. Yamans from the Hakeliah Observatory. They must know of this repeated phenomenon."

Dr. Bertram picked up the landline phone and called Professor Ronald Yamans.

"I thought you would be calling, Theodore. Our computer translates the same rudimentary diagram identical to November 27 of last year."

Dr. Bertram interrupted, "But Ronald, track the diagram to the Kuiper Belt. If you look closely you'll agree the fractal geometry stops right at that point. But, my dear colleague, trace the diagram towards the Orion constellation from there."

Professor Yamans put him on hold for one minute as he let Dr. Hewitt extend the diagram. The data came back and Dr. Yamans shrugged and said into the phone, "I've done what you said Theodore, and I think you're starting to suffer from dementia. It does not coincide one bit."

Dr. Bertram laughed. "DEMENTIA. I thought you'd be a little kinder, Ronald. Now take from the area where the geometry stops by the Kuiper Belt and simply turn it upside down. REMEMBER, just from the Belt to Orion's constellation. Now, what do you see?"

Professor Yamans' eyes swelled from his head. He checked, then double checked. "Holy Galileo. It's the same fractal geometry, but only in reverse telemetry."

Bertram laughed wholeheartedly this time. "Not bad for someone about to be stricken with Alzheimer s disease."

The two brilliant scientists went over the diagrams by phone for the next two hours. Dr. Yamans told Dr. Bertram, "Theodore, for two scientists who use their brains and are trying to figure out the secrets of the universe, why don't we just converse on our computer screens? That way we can put our phones down and talk hands-free. You do have an eye-camera on that thing, don't you?"

Dr. Bertram replied, "Yes we do. It's one of those things these cheapskates allow in our budget."

The men reverted to their computers and concluded their findings little by little. After a while Dr. Yamaguchi said to Professor Yamans, "Ronald, we need to let NASA know what is going on. Back in November of last year the solar flare reached us in a matter of 51 hours. Many of the satellites that weren't shrouded with shields were rendered useless. Many of the big tele-communication giants lost what amounted to billions because they weren't alerted to deploy their shields."

Sato told his other three colleagues, "Our other colleague, Professor Jeffrey Pearson, asked me to call him immediately if similar circumstances were about to occur."

Bertram looked at the diagram and saw the grid line jump to the surface of the Earth. He then studied the grid from November and saw the same exact thing. Only one line of configuration went to the surface of the Earth in the diagram in front of them. He saw in both instances that they pointed to the region of East Hampton, New York. Rubbing his chin with his left hand he thought out loud, "What have you been up to, Jeffrey? Have you found the goose that lays the golden eggs? Have you found the Higgs particle and are keeping it to yourself?"

All of the scientists looked at the line heading down to East Hampton and began to wonder the same thing.

Time: 17:35 hours. June 7, 2011. Honolulu, Hawaii.

Time: 11:00 hours. June 7, 2011. Dusseldorf, Germany.

Inside Professor Pearson's office the Professor and his science and technological team were starting a meeting with Commander John Orion, and his fiancée, Lieutenant Commander Lanny Cromwell. Pearson greeted everyone and gave the floor to Professor Heinrich Kruger.

Kruger pushed the enter button on the processor pad and the screen showed Orion and the two dogs in the middle of the transformation period. Orion and the wolves displayed frightening gnarling and grimacing during the entire process. What it seemed to indicated is that all three of them were one together, experiencing the extreme metamorphosis. Even when they levitated their emotional being was resolved together.

Lanny became uneasy and cried out, "All right, we've seen this before. Can we get to the point? I'm not at all comfortable having to see this again."

Orion jumped in. "Neither am I. I was there, remember? Professor, what is the point to all this?"

Dr. Kruger froze the picture. "Precisely. It bothers you, and that's the point. John, look at those two animals growling. Their faces look as though they are tearing apart an elk. John, you're human, and by that I mean you are subject to complacency and reason. You also have incredible powers that would make Superman unhinge. Maybe you're just learning to fly, but you defy gravity just as his character does. Our question is, when these two animals are finished in a rejuvenation process will they be more modified in the instincts of wolves and be uncontrollable? Johnny, the evolution of dogs goes back to the wolf. They're born hunters and killers. Now what happens if you and Lanny can't control them or their natural instinct to hunt overtakes them? We are not doing this to be mean and insensitive. But us regular humans don't want to be on their menu, if you know what we mean?"

Orion and Lanny looked at each other and grew concerned. They knew the Professors were completely right. A tear appeared on Lanny's right eye and she put her hand over her nose and mouth. She then said, "Poppa, what do you want us to do?"

"Right now nothing, sweetheart. But when Romy and Remy revive in a couple of hours we can only have John in a secured room with them."

Lanny's face was bewildered. "What do you mean, a couple hours? I thought they still had another day."

"No Lanny. If it were your fiancé, it would. But because of the difference in anatomies it will be at 16: 00. You're going to be here and not flying the Trident. Lars is going to be with Valerie as she pilots the super jet. By no means does this mean that you are no longer captain of the Trident. We just need you here to see the interaction between both of you and your dogs."

At that instant the buzzer from outside the office chimed. Pearson pressed the button on the console. "What is it, Kendra? Plus, I hope you haven't been listening in."

Kendra replied, "Of course not, Daddy. A Professor Theodore Bertram is on the line and says it's of the utmost importance, something about a matter of life and death."

"All right, honey, patch me through with him on the monitor." Pearson then told everyone to hold on and hit the receiver button on the processor. Instantly the face of Dr. Bertram appeared on the screen.

Bertram immediately said, "I'm sorry to interrupt your meeting, Jeffrey. But you did tell us to contact you if anything out of the ordinary should arise."

Everybody in the room looked onto the screen to see three other scientists behind Dr. Bertram.

Pearson replied, "Well shoot, Ted. Now we're all in suspense."

With a twinge in his eye Bertram said, "Remember last November when the Earth was hit by a seismic 2 solar flare? Remember how it crippled dozens of telecommunications satellites from around the planet?"

Pearson and everyone in the room raised their eyebrows all at once. Then with a choked up voice Pearson replied, I... I... I remember it very well." Still playing coy Pearson continued. "Well if you will, Ted, please get to the point."

The other three scientists on the screen with Dr. Bertram appeared to be wearing shit-eating grins.

"You see Jeffrey... ah yes. The same exact thing has happened all over again. Since you told me to call you before we inform NASA, you wouldn't happened to know anything about this, WOULD YA?"

Professor Pearson smiled at his colleagues. "Ted, Sato, and Ronald, you look like three cats that have just swallowed birds. Are you accusing me of something?"

Dr. Bertram smiled just a little more deviously. "By no means, my longtime friend. It's just that the same readings show the same exact fractal geometry as it did on twenty-seventh of November of last year. Plus the diagram spread its geometry all the way to the Orion constellation. Only one point of reference shoots straight down to the topography of our planet. Guess where it points to?"

Everybody in Pearson's office tried to act inconspicuous. The Professor then donned his own shit-eating grin. "Well, Teddy, don't keep us in suspense. WHERE? Wait a second, the fractal geometry goes out into the Orion constellation? Then it's not the same as in November. You remember, it stopped at the Kuiper Belt."

Bertram began laughing and the others joined in behind him. "Thought that would get your attention. We didn't notice the first time, but maybe something in the gravitational pull from the Kuiper Belt and the Oort cloud made the optical telemetry reversed. If you don't believe me, just divide the area from the Kuiper onto the constellation and turn it upside down."

Dr. Darfuir frantically began using his charts and turned one side of them upside down. He looked up at Pearson in amazement. "JEFFREY, oh my God, he's right. It's exactly the same from the sun to the belt and has been staring us in the face the whole time."

Bertram immediately cut in. "Jeffrey, level with us. You know and I know all your nanotechnology is composed of fractal geometry. You even told me yourself that Dr. Benoit Mandelbrot s research is undeniably true, without question. If so tell us, have you discovered the Higgs particle? Come on, they've been trying to duplicate the antimatter parallel inside seventeen miles of giant tunnels for years. But yet we are picking up a gravitational pull from the Earth that grabs energy from the sun and throws it out beyond into different galaxies."

Pearson looked into the screen. "What you've just relayed, Ted, is new to me. You've all been close to me for years and have had faith in my research. But bear with me, I need to look into this myself. Would all of you like to come to Dusseldorf and go over your findings with me and my staff?"

The four scientists on the other end began whispering. Professor Bertram came back and said, "Jeffrey, Ronald and Dave came over just a short while ago from the other island. I guess we'll make arrangements to fly out of Honolulu."

Dr. Pearson then jumped in. "Don't worry about that, Ted. I have a corporate jet that will fly both of you from there. First-class, of course."

Professor Bertram still wore that shit-eating grin. Why thank you, Dr. Pearson. See you in Germany.

The screen faded to black and then reverted to the frozen still of Orion and the wolves.

Pearson said to Dr. Darfuir, "Kamal, shut that off. We've got other things to worry about."

Orion's face was puzzled. "What the hell is going on, Doc? Fractal geometry, Kuiper Belt you got me. I'm completely in the dark."

Pearson replied, "John, the Icarus Project may be the reason we're having solar flares from the sun so consistently. NO, as a matter-of-fact, IT IS THE REASON WHY that's HAPPENING! John, concentrate and ask the supercomputer. I'm sure it will indulge the new information right to you."

Orion closed his eyes and concentrated. Within two minutes he came out of his trance and looked concerned.

He told Lanny, "The mixture of the electron generator and my force has created a quark in the space outside Earth's atmosphere and onward into the voids of the galaxy. This was immediately confirmed when they used the same process on the wolves. We are stepping into boundaries of the unknown and the science experiments must stop immediately because it may endanger the Earth itself."

Time: 13:20 hours. June 7, 2011. Dusseldorf, Germany.

CHAPTER SEVENTEEN: HEART OF THE HUNTER

Time: 15:50 hours. June 7, 2011. Dusseldorf, Germany.

With the day already full of surprises, Lanny Cromwell began to have stomach pains. As she and Orion entered the room where their beloved pets were going to be revived, Lanny placed a kiss on each of them and then headed up to the observation gallery to watch.

Dr. Darfuir had already taken off the Portison helmets and the Guardian components. Orion took a look above and saw Professor Pearson nod his head for him to start speaking to the animals.

"Romulus, Remus, it's me boys. Come on, wake up, time to get up."

Nothing happened at first, but suddenly Romulus' tail began to wag.

Lanny turned on the microphone at the top of the gallery. "Come on Romy, you too, Remy. Mama needs you to get up."

The wolves automatically opened their eyes and the purple glow filled the room.

By this time Lanny's stomach felt even a little more nauseous.

The dogs sat upright on the tables and Orion picked up Remus and put him beside his brother on the other table. Both of them licked him on the face, showing him their love.

Lanny said through the microphone, "Hey, babies, Mommy is up here. Come on boys, look up here."

Both animals whimpered for her and a second later levitated themselves to the top of the gallery. They both start licking the see-through Plexiglas window.

Orion was right behind them and said to Dr. Kruger, "Here are your killers, Professor." As Orion floated next to them, he petted them on the back of their heads.

Lanny noticed her father smiling with contentment. "See Poppa, everything still stays in their beautiful hearts. They know who I am."

Pearson replied, They sure do, and they know your beautiful heart as well.

Lanny jumped up from her seat. "I have to go down and be there with my boys." She scurried towards the stairway, but before reaching it heard a crash behind her. Both wolves had smashed the glass to follow her. Lanny fell to her knees laughing as they both licked her face and whined to show her their love.

The purple glow suddenly disappeared as Orion walked up with the others. He looked at both wolves and they immediately looked back. Through mental telepathy he commanded them to sit, and both complied. Orion mentally ordered them to come over and stand next to him and they instantly obeyed.

Lanny and her father were in complete awe along with all who had just witnessed the scene.

Pearson was stymied by just what occurred and conveyed to Orion, "John, we need to do something about them. I can't have them smashing through everything every time you or Lanny go somewhere. Do you think you can come up with some way to contain them?"

Lanny, not paying attention to what her father said, telepathically ordered the dogs to come to her. They both instantly obeyed and sat right next to her.

Everyone now looked at her in amazement.

"Did you just think that, baby?" asked Orion.

"I sure did, Johnny. WAIT, I want to try something." She began to walk away and as soon as the dogs tried to follow she mentally ordered them to stay. They instantly halted in their tracks and sat down.

Lanny said to Orion, "I don't know why, Johnny, but they know everything I'm thinking when I want them to."

Pearson gave them a quick scenario. "Well Lanny, if you remember it was your DNA that multiplied itself inside Orion's invulnerable body. From where I'm standing, both your pets have received the same."

Lanny replied, "Daddy, if one of us is with them at all times we will have no problem controlling what they do."

The Professor responded, "Yeah, but sweetheart, what happens when both of you are sent out on a delicate mission?"

Orion walked over to his girl and the dogs. "I guess the KIDS go with us."

Pearson smiled, then got on his knees and beckoned to the wolves. "Come here, you two troublemakers."

The dogs ran over to lick him as they whimpered.

He looked up at Orion. "I guess we have no choice. I'm going to call our building and construction department and have them create blueprints for a kennel connected to your house." He checked his watch. "Oh God, it's already five o clock. I've got to put our plan in motion to get Carl to go with me into town. Okay, let's get out of here for now."

The Professors took the stairs in front of Pearson, Orion and Lanny. Lanny followed and heard her father say to her fiancé, "Wait one second. Maybe they'll pick up signals with my own telepathy."

Lanny, being only seven steps down, whispered to Dr. Stellarnberg to stop the others and turn around and watch. She barely saw her father at the top of the stairs as he put his hand to his head and began to concentrate. She put her fingertip to her mouth, silently telling everyone not to laugh. Then she concentrated and the dogs went running past the Professor.

"DID YOU SEE THAT? I just telepathically conveyed for them to come, and they came," shouted the Professor.

Lanny put her hand fully over her mouth to keep herself from busting out. She regained her composure as her father and Orion walked down the stairs, and turned around to see his colleagues still laughing. She waved for them to stop and move downstairs.

Dr. Darfuir said to her quietly, "Shame on you my dear, but I must admit I thought it to be hilarious."

They then headed to the main elevator and the main floor of the hospital triage unit. When the door opened, everybody on the main floor saw the two very large wolves exit the elevator with the entourage. People began to pin themselves up against a wall as the odd group made their way down the corridor.

Coming in to the building was none other than Captain James Malloy. When he opened the door he saw the entourage. Lanny moved to the side to talk to one of the nurses and he spotted the two wolves. Having had a bad experience in Vietnam with dogs, he stood rigid and tensed up.

Both wolves seemed to interpret his feelings and came over to lick him. Previously they would have been apprehensive, but through their owner s mind they know he was friend and confidant.

Orion said to his commanding officer, "Skipper, don't be so uptight with them. Believe you me, they'll protect you with their lives if they have to. So give them a break, huh?"

Malloy slowly bent to one knee and both wolves start licking him with love.

"See? What did I tell you!" said Orion.

Malloy replied, "You sure they're not just testing the goods before they eat?"

Lanny walked over and said to Malloy, "Skipper, they're wolves, remember? They would be picking your bones by now. Wolves don't taste test. They know we love you, so they love you too."

Malloy relaxed. "By the way commander, Benny is meeting me and you in my office in about forty-five minutes. We need to go over some of our scenarios before that bastard strikes again."

Orion's face turned serious. "That's affirmative, Skipper. I'll be there in forty-five.

Lanny whispered to the Malloy, "Skipper, has there been any information on the whereabouts of the children?"

Malloy looked disgusted. "Not one single clue. Eagle One has conveyed to me that the parents are putting pressure on NATO to tell us not to interfere. Do you believe they've asked to have us fired upon if there is even an inclination of us getting involved? After all we did in New York City seven months ago HOW QUICKLY THEY FORGET!"

Lanny put her arm around her commanding officer. "Skipper, can you blame them? What would you do if it was Tessie, Mazzy or Eugene?"

Malloy lifted his head. "How do you always know what to say to me, Commander?"

"That's because I love you, Skipper," she answered.

Malloy grinned. "Back at ya, girl."

Lanny asked, "Are you and Marilyn coming to the Rats Kellar for Carl's surprise party tonight?"

Malloy responded, "Without a doubt. She's really excited to have a night out with everybody, especially without having to psychoanalyze them. You have to see her get pissed off when I tell her she can't use anybody's real name whenever they're in battle dress uniform. It's even funnier when I remind her of that as we cross over from the east to the west side of the base."

Lanny said, "Captain, it took me months and tons of push-ups to get used to it, too. I bet she's never done one push-up, huh?"

Malloy smiled. "That is not only none of your business, but a privilege of command."

Lanny retorted snidely, "In other words, no!"

Malloy said, "Don't you have to be somewhere, Lieutenant Commander Cromwell?"

Lanny went to attention. "That I do, Sir."

Malloy growled, "Then get to it NOW."

Lanny smiled. "Aye aye, Sir." She ran out of the building while Orion and the Captain shared a laugh.

Malloy, laughing, said to Orion, "You're very lucky man, Commander."

Orion smiled. "Don't I know it. Come on, Skipper, I don't know about you but I need something quick to eat. Let's grab a coffee and a snack before the briefing."

The executive officer and his captain headed off to the commissary store in the back of the building.

The attack aircraft Viking Avenger came in from the south. Lady Hawke told Merlin (Benny Kramer) to let the unit know they were about to land.

Condor (Carl Bingham) began the landing sequence by initiating the drop of the landing gear. He applied the flaps as they approached the secret airbase in Germany. On the tarmac was the sister ship to the Avenger, the Blazing Trident, and she was almost completely fueled for Sordi towards the African continent.

Time: 17:45 hours. June 7, 2011. Dusseldorf, Germany.

Time: 18:15 hours. June 7, 2011. Dusseldorf, Germany.

In downtown Dusseldorf, Gerta Schmidt, her sister Ingrid Friedrich and their niece Holly were preparing the Rats Kellar restaurant for Carl Livingston's surprise birthday party. Gerta walked in the kitchen and saw her boyfriend, the Professor, sampling hors d'oeuvres from different trays. As he went for the blintzes, she smacked his hand away. "Jeffrey, I just gave you a large piece of apple strudel. Can't you wait for our guests to arrive?"

Her brother-in-law Bader Friedrich laughed as he and his kitchen staff loaded ice into giant wash tubs of the finest brewed beer in Germany. The bottles clinked together and Bader said to Gerta, "Oh, leave him alone. He doesn't drink, so let him indulge in the one thing he likes doing best."

She patted him on the ass as her niece entered the kitchen to get more beer mugs. Holly, just catching the last bit of what was going on, said, "Aunt Gerta, control yourself! And you, Professor, sit in one of those ice basins. This is a family restaurant."

Everyone in the kitchen laughed as Ingrid entered. "WHAT THE HELL IS GOING ON? Let's move! Kamal will be bringing the birthday boy before you know it."

Everyone hurried so Ingrid wouldn't freak out.

Back at the base Dr. Darfuir was keeping Carl busy with computerized charts of the fractal geometry from the fifth of June. They tried to get a timeline on when the cosmic radiation from the solar flare would hit Earth. Carl had just turned thirty-five and was one of the best mathematicians around.

Over at the airfield on the western side of the base, a C-5 Galaxy had just landed from Norfolk, Virginia. Getting off the plane were Kyle Duffy with the two new members of the Global Garrison, Darnell Crawford and Michael Wong. Both new members were discharged Navy Seals and tops in their fields of expertise.

Crawford was one of the best demolition experts ever to come out of the Navy. He was also a fifth degree black belt in jujitsu. This is one of the reasons Malloy gave him his code name BOOMER.

Michael Wong was a true master in the Korean martial art of Tae Kwon Do, Tang Soo Doo, and Moo Duk Kwan. He was also an expert in the ancient knife fighting form of Sang-Gee. Malloy had his name picked well before Wong was discharged: MANTIS. Michael s father, Jhoon Lee Wong was also a master and personally taught his boy. He was a South Korean

Marine who taught martial arts to the Navy SEALs and Force Recon Marines for the United States. When Michael Wong was twelve his father was murdered by a North Korean operative in reprisal for teaching their sacred ancient arts to the Americans.

On his twelfth birthday Michael was competing in the world Tae Kwon Do championship as his father watched from the audience. From behind Jhoon Lee Wong an assassin killed him instantly with a blow dart dipped in deadly poison. Michael s relatives raised him until he reached the age of eighteen, when he applied for citizenship. The Navy Department let him join while he worked himself up to be one of the most aspiring sailors they'd ever encountered. At the age of twenty-one he was given the chance to go to CRT BUDs training. He was the top graduate in his class and he stayed in the Navy for another seven years until Malloy approached him to join his secret organization.

Deep down, Wong wanted to get the coward who killed his father.

The two new members were now on their way up to the Skipper's office. From there they would swear their allegiance to the Global Garrison and sign the same contracts as everyone else. They would follow all rules and regulations given to them by their superior officers. They would also dedicate themselves to rid the world of all evil terrorists, especially Al Qaeda.

The Global Garrison was formed to protect the entire planet. According to the charter, no planet, country, or individual could take precedent unless in imminent danger of being destroyed. Kyle filled them both in on the details of the contracts and charter. They couldn't wait to sign on.

The three of them entered the Main building where the security chief had his office on the third floor. Kyle and the two new recruits got off the elevator and walked straight to Malloy's office. Kyle knocked and the Skipper told them to enter. Kyle opened the door and walked in ahead of them both.

"The two new members are here, Sir," Kyle announced.

The captain was talking with Orion. "That will be all, Puma. We'll take it from here."

Kyle saluted. "Aye aye, Sir."

Malloy returned the salute and Kyle did an about-face and left. Crawford and Wong walked up to the front of Malloy's desk and instantly stood at attention.

Darnell saluted first. "Petty Officer First Class Crawford, reporting for duty, Sir."

Immediately Michael Wong repeated, "Petty Officer First Class Wong, reporting for duty, Sir."

Malloy shook their hands in approval. "At ease, gentlemen. You haven't signed your John Hancock s yet. Have a seat. I'd like to introduce you to my executive officer, Commander John Orion. Once you put on your battle dress uniform along with the rest of us, you will refer to everyone only by their designated call sign name. Since none of us are in BDUs, you don't have too at this moment. But you will read the charter and be given the call signs of the active members of this organization. I was given your clothing size over two months ago. On the western side of the base in hangar four you'll find your new uniforms. The duty officer will fill you in on all protocols. He'll go over every scenario you must follow. My orders supersede those of anyone's except for our big boss, Dr. Jeffrey Pearson. You'll meet him later. In the meantime, I need you to look over your contracts in the other room. If you don't think you can comply, just bring them back in unsigned and I will thank you for your time."

Malloy then handed them their paperwork and they walked into the adjacent soundproof room.

As they shut the door, Orion said, "Twenty bucks they're back in five."

Malloy replied, "It's like you're just giving me the money, shithead."

Orion said, "Oh yeah? Then put your money where your mouth is."

Malloy took out an Andrew Jackson and put it between his teeth. Just as Orion went to do the same thing, the door opened and the new recruits put their signed contracts on his desk. Orion laughed and grabbed the twenty out of Malloy's mouth.

Crawford, bewildered asked, "What's this? Some kind of indoctrination thing?"

Malloy, the sore loser, replied, "No Boomer, our executive officer thinks he's a know it all. All right, you guys, Puma is outside waiting to take you over to the restricted side of the base. Go on now, get out of here so this fucking hyena will finally shut his trap."

Both of them saluted their superiors and headed for the door.

Orion yelled, "One minute, gentlemen."

They turned around.

"WELCOME ABOARD," said Orion proudly. "You are now part of the most elite organization in the world."

Both of them replied, "Hoo Yah!"

Benny Kramer passed them as they exited. He knocked at Malloy's open door. "Those the new guys, Skipper?"

Malloy said to Orion first, "All right, enough. You got me this time. But don't let it go to your head." Then he looked at Benny. "Yeah Senior Chief, they just signed. Come on buddy, let's see what you and laughing boy here have come up with."

The trio pondered three different scenarios for about twenty-five minutes. The phone rang and Malloy picked it up. On the other end was Marilyn Carmichael talking so loudly that Orion and Benny overheard.

Malloy said, "I'm leaving right now, baby. Yes, honey, yeah, I told you

I'm coming right now. Love you too." He hung up and announced, "Shit! I forgot Carl's birthday party. Remember?"

All three of them bolted out the door. As they got into the Land Rover, Orion and Benny's cell phones rang at the same time.

Orion answered, "I'm on my way right now, Lanny. Of course not. I'll be there in a minute."

Benny was now talking with Tiri and his bullshitting was just as good as Orion s.

At the same time Malloy heard both of them say, "LOVE YOU TOO." As they hung up simultaneously, Malloy commented, "You think we should be ashamed of ourselves?

Benny laughed, "The illusion only works if you maintain the deception at its fullest"

Orion responded, "I guess that means we're all in the doghouse."

Benny lifted his eyes to look over the roof of the car. "Without a fucking doubt."

Time: 19:00 hours. June 7, 2011. Germany.

Time: 19:10 hours. June 7, 2011. Dusseldorf, Germany.

Photographs were taken of a lone individual atop the mountain forty miles from the coastal town of Tajura, Libya. The attack aircraft, Blazing Trident, flew over the Gulf of Sidra on its way home to Germany. A purple light flashed on the console of the jet. Valerie Queen looked over at the encrypted sequence of numbers to see that Eagle One (Admiral Fischer) was making contact.

She pushed the relay button. "This is Duchess, active captain of the Blazing Trident. We read you, Eagle One."

The screen console showed an image of Fischer. "Duchess, we have just received a compelling message from our intelligence chief. Another cargo vessel, Syrene Majestic, is about to be attacked. It's cargo consists of 80,000,000 gallons of number two crude oil. But on the deck they also have dozens of containers of magnesium and cobalt stored in the stern of the ship. From our anonymous tip, we learned they're going to set it ablaze as it approaches the Straits of Gibraltar. SOCOM has been alerted. Seal team two is being deployed as we speak. The problem is, they're coming out of the Aegean and somehow I have this feeling your strike team is quite a bit closer. Am I right, Duchess?"

Valerie hit transmit button. "That's affirmative, Sir. I am now setting course for the exact coordinates relayed by your laptop. I'm conveying the alert to my commanding officer. Please do the same with Seal Team 2."

Admiral Fischer said, "That's a Roger, Duchess. Everybody watch your six, OVER."

"That we will, Sir. OVER AND OUT." Valerie looked at Trudy. "What do you think, honey?"

Trudy looked back from the navigator's chair. "I don't know what to think of it, doll. Seems a little too convenient. I'll raise the Skipper on the horn. Maybe it's a trap, but we still have time for him to send back up. Seal Team 2 is too far away to reach us in time. I'm sending out a general alert."

The copilot David Banks (ALBATROSS) agreed with Trudy and put the Blazing Trident in cloaking mode.

Time: 19:23 hours. Dusseldorf, Germany.

Time: 19:40 hours. June, 2011. Dusseldorf, Germany.

Orion and Lanny were the last ones to arrive at the Rats Kellar restaurant in downtown Dusseldorf. They rushed inside just as Dr. Darfuir's car appeared down the street in the distance. Lanny smiled as Orion opened the door to the restaurant for her. As they entered Orion noticed Malloy's concerned face.

Malloy said to Orion and Lanny, "The Duke just sent out the GENERAL ALARM. Come on, let's go. Malloy spotted Kendra starting to follow. Go with your father to operations. I need you on the super computer with me. I'll be there as soon as they're airborne."

Kendra's face was full of disappointment as she conveyed to her uncle, "Uncle Jimmy, you're just keeping me here because of my dad. How can I prove myself to the others if you won't give me a chance?"

Malloy quickly replied, "Listen Baroness, only you, Lanny, Valerie and Claire know how to use the encryptor. The Duchess is already in the air, Claire's flying the Viking Avenger, and Lanny is the emergency doctor on call. So that leaves you. Plus, don't worry you're going to get what you ask for. But for now, being on the computer is just as vital to the operation."

As they went inside they ran into Dr. Darfuir and Carl. Malloy told Carl he needed him in operations and that they would make up for his surprise birthday party.

Time: 19:50 hours. June 7, 2011. Dusseldorf, Germany.

JOHN PETER FERRIS

CHAPTER EIGHTEEN: TO KNOW THINE ENEMY

Time: 18:15 hours. June 7, 2011. Malaga, Spain.

Just south of the coastal town of Malaga, Spain, thirty-two terrorists commandeered the oil and cargo freighter Syrene Majestic. They shot and killed all on board except the helmsman and the engine room chief. Molaan Shavaaz was able to come aboard in Bizerte, Tunisia with forged seamen engineering credentials. The captain, Enrie Machera, put him to work immediately in the engine room.

The head chief of what was called the "black gang" worked in an area near the main turbines. About half an hour earlier, Molaan snuck up on the shaft engineers and shot them in cold blood. He then cut the power to the engines. Waiting in a shrimp boat only two miles away, his barrage of terrorists came to the Syrene Majestic and boarded her. All of them carried forty pound sacks of phosphorus powder and loaded them on a hoist they set up soon as the ship was theirs.

Mustaffa Khaldif had given them orders to set up machine-gun positions on the stern and bow of the ship. He also wanted emplacements in the center and at both starboard and port side.

The other henchmen onboard were opening the marked containers that had magnesium inside. They poured the powder all over the magnesium, when one of them dropped instantly to the ground from a silent bullet from the east.

The Duchess had snuck up on the ship and maintained a hover while they made their assault from the stern. Albatross (David Banks), then took the Blazing Trident and began circling the endangered ship.

They spread out into two fire teams: Alpha Team consisted of Trudeaux along with Valerie, Zorro (Carlos Alvarez), Mustang (Hansy), Cuda (Kada Bondi), and the Griffen (Patrick Tinsdale). Delta Team consisted of Dante (Joshua Golon), Maverick (Michael Maguiness), Rhino (Calvin Thomas),

Gunner (Gunnar Mientz), Galahad (Bobby Palladin), and Luna (Lunsi Paal).

Gunnar started off the firefight with a suppressed round into the first terrorist pouring the phosphorus onto the magnesium. But a PRK opened up on them and pinned them down against the rear of the containers.

Galahad said to Gunner, "We've been set up, Gunner. I'm going to pop smoke then we'll split into three s. We need to get the PRK up on the bridge."

Back in Mocha, Yemen, Abdullah Musheen and Mustaffa Khaldif watched the action going down from their giant screen. Musheen said to Khaldif, "Where is their android? Do they not think the main waterway to the Atlantic is important enough?"

They saw from their hidden cameras that Rhino was slowly creeping up the stairs to the bridge. Mustaffa yelled into the microphone, "Sabaz, one of them is sneaking up the stairs behind you."

Immediately the man shooting the PRK ran towards the stairs and aimed at Rhino, who dove off as bullets strafed the stairs and barely missed him. Maverick fired at Sabaz so Rhino could get behind him to safety.

The Duchess (Valerie Queen) made ground towards the middle of the deck just as the Duke (Michael Trudeaux) saw the terrorist manning a 30 caliber machine gun, aiming right for her. He tackled her and flew past a lifeboat entry station. Bullets were now pinning both Alpha and Delta teams to the deck.

Valerie looked at her boyfriend. "I think I Charlie-horsed my knee, honey.

Trudy asked, Duchess, do you want me to carry you?"

She gave him a quick kiss. "No baby, but we need to knock out that 30 Cal. I'm going to draw his fire, then when I fire back one of you need to pincer him from the left and flush him towards me. Then I'll take him out."

Suddenly an explosion came from the rear of the ship. The two end containers were completely engulfed with the brightest burning fire they had ever seen.

But back in Yemen Musheen screamed, "WHERE IS THIS SO-CALLED SUPER ROBOT? I'm getting fucking bored."

From a distance a glowing purple light came out of the northeast. Suddenly the Viking Avenger was right on top of them and began to hover in place as the rear door opened. Swooping down from above Orion took on tremendous gunfire from every direction. The bullets dropped around him as he made his way to the burning containers.

Musheen and Khaldif's faces were in awe as he shoved an unlit container into two that were ablaze. Orion pushed it until both of the containers fell off the ship. Some of the terrorist became so frightened they ran towards the front of the ship, right into Alpha Team s clutches.

In the middle of the ship the terrorist manning the 30 caliber trained the gun on Orion. The Duchess saw her opportunity and fired a double tap that killed him instantly. Orion now hovered above the ship about fifteen feet in the air. The purple light glowing from his angry eyes and body seemed to mesmerize all that looked upon him.

Benny, Lars, Kyle and Lanny were now on the deck gathering up the capitulated enemy with the other two teams. Orion floated over to the man who was manning the PRK on the bridge.

Sabaz held his hands up. "Please don't kill me! I give up. Please, I have a wife and children."

Orion looked around at the bodies of the dead crewman and replied, So did these brave men, you piece of shit." Orion grabbed him, flew to the side of the ship and hung him above the water. "I'm only going to ask you once who is in charge here and who sent you."

Sabaz screamed with fear. "Molaan Shavaaz is in charge. We all work for Mustaffa Khaldif."

Orion threw him to the deck of the Syrene Majestic and told Lanny to cuff him. As Lanny finished Merlin brought another cuffed terrorist to Orion. "Talon, it didn't take long for these assholes to give him up. This is Molaan Shavaaz."

Then a weird squelching sound came over the loudspeakers of the ship. A television screen lit up and was hard to see at first. On the screen was a man with a neckerchief in front of his face.

He looked at Orion. "VERY, VERY Impressive."

Orion landed in front of the screen and his purple glow disappeared.

"Ahh, that's more like it, face-to-face," smirked Musheen.

Orion replied angrily, "This ain't face-to-face, Musheen. No need for that rag to cover your ugly mug. We already know what you look like."

Musheen ripped the neckerchief off. "Now it's your turn."

Lanny, Valerie, Benny, and Bobby came in front of the screen. Lanny said to Musheen, "Oh, wouldn't you like that, you darn coward. Where are the children? The great terrorist Abdullah Musheen is so desperate he needs to torture and kidnap children for his conquests. You are nothing to the people of Islam. You say you serve Allah. How pathetic. You actually believe you're doing this in his name?"

Musheen screamed, "SHUT UP, WHORE. I'm not talking to you." He looked at Orion carefully. "Well, I can clearly see you're not a robot. So you must be cybernetic organism. Yes, that's what you are, a cybernetic FREAK. Enjoy your time on Earth, FREAK. Soon they'll have no more need of you and will shut you down and make you their slave."

In the distance was the familiar sound of a Chinook helicopter coming in. Musheen seemed to be aware of it too. "Your friends are on their way, so let's get to the point. If I see, smell, or even think you're coming to rescue these fucking brats, I will throw them to their deaths. Do you hear me, FREAK? You or any of your so-called Global Garrison make any attempt, and they die right away." Then he turned his attention to Lanny. "And you, whore, I serve the devil himself, not Allah. Allah has abandoned his people, whereas I have not. One day I will unmask all of you. But in the meantime, heed my warning."

The screen faded to black as the Chinook's motors became clearer. Orion said to Bobby, "Put this Molaan Shavaaz in the Avenger and blindfold him. I got a plan that just might work."

Merlin, overhearing, said to Orion, "Are you doing what I think you're going to do, Talon?"

Orion turned to Benny. "Well, I learned from the master and it seems you've rubbed off on me. Now come on, let's get him in the Avenger before our old brothers in arms start showing up. Tell Lady Hawke to contact Eagle One. Let him know we have taken the ship back from Al Qaeda. Tell the Skipper we'll be on our way back as soon as we turn the prisoners over to Seal Team 2."

Four minutes later a chopper hovered above the Syrene Majestic. Navy SEALs then began fast roping to the deck below and took over the manacled prisoners. Lieutenant Teddy Riedell was in charge and heard Orion's voice. It struck a chord and he vaguely wondered if he might have served in BUDs with Orion. Riedell was Billy Stokes first swim buddy in his ocean drops and earned the nickname "Spanky" because he always wanted to be in charge.

Riedell put his hand out to shake Orion's. "It's an honor to meet you, Commander. I don't know if you know, but everything that just happened was broadcasted around the world."

Orion's face became worried. "It's a pleasure to meet you too, Lieutenant."

Riedell jumped in. "Oh I'm sorry Commander Talon. It's Riedell, Lieutenant Commander Riedell. Do I know you? Your voice seems quite familiar."

Orion smiled but said, "Not really, Lieutenant Commander Riedell. I left the military a long time ago."

Riedell added, "Admiral Mike McRaven informed me that Naval Intelligence picked up Musheen's signal four points southeast of his position in Afghanistan."

Orion nodded. "That figures, the Gulf of Aden. How much do you want to bet the source is Yemen?"

Riedell replied, "That's exactly what I was thinking."

Orion then turned the ship over to Riedell. "Maybe we'll work together sometime in the future, Commander."

"I would like that a real lot, Talon." Riedell saluted him and Orion returned it. He then lifted off the deck of the Syrene Majestic and flew into the rear of the Viking Avenger. Everyone on the deck of the ship had their mouths opened in awe.

The super jet then hurtled across the water and disappeared towards the north. The Aegis class Missile Cruiser USS Antietam arrived with a small task force in tow. Captain Jason Pritchard had his radioman raise Lieutenant Commander Riedell on the ship's private magna phone.

On the deck Riedell hit his Comm button on his Biv-pack. "This is 1 Hotel Sierra standing by to be boarded."

Gunnery Sergeant Lymon and his fifth Marines were coming alongside to relieve him of the prisoners and Sergeant Lymon answered, "SOCOM has just contacted us and you are to be deployed with your team immediately. The Libyan rebels have asked NATO forces to help keep the oil fields at Benghazi safe from Qaddafi's flotilla. Supposedly they have set limpet mines in the outer barriers. Admiral Maguire is sending coded transmission to you once you're aboard the Sea Knight."

Riedell replied, "That's a copy 1 Alpha Romeo. Will comply soon as your devil dogs take over."

Pritchard then handed the headset back to the ship's radioman. He headed back outside and picked up his binoculars to watch the fifth Marines as they boarded the rescued ship.

Time: 21:40 hours. June 7, 2011. Malaga, Spain.

JOHN PETER FERRIS

CHAPTER NINETEEN: RUN RABBIT RUN

Time: 07:10 hours. June 8, 2011. Dusseldorf, Germany.

After a wild night the Garrison unit made their way to the mess hall. Valerie Queen still had a slight limp from her boyfriend tackling her out of the way of a 30 caliber machine gun. Orion walked in with Lanny and Kendra and they noticed it right away.

Lanny walked over to the Duchess. "I want to see you in the infirmary right after breakfast, Duchess."

Valerie looked at her sister and replied, "It's just a little bruising, Lady Bee. I'll be fine. Besides, I've suffered worse."

Lanny gave her that motherly look. "I'll be the judge of that and that's an order. Okay, sweetie?"

Valerie laughed. "Okay sis, but I don't want to be pulled from the duty roster. I don't care how much it hurts. I'm going to be there when we rescue those kids."

Lanny replied, "I know that, girl. But I still might have to give you a cortisone shot to make it more comfortable, OKAY?"

Valerie hugged Lanny. "Thank you, sis."

They then headed for the food line and Orion conveyed to Kendra, "Did you look at the duty roster yesterday, Baroness?"

Kendra, surprised, answered, "I didn't get a chance to yet, Talon."

Orion with a devilish grin said, "You're with Alpha team this afternoon. It's your time to shine, girl."

Kendra jumped for joy and hugged Orion as her boot heel got tangled on the running board beneath her. Orion caught her before she fell. I hope you keep better balance and composure when you're deployed.

Kendra replied, "Oh, I promise. You can count on me, Sir."

Orion gave her a stern look. "I need you to focus, little sister, when you're out there. Okay?"

She affirmed as Lanny congratulated her.

The mess hall was now almost full and everyone accounted for when Captain Malloy came in and headed for the center of the room.

"EVERYONE LISTEN UP. I've just gotten a communique from Eagle One. It seems Musheen had the whole rescue mission broadcasted worldwide. Everyone on the planet saw his demands and the threats he imposed on us. Because of that, Eagle Two has told us to STAND DOWN. Too much political pressure from Washington has set the precedent. If we're even seen trying to countermand these orders I was told we could be fired upon. Well, what do we say to that, ladies and gents?"

From all around the room came comments like, "Fuck that," and "No freaking way," and "Who the hell do they think they are?"

Then finally from Claire, "I'll go by myself if I have too. Those babies are counting on us."

Malloy came over and put his arm around his niece. "That's my girl. Now if anyone of you feel opposed to Lady Hawke's philosophy, speak now. If not let me hear a big FUCK THEM."

The whole room, except for Lanny, screamed, "FUCK THEM."

Malloy looked at Lanny and held an open hand to his ear. "I can't stand cussing, but frig them," she said.

Malloy looked disappointed. "WHAT?"

She looked at her commanding officer. "All right, FUCK THEM."

Everybody started laughing hysterically and began clapping at the girl who just refused to curse. The only time she used foul language was in front of Orion, who kidded her, "Are you going to kiss me with that filthy mouth?"

Lanny smiled and slapped him on the shoulder.

He then planted a giant kiss on her lips. "Nope, nothing changed. Still delicious as ever."

Malloy walked over and said to Orion, "Merlin and Tank have the prisoner in the interrogation room. After breakfast meet me there. We then will initiate the plan you and Merlin devised."

Orion nodded. "Aye aye, Sir."

Kendra asked Lanny if this changed their mission. Lanny reassured her that she'd still be with them when they took off at 1300. Then from the side door of the cafeteria walked in Lieutenant Seka Sharon. She was the operator secretly known as the Nightingale and had been with the Israeli Secret Service the Mossad for eight years. With her was another operator from the IDF, Staff Sergeant Guri Hertzig, call sign SHOFAR. For years they had blended into the North African terrain as wealthy Turkish aristocrats and were a little weary of anyone affiliated with the CIA. But what intrigued the Nightingale to come aboard was the discovery that her dear friend and confidant by the name of Valerie Queen had also joined.

Nightingale wondered why Queen just disappeared right off the map. Now she knew why and couldn't wait to reunite with one of her closest friends."

Valerie reached for the pepper on the table and looked up to see Seka. "Oh my God, I don't believe my eyes."

Valerie walked towards her not remembering that she was still wearing a mask and that Seka would not recognize her. She held on for a second and waited for her friend to come by.

As Seka neared, her brow squinted a bit at something familiar about the masked woman in front.

Valerie said just as she was about to pass, "Well, well, well. If it isn't that famous secret agent Nightingale."

Seka turned in surprise and recognized the voice immediately. "Ahh, you must be the one they call the Duchess, am I correct?" They hugged as Seka whispered in her ear, "How you doing, Val?"

Valerie whispered back, "God, it's good to see you, Seka." She had her join them. Seka and Guri sat with Valerie and Trudy near Orion and Lanny's table, which was filled with Kendra, Bobby and Claire.

Seka and Guri met with Orion and Bobby an hour before. Malloy introduced them as they were coming in from their run. Malloy then took them over to operations to have them fitted for their special uniforms. Seka and Guri were part of Orion and Benny's plan to deceive Molaan Shavaaz. Part of their craft as actors and illusionists enabled them to gain entry into an enemy's inner circle.

Seka was another gorgeous raven-haired beauty who had men eating out of her hand. Joshua Golon always told her she should go to Hollywood because she was definitely an Academy award winner. One time in Morocco her and Valerie disguised themselves as high-priced call girls and captured two of the most wanted Al Qaeda money launderers in that part of the world. The criminals begged to get away as Seka threatened to castrate them. Malloy had heard of her exploits and wanted her in the organization immediately.

Seka asked Valerie why they were wearing masks in the mess hall. Trudy explained that Captain Malloy wanted it this way, even though the mess hall was located the center of the base. For security reasons masks had to be worn when they dressed in battle dress uniform from the center to the west side of the base. Since they were not in uniform yet, they were exempt for now.

Meanwhile, coming in from the east was a Boeing 747 jet owned by the science division of the Corporation. On board were two astrophysicists from the Hawaiian Islands. Professor Theodore Bertram and Professor Ronald Yamans began walking down the passenger ramp and were greeted by Jeffrey Pearson himself.

Ted Bertram and Pearson had known each other most of their scientific lives. They both attended science conventions all over the world and had shared more than one thesis on multiple topics, from nanotube construction to the theories of how to create artificial gravity in space.

Dr. Yamans had only met Pearson once and that was at the propulsion laboratory in Grand Island, Nebraska. Yamans was there to support the theory of Ionic Plasma Propulsion over that of fossil fuel and nuclear generators that would need water to keep them cooled. This was over two years ago when NASA engineers were listening to some of the best scientists in the world and had left everyone in the dark since. The proposals were given, but to this day no one knew of their decision. A lot was riding on it.

Because of the manned mission to Mars, Dr. Yamans heard of the launch of the Perseus prototype into space and now wanted to go over the findings in great detail. Pearson shook his two colleagues' hands and they boarded the waiting limousine to take them over to the guarded laboratory. Bertram and Yamans got a clear look at the ramp that took the Perseus spacecraft into space. They then came to the center gate that separated the west side to the east side of the complex.

As they pulled up to the Main building, Professors Stellarnberg, Livingston and Kruger were there to greet them. Professor Kruger told Pearson that Orion and the two wolves were with Dr. Darfuir down below in the operations laboratory. Pearson led them through the corridor to the private elevator, then peered into the eye scan monitor next to it. The voice print analyzer asked for voice recognition and Pearson spoke his name. The elevator s motor kicked in and they descended to the subterranean laboratory below.

Pearson brought them across a vast and intricate facility the size of a football field. As they approached the walled-in area to the right they heard, "Calm down, boys. It's only grandpa coming."

Dr. Darfuir opened the door and greeted the Professor just before he walked in. "We're all ready for you, Jeffrey."

But as the two scientists from Hawaii entered, the two wolves bared their teeth and started growling. Then their eyes began to emit the purple rays of light.

Immediately Orion yelled to his wolves, "STOP! They are friends. Calm down."

Both Dr. Bertram and Dr. Yamans had hair standing up on end. Pearson and Kruger helped their renowned colleagues to chairs on the other side of the room.

Bertram looked at Pearson and asked loudly, "WHAT THE HELL OF YOU BEEN DOING HERE?"

Slowly and surely Pearson and his team of scientists began to explain everything from November to the present and showed their colleagues the accumulated computer disks.

Dr. Ronald Yamans had a hard time taking it all in. That's when Dr. Darfuir whispered something to Orion, who began to concentrate. He lifted off the floor and almost nearly touched the twelve foot ceiling. The wolves automatically floated up to be with their master. Orion looked at both and they descended and sit on the floor. Orion then came down and the purple rays of light stopped generating.

Pearson asked the scientists to walk out to the construction area. "Do something!" he whispered to Orion.

Orion started glowing again and lifted a three ton forklift like it was a child's bicycle.

The two scientists from Hawaii were flabbergasted as they looked at each other in disbelief.

"If this is brought to life publicly, the lives of Orion and his companions will definitely be risk. Even though nothing to date has been able to harm him, who can say what some military war department would try to do? Pearson told them in confidence."

They returned to Pearson's office and he picked up the phone on his desk. "All right, sweetheart come down. We're ready for you."

The motor on the private elevator kicked in and door opened. Out stepped Lanny Cromwell, attired just like her boyfriend in battle dress uniform. Even with her mask on it was obvious what an attractive woman she was. She put on a big smile as she spotted her two dogs, then concentrated. The two animals rushed to her.

Pearson said, "You and John can both remove your masks. Our secret is safe with my two dear friends here."

Lanny punched her own personal code into her left gauntlet of her uniform. The electro-magnetic lock disengaged behind her head and she pulled off the mask. They saw her gorgeous blue eyes and facial features.

Pearson then said, "Teddy, Ronald, this is my daughter Lieutenant Commander Lanny Cromwell. She's soon to be the future Mrs. John Orion. These are both my children whom I love very much and I would do anything and everything to protect them."

The two scientists gazed at the couple and seemed worried about their safety. They then witnessed a love that was clearly abundant and their hearts began to melt. They then both explicitly vowed to keep this secret safe from the entire world.

Orion looked at their two wolves and telepathically instructed them to go over by Bertram and Yamans. Both dogs began licking them and making them feel at ease.

Dr. Bertram asked, "Are you sure they're not just taste-testing us before they decide to eat us?"

Orion said snidely, "Funny, you and my commanding officer seem to think alike."

Lanny scolded him and reassured the two men, "Just ignore him. He can be an idiot sometimes."

Orion grabbed her and gave her a big kiss. "Yeah, but I'm your idiot."

Lanny turned a smug face towards the scientists. "See what I mean?"

Carl Livingston cut in. "Gentlemen, not meaning to change the subject but we have a cosmic storm heading this way as I speak."

Pearson and Bertram immediately scoured over Livingston's new chart predictions and saw the time of arrival was just fourteen hours away. The last one in November didn't subside for at least ten hours. This time because of their notification to NASA, a lot of the satellites could be shielded from the harmful rays before it hit. NASA had already put the shields in place around the Hubble telescope. They also alerted the astronauts aboard the international space station to take cover in the safe room. Last time, the astronauts had just barely made it to safety.

Orion looked at his watch and told Professor Pearson that he had to meet Malloy on the west side of the base. He kissed Lanny and told her he'd see her at lunch before they went on recon at thirteen hundred.

Lanny helped her father entertain their friends from Hawaii.

Over at the interrogation and holding cells at hangar three Tank had Molaan Shavaaz against the wall and slammed him hard, then threw him to the ground. That's when Merlin winked at Tank while Molaan was not looking.

"One moment, Tank. I'm starting to believe him. He would've talked by now if he knew where Musheen was."

Shavaaz with a bloody lip screamed out, "YES, YES! I don't know where he is. He's constantly moving from place to place. I swear by Allah. Please don't let him beat me anymore."

From behind Guri Hertzig shoved a syringe to the side of Shavaaz throat. The terrorist immediately fell unconscious.

"Quick, put him on the table so we can go to work. I'm going to make an incision where he's already bruised up. Then I'll put the micro transponder in. He'll think the irritation is from the beating. The small tiny power source will transmit to us for only eighteen hours before it goes dead. I'm sure this prick will lead us to them in that amount of time."

Orion and Captain Malloy walked in as Guri was closing the area around the incision. Malloy asked Guri, "Have you given him our little present?"

Guri smiled, then pointed to the transceiver on the nearby table. He elaborated, "Our little knockout cocktail is only good for twenty minutes at best. Get Seka ready for her debut."

Orion confirmed, "Already done."

Valerie smacked her around a little to make it more convincing.

"Now I get to see our leading lady at work," said Malloy, who then told

Tank to follow him and Orion out to hanger four. From there they would watch the whole performance on hidden camera.

Benny moved the unconscious terrorist to an old army cot and waited for him to wake. Shavaaz was handcuffed to a one inch thick metal ring cemented to a series of rings set into the hangar wall. Inside the room was an intricate number of hidden cameras and next door a galvanized steel holding pen. It was more like a metal cage then a prison cell.

They were keeping Romulus and Remus there until the wolves busted the metal grated roof that covered the top of the cage. When this happened, they would have to be moved in with Orion and Lanny while the new housing units were still being built. This gave Orion the idea to leave it purposely broken for an escape while still having the appearance of a well-fortified holding cell.

It was the Nightingale's job to pretend to find it accidentally.

Shavaaz's eyes began to move and he slowly revived from the knockout cocktail. He noticed the right side of his head hurt with a stinging pain. His left wrist was cuffed to the metal ring in the wall.

Benny smiled as Shavaaz started to sit up.

Looking at the masked man in front of him Shavaaz asked, "What the hell did you shoot me up with?"

Benny got out of the chair. "Just a little bit of sodium pentothal. You know, the shit that makes people tell the truth. Oh we couldn't shut you up after a while. You told us everything from your liking little boys to the hiding places of some of your shit brothers."

Shavaaz laughed. "I guess you must think I was born yesterday. How can I give you information that I am not aware of? You're wasting your time. His Excellency has fooled you time and time again. Since I have no further use for your commando dress-up party, send me off to wherever you're going to send me."

Benny gave him a dirty look just as a small ambulance pulled into the hanger's giant open door. Driving was Lars, who pulled right up next to a Jeep Commander and then got out. On the passenger side was Valerie Queen who also exited. They went to the back and propped open both doors. Lars pulled out unfolded wheelchair and suddenly Seka came hurtling out and slammed to the ground all disheveled and cut up.

Valerie kicked her in the stomach. "Come on, bitch. Get up so I give you what you and your buddies did to those poor innocent people. BABY KILLER! Come on, get up."

Lars stopped her just as she was about to kick the prisoner again. "DUCHESS, I know what she's done, but she can't walk, remember. The good thing is, she'll never walk again. The Nigerians want her back for trial anyway. She'll be beheaded when we turn her over to them." Lars then cradled Seka in his arms and put her into the wheelchair.

Seka was sniveling and crying uncontrollably. "Please, I had no idea what they were going to do. I'm telling you, I was only driving the car."

Benny yelled, "Sure you did, bitch." Then he made a chopping motion alluding to her upcoming beheading and opened the metal cage door so Lars could wheel her in.

Shavaaz saw how badly she had been beaten. "You know this is against the Geneva convention."

Lars with an angry face said to Benny, "Merlin, give me the keys to his cuffs."

Benny handed Lars the keys and Lars unhooked Shavaaz, then backhanded him across the cell. "WE don't FOLLOW ANY FUCKING GENEVA CONVENTION. We do what the fuck we feel like."

Benny then interrupted him. "Yo, Tank, I'm friggin' hungry. Let's go eat. Besides, the doc wants to examine her to see how bad that back is anyway. You can beat him to death when we get back. We have no further use for them anyway."

Lars threw Shavaaz inside the cage with Seka and watched him painfully get up. Lars locked the metal door and gave both prisoners an evil laugh. "I'll be back in an hour, muffin. Then I'll stir and batter you. Ha, ha, ha."

Benny, Valerie, and Lars hopped into the Jeep Commander and drove off laughing.

As the Jeep vanished through the hangar door, Seka said with a gasp, "We've got to get out of here before they kill us. The big one over there snapped my cousin s neck. We have to figure a way out of here before they get back." Seka stood up and began to walk around, slowly checking the outer perimeters of their cage.

Shavaaz's eyes opened wide with confusion. "Holy Shit, you are able to walk."

"Of course I can," she replied sarcastically. "If that bitch knew it she would really lay into me. That bomb had a shockwave big enough for me to fake this injury. These scumbags caught us as we were just about to cross the border into Ghana. I was laying down in the back of the truck when we were captured. From then, on I pretended not to be able to walk. But still that phony hair colored cunt smashed me around. My cousin Tarkees was tortured for hours in front of me. That big piece of shit killed him even after he told them what they wanted to hear. My back is killing me but I still need to get out of here. They know where the next target is."

Shavaaz asked, "Who are you, my dear?"

"My name is Shuri Hawassi. I am an Egyptian freedom fighter. Since they overthrew the government my organization has been trying to get rid of Western influences in the country."

Shavaaz looked at her with regret. "Unless you have strong bolt cutters, Shuri, I think we are doomed,"

Seka replied, Do not think that way. What is your name, anyway?"

"I am called Molaan. You are very beautiful, Shuri."

Seka put on a shy look. "Why thank you, Molaan. But I need to get out of here. I'd rather die than have myself raped in prison for the rest of my life."

Seka then started testing the steel mesh around the enclosure. After five minutes, she looked disappointed and sat back on the cot. With her hand to her forehead, she said, "By Allah, this is hopeless." Then with tears coming from her eyes, she leaned up against the wall and looked up at the ceiling.

"Wait! What about the top of this birdcage? Maybe it's worth a try. Molaan, help me. See if the top of this cell is secure."

Molaan stood on his cot and pushed on the ceiling grate. With a surprised look he noticed that it moved and grabbed one of the folded-up cots, then pushed it upwards against the meshed ceiling. It rose with no problem.

"Look at this, Shuri. These imbeciles have made it easy for us and they don't even know it." He hugged her. "Allah is here with us, Shuri. I'll climb out of here and find something to get this door open."

After about six minutes of maneuvering he was able to squeeze himself through the top of their cell to freedom, knowing he had to move fast. In his mind he knew the hour was almost up and started smashing a fence pipe against the lock of the door that kept Shuri imprisoned. After another five minutes he dropped the pipe and looked disgusted.

"I don't know what to do, Shuri. They'll be back soon and I'm getting nowhere. I can't leave you behind."

Seka said, "You have to leave, Molaan. I could never make it through the ceiling of this cage, anyway. They'll be here soon. You must get away. I need for you to contact my sleeper cell and get word to them. You must tell my superior that INTERPOL now knows of our plans to attack the American Embassy in Paris."

She had him memorize a phone number and told him to only talk to a man named Daehli and say "The laundry is ruined."

Molaan then headed towards the open door but stopped and looked into the ambulance. The keys were still in the ignition and he laughed and opened the driver s door. Then he noticed an EMT uniform shirt and with cap lying next to a folded up gurney. He dressed quickly, started the engine and hit the gas. As he rolled out of the hangar and approached the western gate he became nervous, but the security staff just waved him on through. He gleefully made his way south to imminent freedom.

When he stopped at a light twenty minutes into his journey he saw a large four foot case with the writing GUARDIAN COMPONENT, marked ANIMAL ONE. He wondered what the hell was in the case as he drove on.

Time: 11:14 hours. June 8, 2011. Dusseldorf, Germany.

Time: 12:03 Hours. June 8, 2011. El Hambra Mountains, Libya.

A courier arrived at the mountain hideaway where ten kidnapped children from around the world were being held hostage. Omar Khaldif was there to meet the messenger. As he opened the note a look of concern came over him. He then crumbled the message and walked towards where the kids were being held.

CHAPTER TWENTY: KILL THE MESSENGER

Time: 14:30 hours. June 8, 2011. Heidelberg, Germany.

The Al Qaeda operative Molaan Shavaaz had escaped his captors and was now heading east away from the main highway. He noticed that up ahead a motorist was changing a flat on his BMW. The man was an elderly gentleman in his late 60s. Shavaaz slowed down and pulled in front of the BMW, then got out.

The old man grabbed the tire iron, seeing that the man approaching was not of German descent.

Shavaaz asked in English, "Do you need help?"

The old man, as best he could, told Shavaaz that he didn't speak English.

Shavaaz, who spoke French, asked the same thing again.

The old man replied in French that he was just finishing up his task.

Shavaaz politely said, "I think I'm lost."

The old man asked where he was going.

"Baden-Baden," said Shavaaz.

Smiling, the old man told him he was going the wrong way and that this was the road to Stuttgart. He instructed Shavaaz to turn around and head back to Mannheim, and then go south straight to Baden-Baden. He also asked why Shavaaz was driving an ambulance from Dusseldorf this far south.

"I'm transporting a frozen kidney and need to reach Baden-Baden as quickly as possible," Shavaaz explained.

"You should hurry. New construction starts every day on that highway two hours from now," urged the old man.

"Merci beaucoup," said Shavaaz, who got back into the ambulance. He pulled a little further down the road, then made a U-turn and stopped.

The old man saw this and wondered why Shavaaz had stopped. He saw

Shavaaz look around the ambulance, then shut his trunk and slowly pull away.

The old man finished fixing his flat tire then made his way back to the driver s side of his BMW. The ambulance sped up at a high rate of speed. But just as the old man believed everything was all right, the ambulance at the last second veered off and slammed into him. He was killed instantly as he flew into the bushes nearby.

Shavaaz immediately pulled to the back of the BMW and walked over to the dead old man. He reached into the corpse's pockets to find the keys and opened both the trunk of the BMW and the back of the ambulance. He grabbed a large case marked GUARDIAN COMPONENT and threw it into the trunk of the BMW and quickly retrieved the dead man from the bushes and put him in the back of the ambulance.

Shavaaz took off the cap and shirt and threw that in the ambulance, also. He helped himself to medical supplies, then looked inside the BMW and put the old man's cell phone inside his pocket. He then closed the back of the ambulance and drove it into the woods to hide it as best he could.

"Danke schoen, you schweinhund." He jumped into the BMW and headed back towards Mannheim. When he finally arrived, he made a left and headed south towards Baden-Baden. Then he pulled the cell phone from his pocket and called Faraz Saphan, Mustaffa Khaldif's head lieutenant.

Shavaaz explained his situation and told Faraz he needed papers and a passport to get out of the country.

Faraz told Molaan to go to the Braunstein resort in Baden-Baden. A cottage right at the edge of the Black Forest would have reservations already made for him. He reminded Shavaaz to make sure the car was ditched in the forest.

"I will leave Zurich immediately and be there in three hours."

"Talk to no one until I get there. I'm making arrangements to get you out of Germany," instructed Saphan.

Time: 15:45 hours. June 8, 2011. Mannheim, Germany.

Time: 10:10 hours. June 8, 2011. NBC news Washington Bureau office, District of Columbia.

A messenger from the Al Jazeera s Washington DC office handed a manila envelope to Hannah Delguidice, secretary of the chief editor of publications and broadcasting. Hannah opened the envelope to see a piece of paper that read: PLAY ME NOW. From the sealed plastic DVD jacket she shook out a DVD and inserted it in her computer. It began the playing sequences from a masked terrorist from a broadcast of four days prior.

She blurted out in the busy news office, "OH MY GOD."

Her assistant came over just as Hannah ejected the DVD and put it back in the jacket. She rushed over to the office of her boss, Leo Kretsky, and charged in.

"Leo, this just came in from our friends over at Al Jazeera."

Leo loaded the DVD and his brow furrowed with worry. "Are we the only news channel with this right now?"

Hannah replied, "Chief, I just got it five minutes ago from Yuli. He's the only one from Al Jazeera who delivers packages to me."

"Have Frieda call Andrea Mitchell and tell her we've got something big," ordered Leo.

Hannah reminded him that Andrea was out of the country on assignment. Leo then grabbed his open line to the White House and got his bureau chief on the line.

Patty Carpino answered the phone and listened to her boss for the next two minutes. "I'll alert the White House Press Secretary," she told Leo.

"A young woman was beheaded on the disc and I'm calling the Censor Chief," informed Leo. He hung up with Patty and instructed Hannah to have her assistant call Harold Laramie, who needed to get up there pronto.

Hannah opened Leo's door and yelled to Frieda Kaufmann, "Summon Mr. Laramie to the chief's office."

Leo asked Frieda to burn two copies of the DVD before Laramie arrived from downstairs. "I wonder what the president is going to want to do when he sees this," he added.

Time: 10:45 hours. June 8, 2011. Washington DC.

Time: 17:00 hours. June 8, 2011. Dusseldorf, Germany.

Kendra Pearson was just about to change out of her battle dress uniform when she heard the commotion coming from outside the women's locker room. She had just finished her first ocean drop with flying colors, but swallowing a bit too much salt water on her first time out didn't agree with her stomach.

As she made her way into the hangar she saw most of Alpha team around the television with their faces in a state of shock. She looked at image of one of the chaperones, Kerry Bannister, who was kidnapped along with the children.

Kerry Bannister had eaten dinner with Kendra and Claire the first night on the Queen Beatrice. All of them became very good friends and Kendra wondered why her photograph was on television in Germany.

From the front of the hangar Bobby and Claire approached Kendra with sympathetic faces. Tears rolled from Claire's eyes as she told them Kerry had been beheaded by Al Qaeda as a reminder to the world that Musheen meant business. Worse, it was done in front of the children to create more horror for the world to see.

The voiceprint from the masked man who executed Kerry came back 91% positive as belonging to Omar Khaldif. Claire told Kendra that they edited the beheading, but not the screaming children. Right after the beheading, and over the screams of the children, Khaldif reiterated the same demands his boss Musheen had conveyed. Once he was done talking the DVD faded to black for about five seconds, then Musheen reappeared still hiding behind a stupid polka-dotted neckerchief he always wore.

Kendra stared at the television as CNN repeated the broadcast and painfully watched the horrifying replay. But then she noticed Carly, who was not screaming. It was obvious she was horrified but was doing something with her hands. Kendra yelled out, "Is there any way we can get a copy of this?"

Claire looked at her sister, bewildered. "Yeah, but why, Kendra?"

"Claire, you didn't see what she was doing with her hands. CLAIRE, she was using sign language! She showed me once how good she was at it, especially when she was talking with the deaf girl from Greece. I need to see it right away because Poppa showed me how to sign a long time ago."

Claire ran to the phone directly connected to Malloy's security office and punched her clearance card into the side of it. She told Kendra to get out of her uniform, because they were going to the Skipper's office on the other side of the base.

Kendra sped off to the locker room as Malloy picked up.

"What's up, Lady Hawke?"

Claire replied, "Our Baroness has just picked up something on a recent Al Qaeda broadcast, Sir. We'll be arriving in about ten minutes."

Lanny followed her little sister into the locker room just in time to see Kendra tossing her cookies.

Orion noticed you turning pale just before we got back. "Here, take these." Lanny gave Kendra her two pills. "Orion said not to be ashamed. He barfed too on his first time out on ocean drop. Next time, you learn to keep your trap shut. "

They both laughed as Kendra removed her secured mask from her face, pulled off her gauntlets and hurried out of her uniform. They ran to the awaiting Jeep. Lanny hit the gas and sped across the giant airfield to the center checkpoint. The guard waved them through without a problem.

As Claire reflected on Kerry she start sniffling with despair.

Kendra comforted her. "I know, sweetie. I was really fond of her too."

Claire then looked at Kendra and Lanny. "Why are they killing people who would never even hurt a fly?"

"BECAUSE they're friggin' cowards," exclaimed Lanny angrily. "They only go after those who can't defend themselves. Look what they did at the World Trade Center. They had a day care center there too. Try not to let it eat you up honey. I know we'll get those creeps."

Lanny raced up to the main building and pulled right up to their father who waited at the door. They ran to greet him and then headed for Malloy's office. When they get there Kendra knocked on the commanding officer's door.

Malloy yelled, "Professor, you know you don't have to knock. Bring your three brats in with you too."

They all walked in to see the captain looking at the eight surveillance security screens on his wall and realized this is how he knew it was them. But they also noticed Orion and Benny looking at a large GPS computer.

Guri Hertzig pointed to an area and said, "He hasn't moved from that spot now for about twenty minutes. I'll bet you anything he's waiting for a contact so he can get out of the country."

Lanny walked over. "What are you guys doing?"

Benny replied, "We tagged our prisoner with a tracking device when he was unconscious. Now that we've let our little rabbit escape we're hoping he'll lead us back to their lair. Right now he's at the northern edge of the black forest and seems to have stopped for a while. Once we see that he's left the country we're hoping he'll lead us to the other assholes who are holding the kids."

Malloy asked Kendra, "Claire tells me you saw something on the broadcast. What did you see, girl?"

Kendra asked Malloy to replay the broadcast. As everyone watched they all seem puzzled until the edited version of the beheading came into view.

"Make it go into slow motion," she instructed. "There. See? Carly is using her hands. Poppa, look at her hands."

Pearson realized the little girl was using sign language and began to interpret: I am in Libya. We are being held two hours South of the ocean.

But as she made the sign of an M and a T the tape faded to black, and then five seconds later Musheen appeared.

Benny looked at the Skipper. "A very smart and brave little girl there. But two hours south of the ocean? Well, we know the ocean reference means the Gulf of Sidra. But that's a huge spread of water with over 1000 miles of coastline. If only we could see more of her message. "

Malloy's face became distraught. "We are now running out of time. In five hours that solar flare will be hitting the Earth and all satellite communications will be rendered useless. I don't know how Musheen knew about it, but he does. Otherwise he would have told us the drop-off point ahead of time." Malloy stood and walked around. As he peered outside his window he spoke to himself. "Just what are you up to, you fucking evil bastard?"

Guri then reminded the Skipper, "Captain, remember that we've been warned not to interfere."

"I KNOW, I KNOW," came Malloy's curt reply. "Jeffrey, do you actually think that spray you and Dr. Darfuir have concocted will work?"

The Professor responded, "Well Jim, I know when we combined a phenol and chorominium compound, the chorominium spray turned a glowing purple when exposed to the uranium. They will not be able to pick up on the chorominium element because it gives out no residual effect. But once you add the depleted uranium to the equation, it reacts instantaneously. I've made just enough for you to give to Eagle One. So if you're going to mark the gold and diamonds you better get it to them now."

Malloy nodded. "I will send it by courier to the naval office in Marseille. I'll let Eagle One know of our plan. Since they want the gold and diamonds put on a mining barge anchored fifty miles south of the island of Malta, this probably means they plan to transfer their booty to another seagoing vessel. How much do you want to bet it'll be a certain hijacked Russian submarine?"

Lanny interjected, "Can't the Navy trail them without being detected?"

Benny, disgusted, replied, "We wish it was that easy. But Musheen explicitly said that any sign of a warship or submarine would constitute deception. He said he would instantly retaliate by killing the children. The one thing that really pisses me off is that he now says he'll do it in front of the world. Eagle One has already conveyed to us that an unusual amount of fishing and recreation boats are now starting to clutter that area of the Med. Most likely, they're his watchdogs to make sure there are no unexpected surprises from us."

Malloy cut in. "Now it would be another thing if we knew where they were going to unload it… "

A knock interrupted. Malloy looked at the security screens and saw Dr. Darfuir with Shaleem standing in front of his door. He hit the unlock switch. "Come on in Professor. We've been waiting for both of you."

Both entered and Shaleem smiled as she saw Lanny. Lanny's face lit up and she asked Dr. Darfuir, "Professor, how is our patient doing today?"

Darfuir replied, "She is getting much stronger day by day."

Lanny walked over and kissed Shaleem on the cheek. "Glad to see you, Shasha."

"And I am so glad to see you too, Lanny," replied the princess.

Dr. Darfuir said, 'Well Jeffrey, I told her what you needed her to do and she immediately agreed and can't wait to get started."

Professor Pearson pulled out a little box and opened it, then dropped about twenty sparkling diamonds into his hand. He put them on the Skipper's table as Dr. Darfuir handed him a spray bottle. Pearson explained as he sprayed the diamonds with the special concoction, "Kamal and I have devised this solution of phenol and the element from the mountain in the Congo. Now that I have sprayed the material onto these precious stones, I'll introduce them to depleted and safe amounts of the element uranium."

As he sprinkled a minute mist from another spray bottle, Orion began to illuminate with the rays of purple light. But at the same time Shaleem pulled out the sacred amulet she had worn since she was a little girl. The talisman was also radiating the same recognizable glow that came from Orion.

Everybody in the room was in awe.

Malloy interrupted, "We have proposed to Eagle One that the gold and diamonds be put in crates with metal banding around them composed of a very small amount of the depleted uranium. There won't be a high enough concentration radioactivity to alarm the terrorists. But the combination of the metal banding and the solution sprayed onto the gold and diamonds will be able to illuminate the princess' amulet as well as our executive officer's impregnable body. Now I want you to watch what happens when gold is introduced to both solutions."

Kendra reluctantly came forward and handed her father a velvet purple ring box. Pearson said to Orion and Lanny, "Both of you come to me now."

Orion and Lanny looked at each other with bewilderment and walked straight over to the Professor. Pearson elaborated as he opened the box, Kendra's mother Arlene and I were married with these rings. You are both my children now, and you would both honor me and Kendra if you would accept them for your upcoming wedding."

Lanny immediately began to cry as Orion hugged the man who had given him a new life. Claire and Kendra both came over crying and began hugging all of them together.

Malloy interrupted. "Ahem, ah, Jeffrey to the business at hand please."

Pearson said, "You're right, James. Just one second. I want to make sure they fit."

How weird that the rings fit them perfectly. Lanny looked at Kendra. "Are you sure, little sister? This ring should be yours on all accounts."

Kendra hugged Lanny and tearfully replied, "If it wasn't for Johnny coming to save my life, I wouldn't be here to share in your joy. You're my big sister and he's my big brother and I love both of you beyond compare. So please, in the memory of Arlene Pearson and Margaret Vanderkamp, accept these rings."

Lanny hugged her as she also looked at Claire. "With all my heart."

Malloy yelled, "Okay, now that you're done and it's all over, THE RINGS, PLEASE."

Claire once again put her foot in her mouth. "What a fucking grouch." Then she caught herself. "Ooh, I'm sorry, Skipper."

Malloy slapped his right palm to his forehead. "Please, can we continue?"

Orion and Lanny laid their new rings on the top of the table as the Professor sprayed them with the Chorominium solution. He then sprayed more of the same solution of depleted uranium onto the rings. Immediately the glow became so strong that Malloy had to cover them with books.

Orion and the amulet still glowed, but not as much.

Dr. Darfuir yelled, "Put the rings back into the box!"

Orion pulled the books off and neatly tucked the two rings into the velvet box. The glow around him and Shaleem's talisman stopped immediately.

Pearson instructed Malloy to put them in a safe.

Malloy with a smile said, I think, boys and girls, this just might work. He asked Dr. Darfuir, Is she able to travel?

Darfuir answered, Why don't you ask her?

Shaleem looked at Malloy. "Oh, I'm just fine and I'm going to do everything possible to catch my father's murderers."

All the sudden Guri yelled, "The signal just went dead."

Orion walked over and asked with concern, "Are you sure, Guri? Maybe it's just a slight malfunction."

Guri replied, "I'm afraid not, Commander. This only happens if it's removed or the subject is dead."

Benny gasped with disbelief. "What else can go wrong now? We better pray this spray will work."

Time: 18:30 hours. June 8, 2011. Dusseldorf, Germany.

Time: 18:12 hours. June 8, 2011. Baden-Baden, Germany (northern edge of the Black Forest).

A knock finally came to the cottage door where Molaan Shavaaz had been waiting for the arrival of his other comrade of evil. Molaan approached the door holding a large knife from the kitchen drawer. "Who is it?"

From outside the door he heard, "It's me, Faraz. Open the door quickly, Molaan. We don't want to arouse suspicion."

The door opened and both men hugged each other with respect.

Faraz said, "Allah be praised. Thank God you were able to escape your captors. Tell me, have you talked to anyone else since your escape?"

Molaan replied, "No Faraz. I've done just as you instructed. But I've stolen something that this so-called Global Garrison neglectfully forgot to put away." He showed Faraz the large case marked GUARDIAN COMPONENT: Animal One.

Faraz opened the case inscripted with TOP-SECRET. He removed the cover to see a computer DVD disc setting atop a weird looking harness with the strange metal discs placed all around it in different sequence.

"Molaan, go and shower right away. We have a long journey ahead of us and must leave as soon as possible. Transportation has been set up, so hurry."

Molaan rushed into the bathroom and got undressed. Faraz heard the shower turn on and waited thirty seconds before walking into the bathroom. He opened the shower curtain holding a Sig Sauer 40 caliber pistol with a silencer on the end.

"Final destination, ahh yes, Nirvana," he mocked as he shot Molaan, whose dead body crumpled to the bottom of the tub. Faraz walked back to the other room. He re-packed the case and walked out the door, locking it behind him.

Time: 18:35 hours. June 8, 2011. Baden Baden, Germany.

Time: 23:25 hours. June 8, 2011. Dusseldorf, Germany.

Solar shields were implemented around the three main telecommunication and spy satellites. Professor Stellarnberg activated 18 VLF antennas to try and compensate for lost communications. He then contacted the two new bases being constructed in Upernavik, Greenland and the other in the vicinity of the Mauritius Islands. Once that was done he activated the VHF antennas to work at different intervals from the VLFs.

After twenty-nine minutes all of the sixteen outposts around the world checked in to confirm they were in working order. Stellarnberg looked at the wall clock: 24:00 hours, the Witching Hour.

JOHN PETER FERRIS

CHAPTER TWENTY-ONE: SHINE ON, YOU CRAZY DIAMOND

Time: 07:05 hours. June 9, 2011. Dusseldorf, Germany.

Inside the mess hall on the western side of the base the units of the Global Garrison gathered to eat. All television, cell phones, or any computerized gadgets that relied on satellite interface were now rendered useless. Confusion and disorientation convened throughout the elite organization.

Malloy had since doubled the guard around the entire perimeter of the bases worldwide. He now arrived at the chow hall to see utter chaos amongst his elite troops. Knowing something like this might happen, he came prepared, carrying a bullhorn, which he used as he stood on the officer's table.

A loud burst wafted across the cafeteria and had everybody shutting up and looking at the captain.

"People, listen up. I kind of told all of you what to expect yesterday. Seems no one took it to heart. We still have an expected eight to ten more hours of this shit. Now this goes for everybody. I need all of you at your very best. In three hours the ransom will already have been delivered. Now we have no way of communicating because of the cosmic radiation. All satellites around the world are completely shielded. We have to do everything old-school. I did it in Nam and so did everybody else back in those days. We need comprehensive teamwork because the outside world thinks after the ransom is paid, the bastards will let those innocent kids go. We know better. They'll kill them soon as their hands are on the booty. Lady Hawke, I want you to assemble Alpha team. Make sure all their weapons and gear are stowed. Galahad and Merlin, make sure there are comfortable accommodations for Sasha because she's going with you.

Wheels up in forty-five, so eat real fast."

Malloy then gestured for Orion to come over. As they talked Wolfman and Dante came into the hall. Lanny and Tank began watching what was going on, because the Blazing Trident was set to follow the Viking Avenger an hour after their takeoff.

Suddenly, Patrick Tinsdale came in followed by the British contingent of the units. Orion and Falcon were the mission commanders on the Blazing Trident. The Duchess and Luna were also with them. Cuda would be going with Lady Hawke at her request.

Once Wolfman finished showing Malloy the photographs he slipped them back in a folder and headed over to share them with Lanny. He sat down across from her and Galahad and gestured for Merlin to look, also.

"You guys, look at this picture taken when the Duchess flew over the El Hambra Mountains the other day. We caught a glimpse of a man at the top of this particular bluff. Notice he's armed with an AK-47, but he's in the middle of nowhere. Also look in his left hand. He's holding a walkie-talkie. Come on, these things are only good for a twelve mile radius. If that's true, Lady Bee, what we need of you to do is fly over again at the same point, but at a much lower altitude to photograph this time. Also, make sure you implement the bafflers because we need you to be silent, as well. Lady Hawke is going to fly the Libyan coastline in the meantime. At 13:30 hours both of you will be back here so we can review our intelligence. After that we'll plan our strategy from there. The reason we want you to fly over is so Talon can be with you. We need to have the Trident cloaked so she can't be seen.'

Then he looked at Claire. "I'm going to be with you in the Avenger. Since we can't scout the area of the Med that is off-limits for now, we'll scout the outer reaches of the North African coastline. Hopefully the princess' amulet will illuminate and give away the enemy's position."

He then informed that they would undertake in-flight refueling with the air units KC-10 and KC-135. Raven (Liam Faraday) and Albatross (David Banks) would be on both VHF and VLF frequencies. They were set to take off right after 15:00 hours. This would be after the mid-day briefings.

They knew they had to stay in the air before the ransom would land in the clutches of Musheen's henchmen. Claire reached across the table and pulled out the photograph of the man on the mountain. She looked one more time and said to the table, "We'll find them."

Time 07:25 hours. June 9, 2011. Dusseldorf, Germany.

Time: 07:00 hours. June 9, 2011. Gulf of Tunis, Carthage, Tunisia.

After hiding out for the past two days, Captain Vladimir Kozlovski got underway and headed out for the Gulf of Tunis to rendezvous with the mining barge anchored fifty miles south of the island of Malta. As the Damocles made its way out to sea, Kozlovski radioed ahead to his spotters who were spread out in positions only Kozlovski knew about.

The spotters were in various types of boats aligned to pick up on any approaching vessel that entered a special designated grid area. But not only boats traveled this grid line. Musheen had deployed single-engine aircraft to safeguard the pickup point.

Omar Khaldif had also given Kozlovski a Geiger counter and different ultraviolet and black lights to see if the ransom had been marked. He was also equipped with the state of the art radio and bug detection devices.

Kozlovski was told by Khaldif that if any type of tampering was done, he should sink the barge and relay word of the deception back to him immediately.

Time: 07:25 hours. June 9, 2011. Carthage, Tunisia.

Time: 08:00 hours. June 9, 2011. 150 miles south of the city of Tajura, Libya.

Omar Khaldif told his men to be prepared just in case they had been deceived by the people who were supposed to be paying the ransom for the safe return of their children. One of his henchmen, Tariq Peshwan, gathered up the kids and brought them to the main part of the mountain. This was where the terrorists watched from six screens to see if anyone was approaching.

Only a hundred feet away was a thirty-five foot opening with two surface-to-air missile battery launchers. Next to each one of them was an American-made Ma Deuce (50 caliber) machine gun. The opening was now closed but would open automatically if the mountain hideout was compromised.

Omar Khaldif had been given orders that if any sign of a rescue attempt were to come to his compound, he was to throw the children eighty feet to their deaths through the thirty-five foot opening. Tariq made the ten children sit against the wall just outside the security camera room. Omar pulled a large Persian saber from out of a case and laid it down on the table where his guards attentively watched for any type of rescue attempt. Omar awaited confirmation of the ransom being paid.

He said to the frightened children, "Now we will see if your parents love you as much as they say they do. If not, they get a consolation prize of having your heads come home in a box." As he went back into the security room Carly tried to comfort them and promised that help was on the way. But Melania Karaditos read her lips, then signed to her that Carly was giving them false hope. Carly immediately reassured her in sign language that their time of rescue was drawing near. The coded sign language assured that the other children would not overhear and would remain calm.

Time: 09:10 hours. June 9, 2011. Tajura, Libya.

Time: 10:08 hours. June 9, 2011. Site of the mining barge fifty miles south of Malta.

The submarine Damocles surfaced alongside the barge containing the ransom of gold and diamonds. Kozlovski told his crewmen to watch the skies for aircraft attack. He then told his men to go over the booty and look for any signs of tampering and markings. They used two different Geiger counters with ultraviolet and special illumination lights to detect any kind of residue on the precious gems and gold, then smiled and told Kozlovski the cargo was safe to put on board the submarine.

Instantly Kozlovski ordered the crew to hurry and load it so they could be underway. Fifteen minutes elapsed and job was just about done. Kozlovski told his chief to cut the anchor line to the mining barge and let it go adrift.

Lifting the last crate of gold, the evil captain looked to the sky and laughed. "They paid up. The rich fucks actually paid up." He then hurried his men down the conning tower and shut the hatch. The Damocles slowly disappeared beneath the calm waves as she headed for the northern coast of Africa.

Time: 10:47 hours. June 9, 2011. 240 miles north of the Libyan coastline.

Time: 11:05 hours. June 9, 2011. Sokna, Libya.

Passing over the vast oasis in Sokna, Libya, Lars Olsen opened the port and starboard camera lenses that were fixed under both wings. The Blazing Trident was about to make its third Sordi reconnaissance pass over.

Seeing the mountains starting to appear in front of them, Lanny implemented the bafflers to the outside engine ports. Lars, being the RIO radio intercept officer today, had to use eye confirmation and land-based maps to navigate the Avenger to a more easterly pattern than the Sordi before. Lanny feared that all the reconnaissance they took all morning was merely a futile attempt at nothing. She conveyed her concerns to Falcon and Orion.

Percy told her to think positively. Percival Nelson, being a devout British Catholic, also knew that Lanny Cromwell had British blood coursing through her veins. He reminded her that God could answer prayers only if the pure of heart accepted it.

Lanny lowered the altitude of the Trident and said, "You're right, Sir. She'll only help if I bring my heart to her."

Percy was astonished, but before he could say anything Orion tapped him on the shoulder. "Oh, you really don't want to go there. I'll explain later."

They then noticed the engines of the Trident eased up and the super jet began to slow down for aerial photographs. Orion knew that was the cue for him to power up and put the Trident into cloaking mode. The mountains were right in front of them and Bedouin tribesmen looked up to see the incredible super jet disappear before their very eyes.

Meanwhile 320 miles to the north the Viking Avenger was about to reverse course and head back west along the Libyan coastline. With each Sordi the Avenger had taken Claire had also lowered altitude for readjustment.

Wolfman reminded her that she shouldn't go too low, otherwise the rebel forces fighting Qaddafi's army might mistake them for his forces. After having just passed Tobruk, they approached the city of Bardia. Wolfman raised Dante on the VHF antenna and reported no success at this time, and to let the Skipper know that they would RTB (return to base) after the next run.

Now to the South of them Lanny had the Blazing Trident close to the area where Valerie flew days before. She pressed the onboard cameras and the shutters began to take dozens of pictures as they flew over.

From the back came Luna who had been peering through a pair of high resonance binoculars to the ground below. He conveyed to Orion and Percy that he had seen what appeared to be three, maybe four, men on top of the mountain below.

Orion immediately asked Lanny if she could turn around and repeat the flyover. She smiled at her fiancé and began to drop the left wing to do so. The warriors resembled lions spotting prey. The glow from Orion's eyes become more eerie and mystified. In the cockpit Lanny, Lars and Carl felt the thrill of the chase. Percy called Paddy Tinsdale over and showed him the mountain terrain below.

As they passed over the spot where the men were seen Falcon asked the Griffen, "Do you think you're flying suits could put you right there from thirty miles out?"

Paddy replied, "Well, as long as you drop us from 25,000 feet with oxygen and stabilizers, they'll never know what hit them. "

Hans von Dietrich had his doubts. "You must have a damn ego, or you're just crazy enough to think that.

Maverick started laughing. "He's the best HAHO and HALO jumper I've ever seen and I'll bet you he's probably more proficient in those funny-looking suits."

Paddy put on a crazy face. "Nah, Maverick, I'm just fucking nuts."

Boomer (Darnell Crawford) and Mantis (Michael Wong) yelled from the back, "We must be nuts too, because we're going with you. The new guy back at the base is probably also doing it."

Orion, still concentrating, asked, "What new guy?"

Mantis told Orion that the Skipper said it was a surprise.

Now as the mountain range slowly began to fade, Lanny pushed the throttle forward and the wheel back. The Blazing Trident climbed and disappeared as they headed back to base.

Meanwhile, the Viking Avenger passed into the Gulf of Gabes in

Tunisia and the Princess Shaleem's talisman started to light up, but very weakly on and off.

Wolfman told the RIO, Michael Trudeaux, to mark the area on the map where the amulet illuminated. He looked down at the topography and saw that they just flew over Gabes, Tunisia. He glanced at Claire. "I'll bet you anything they're in the Gulf and the reason we don't have a good fix is because they're still submerged in that damn submarine."

When Claire turned the Avenger around the amulet's signal did the same thing and disappeared while they were over the water. Claire said to Trudy, "I think you're right, Duke. Let's bring this back to the Skipper and see how he wants to call it." Claire then pushed the throttle forward and her wheel back as the Viking Avenger disappeared heading north towards Germany.

Time: 12:02 hours. June 9, 2011. Gulf of Gabes, Tunisia.

Time: 11:47 hours. June 9, 2011. Aboard the submarine Damocles, Gulf of Gabes, Tunisia.

Holding the ransom of diamonds in his hands Kozlovski watched as they become bright. He began to wonder if it was magic or if his evil voyage had been cursed.

CHAPTER TWENTY-TWO: WHERE THERE'S SMOKE, THERE'S FIRE

Time: 14:45 hours. June 9, 2011. Dusseldorf, Germany.

Captain James Malloy, still pondering the danger facing his tactical team of men and women, called the officers of the elite organization to his security office. Once they assembled Malloy passed out duplicate photographs. Each officer held one folder containing their entire reconnaissance mission from earlier that day.

Standing next to Malloy was Master Chief Benjamin Kramer. Benny and Orion were just about to reveal their cultivated plan to the officers who would be carrying out the dangerous mission. Malloy said to Benny, "Merlin, the floor is all yours."

Benny began with, "Everyone, please take your dossiers and examine the first shot from the Trident's camera. This one was taken as the Trident was on approach. If you look closely you'll see metal tubes with smoke coming from them at the eastern side of the slope. Now notice as the Trident is practically over it.

Everybody examined the photo and with the help of the base's photo-lab it was apparent that each position revealed what appeared to be chimneys. Emplaced sentries stood about forty feet from each metal tube. Two of the guards held AK-47s, while the third was at a slightly higher elevation and equipped with a PRK and bipod, twenty meters above their positions.

Benny commented, "How about that? Out in the middle of nowhere somebody needs three heavily armed sentries to guard it? Hmmm, I wonder. Now people, go to the next photograph and you'll all see surveillance from the other side of this particular mountain."

The unit commanders instantly noticed that the other side broke away from the range for at least a mile, then the range continued for another two miles. Enlarged photos revealed numerous carved-out roads leading to this particular mountain.

Benny elaborated, "Notice now how the whole area around the two-mile area had been demolished and excavated. Now, in the next photograph… " He motioned for them to flip to the next one. "You'll see that the top of the summit is also conveniently air-vented and air-conditioned. Unit commanders, notice the enlarged area with commercial-sized blower fans and base compressors for air-conditioning."

Then Benny instructed them to look at the next photo, thermal induced. As they studied it Claire instantly blurted out, "BINGO! Well what do ya know, all lit up like a fireplace for everyone to see. "

The thermal imaging showed little children walking on the other side of the enclosed mountain. In the middle was a tall man wielding an assault rifle and pointing his finger in the direction of the children. As the unit commanders examined the tiny infrared silhouettes Claire said, "That's positively the children. I remember the funny-looking hat little Ruah Kahsesky had on her head. See the odd shape that accents the back rim? You might as well put a glow-in-the-dark nameplates on them." She looked at the Skipper and saw him smiling with enthusiasm.

Percy looked at Lanny and said, "Looks as if your prayer has paid off."

Malloy replied with reservation, "Not so fast, we still have to get to them without tipping off the sons of bitches. We've intercepted a radio transmission that came out of Djerba, Tunisia. From what we've interpreted they are awaiting cover of darkness for the Damocles to surface. Now let me bring your attention to the same photograph, only this time we've used a spectral illumination analysis."

The unit commanders flipped to the next photograph but were confused.

"Okay boys and girls, you're all probably wondering what the big deal is. Well these funny different colors show what elements from which they are derived, plus show us the contour of what it exactly is. Now I turn your attention to the area we just identified where the children are being held."

Everybody saw an area about thirty to forty feet long. It was about eight feet high and didn't start until it was about almost six feet up from the floor.

As the group peered at the image Malloy explained, "Dr. Livingston told me that the blue spot on the screen is solid steel. Now look above the bluish green area."

Everybody noticed an olive green-colored area.

"Carl Livingston, AKA Poindexter, told me this is a composite of nickel and zinc. EVERYBODY, GUESS WHAT? This is a riser that holds a steel picturesque window in place. If you look above the riser, you'll see it's attached to what looks like a beam of steel above it. I also asked our good Professor Livingston what the two things on both sides of this window could be."

Malloy explained that Professor Livingston examined it thoroughly and determined from its compositional make up that it was, in fact, machine gun emplacements and possibly a surface-to-air missile battery.

"Tell me, don't you just love this scientific stuff?" continued Malloy. "Well there's more good news ahead as you turn to the next photograph in your dossiers. "

The unit commanders saw the two-mile opening end as the last mile of mountain range came into view. Benny walked to the front and started to talk.

"Everybody, if you look towards the ground you'll see they've constructed a path just wide enough to get a large truck or bus into their canyon hideout. Now as you look at the next photo I turn your attention thirty feet up and on both sides of the road."

The unit commanders grabbed the next photo and saw it was enlarged. Immediately they noticed circles drawn around about five armed sentries on both sides.

"Well, well, well. What have we got here? Looks as if they're going to stop anyone they want from coming in or out. Benny shut down the computer. We have just one more picture, but it's not from the Trident. Instead it's from the Avenger. Duke, you did the smart thing by activating the onboard cameras as soon as Shasha's amulet began illuminating. Seems we have one more surprise I guess we can all appreciate."

The next photograph revealed a periscope out of the water and in full view. Benny conveyed to all of them, "The Skipper contacted Eagle One just in case it was one of ours. The admiral got back to him to say it was not one of ours. As a matter of fact, right now the battle group task force USS Guadalcanal is secretly enroute to prevent any escape by the stolen submarine. Captain Jason Pritchard is the commander of the battle group aboard USS Antietam."

Malloy conveyed to Lanny, "Lady Bee, you're not flying the Trident tonight. I need you and Dr. Darfuir on the Viking Avenger. You're a skilled surgical nurse and God forbid if any of the team is severely wounded. We need you in theater to help save lives if the need should arise."

Lanny looked at Malloy with pride. "I understand completely Sir, and agree with you all the way. Besides, the Duchess is getting to be one crack ace pilot herself."

Malloy shook his head. "Sorry Duchess, I need you with the Baroness on the assault on the mountain. Those kids have been through a living hell. They'll need the comfort of a female's distinctive voice when we rush them out of there. You understand this can only be to their benefit."

Valerie looked at her commanding officer. "No need to explain, Sir. Besides, someone has got to watch over my little sister."

Kendra smiled at Valerie as Malloy reiterated, "Not just her back everybody's back. IS THAT CLEAR, EVERYONE?"

The unit commanders shouted, "HOO YAH!"

Malloy then told his officers to debrief their units because it would get dark just around 19:40 hours their time. He conveyed that Alpha and Delta teams would be in full gear and on the tarmac at exactly 19:30 hours. Wheels up and take off time would be exactly 19:40 hours.

As they stood to leave Lanny began to feel nauseous, then grabbed her stomach. Orion instantly put his arm around her

"Are you all right, baby? Are you sure you can do this? I mean if you can't, I'm going to tell the Skipper right now."

Lanny's eyes popped out of her head. "No, please don't. I just have an upset stomach. I'll take a couple of Nexiums and will be fine. Come on my love, you know I can't miss this."

Even behind her mask Orion could see her baby blue eyes sparkle. "Okay Commander, but I'm now ordering you to get some rest. So take your pills and then lie down. I'll wake you in an hour before we have to gear up."

Lanny kissed her fiancé passionately. "Thank you, sweetheart. I love you so much."

Orion turned her by her wrist and slapped her softly on her bottom. "You better get some rest because after this is over you're going to need it. I'm getting what I want from you later." He winked at her as she wrapped her left arm around his waist.

Laughingly, she responded, "We will see, we will see."

Time: 15:50 hours. June 9, 2011. Dusseldorf, Germany.

On the airfield to the western side of the base trucks arrived with the special ingredients they would put in the JP-500 jet fuel. This would replenish both of the super jets.

CHAPTER TWENTY-THREE: SUMMIT SALVATION

Time: 19:15 hours. June 9, 2011. Dusseldorf, Germany.

As the units of the elite members to the Global Garrison began to assemble on the tarmac, a Cadillac SUV arrived to send them off. Getting out of the Cadillac were the Professors Pearson, Kruger, Darfuir, Stellarnberg and Livingston. Everyone began to laugh as they spotted Dr. Darfuir in his new battle dress uniform.

Darfuir was a short and pleasantly plump man, his height only five feet four inches. With the mask on he looked like one of those blue meanies from the movie Yellow Submarine. Valerie started singing the famous song when the good doctor reminded them he was still their boss.

Lanny came over and kissed him on the forehead. "Professor, you look adorable in that uniform. Just ignore them, Sir."

Darfuir with a smile said to Lanny, "Thank you, my dear. At least some of you are grown up."

But as he entered the Viking Avenger Lanny couldn't help herself and covered her mouth to conceal the laughter.

Professor Pearson came over to witness the Garrison forming together for their dangerous mission. Looking at his daughters, he first said to Kendra and Claire, "I know Arlene Pearson and Margaret Vanderkamp are looking down at you right now and are so proud of you, as I am at this very moment. I love all you girls so much, so you all better come back to me or I'll be mad at you." He then looked at Valerie and said, "You, my dear, even the toughest of the men fear you. But remember, those fanatics will blow themselves up along with you to cause agony and grief. Duchess, you're in my family now so please come back in one piece."

Then the Professor headed over to Orion and Lanny who were standing with the rest of the units. "Well if you must know, you're all my children now and I would be devastated if anyone of you were killed."

Trudy came over to stand in front of them and the units. "If it weren't for you, I wouldn't have a law degree and I would never have been reunited with my brothers in arms. Don't worry Professor, we have the greatest secret weapon of them all. With Orion and that belt, we will be unstoppable."

Orion looked around and was glad the Skipper hadn't yet arrived. Looking at the entire unit he replied, "So you think it's my belt that carries us into battle, and with its help, victory. But if you think for one minute that we rely on this noble component that replenishes my power, you are surely mistaken. For as the Professor noted, we are now one family and I need every one of you by my side. YOU ARE Orion's BELT. I am nothing without all of you, and never mistake it again. I will die for you, or even alongside you if I have to. So my brothers and sisters, let's go kick some fucking ass."

As Malloy arrived he heard, "Hoo Yah" and lots of cheering coming from every member of the units. Malloy got out and walked over. "You must've said something to enlighten them a bit."

Oh, I just said, "Let's hear it for the Skipper, and they all just went nuts," answered Orion.

Carl Livingston came over and said to Malloy and Orion, "Skipper, within two hours our supercomputer predicts that the cosmic storm will relinquish its grip from around the planet. Just know that not only will the satellites go back online, the rest of the world's will also."

Benny overheard what Carl had just said and came over, adding, "Skipper, we have live television feed cameras on the front and rear of both of these planes, do we not?"

Professor Stellarnberg interrupted. "Yes we do, but only if the jets are flying under pressurized capacity."

Benny thanked the Professor, but pulled Orion and the Skipper to the side for a secret conference. They talked for about three minutes, then both of the Jets began firing up their engines. Malloy had a devilish face, as he and Orion nodded with approval to Benny. That's when Cochise(Joe Coffey) yelled to Orion and Benny, "Commander Talon and Master Chief Merlin, time to go."

Orion and Benny saluted the Skipper and then ran into the back of the Viking Avenger. The Avenger started its taxi towards runway one. Claire initiated the pre-lighting sequence as the super jet made its way out to the area for takeoff. The Blazing Trident began to follow suit as it made its way out to runway two.

Flying the Trident was Condor (Carl Bingham). His copilot was none other than Albatross (David Banks). Banks made a laughing comment, "Feels a little bit like déjà vu, huh Condor?"

Carl smiled. "Sure does. Now let's go get those kids and bring them home safely to their parents."

Aboard the Viking Avenger the Alpha team got a real surprise. Donald Tremaine, Admiral Fischer's second-in-command, stood waiting to greet Orion and Benny as they headed for their seats.

Orion saw him and immediately put on a smile. "Well if it isn't Eagle One's executive officer."

Tremaine replied, "Yeah, but it's ex-executive officer. Lieutenant Commander Firebird reporting for duty, Sir."

Benny piped up, "Nice call sign. I like that, Firebird. Welcome aboard."

Tremaine smiled. "Glad to be part of the family, Merlin."

"The Skipper told us he had a surprise for us. So I guess you're jumping in with Griffen's team," said Merlin.

Firebird responded, "Yeah Merlin, but I'm to land above point B so I can drop lines down to the surface strike team. The wind is coming from the Southwest and right now it's only at eight knots. But without satellite Intel, who knows if it's going to pick up. I just hope the conditions stay the way they are for now. Everything depends on me clearing that drop point and taking out the sentry up top."

Benny laughed. "I think you'll be fine. If the Skipper and the admiral have that much faith in you, so do we. Ah... but do me a favor... "

Firebird grinned. "Sure Merlin, anything."

Benny pointed to his mask and said, "Put your mask on and be glad the Skipper's not here to see you with it off."

Firebird immediately put it on. Thanks, Merlin, I'll catch on.

"Don't worry about it, Firebird, assured Benny. "You're my superior officer. That's my job."

Tremain replied, "Hoo Yah."

Inside the cockpit Claire awaited clearance from the tower to take off. Lars went over the checklist one more time when the tower signaled It's a go. Claire pushed the throttle forward and the Viking Avenger hurtled down the runway. As soon as she was airborne the tower gave clearance for Carl to take off with the Trident. Carl pushed his throttle forward and took off down the runway to follow their sister ship into the sky. Within ten minutes both of the super jets converged on the northern part of the Mediterranean.

Lady Hawke dialed in the coordinates for the Avenger to fly over Algerian air space. She needed to have the Viking Avenger come in from the south. The jump team would deploy once they were thirty miles from the target. The Blazing Trident would be its backup if something went wrong. But it would also be looking out for Qaddafi's Air Force. If they were discovered, Carl's orders were to blow them out of the sky.

Meanwhile, inside the mountain hideout of the evil Omar Khaldif a radio message came in from the lookout sentry on the other side of the canyon. He conveyed to Khaldif's radio operator that the Damocles would surface in exactly one hour. Kozlovski let him know that ransom had been received with no problems whatsoever. Omar Khaldif began to celebrate with his henchmen as the frightened children looked on. But Khaldif wanted confirmation from the two radar units that were in place thirty miles to the west of their position. Hidden in a camouflaged bivouac net to the west of the mountain was a well concealed radar unit watching to see if any rescue attempt was being attempted by NATO forces. Seeing the existing air space was even clear of birds, they radioed back to him the all clear signal.

Back in the mountain fortress Khaldif closed up shop. He told Tariq Peshwan to get the rest of their men together for their journey to Gabes, Tunisia. The radioman told Khaldif that Kozlovski would be moored at the designated spot in the Djerba in ninety minutes. Kozlovski conveyed they were to be underway as soon as they arrived in two and a half hours.

Peshwan asked Khaldif where they are going to release the children.

The evil bastard answered, "We're going to throw them over the wall down by the corridor in a little bit." He laughed as the children gazed at him in horror.

The little boy from Jordan, Yasi Kesmara, told Carly secretly what he just heard. When the other children overheard him they began to cry for their parents.

Carly, keeping a cool head, told them that crying would not help them.

At the bottom of the canyon Khaldif's men removed a giant burlap blanket off the top of a bus that had brought the children there. It was covered with sand and dirt to blend into the surrounding terrain. The men begin gassing up the tank for the upcoming ride.

Time: 21:05 hours. June 9, 2011. Ghadames, Libya.

Flying in from Algerian airspace, the super attack aircraft Viking Avenger crossed southwest over Ghadames, Libya. Looking at their watches, Alpha team synchronized their bezels at five minutes.

Lady Hawke's voice came from the cockpit to the rear of the plane. "Prepare to deploy, GRIFFEN."

Paddy Tinsdale (Griffen) stood up with Boomer (Darnell Crawford), Mantis (Michael Wong), Firebird (Donald Tremain), and Tank (Lars Olsen). Standing by to jump three minutes after were, Benny Kramer (Merlin), Valerie Queen (Duchess), Kendra Pearson (Baroness), Kada Bondi (Cuda), and Mike Maguiness (Mustang). They all fastened their oxygen masks as Joe Coffey (Cochise) opened the vertical rear door for the jump.

Cold air immediately swarmed over the rear cabin. They all checked pressure gauges and adjusted stabilizer valves. Everyone checked each other's gear and chutes before giving the thumbs-up signal.

The purple light went on and Griffen jumped instantly. Following him were Boomer and Mantis, but Firebird looked at his watch to deploy with Benny's team. The only difference was that he would be doing a H.A.L.O. jump while Merlin s team would be doing a H.A.H.O. jump.

Benny's team was to land two miles from the opening to the mountain pass so that the Sentry thirty-five feet up didn't spot them as they landed. But Firebird's job was to come right above the sentry who was armed at the highest point with the PRK machine gun. Once he took him out, Firebird would signal Merlin's team to come forward silently as he lowered ropes to them.

Once Firebird was in the zone, he was to go to the offensive firing position and began shooting the other sentries with his suppressed M-110 Knights assault rifle.

Orion studied his unit proudly and saluted them as they jumped and disappeared into the skies above Libya. He awaited the signal from Tank as Claire began to lower the left wing of the Avenger. She waited until the indicator showed she had done a complete 180 degree turn, then leveled off to bring the super jet back. She then began reducing speed and lowered the altitude while they awaited confirmation.

Time: 21: 20 hours. June 9, 2011. Tajura, Libya.

Above the planet Earth the first satellites back online were those of Pearson Global Technologies. Slowly the danger of the cosmic radiation came to a close. Instantly the satellite components interfaced, lighting up the console of the Viking Avenger and the Blazing Trident.

As this was happening a shadowy figure came up from behind the sentry on the mountain where the kids were being held. Griffen was now only twenty feet behind them. Tinsdale pulled his lanyard release and his chute hurtled away as he slammed into the unwary sentry. Two seconds later and wearing NVGs (night vision goggles), Mantis and Boomer repeated the feat and dispatched the other two sentries.

Two miles across the canyon and coming from above, the sentry holding the PRK was dispatched by Firebird. But just before he was on top of him, the guard decided to look up. Instantly Firebird fired a double tap into his center mass and killed him. Tank looking from the other side breathed a sigh of relief.

Knowing he was being watched by Griffen's team, Firebird gave them the hand signals they had been waiting for.

Tank radioed the Viking Avenger, "Griffen and Firebird both in the roost."

Lanny aboard the Avenger replied, "That's a copy, Tank. Sending in the SANDMAN."

Orion told Cochise to wait a minute while he conferred with Lanny and Claire. He opened the door of the cockpit with the security code and stuck in his head. "Lady Hawke, you know where to position the plane. I'll be there, but just remember, if I'm not onboard the Avenger for at least twenty minutes it will become visible again." Orion eyed both of them closely and continued, "I know it's dangerous, girls, but just keep the bafflers going and hover steady. Now get me in close as you can. My passengers await."

Lanny's face was overwhelmed with concern. "You be careful. I love you and you better come back to me."

Orion smiled and kissed her, then closed the cockpit door.

Claire saw the mountain range ahead and began her descent. Meanwhile on the other side of the canyon, Tank broke through one of the air ducts that lead down into the fortress. Boomer and Mantis were almost through their positioned air ducts, as well. Once done they signaled each other that they were ready.

Tank radioed across the canyon to Firebird, "Tank calling the Wizard."

Benny, who had just reached the top of the ropes that Firebird dropped for him and his team, answered, "Merlin here. I read you loud and clear Tank."

Lars replied, "Hope you and the ladies are ready, because the SANDMAN is on his way."

"We're getting into position, Tank. Wish us luck, answered Benny.

Tank replied, "See you in a few."

Benny handed the headset back to Firebird and signaled for the Duchess and the Baroness to follow him up the slope. Meanwhile the Avenger flew slower as it approached the beginning of the mountain range. Cochise had already opened the vertical door and looked at Orion as he began to illuminate ferociously with the familiar, yet still eerie, purple light. Cochise saluted the impressive hero as he floated out the door and hovered. Orion stayed motionless, then returned his salute. He then swooped his hands to the sides of his thighs and flew towards the mountains below.

Lanny from the copilot's seat beheld the spectacular sight of the man she loved defying the laws of gravity before her very eyes. Below on a small slope of the mountain, three members of the elite Garrison watched in amazement as the silhouetted figure of purple came hurtling towards them. Almost upon them, it slowed down to reveal Orion.

He yelled to all three of them, "Hang on, because here we go!"

Kendra gasped as they were lifted from the slope into the air. Orion bundled all three of them, picked up speed, and headed toward the terrorist hide out.

Inside Carly Sinclair had noticed cans of insecticide by the door. Four cans stood next to a cleaning bucket just under the table that held a coffee pot and microwave oven. Suddenly one of the guards screamed in Arabic. Yasi Kesmara translated for Carly that the purple man had been spotted again. Suddenly confusion and chaos spread throughout the entire fortress.

Carly saw her opportunity and ran to the door, snatching the insecticide cans. She threw them into the microwave oven, then turned to the other kids. "COME ON, LET'S GO," she ordered. "They're here to save us!"

Yasi knew Melania was deaf and grabbed her hand to help her stand. Now all the children were on their feet and glimpsed the television monitors in the other room. They saw an amazing man glowing purple on the screen and flying towards the camera.

Carly instructed the children to run down the corridor outside the opening where she just put the cans into the microwave. One of the men watching the monitors saw them and alerted the other guards. Carly timed herself as she saw the men jump up. She set the microwave at full power and then ran to join her companions in their attempted escape.

The guards entered the now-empty room and were about to exit when the microwave exploded, propelling them to the floor. Meanwhile on the outside, Orion lowered Benny and the girls to the ledge then flew back up to the enormous steel opening. He slammed into it, toppling it inwards. Retrieving his comrades, he brought them inside to find the kids.

Orion told Benny to take the Baroness and go left, while he and the Duchess would go to the right. "Don't worry, the force field will protect you," he assured them.

As Kendra and Benny pressed on to the left, she said, "Merlin, how can the force field protect us if we move farther away?"

"It's all in the plan, sweetheart, don't worry. Now keep your eyes and ears open."

To the right, Orion and Valerie reached the first right turn in the corridor and heard tremendous gunfire. Rushing ahead they saw Paddy, Darnell and Michael firing nonstop toward whatever was coming at them.

"Griffen, how many are there?" asked Orion.

Paddy looked up at his commander. "We took about sixteen of them out, when all of a sudden these things showed up."

Orion looked down the end of the passageway and was astonished at what was coming at him. Two robots standing ten to twelve feet tall were now clanking his way. Orion immediately told his team to head back towards the other opening.

"I'm staying," informed Valerie.

"Leave!" Commanded Orion.

Valerie complied, making it about thirty feet before disobeying and heading into the prone position with her assault rifle.

Standing behind the two giant robots were Omar Khaldif to the left and Tariq Peshwan on the right. Laughing wholeheartedly, Khaldif sneered at Orion. "Like my little play toys, you FREAK? My brother Mustaffa said you would probably make an appearance. So we made these masters of destruction to get rid of you and your pathetic existence."

He pushed one of the controls, instantly causing machine guns to appear from each arm of the two robots. They fired at Orion simultaneously, yet the bullets appeared harmless and simply dropped to the floor. But from behind Orion heard a moaning sound.

One of the fifty caliber rounds hit Valerie's force field. It protected her, but the compression of the force threw her back ten feet into the wall.

Worried, Orion yelled, "Duchess are you all right?"

Valerie regained her composure, just shaken up a little bit.

"When I give you an order, you obey it. Understand me?" yelled Orion.

"I'm sorry boss," she apologized.

"No problem, sweetheart. Now get back towards the Avenger. I'll be fine."

Valerie picked up her Beowulf assault rifle. "I'm going to help Merlin," she informed before running toward the other side of the corridor.

Khaldif sneered, "How touching, but none of you are going to make it out of here alive. Now, Tariq!"

Suddenly 40 mm grenades come flying at Orion like a machine gun. Explosions occurred everywhere as the mountain crumpled in ruins. As the smoke began to clear, no sign of Orion was evident.

Khaldif and Peshwan yelled joyously, "WE'VE KILLED THE SON OF A BITCH!" They jumped up and down with glee until Orion walked up and tore an arm off a robot. He smashed it like a tin garbage pail.

Khaldif and Peshwan ran in horror fearing what he might do to them.

After dismembering the robots, Orion pressed the transmitter button on his Biv-Pack and asked, "Did you get that, baby?"

From the other end came Lanny's voice. "Sure did, show off! Come on honey, let's get these kids back to their parents."

Orion replied, "I'm on my way, Lady Bee." Spotting an opening created by the grenade blast, he illuminated and flew outside as the powerful glow engulfed his body.

On the other side of the compound it appeared Carly's escape plan only half worked. Some of the children did not follow her as she instructed and could not be found. Carly, Yasi, and Melania were captured by Khaldif's men right in front of the wall, now missing its steel opening.

Khaldif and Peshwan laughed hysterically as Khaldif taunted, "Thought you could escape, you little rich bitch?"

Khaldif then looked at five of his men. "What happened to that assault team?"

His radio operator replied, "I don't know. They just left. But your Excellency, we've just gotten word from the Damocles and it seems they are surrounded in the harbor."

"What have you done with the other children?" demanded Khaldif.

Smiling, one of his men responded, "Some of them may be hiding. But we just threw two of them over the wall to their deaths."

"Well, what are you waiting for? Let these three join them!" ordered Khalif.

All the sudden, Benny came around the corner and was instantly disarmed by Khaldif's men.

"Remember me, Omar?" challenged Benny.

Khaldif instantly recognized his voice. "Oh by Allah, my enemy is delivered unto me. Yes, you are the Jew who pretended to be Muslim. I thought we killed you, Fashir, back at the Holland Tunnel. I guess the magic tricks you performed for those old hags back at the mosque in Jersey aren't working now. Your illusions aren't going to help you and these fucking brats now, are they?"

"Let them go, Omar. It's me you want," spat Benny.

Khaldif replied, "I've caught all of you! Now Tariq, throw the boy over the wall."

Little Yasi's tears streamed out of his eyes as he screamed for his mother and sailed over the wall.

"Save the Cullen girl for last," ordered Khaldif who then ordered Tariq to throw the little deaf girl over the wall. Melania was immediately tossed to her doom.

As Carly screamed for her daddy, Benny picked her up.

"Drop her!" Omar yelled.

Benny countered, "Let me jump with her to ease her fear."

Khaldif and his men laughed hysterically. "Go ahead Jew, show the little bitch how to swan dive," enticed Khaldif.

Benny climbed atop the 68 inch wall. "Hand me the girl."

As they handed over Carly he whispered, "Do you trust me?

She was about to answer when one of Khaldif's men from the monitoring room yelled, "This is being broadcast all over the world! I don't know what's going on, but I see the kids coming out the window and then they just disappear."

Carly nervously said to the strange masked man, "I do trust you."

Benny said to the evil Khaldif, "How about this trick, Omar? ABRACADABRA." He climbed to the ledge with Carly and jumped from the wall, hand-in-hand.

The man from the monitoring booth showed Khaldif a view from his laptop, revealing that Benny and the little girl started to fall but then immediately disappeared. Khaldif spun around and sprinted for the small ladder that led to the 50 caliber machine gun and looked out. There in front of him was the super jet Viking Avenger hovering in place as the elite crew strapped all of the children safely into their seats.

Khaldif's eyes become enraged as he spotted Orion, feeling humiliation that the whole world was watching a miraculous rescue eighty feet above the ground. In a spiraling rage he set the breech of the 50 caliber.

Shots rang out twice, but it wasn't Orion or the children who caught the bullets. Instead, Khaldif slumped over the machine gun. The Baroness lowered her smoking M4 assault rifle and yelled, "Let's get out of here quick!"

Cochise shut the door and pressed the intercom button. "We're ready whenever you are, Lady Hawke."

The loudspeaker answered, "Make sure all the children are strapped in securely, because here we go."

Carly's face lit up. "Claire!"

The woman next to her tapped the girl s shoulder. "Shhh, Carly, don't say any names.

Carly teared up and without making a sound mouthed, "Kendra."

Kendra pulled her closer and put her finger in front of her lips.

"I knew you would come for all of us," whispered Carly, still crying.

Claire pushed on the throttle and hit the transmitter button on the console. "USS Antietam, this is Lady Hawke of the Global Garrison. You are now cleared to fire on those coordinates we sent you."

Over the loudspeaker of the Viking Avenger came, "That's a copy Lady Hawke. Congratulations to you and your commendable team."

From the A.S.R.O.C missile battery aboard the USS Antietam, two Tomahawk cruise missiles were unleashed. This was broadcast to demonstrate that the unified world meant business and would not tolerate the atrocities of Al Qaeda. On the other side of the canyon, the Viking Avenger hovered while Orion brought the rest of the unit on board.

Claire spotted two inbound objects on the radar screen heading their way. "Everybody hang on! None of you have had a ride like this."

Orion, who always loved a thrill ride, played a CD from the group Kansas, plugging it into the main intercom. The ending melody of Sweet Child of Innocence floated in the cabin as the Viking Avenger hurtled into the sky.

Claire looked into the rear viewing cameras to witness the mountain fortress being blasted from the face of the Earth. In tears, she commented, "This is for Lena, Sharisse and Kerry."

From over the radio came, "Viking Avenger, this is Captain Jason Pritchard, Commander of the USS Antietam, over."

Claire hit the console button to transfer to her headset. "We hear you Captain Pritchard. This is Lady Hawke, captain of the battle aircraft Viking Avenger, over."

Pritchard then said, "Lady Hawke, Eagle One has advised that you contact your commanding officer, over."

"That's a copy, captain, will do," replied Claire. "Please advise Eagle One that all the children are present and accounted for, over."

All over the world people were listening to the transmission and burst into cheering. The children's safety came as an answered prayer and the president standing in the Oval Office slumped back into his chair with a sigh of relief.

Captain Pritchard replied, "Roger, Lady Hawke, over and out."

Obsessing over their television in Mocha, Abdullah Musheen and Mustaffa Khaldif were in a rage. Tears of anger flowed from Mustaffa's eyes. They've killed my brother! I don't care what it takes, but I'm going to make them wish they were never born. OH ALLAH, give us the strength to carry out our sacred Jihad against these infidels."

Musheen comforted him. "We will avenge the death of your brother, Mustaffa. His sacrifice has given him martyrdom. His name will be spoken in reverence to Allah. We will destroy that freak of nature and his so-called Army. Then we will bring the West to their knees."

Now flying a low ceiling above the Gulf of Gabes, the Viking Avenger came upon another delightful scene. Below the forces of the U.S. Navy and Tunisian Navy were leading Captain Vladimir Kozlovski from his submarine. They took him onto the deck of one of the destroyers from the USS Guadalcanal battle group. Coming alongside the Avenger was the Blazing Trident, contacting Claire as they rode alongside. An encrypted message came across instructing them to go to a secure channel.

Lanny immediately turned on an outside jamming signal to prevent anyone but the Trident from listening. Pressing the transmission button she said, "Nice to see you, Condor. Hope you're keeping good care of my aircraft, over."

Carl laughed and replied, "Your baby is safe with me, Lady Bee, over."

"How did they get him to surrender, over?" asked Lanny.

Carl replied, "Well, we kind of blew up a proximity mine about forty feet in front of them, over."

Lanny laughed. "Yeah, I guess that would kind of do it, over."

"What I would do to see Kozlovski when he comes face-to-face with Vladimir Putin. I would pay to see that, over," commented Carl.

Lanny laughed again, but then wanted to know why the Skipper was keeping them airborne. Carl explained that if they turned the kids over in Germany, the captain was afraid of being compromised at the secret base.

Claire overheard and told Lanny to contact the Skipper because she had a good (but crazy) idea.

Lanny relayed this to Carl and then broke communication as Claire asked Valerie to come up to the cockpit. The Skipper called in and Claire shared her plan.

"If you can convince your two friends, I'm all for it. I'll tell your father to wait for his call," said the Skipper.

Valerie reentered the cockpit, but at that instant Lanny grabbed her stomach in pain, this time almost doubling over.

"LANNY, WHAT'S WRONG?" screamed Valerie.

Orion with his keen sense of hearing zoomed into the cockpit. No one in the back had any idea what was going on. Orion grabbed Lanny out of her copilot seat and immediately took her to the rear for an examination from Dr. Darfuir.

Orion's face was full of concern. "Doc, do something! She looks terrible. What's wrong with her? Please help her!"

Professor Darfuir replied in a calm voice, "Hold on there, son. Let us have a look." After an intensive five minute exam with his stethoscope Dr. Darfuir looked delighted. "My child, have you been feeling nauseous in the morning?"

Lanny replied, "Yes doctor, and just recently a little more each day."

"Has your appetite increased and do you crave foods you don't normally eat?"

"Yeah Professor, but what has that got to do with it?"

"Did you not tell me you are unable to conceive children?"

"Yes, I was told that long ago. It's impossible."

Dr. Darfuir exclaimed, "IMPOSSIBLE MY ASS! My dear, not only are you pregnant, but there are two heartbeats!"

Kendra instantly screamed in joy, "Oh my God, I'm going to be an aunt!"

Orion was flustered and stuttered, "I'mmm… gonnnna… be… a… daddy?"

Feeling weak at the knees he bent over to see the happiness in his woman's eyes, then kissed her passionately. "I love you, baby!" he rejoiced.

Word reached Claire inside the cockpit and tears came to her and Valerie s faces. Claire told Valerie to make a very special phone call. Valerie punched a coded sequence into her phone then dialed the number. The phone rang about four times before someone picked up on the other side.

"What's up girl? Are you watching all the excitement on TV?"

Valerie cut her off. "PIPPA we need a very, very, big, big favor. Do you think you can call Katie and ask her to talk to her father-in-law? He's great buddies with my father, and this is more important than you'll ever believe." Valerie explained that Kate's father-in-law must get back to her father right away.

At that precise moment in the rear of the Viking Avenger while everyone celebrated, Orion stood up and announced, "I'm going to be a dad." Then he fainted, but before hitting the floor hovered ten inches from the deck.

Lanny said loudly, "THE INDESTRUCTIBLE TALON can defeat almost anything—but is a wuss when it comes to children." Everybody laughed hysterically as they reveled in the momentous occasion.

CHAPTER TWENTY-FOUR: FROM THE MOUTHS OF BABES

Time: 23:11 hours. June 9, 2011. London, England.

At Heathrow International Airport in the United Kingdom, the Viking Avenger and Blazing Trident taxied to a specific area. Reporters from all over the world tried to glimpse the group of men and women who had just achieved the impossible. Only a select group of reporters and photographers were allowed to see the children disembark from the jets.

Their parents eagerly awaited as the two jets finally come to a stop. The eerie purple strobe lights had everyone in awe, and photographers flashed their cameras as the rear vertical door slowly opened and hit the ground. As their parents slowly approached the rear of the Viking Avenger, the children came running with arms wide open.

Part of the royal family was also in the crowd. Cochise (Joseph Coffey) approached the Princess of Cambridge and her sister Pippa only to be stopped by guards. Immediately the Princess called them off.

The royal females talked with Cochise and then followed him into the jet to see first-hand the tired but amazing unit. A woman in a unique uniform and mask caught their attention.

"Lanny!" cried Pippa.

Lanny smiled from the comfortable bed. "Yeah, it's us, Pippa. Tell your military thanks for letting us land here."

"That's no problem at all, girlfriend," responded Kate. "But this is very hard to take in. It seems our friends are part of an elite secret organization that has been stunning the world since last year." She leaned over and kissed Lanny on the forehead. "I just picked out my dress for your upcoming wedding, and now I hear you're expecting."

Kate looked around recognized Orion behind his mask. "And you,

Tarzan, you have to take it easy with my girl here. Oh my God, TWINS!"
Then standing, she said, "Don't worry about your secret, it will always be
safe with us."

A strawberry blonde head could only be one person and Kate headed to
Valerie and hugged her. I know our countrymen and women of Great
Britain are proud of the noble warrior born here. I've never been so proud
of your service.

Valerie in tears replied, "Thank you, your Highness."

Kate then laughed, "Don't pull that 'your highness' shit with me,
girlfriend." They hugged and conversed with everybody for another three
minutes.

Lanny told Kate and Pippa, "We'll call you in about two weeks after we
get some rest back in the states."

"Will you do a photo op for the London press?" asked Kate.

Lanny threw her feet around and got up.

"Lay down!" scolded Orion.

She shot him the look. He shut up immediately.

"Get ready everyone," she commanded.

Claire called the Trident and instructed Condor to bring their unit to the
outer edge of their vertical door. Valerie asked Kate if she would introduce
them as the Global Garrison and not disclose any names.

Kate agreed and headed out with her sister. With the podium set up she
tested the mike. "Ladies, gentlemen and members of the press, I just had a
delightful conversation with these extraordinary and incredibly brave
members of a noble and distinct organization. They are mysterious to us all
and remain anonymous not only to protect themselves, but to relay to us an
understanding of cooperation amongst the peaceful countries of our planet.
They've asked us to let them coexist and be helpful in any way that
preserves the prosperity of our unpredictable world. I've asked them to
confer with the press. But please make it quick, for I am told they have
pressing business awaiting them elsewhere. So ladies and gentlemen, I give
you the Global Garrison."

The unique unit walked in unison down the ramps of the two
formidable jets. Flashes of light added brilliance to a dark night sky. Orion's
eerie light engulfed his body. But now the light completely enveloped
Lanny's body the same way. Surrounding the tarmac were sounds of gasps.

As the reporters tried to ask questions, a little girl shouted from behind,
"EXCUSE ME, EXCUSE ME!"

The reporters parted the path as Carly Sinclair made her way to the
podium. Waiting by the large limousine in the background was Professor
Jeffrey Pearson, Captain James Malloy and Carly's ecstatic parents.

The girl walked onto the stage but was still too small to reach the
microphone. Kendra lifted her up and walked to the mike as both of them

smiled at each other.

"I really don't think it's fair that you ask them anything," said the girl. "First of all, me and the other kids heard broadcasts from our room as we were being held by those evil men. They said if the Global Garrison made any attempt to rescue us, they'd be fired upon. If it wasn't for them, we probably would've been killed along with Kerry, Sharisse and Lena."

She paused and took a quick breath. "No, I really don't think you deserve to talk to them now. It's bad enough that there was squabbling over money for the safe return of kids with wealthy parents. But you shame yourselves by making the poor kids look expendable for the world to see. The little time I had amongst my new friends gave me a purpose. I will dedicate my life from now on to make sure every human being is given the same value as all of the people of this planet. I'm just wondering how God can put up with the selfishness around our globe. How can God trust us when we don't even trust each other?"

Her brow furrowed as she concentrated on her words, the sincerity pouring out. "The hurt and pain we deliver upon our fellow human beings is despicable. We need God's eternal wisdom." She began to cry and her chin trembled. "I thank you with all my heart for saving my life," she said as she looked at Kendra. Then she looked out at elite unit and implored them directly, "BUT PLEASE NEVER BECOME LIKE THEM."

As the girl rested her face against Kendra's shoulder, Kendra whispered, "That will never happen, baby sister."

Everybody was dumbfounded at the beautiful words—words that had them thinking twice. Kendra quietly told Carly how proud she was of her, then added, "Go to the car. You'll see Dr. Pearson and your parents."

Carly kissed Kendra and scampered off to be with her mom and dad.

Valerie stepped up. "I guess you all heard that brave little girl, and you can believe it when I say we'll do just what she says. As far as we're concerned, we are around to protect those who can't protect themselves. If you still behave like idiots, then your destiny is to contend with your own greed. Our commanding officer told us that once we joined, there was nothing on Earth that would deter us. We are not guns for hire, but serve notice to all: we will go after anyone who destroys people of good will. We will not be a part of your ridiculous squabbles unless you deliberately kill the innocent. So next time if you think you can give us an ultimatum, remember it will fall upon deaf ears."

Valerie stepped away from the podium and spotted Malloy, who nodded in approval.

The Garrison made its way towards the rear entrance of the Jets. One reporter ran at them yelling rabidly, "WHAT THE HELL DO YOU CALL THAT? Who appointed all of you God? That's all there is to it, you all coming here dressed up like Batman. All of you are pathetic!"

Valerie made her away over and asked, "To whom am I speaking?"

"Ralph Billings from the London Inquisitor."

Valerie stoically responded, "Well Ralph, you should clean out your dirty ears, and by the way... " She punched him and he landed square on his ass. "Nobody but nobody badmouths the Caped Crusader."

Everyone broke out in laughter as Orion and the Global Garrison turned back toward the super jets. The roar of the powerful engines could be heard for miles as they asked Heathrow's tower for permission to take off.

Just as the Viking Avenger was about to take off, Orion laughed. "Do you believe that the future Queen of England just called me Tarzan?"

Michael Wong replied, "Good, Commander. I have the perfect music for the occasion."

The engines fired up as they hurtled into the heavens with Raise Your Glass booming over the loud speakers in both aircrafts. People all over London were awestruck as both crafts disappeared into the clouds.

THOSE WHO ENGINEER ARROGANCE ONLY SUCCUMB TO IGNORANCE. ~ John Peter Ferris

COMING SOON!
ORION'S BELT: FULL MOON FEVER

Don't miss all the action in Episode Three as our hero evolves in an ever more dangerous world.

Go to www.johnpeterferris.com for more information.

www.ingramcontent.com/pod-product-compliance
Lightning Source LLC
Chambersburg PA
CBHW060134130626
46556CB00006B/2338